THREE BLIND DATES

A DATING BY NUMBERS NOVEL

USA TODAY BESTSELLING AUTHOR
MEGHAN QUINN

Published by Hot-Lanta Publishing
Copyright 2018
Cover design by RBA Designs

This book is licensed for your personal enjoyment only. This book may not be re-sold or given away to other people. If you would like to share this book with another person, please purchase an additional copy for each person. If you're reading this book and did not purchase it, or it was not purchased for your use only, then please return it and purchase your own copy. Thank you for respecting the hard work of this author. To obtain permission to excerpt portions of the text, please contact the author at meghan.quinn.author@gmail.com

This book is licensed for your personal enjoyment only.

All characters in this book are fiction and figments of the author's imagination.

www.authormeghanquinn.com

Copyright © 2018 Meghan Quinn
All rights reserved.

Three Blind Dates
Meghan Quinn

PROLOGUE

NOELY

"Just state my name?"

"Yeah. Gives us a quick rundown on who you are, what you do, your interests, and what you're looking for in a man."

I nod and clear my throat. Sitting tall, my hands resting in my lap, I speak directly into the camera...

"Hi, I'm Noely Clark, and I'm one of your Good Morning, Malibu hosts. As you know, I'm single and in the market for love. As a twenty-seven-year-old woman who has had her fair share of rotten relationships, hookups, and dates, I want to try something new. I want to be thrust into a program where my celebrity status isn't the first thing someone knows about me, where I can be known for who I am as a person rather than how I'm represented on TV."

"And who is the person you want to be known for?"

Tilting my head to the side, I purse my lips, thinking of my answer. "Just a regular girl who loves Tom Hanks, would do just about anything adventurous, and would rather be seen eating nachos at a hockey game than enjoying a chardonnay during a classic night at the opera."

"And what are you looking for in a man?"

Taking a deep breath, I look straight into the camera. "Someone who will cuddle on my couch and watch a classic romcom with me. Someone who will challenge me. Someone who is respectful and courteous to others but also has no qualms about shouting at an official while pounding on the glass at a hockey game. We don't have to be a perfect match, because when is that really the case? But I want our match to be close with a little bit of wiggle room for some give and take, because what's love without a little bit of compromise, without being able to adapt to your partner and love what they love? It's the people in our life who mold us, and I'm far from being molded completely."

Part One

THE SUIT

CHAPTER ONE

NOELY

"Noely, my office. Now."

The slam of my producer's metal door echoes through the set, shaking the blaring lights hanging above me.

"Yikes, that doesn't sound good," Dylan, my co-host, says with a slight crease in her brow. Looking behind her, she eyes the door Kevin, our producer, flew through on what seemed like a rampage. "I think you might have poked the bear."

"Seems that way." I look at the door, nerves starting to shake my coffee hand.

"What do you think it is this time?"

This time . . . *Yeah*, this isn't my first offense.

I wrack my brain for what I've done in the last twenty-four hours that could land me in Kevin's office.

"It could be a plethora of things."

Like I said, not my first offense. If I wasn't so loved by the viewers, I'm almost positive Kevin would have fired me three months in on the job. But two years later I'm still the youngest co-host for a morning show in the country. Maybe my youth is the thing getting me in trouble . . . I do tend to push the limits on what's acceptable in Kevin's eyes.

Dylan looks me over and pokes my boob. "Maybe it's your dress you wore today. It's really low-cut."

I adjust the straps that continue to pull apart, giving my boobs their own personal morning show. "Carla in wardrobe said it was fine."

"Carla also thinks conservative dressing is wearing a bra over a T-shirt, so you can't take her word for it." Dylan thinks for a second. "Maybe it's because you said penis on air this morning."

"I can say penis." Ehh . . . can't I? I make a mental note to look over the list of words I can't say on air again. "It's not like I said cock or throbbing man sword. I used the medical term. Penis. That's legit."

"Yeah, about a guy who was jogging by you this morning. You said his penis was swaying like the wrecking ball in Miley Cyrus's music video and he needed to wear man panties rather than free-ballin' it."

I chuckle and shake my head. "I mean . . . women in Malibu have to be warned. I'm lucky I was able to swerve away from such an attack. I could have been bruised if that thing caught me in the arm. Bruised, Dylan. BRUISED!"

Dylan rolls her eyes just as Kevin pops out of his office and grips the doorway, his bald brow spitting fire in my direction. "Noely, what the hell do you not understand about the word *now*? That doesn't mean when you feel like it, it means right fucking *now*."

Oh. Crap.

"Yep, sorry." I scramble to stand in my ridiculously tall heels and cringe at Dylan, who is covering her mouth and chuckling at my less than graceful attempt to stand. "Be right there, bossman. Just . . . one . . . second," I grunt, righting my shoes. Brushing my skirt over my legs and with my head held high, I walk into his office where I quietly shut the door, not wanting to make more of a scene than necessary.

THREE BLIND DATES

"Sit." Kevin points to a chair in front of his desk with the pencil in his hand. "And if you know what's good for you, keep your mouth shut."

Okay, this could be about the penis or the dress, but then again, I've said vagina on air before and that didn't seem to get the same reaction. And I've worn worse on the show. This has to be something else. Something I'm not thinking of. Something that—

"Explain this." A white CD case is tossed onto Kevin's desk in front of me. He leans back in his chair and bites on his pencil, waiting for an answer.

I eye the CD and start to panic. What the hell is on *that*? In a digital world, where anyone could record anything, I'm actually quite terrified.

It could be as innocent as me scratching my boob while going for a walk, or it could be . . . *oh, hell*.

Please don't let it be a sex tape. Please don't let it be a sex tape.

And before you start judging me for even considering that CD to be a sex tape, let me tell you, there are creeps out in this world who will do things like hide cameras in teddy bears kept on their bedroom chair. I could have been filmed without my knowledge. That's the only way it could be a sex tape, as I'm not stupid enough to do one on my own. I was a journalism major, after all, but I did date some questionable men.

Very questionable . . .

There was Roofus the Doofus with the coifed bouffant and gold tooth. Charlie Three Nips with the penchant to say supposedly in every sentence. And Ryan Big Beard who asked me to condition and braid his wiry man hair every night we were together. The first time was endearing; the second, third, and fourth were just plain creepy.

Clearly not winners, clearly the kind of creeps who could pull a stunt like this. Especially Charlie. You can NEVER trust a man with three nipples. Write that down, ladies: three nipples is a no-go, even if they are fun to touch. Love tweaking that nubbin.

My hands fidget on my lap, my nerves kicking up a wave of

"oh, Gods" in my head and not the good kind. I bite my bottom lip and look at the tape, trying to telepathically read what's been burned on it. "Eh . . . is it my audition tape?" I ask cutely with a smile.

"No," Kevin deadpans, not falling for my charms.

At least I know I can say penis and not get in trouble, so that's one thing to celebrate. And hooray, this dress is A-okay. Gives self a mental thumbs up.

Clearing my throat, I sit back in my seat and steady my shoulders. "Well then, I'm afraid I'm just as lost as you are."

"I'm not lost, I know exactly what's on that CD."

Gulp. Oh God, I'm being blackmailed. I just know it.

Swallowing hard, I politely ask while daintily running my finger along his desk, "Care to share?"

"Does this ring a bell?" Talking in a small girl voice—I think he's trying to impersonate me and it's horrendous—he says, "Hi, my name is Noely Clark, I'm a spicy yet mature twenty-seven-year-old who enjoys a good burger and milkshake combination, and I'm a morning show host on Good Morning, Malibu, and I'm looking for love."

Oh.

Shit.

"Ha, ha." I nervously laugh, my eyes looking everywhere but at Kevin.

How the hell did he find that tape? The only people who knew about it were Carlton, Dylan, and the girl who helped make it. I swear to the freckle on my right breast if Dylan left that lying around her office last night I'm going to kill her. Like *Jason with a chainsaw* kind of murder.

"Can you please tell me why you're using company resources to 'find love'?"

I want it to be known, I don't like the way he condescendingly used air quotes when he said find love, but I'm smart enough to realize that's not something I should bring up at this moment in time.

"And don't lie to me, Noely. You're already on thin ice with me."

Crap.

I bite the inside of my cheek, not wanting to get into this with Kevin since he's the last man who would understand where I'm coming from, but I can't think of any other reason other than the truth, something apparently he wants to hear.

Let it be known, when he rolls his eyes at me, I really don't want to tell him.

Adjusting myself in my chair, I slip my hands under my thighs and lean slightly forward. "Have you heard of *Going in Blind*, the new restaurant in town?"

Squinting at me in observation, Kevin shakes his head. His face isn't purple yet, so I'm going to assume he's more curious than angry right now. I better deliver.

"Well, I was approached by their public relations consultant a few days ago. It's a restaurant where the sole focus is blind dates. They have an app where you create a profile and they match you with other individuals of your likeness. You then attend a blind date with them in the restaurant. You're required to put together a dating video for your profile so the matchmakers can get a feel for your personality, and to also see if you're taking the program seriously. They didn't want it to be a hookup app. Since I'm notoriously single, they thought I might want to give it a try."

With the eraser of the pencil pushed against his chin now, Kevin nods and then sits forward. "And you used company resources to create the video."

"Well . . . I wanted good lighting."

Kevin rolls his eyes.

See, told you he would.

"Was that not okay?"

"Depends." There is a glint in his eyes. I don't think I'm going to like what comes out of his mouth next. "Company materials and resources were used to make this video, which means, that video is company property."

How many "oh God" moments can one person have in the matter of five minutes? I'm guessing I'm over my limit.

"Are you going to say what I think you're going to say?"

You know that smile the Grinch gets when he gets an idea, an awful idea, a wonderfully awful idea? Yeah, that's the kind of grin Kevin is sporting right about now.

He tosses the pencil on his desk and places both his hands behind his head, striking a very casual and confident pose. "Looks like we're going to have a new segment for the show."

Yep, exactly what I thought he was going to say.

"Going in Blind with Noely Clark. I think it has a nice ring to it, don't you think?"

Mentally I turn my nose up at the title. I think it's a horseshit segment title. Entirely too long and nothing rhymes.

Needing to try to nip this in the bud before it turns into an on-screen dating session with yours truly, I lift my chin and say, "You know, Kevin, I respect your idea to spice things up on the show. If you're not coming up with new ideas then the show goes stale, so kudos to you." I give him a small clap with just the tips of my fingers. "But I'm going to have to suggest you nix the dating segment. Don't you think it reads a little desperate? Kind of, you know, trying too hard?"

"Not even a little. With sweeps coming up, I think it's the perfect idea."

I move my hands up and down as if I'm weighing two objects and scrunch my lips to my nose. "Or . . . how about running that dog in the bellhop costume segment again? I mean, that was a real winner." I chuckle and shake my head. "How do you tip a dog bellhop? With dog-lar bills." I slap my knee. "Oh, that is just pure comedy right there."

"Or we do the dating segment, and you listen to what I'm saying."

Wanting to reason with him, I fold my hands on my lap and use my most sincere begging voice. "Kevin, I really don't feel comfortable putting my dating life out there. It's been rough as it is, trying to find someone to settle down with. That's why I wanted to try this program, so I could be matched with someone, through a trusted system, without all the nonsense of dealing with my celebrity and hectic schedule. I truly want to find someone, and I'd rather not splash it all over television."

Rocking ever so slightly in his chair, Kevin rubs his jaw, studying me before he puts one hand on his desk. "Let me know what the company says about your video and what the next steps are. I look forward to hearing about your progress with this program. Also, put me in touch with the publicist you worked with. I want to see if they want to pay for some marketing. Let's reconvene next Friday." He demonically winks at me. "Happy dating."

And with that I'm dismissed. Looks like my sincere begging got me nowhere. I stand from my chair and head for Kevin's office door when he stops me. "And don't play the *woe is me* card, Noely. You're getting away with murder on this one, and you know it. Company property and resources are not to be messed around with for personal gain. Consider your dating segment paying your penance." He clears his throat and says, "See you tomorrow morning."

Squeezing my eyes shut, knowing he's right even though I hate him for it, I see myself out of his office and head to where I left Dylan, in our director's chairs.

I slump down in my chair, kick off my heels, and place my arms on the armrests.

"Were you fired?" Dylan asks, sounding very concerned.

I sigh heavily. "No. If I was fired, I doubt I would be hanging out in my chair."

"Some people handle termination differently." She looks around and asks, "So what happened? Was it the dress or because you said penis?"

"Neither." Turning my head, I lean it against the flimsy back of my chair and ask, "What did you do with that dating tape yesterday?"

"I put it in your mailbox, why?"

I blow out a frustrated breath. "Did you put it in mine or did you put it in Kevin's like that last time you put a coupon for buy-one-get-one-free FroYo at Penguin's Palace?"

Dylan chews on the side of her cheek as she thinks. "You know, I can't remember now. Why, does this have to do with the video?"

"Yes!" I throw my hands in the air exasperated. "That dickhead of a producer of ours is forcing—"

"Best keep your voice down, Noely. You won't want people to hear you," Kevin says, walking by with his briefcase in hand, causing my entire body to redden from embarrassment. "And for the record, don't say penis again on air and burn that dress. If you wear it again, you will be fired. We are a morning show, not a gentleman's club in Ventura. See you tomorrow, ladies." He waves over his head, leaving me in a wake of utter humiliation.

"Oh my God," I mutter, my hands over my face now.

"That was embarrassing," Dylan points out. She's five years older than me, is married with two kids, but I swear, there are times when I feel more put together than she is.

Speaking through my hands, wanting to get this all out in the open, I say, "Kevin found the tape, and since I used company resources to make it, it was either fire me or make me use the tape as a sweeps segment."

"Nooooo," Dylan drags out, with a smile. I have a strong urge to wipe that smile right off her face.

"Yes. And do you know what's really terrible about all of this? I decided to join this program because I really wanted to meet someone. I wasn't doing this just to do it. I was doing this, hoping to actually find someone to settle down with."

"Who says you still can't do that?"

"Come on, who are you kidding?" I sit up in my chair and level with Dylan. "Kevin is going to turn this into an entire production. I can see it now: cameras on my dates, zooming in on a possible good-night kiss, interviews of unsuspecting guys. No one is going to want to be with me while going through all of that."

THREE BLIND DATES

Dylan shrugs. "I don't know. If the men in this program are as serious as they claim to be, they might understand the predicament you're in. Plus, think about all the women you can encourage by taking a leap and joining this blind date restaurant project. You might become an inspiration."

And that's so Dylan. To put a positive spin on something that seems so bleak.

A dating inspiration? I could jump on board with that.

CHAPTER TWO

NOELY

"Are you signed in?" Lynn, the publicist for *Going in Blind* asks me.

"I am." I'm sitting on my couch in a pair of rainbow shorts and a black tank top, a pint of cookie dough next to me, and two phones in hand. One is connected to Lynn and the other is displaying the *Going in Blind* dating app.

"Perfect. As you can see, it's pretty self-explanatory. Your profile is already set up with your avatar and the information you gave us. The video you made is just for us, so other daters won't be able to see it. We want all daters to really go into this program just like any other blind date, not knowing much about looks but only information a friend might tell you about them."

"Makes sense. What about my name; did my handle choice pass?"

"Yes, ma'am. You can see it at the top there."

In the top right corner, there is a picture of a Christmas tree—my avatar—and next to it, written in pink is my handle: ShopGirl.

I smile to myself.

THREE BLIND DATES

I know what you're thinking. What the hell does ShopGirl have to do with me, a co-host of a morning show? Let me ask you a question. Have you ever seen *You've Got Mail*, the best romantic comedy ever produced? If you haven't, stop what you're doing and go watch it now. I'm not kidding, go watch it.

If you are well versed in the world of romcom, then you know ShopGirl was Meg Ryan's handle in the movie. I figure if Kathleen Kelly, the owner of The Shop Around the Corner, could find love through an unconventional way, so can I. Let's just call it a little hint of luck.

And the Christmas tree avatar, well that's just a play on my name . . . you know, Noely, Noel, Christmas, Christmas tree. Clever, so freaking clever.

"That excites me. I'm glad it was available."

"Yes, since we're just getting started, we still have a lot of usernames available. So if you click on your profile avatar at the top, you will see all the information you gave us about yourself is listed."

Blonde hair, hazel eyes, five five, and an extrovert. Loves a good corn on the cob (the food), enjoys hockey and baseball, is infatuated with Tom Hanks, and will tell you if there is food in your teeth—it's the neighborly thing to do, after all.

I'm happy with it. We really didn't get to say much, only the very basics and had about fifty characters to use for a brief description about ourselves. I think I did a pretty good job.

"It looks good. What's next?" I take a scoop out of my raw cookie dough pint and plop it in my mouth. I went to the spin studio today, cookie dough is my reward.

"Since we have everything set to go on your end, we're going to run your profile through our system and set you up with some dates. The system might give you multiple dates, or one at first, depends on the matches, but the first one will be the person who best matches your personality and what you're looking for in a man. That's what we've witnessed within our beta testing so far."

"So you're saying my first match should be the man of my dreams?"

Lynn chuckles. "Well, not necessarily, but he should be pretty darn close. Once you both match up, there will be a time and date offered on the app to have dinner at the restaurant. If you accept the date, you must attend. If you're a no-show, you will be kicked out of the program. We don't want people to get discouraged from dates not showing up. This is so daters can truly find their match."

"That's so great to hear. Will there be a way to talk to the person before the date? I see there is a messenger app on here."

"There is. You can talk to the person before you meet, but we encourage our daters to wait until the actual date for a more authentic experience."

Authentic means awkward, but hey, I want to do this the real way, so I'll stay away from messaging my dates.

"Awesome. Anything else I need to know?"

Lynn pauses, and I'm sure she's looking at some sort of checklist. I would too if I was doing her job. "Yes, at the end of the date, the app will ask you if you want to meet with your date again. If you say yes, the app will suggest three second-date options around the city based on your compatibility and interests."

"Wow, really?"

"Yeah. We're committed to making this process easy on our daters so we offer ideas for your second date. But after the second date, you're on your own."

"That's fair." I chuckle. Feeling a little invigorated, slightly nauseous, and a tad excited, I say, "I can't wait to get started. Do you think there'll be a match for me soon?"

"We work pretty fast on our end. Within twenty-four hours you should have a notification on the app."

"Wow. You do work fast. I can't wait."

"We're glad we can accommodate you, Miss Clark." Lynn pauses, and I shove more cookie dough in my mouth. Two more bites and then I'm going to put it away—can't be having cookie dough stomach rolls on my date. "I did have a chance to talk to your boss, Mr. Stein. He wanted to put together a piece on the restaurant and use you as a test subject." Of course he did. I hold back the huff that wants to escape. "I informed him that filming is not permitted in our restaurant, but if he wants to do a piece on our dating program we would be more than happy to sit with him and give him a one-on-one interview."

Well, thank you, Lynn.

Smiling inwardly, I say, "You know, that's a relief, Lynn. I wanted to keep this side of my life private, so I'm happy I won't have to share my dating experience with the world, at least firsthand. I'm sure I'll be asked about it, but at least I'll have some privacy from how awkward I'm sure I'll be."

"Glad to help. But I do want to ask you a question. You're in this for the right reasons, right? I would hate for you to be matched with someone when this is just publicity for you."

I sit up and loathe that I have to prove my sincerity. *Thanks, Kevin. Turd.* "I'm absolutely in this for the right reasons. I honestly didn't want anyone at my job to know because this is personal. But also because I knew they'd want to use it to the show's advantage. I'm truly sorry Kevin got hold of it. I hope *he* didn't upset you."

"Not at all. We set the ground rules, and he can take us up on the interview if he wants. His choice."

"He will. I have no doubt in my mind." I let out a long sigh and say, "I have an early morning so I need to go. Thank you for taking the time to walk me through the app. I'm easily confused, so I wanted to make sure I wasn't setting up a date with a trout set to be one of your main courses."

Lynn chuckles. "I can guarantee that will never happen. Have a good night, Miss Clark, and if you have any questions, please don't hesitate to ask."

I say my thank yous and good nights and hang up. Tossing my work phone to the side, I bring my personal phone close to me and lean back on the couch, getting comfortable, willing the phone to notify me with a match.

I know it will take a little bit of time, but I'm all about instant gratification and therefore have zero patience. Continuing to refresh my dashboard, I talk to my phone. "Who's going to be my ultimate match? Are you going to be a laid-back surfer boy who's lived his whole life in Malibu? Are you going to be a teacher with a thick stapler in your pants?" I giggle to myself. "Maybe a doctor who loves doing pelvic exams. Wouldn't mind one of those."

After refreshing my dashboard about twenty times, I black out my phone and toss it to the side with the other one. Closing my eyes, I rest my head on the couch cushion and think about the possibility of actually meeting someone. I don't know when it happened exactly, but coming home one night recently, as I entered my apartment, it struck me how quiet it was. I am surrounded by noise at work, so you'd think I'd want quiet when I get home. But it wasn't *that* sort of quiet. It was the quiet that confirms no one awaits you as you walk through the door. The quiet that confirms you'll be cooking and eating dinner on your own *again* tonight. The quiet that bounces off the walls when you watch TV and laugh at the stupid humor. The quiet in bed when no one farts next to you. *Oh, hang on. That one I want to keep.* The quiet I don't want or like anymore is the one that is my everyday quiet. *Because it's become ... lonely.*

I haven't had the best of luck in the dating department. Clearly my radar for good men is terrible. I attract the worst kind of men from the clingers, to the stealers—yes, I've had men steal from me before—to the perpetual criers. And now that I'm "famous" in Malibu for my morning talk show, the pool of good men has really narrowed.

All I want is someone amusing who can laugh with me, a man who can also connect with me on an intellectual level. If he happens to be handsome, with big hands, impeccable style, and a deep voice that can rock my socks off in bed, then hey, I'll take it.

CHAPTER THREE

NOELY

"And we're out. Good show, everyone," Marcia, one of our producers announces.

I turn toward Dylan, who's already reaching into her dress and unclasping her bra. The production crew rotates around us, cleaning up and preparing for tomorrow's show, ignoring Dylan's impending freeing of her breasts. They're used to it by now. They know, when the show's over and the red light has been turned off, Dylan is reaching into her shirt or dress and taking off her bra. I just wish when she did it, she didn't grunt like a pig digging for truffles.

"Can you wait to do that when you're in your dressing room?"

"Never," she huffs, moving from side to side. "This sucker is really gluing itself together. Lend a girl a hand." She nods for me to help her out.

"Yeah, I'll pass." I pull out the drawer to the coffee table in front of us and snag my phone. I forgot it was in my hand when I walked on set and quickly stored it away before we went live.

Five text messages, most likely all from my brother, a few emails and . . .

"Gah! A notification!" I squeal and quickly open up the *Going in Blind* app.

"A notification? For . . . what?" Dylan grunts.

"Going in Blind. I have a match."

With hands digging in the front of her dress, through her sleeves, Dylan turns toward me in slow motion, hands stilled, eyes wide. "You have a match. Oh my God, who is it? What does he look like? What does he do? Tell me all the things," she practically yells.

"Let me look." I can't type my password quick enough into my phone, but once I do, I open up the app and wait impatiently as it loads. Finally, it pops up and a heart appears on the screen with an announcement that I've been matched with someone.

Oh how wonderfully exhilarating.

If that isn't something magical to see play out on my phone, I don't know what is.

Dylan leans over. "What does it say? Who is it? What's his name?"

"It doesn't tell you names or anything like that." The screen shifts to the man's profile. The avatar is a business tie. Interesting. The man's handle: WindsorKnot. Okay, so he's a businessman.

"What does it tell you? Come on." Dylan nudges me with her shoulder since her hands are still in the front of her dress.

"Let's see, the guy's handle is WindsorKnot, he has brown hair, brown eyes. He's six three and has a type-A personality."

"Anal retentive, that's what that means." Dylan rolls her eyes. "Chad has a type-A personality, which makes living with him a real treat at times."

"Type-A personalities can be very attractive." So can brown hair and brown eyes. Tall, dark, and handsome, just the way I like them. Well, I don't know if he's handsome, but I'm going to assume he is. Reading the rest of his profile, I say, "He's allergic to pineapple, had a cat once named Pineapple, and his favorite actor is . . ." I screech. "It's Tom Hanks. His favorite actor is Tom Hanks. Isn't that amazing?"

A complacent look crosses Dylan's face. "So you have one thing in common. That doesn't get me past the whole pineapple thing. First of all, who's allergic to pineapple? And when he says he's allergic to pineapple, is he talking about the fruit, or his dead cat? Can you see how that's confusing?"

That is slightly confusing to put on a dating profile and a little weird, but maybe it just means the guy has a sense of humor. There has to be more to this man than what's on his profile, because the system seems to think we are a great match. I mean, we both made clear our love for Tom Hanks, so that has to be a positive right there.

"I think I'm going to go for it."

Dylan shifts next to me and then flings her arm up in the air, bra in hand. "Ah-ha, I got you, you wryly beast." She tosses her bra to the side and leans back on the couch, pretending to smoke a cigarette, as if she just had the wrestling match of a lifetime. "You're going on a date?"

"Why not?" I shrug. "I told myself I'd give every date a chance. I'm intrigued by this non-pineapple-eating businessman." Without giving it a second thought, I answer yes to a date and the screen gives me three different times to secure at the restaurant. I answer open to all times. It's polite to be flexible; at least that's what I tell myself. *I'm not desperate at all.*

"You're really doing this?"

"I am. I think this could be it for me."

I'd be a fool to not at least give it a try.

~

"Why doesn't this app tell me more?" I scream into my phone, holding it close to my face and shaking it.

I'm an hour from my date, I have one leg shaved, my hair is halfway curled, I have no makeup on, and I'm bleaching my non-existent mustache because Dylan said to do it "just in case." All I want is a little bit of a clue as to who I'm going out with tonight.

Just a hint. I know this is supposed to be a blind date, but I have so many questions. Does he like boobs or butts better? My outfit depends on it. If it's boobs, then strap me up with a push-up bra. If it's butt, then shuck the underwear, I'm going commando.

Damn you, app! Is it boobs or butt? I mentally shake my fist in the air.

I was half tempted to message him, so damn tempted to strike up a conversation before we met. Dear sir, do you prefer the bouncy breast or the bubbly butt? Please respond as soon as possible because my outfit depends on it. But despite my psychotic obsessing, I held back. I wanted the organic *Going in Blind* dating experience and I'll be honest, not my best idea because I'm not loving it. Organic is sometimes not always best, because hell on a high horse, this is stressful.

"How long have you had the bleach on?" Dylan asks, walking into my bedroom with a bag of chips in hand. We might be morning hosts, but we're also junk food fanatics.

"I don't know, like twenty minutes."

Dylan is mid-chew when she says, "Twenty minutes? It's only supposed to be ten. You're bleaching your skin now."

"What?" I fling my body toward my bathroom and bury my face under the facet of my sink, spraying my face and half-done hair with water, trying to clean all the bleach off my upper lip.

Chuckling behind me, Dylan shakes her head. "I'm just kidding. You can't bleach your skin with that stuff."

Standing from the faucet, face dripping, I turn on Dylan and reach out my hand only to clasp it around her neck. "I'm going to kill you."

Laughing some more, Dylan swats me away. "Come on, you need to lighten up. It's just a date. What's the worst that can happen?"

I turn toward the mirror and examine my upper lip. "I could show up with a bleached upper lip, looking like Santa Claus with a porn stash, scaring my poor date away." Standing straight, I motion to my wet hair, unshaved leg, and possibly bleached upper lip.

THREE BLIND DATES

Hysterically and high-pitched, I say, "This is not a good look for me!"

Dylan covers her mouth and snorts. Her shoulders shake with her silent laughter. I know she means well, hell, I would laugh at her if she were in my place, but right now all I want to do is bleach the hell out of her nostrils.

I sigh and rest my hands on my bathroom counter. "I really want this to work out, Dylan. I miss being in a relationship, being able to rely on someone, connecting with someone. I miss intimacy. And hell, I miss sex."

Sensing my seriousness, Dylan places her salt-covered hand on my back—thankfully I'm wearing my robe. "You're getting yourself worked up, sweetie. You need to relax. If this guy isn't the guy, it isn't the end of the world."

"But Lynn said my first match is the match I'm meant to be with..."

"She said that?" Dylan's questioning look tells me she doesn't quite believe that statement.

I nibble on my lip. "Well, something like that." Going back to my tub, I start to shave the other leg. "According to the program, he's supposed to be the best match for me."

"Yeah, within the program right now. There might be others who give it a try later, too. There are millions of guys who aren't doing this *Going in Blind* thing, just remember that." She has a valid point. "If you go on these three dates and nothing happens, then nothing happens. It's okay. It doesn't mean you're destined to a life of solitude and loneliness. It means the right guy might be later in your future. Don't put too much pressure on yourself over this, okay? Kevin can't interfere, but he'll prod you afterward, and as this is for fun, enjoy it. And hey, if you get some free meals out of it, that's a score in my book." Dylan reaches into her bag of chips and stuffs her mouth. If only the viewers knew the real Dylan. She seems so refined on television, but in person, she has no qualms about picking her teeth with a toothpick at the dinner table.

Believe me, it's a nighttime ritual. And weirdly, her candidness is what makes us such great friends.

Settled slightly, I continue to shave my leg. "Will you help me get my hair back in gear? I don't want to be late."

"Sure." She wipes her hands on her yoga pants and reaches for the hair dryer.

"Hold up." I turn toward her, razor in hand. "Wash your chip-covered hands first, and please don't bring that hair dryer near me while I'm in the tub shaving my legs."

Playfully, Dylan chuckles at her mistake. "Not into getting electrocuted today?"

"Not so much." My phone beeps on the counter. I nod at it and say, "Can you see what that is . . . but wash your hands first."

Dylan unabashedly rolls her eyes. "So particular."

"Use soap," I say as the water is turned on.

"I'm not a child." Dylan washes her hands quickly, snags my phone, and says, "It's a notification from your *Going in Blind* app."

"What?" I wash the soap off my leg and dry myself off. "Is the guy cancelling? I bet he's cancelling. Is that what it is? Just tell me and end my misery."

"Good God, woman. Get a hold of yourself." Dylan presses on my phone a few times and smiles to herself.

Eagerly and nervously I ask, "What is it?"

Smile plastered across her face, she turns toward me and leans against my bathroom counter. "It's a message from WindsorKnot. He says, 'Can't wait to meet you in an hour. Hope you're as nervous as I am.'"

Rays of heat course up my back as my stomach does a little flutter. That's cute and *exactly* what I needed. There's nothing worse than being a fumbling mess next to an overly confident person. "That's . . . kind of cute, isn't it?"

"Very cute. He even used a smile emoji."

"Did he really?" I snag my phone. And there it is, a smile emoji. "You know, there's something to be said about a man who doesn't mind using a smile emoji. Makes him seem like he has a sensitive side."

"Chad uses emojis. The pointing finger one and okay sign, which indicates his intentions for the night."

"That's . . . sweet?" Staring at the message, I ask, "Should I send him something back? I said I wouldn't partake in talking before the date."

"Yeah, but you don't want to be rude. Just send him a quick message, especially since he said he was nervous."

I flatten my lips. "You're right." Thinking for a second, I quickly type something as I read it out loud. "Can't wait to meet you. Might be beating you in the nerves department. *Wink emoji.*" I press send and take a seat at my vanity. "Short and flirty, right?"

"Perfect. Now, let's do a low bun with your hair, because I don't think we have time to curl it all."

"Work your magic, Dyl. I've got to get out of here in fifteen."

CHAPTER FOUR

NOELY

I didn't realize how close I was to the restaurant because I'm ten minutes early. Does that make me seem desperate? No, I chastise myself. It shows that I respect the other person's time . . . *right?*

God, dating is the worst. There are so many unspoken rules you have to follow to not look desperate, or to not look like a psycho, or a creep, or horny, or—

"Can I help you, miss?"

Straightening up, I turn toward the hostess stand, which is a beautifully carved piece of wood. Standing behind it is an exotic, tall woman with long black hair, stunning grey eyes, and a massive engagement ring on her hand. *Please tell me she got that rock from dating someone in this program.*

Don't get me wrong. It's not that happiness for my life is dependent on getting married, but to see a success story in the flesh—particularly for me—would be encouraging.

"Hi, yes, I'm Noely Clark. I have a date at seven tonight with"—I lean forward, feeling silly and whisper—"with WindsorKnot."

Her smile is kind and reassuring, making me feel a little calmer. "Yes, Miss Clark, I have you here for seven. You're date hasn't arrived yet, so can I show you to the bar for a drink while you wait?"

"That would be lovely, thank you."

With my clutch tucked under my arm, I follow tall, dark, and beautiful to the bar where a very handsome Asian man is standing with a towel draped over his shoulder and a bright grin on his face. He's wearing a button-up shirt with rolled sleeves, a brown vest covering his chest, which totally channels his inner Justin Timberlake.

"Danny, this is Miss Clark. She has a reservation at seven. Would you be so kind to make her whatever drink she would like?"

"Of course." He winks at the hostess who presses her warm hand on my arm.

"Enjoy, Miss Clark. If you have any questions, please feel free to ask. My name is Veronica, this is Danny, and we will be happy to serve you in any way." With a parting grin, she moves back to her hostess spot.

Well, she's nice.

"Miss Clark, please take a seat. What would you like?"

My tight, formfitting red dress makes my hop onto the bar stool a difficult task, but with a pleading prayer to the dress gods and a swift jump, I situate myself, only breaking a minor sweat.

I let out a sigh of relief and place my hands on the bar in front of me, scanning the glitzy bottles of "muscle relaxant." "Hmm . . . how about a Moscow Mule?"

"Coming right up." He gets to work and I watch as he magically floats around the bar, pulling the ingredients. "We recently bought new copper mugs, and I've been dying to use them."

"Yeah? Am I the first?"

Winking, he says, "You are."

If I didn't know any better, I would say Danny is a bit of a flirt. Either that or he's super friendly. *Or simply made to be a bartender.*

From beneath the bar, Danny pulls out a shiny, hammered-copper mug, and I'm instantly taken by the design. So sleek, just like its surroundings. The restaurant, with its white exposed brick, natural wood features, electric colors, and stone tabletops, is sexy, yet inviting. The friendly waitstaff is an absolute bonus. Every table is cornered off in its own spot, never getting too close to the other tables around it, and the mood lighting is on point with dim Edison bulb lights hanging from the ceiling and tabletop candles. I'm feeling the mood.

Despite the welcoming atmosphere, I can't help but feel nervous, even after my brief exchange with WindsorKnot. There's something to say about a blind date: the anticipation, the unknown, the knowledge that you're having dinner with someone to possibly form a romantic relationship. It's intimidating, but exhilarating all at the same time.

Could this be the last time I ever go on a first date? Will he like me? Will he want to get to know me?

Butterflies float around in my stomach and my cheeks heat as Danny places a napkin in front of me, topped by my drink with a lime slice on the side.

"Here you go, Miss Clark. Please enjoy."

I smile politely. "Thank you." When I take a sip, I'm instantly assaulted by the ginger-lime combination. *Perfect.* "This is fantastic."

"Good." Danny winks again and like an old-time bartender, starts drying a tumbler with the towel hanging over his shoulder. Eyeing me for a second, he asks, "A little nervous?"

After taking a sip from my drink, I lick my lips and nod. "Just a little." I scrunch my nose, squinting ever so slightly. "Is it obvious?"

"Nah, you look pretty chill compared to a lot of blind daters I see come through the door."

"Oh, I'm sure you see a lot of different reactions to these dates." I lean forward, the cold wood of the bar cooling my sweaty hands, and whisper, "Any good stories you can tell me?"

Danny chuckles quietly and leans forward himself, taking a

look from side to side before answering. "Plenty, but looks like your date just arrived."

My date just arrived?

The temperature in the room seems to go up a thousand degrees as my body seizes and my shoulders tense. "Oh God, can you see him? Is he hot? What does he look like? Should I turn around? No, I shouldn't, he would know I was checking him out." Whispering a little louder, I ask again, "Just tell me, is he cute?"

Danny's eyes scan over my head and his smile stretches across his face. "That's for you to judge, not me." *Damn you, Danny.*

Oh Christ, I'm not ready.

That's right, I'm not freaking ready for this.

I get it, I know I said I was ready, that I wanted to do this, that I was all-in, that I wanted to find my soul mate, but now that I'm here, seconds from meeting "the one," I'm pretty sure I'm going to throw up. Yep, I'm going to throw up. I can feel it rising.

Oh God, I'm going to retch all over him, right on his shoes. I know it. It's bound to happen.

"Relax, you're going to have fun," Danny whispers before he turns to the bottles behind him.

As if the light hairs on my arm can sense it, they stand at attention as the sound of faint footsteps come closer.

Click, click, click. The cement floor leaves zero room for sneaking up on anyone.

Don't throw up, don't throw up. Think compliments, think pleasantries, think—

"Hello."

Smooth molasses drips over my shoulders as the most velvet of voices I've ever heard echoes behind me, pulling me away from the death grip on my copper mug and turning me in my seat to face one of the most handsome and polished men I've ever seen.

Immediately I'm drawn to his dark-chocolate eyes, so shadowy I'm having a hard time deciphering where his irises begin and his pupils end. His strong, square jaw is peppered in well-maintained scruff, and his hair is just long enough to show

how thick and full it is. And his style? Impeccable. A navy-blue suit wraps around his broad shoulders and long legs, while a white-pressed button-up shirt shows off a triangle of tan skin below his neck.

Sexy.

Handsome.

Everything I could ask for.

Clearing my throat, I awkwardly wave and say, "Hi."

Smiling sincerely, he holds his large hand out to me and says, "I'm Jack, also known as WindsorKnot. Veronica told me you were ShopGirl."

"Yes, that's me, but you can call me Noely."

"Noely," he repeats, as if testing the sound on his tongue. "Beautiful name."

Yep, hearing him say my name and beautiful together, makes my cheeks flush. I've barely said a word to this man and I'm already blushing madly.

"Thank you." I hold back the giggle that wants to escape.

He motions to the bar stool next to me. "May I join you?"

"Oh, of course." I move my clutch to the other side of the bar, making room for him.

Motioning to the bartender, he politely shakes the man's hand and says, "Jack."

"Danny. What can I get you, sir?"

Jack eyes the drink in my condensation-covered hands and says, "I'll have what the lady is having."

"Right away."

Danny gets to work once again as Jack turns in his stool to face me, one hand on the back of his seat, the other on the bar to his side.

A casual pose for someone comfortable with his surroundings.

Not to mention, he's giving off a confident vibe, a vibe I couldn't have predicted from the man who messaged me earlier while I was getting ready. I half expected for him to show up, already sweating with a nervous shake in his hands. But not Jack, not the man in front of me. He's stoic almost, comfortable in his own skin, unbothered by the situation we're in.

Unlike me.

My nerves ratchet up all kinds of embarrassing reactions caused by the gorgeous man in front of me. I can feel it, there's no denying it, especially by the way I'm tongue-tied, unable to say anything . . . I'm awkward.

Ah, I'm awkward!

I'm the antithesis of who I wanted to portray. I've thought about this moment, this date, the first one, in my mind . . . God, was I sexy and smooth with hair flipping, chest puffed out, and a stray finger grazing my date's arm.

Instead, I'm clammed up like a fetus, hair pulled behind my neck leaving me with a twitch instead of a hair flip, and my fingers, let's just say they're glued to my copper mug right now. There is no finger running, and my smile? There is no ease in my lips. It's more like my brain is telling my lips to show off my teeth rather than look like a prize to be won.

I blame *Going in Blind!* They set me up with someone entirely too good-looking. How is a girl supposed to function when Mr. Impeccably Dressed with the Strong Jaw is staring into your eyes, studying your every move? It's impossible.

Leaning forward, Jack brings his head closer to mine, enveloping me in his fresh scent. "I don't know about you, but I'm really nervous right now."

"Really?" I ask, swallowing hard from how close he is. "You don't look like you are."

He chuckles. "After many years in the boardroom, hiding your external reaction to situations becomes second nature. Believe me, the moment I saw you, my stomach started flipping."

Handsome and suave. Okay, where did they find this man and what the hell do we have in common—besides Tom Hanks—that could possibly have matched us? I'm feeling like Kraft Singles compared to his Camembert.

Trying to pull myself together and act like somewhat of an

adult and not a sputtering barely blossoming tween, I ask, "Boardroom. Does that mean my assumption of you being a businessman is true?" I lift an inquisitive eyebrow at him right before I take a sip from my drink, holding the mug with both hands to avoid revealing the unsteady shake roaring through my bones.

"I guess I didn't do a good job hiding it, did I?" The boyish charm that follows his statement is endearing, especially the little peek of dimples in his cheeks. *Dimples, the kryptonite for every woman.*

"Not so much. I don't think you can deny it with the handle *WindsorKnot*. Not sure there was a lot of competition with that name choice."

Danny hands Jack his drink, which he takes with a grateful nod in Danny's direction. In fascination, I watch his lips wrap over the ledge of the cup, soft and wet. Sexy, so, so sexy.

After he swallows, the liquid falling down the thick column of his neck, he asks, "What, you don't think WindsorKnot is a popular name choice?"

"Not even in the slightest." I chuckle. He joins me, and the sound mixed with mine sounds harmonious, like the two noises were meant to be mixed together. Oh, I want to hear him laugh again . . . badly.

"All right, what about your name? ShopGirl. Does that have anything to do with your profession?"

I should be slightly insulted that he doesn't recognize me from my morning show, but then again, if he's a businessman, my nine o'clock airing time doesn't necessary mesh with his schedule.

Shaking my head, I take a quick sip from my drink and set the mug on the bar, letting my hands defrost from the chill of the copper casing. "Not even in the slightest. Let me ask you, Jack . . ." Did I mention I really like his name? It's strong, yet traditional. "Have you ever seen the movie *You've Got Mail?*"

A slow, knowing smile starts to unfold over his lips. Casually, he sips from his mug, his eyes trained on me, his gaze unfaltering. Oh boy, he's dangerous. With those eyes and that look, yep, I'm surprised I haven't pulled a Dylan yet and ripped my bra off in public.

When he pulls his mug away, he asks, "Have you failed to remember what's on my profile? Tom Hanks, he's my main man. I've watched every single one of his movies more than once, *You've Got Mail* being in my top-five Hanks movies."

I mentally applaud *Going in Blind*. No, an applaud is to tame, I need something more meaningful. I mentally ass slap them, right on the glute, hand to skin, leaving a red mark, a red mark of love. Nothing says thank you like a branded red-slap to the old buttocks.

"So then you know about ShopGirl?"

He nods. "It makes so much sense now." He pauses and then asks, "Would you say *You've Got Mail* is your favorite movie?"

I don't even skip a beat. "Hands down, the best."

Another smile peeks over the rim of his mug. "I might just have to kiss the people who set up this date."

Same freaking here, and not just because he loves *You've Got Mail*.

"Noely, Jack, your table is ready if you would like to follow me," Veronica says, motioning to the dining space.

Like a gentleman, Jack helps me from my stool and places his hand on my lower back, guiding me behind Veronica. The feel of his hot palm against my dress doesn't go unnoticed, neither does the unexpected craving for him to lower his hand a few inches.

Veronica guides us to the back of the restaurant, to a quaint table in front of exposed brick, lightly covered by vibrant hues of red. Jack guides me to my chair and pulls it out for me. His hand rests on the back of the chair when I sit and he carefully helps me scoot in.

I don't think I've ever had a man do that for me before, it was . . . different, but nice. Really nice.

Jack waits to take his seat as Veronica speaks. "Your waiter's name is Dennis. He'll be over to take any other drink orders you might have. Please let us know if you need anything."

"Thank you, Veronica," Jack says politely. Once she leaves, he takes a seat, unfolds the napkin in front of him, and places it on his lap. There is an air of elegance about him, a manner I'm not familiar with, but also not opposed to either given my track record of dates. Wanting to follow his lead, I do the same with my napkin.

A single piece of cardstock rests on each of our plates indicating our dinner choices for the night. There are only three options: steak, lobster, and pasta. I'm surprised we don't have more choices given the hype of the restaurant, but after reading over the menu, I realize it doesn't matter how many options there are, I want all of them.

"This place is so nice." I look around, trying to start some kind of conversation. I eye Jack and ask, "Is this your first date? Or have you been on others?"

That smile shows up again and I can't help but want to sigh. "First one, what about you?"

"Me too. I guess we're popping each other's cherries." The moment the words leave my lips, I cringe, but the crease in my brow is quickly washed away by Jack's chuckle.

"Yeah, I guess you're right." Leaning forward, he bites on his lower lip and says, "Please be gentle."

I pat his hand that's on the table. "Don't worry, I'll use lube."

He throws his head back and a good hearty laugh escapes him. God, I'm starting to become addicted to that sound.

"Kinky, should I be worried?" he finally asks when his laughter dies down.

"I'd watch your six." I wink at him and turn back to the menu. "What are you going to get? I'm having a hard time deciding."

He studies the menu, the intensity in his gaze strong, intimidating. I would fear him in the boardroom. "I'm a steak man myself, so I'll probably go with that. Do you like meat, Noely?"

Did he mean to phrase his sentence like that?

From the raise in his brow and the playful look in his eyes, I'm going to guess, yes. Okay, this conversation has gone from nervous, awkward talk to sexual innuendos in the matter of seconds. This is my kind of date.

Not wanting to scare him away, I refrain from jumping up on the table and shaking my ass in his face while screaming I love meat. He might seem easygoing, but getting slapped in the face by a red-clad derriere might not scream best first date ever. Instead, I nod and say, "Yeah, I think I might join you with your steak choice."

He nods and gathers my menu. "Do you mind if I order for you?"

"Not at all. Medium-rare please."

Dennis arrives soon after and takes our order. In awe, I watch Jack sophistically order our steaks, both medium-rare. I don't think I've ever been out with such a cultured man.

When Dennis disappears, I swear the mood lighting changes, the lights dimming, casting a romantic glow over the diners. The feeling around us becomes exponentially more intimate with blue and teal uplighting reflecting off the white brick walls and the lights above us dulling, making the tea lights at our table become more prevalent.

"So, want to play cards?" Jack asks, kind of out of the blue.

"What?" I chuckle, caught off guard.

He nods to the wine list next to the salt and pepper shakers and a small white vase of pink peonies. Nestled between them is what I'm going to assume is a deck of cards in a metal tin. Without an answer from me, he pulls out the deck and starts shuffling while eyeing a small card in the box.

Still shuffling, he glances up at me. "It's Crazy Eights with questions. Have you ever played?"

"Never."

But hell if I'm not intrigued. I'm on my first blind date with a drop-dead-gorgeous and humorous man . . . and we're about to play cards. I didn't predict this night to start out like this, but I'm really glad it has. Let the questions begin.

CHAPTER FIVE

NOELY

Okay, this is going to seem like a really weird thing to get all hot and bothered over, but can I just take a moment to say the way Jack is shuffling those cards, the way his large hands make the cards look minuscule, or the way his fingers gently shuffle with precision—it's kind of a turn-on. No, not kind of, it *is* a turn-on.

I know . . . weird.

But I mean, fingers, gentle fingers, large fingers. Thick man fingers.

See what I'm getting at here?

Clearing my throat and trying not to stare too long at his hands, I say, "I've played Crazy Eights before, but not this version."

"Same, but it seems pretty self-explanatory. Looks like each card has a question on it. According to the rules, if I lay down a card, you have to answer the question and vice versa. If we lay down an eight, we get to ask the other person any question we would like and they have to answer . . . within reason."

"Within reason?" I ask with a smirk.

"Well, I mean, nothing embarrassing like . . ." He pauses as he tries to think of an embarrassing question. He must have thought of something he doesn't want to share because he ends up chuckling and shaking his head right before he starts to deal the cards.

"Ready?" he asks. "You can go first."

"Hold on, what was going to be our embarrassing question example?"

"You don't want to know."

"I really do."

Sighing, he shakes his head and leans back in his chair. "I have a feeling I'm not going to be able to get away with anything where you're concerned."

"It's good you realize that now." I grin and sip from my mug.

He pauses, his eyes bouncing back and forth between mine, trying to read me. "My example question was"—he shakes his head some more and then huffs—"something stupid like, did you plan on returning that dress after our date?"

Immediately I feel my cheeks heat. *Oh. My. God.* You know those times you have that nagging sensation that something doesn't quite feel right? Like, *Why does this dress feel as though something is sticking out of the left shoulder strap?* Next time. *Do. Something. About. It.* I reach to the side of my shoulder, and there it is. The *unwelcome* piece of dreaded cardboard that I embarrassing forgot to take off before I put on the dress. I was in such a whirlwind of not wanting to be late that I completely forgot.

Red doesn't even begin to describe the color eclipsing my cheeks.

Not even thinking, I yank on the tag and pop it off with one swift pull. I shove the tag in my clutch and smile awkwardly. "Well, that would be an embarrassing question, now, wouldn't it?" Trying to even the playing field, I ask, "So, would something like did you know you've had a toothpaste ring around your lips this entire time fall along the lines of embarrassing?"

Jack's face blanches as he quickly wipes around his mouth, causing me to laugh obnoxiously louder than I wanted. Waving my hand in front of me, I say, "I wasn't talking about you. Its just an example."

His hand stops mid wipe and his eyes mirthfully narrow in on me. "Oh, you little tease."

I chuckle a little harder. "Hey, at least yours was only a joke. I was the one with a tag hanging off my clothes. Be glad you didn't walk in here with your fly down or something."

"Now that would have been unrecoverable." He pauses for a second and bites his bottom lip. "Now you have me growing paranoid over not zipping my fly. Would it be entirely too rude if I did a quick zip check?"

"Not if you check my teeth for lipstick."

"Deal."

He looks down at his crotch, gives himself a fist pump for clearly zipping up, and then turns to me. I smile brightly and I'm given a thumbs up. "All clear."

"Well, thank God for us being able to pull ourselves together enough for this date . . . minus the clothing tag."

He waves me off. "We'll veto that mistake from this date. You were trying to make a good impression with a new dress and forgot one minor detail. The intention was there."

"So honorable." I press my hand to my chest and then pick up my cards, sorting them by suit.

Eying me over his cards, I notice Jack studying me, his dark, penetrable eyes burning through me. He's an interesting man, because some moments, I can see the businessman in him, the intensity I'm sure he uses at work, or a sense of sophistication one would have after spending many years wining and dining potential partners. But there is also a soft, easygoing side to him, and that's the side I like the best, even though his intense stare sets off a flight of birds in my stomach.

Instead of returning his look, I focus on my cards. What I wouldn't give to know what's going through his mind right now. What he must be thinking. What he's assessing about me. I'm sure he's good at reading people—he has to be in order to be a successful businessman. Does he think I'm funny, or a bit of a spaz? I really hope he thinks I'm more funny, endearing, rather than the crazy who wears dresses with tags.

But to put things in perspective, it could have been a lot worse. I could have had toilet paper hanging out the bottom of my dress. Impossible you may think? Nope, unfortunately, it's not . . .

"Ladies first." He flips over the top card on the deck and motions for me to go.

Five of clubs. Thankfully I have a five of hearts, so I place it over the card and read the question out loud for Jack to answer. "You can invite one boy band member to dinner, who is it and why?" I quirk my lip to the side in confusion and then look up at Jack. "What kind of questions are these?"

Laughing, he scratches his jaw, the sound of his nails running over his scruff, igniting a warm feeling inside me. "I have no idea but I feel like we're about to get to know each other on a much deeper level."

"Seems like it." I lean back in my chair and pointedly look at him. "Well . . ."

Sighing, he capitulates even though he seems entirely too resistant. "From any boy band?" He scratches his jaw again, his eyes trained to the ceiling, deep in thought. "This question sucks." He chuckles. "But if I have to choose . . . Mark Wahlberg because he seems like he'd be pretty chill to hang out with."

"Marky Mark?" I ask incredulously. "He wasn't in a boy band."

"Yes, he was," Jack counters, with more passion than I expected. "Marky Mark and the Funky Bunch. They're a bunch of boys in a band of sorts. So that works." Tapping the table, he asks, "Were you expecting me to say something else, like Joey Fatone from *NSYNC?"

"Not even in the slightest. Judging from your impeccably tailored suit and chivalry, I would have guessed someone classic like Paul McCartney or John Lennon."

He blanches in the best way possible, as if I just turned on a light bulb in his head, and he's now realizing he made a big mistake.

"Ohhh," he draws out thoughtfully. "I never even thought about The Beatles."

"No, instead, your mind goes straight to Marky Mark and the Funky Bunch." I can't help it, I laugh. "Should I be worried?"

"Maybe a little." He rubs his jaw some more. "I change my answer to Paul McCartney."

"You can't change your answer now. You've already put Marky Mark out into the universe. You can't take something like that back."

Humor is in his eyes as he shakes his head. "You're brutal." Staring at his cards, he lays down a heart and reads the question out loud. "Pear or apple?" His brow creases together and he looks at me with the cutest expression I've ever seen. "Pear or apple? I have to answer about my favorite boy band member and you get to tell me if you prefer a pear or an apple? How is that even fair?"

Chuckling, I say, "The cards have spoken." I press my finger to my chin and contemplate my question. "Pear or apple. Pear of apple, hmm . . . that's a real doozy."

"Oh, come on." Jack leans back in his chair and crosses his arms.

Laughing, I answer, "Pear."

"I can't even believe you were able to make such a tough decision." Sarcasm drips from his mouth. *And I like it.*

I press my palm against my chest. "How dare you? I barely made it through that question. I might need another Moscow Mule after that."

"I might need another Moscow Mule if I keep getting questions like what boy band member do you want to take to dinner."

God, he's funny and so easygoing. I don't know why, but going into this date I thought he'd be a little more uptight. Maybe because his handle was WindsorKnot. Either way, I'm relieved.

Eyeing his heart, I lay down another on top of his and burst out into laughter when I read his question. "What's your most embarrassing moment to date?"

THREE BLIND DATES

He tosses his cards on the table, face down, and calls to our waiter. "Another Moscow Mule, please."

A fit of giggles takes over me, filling the air between us as his smile stretches across his face. Who knew blind dates could be so fun?

~

Half my steak is gone, I've had two Moscow Mules, and my grilled veggies have been consumed. The man sitting in front of me has charmed me all night with his quick wit, out of nowhere intensity, and funny facial expressions. And I can't help but wonder, where did this man come from and how has it taken me this long to meet him? *Why is he still available?*

Jack sets his knife and fork down and studies me for a second. "So, I know you like pears, your favorite movie is *You've Got Mail*, you were born in Escondido, and if you had to pick, you would choose *The wedding Singer* Drew Barrymore over *Fifty First Dates* Drew Barrymore."

"There's just something about her close call with becoming Julia Gulia that makes me want to be her friend."

"Totally understandable." He pauses, his head tilted to the side when he asks, "What about you though, do you enjoy being a TV host?"

"Ah, so you do know who I am."

Sheepishly he smiles. "I was playing it cool." *This guy is too cute.*

"I appreciate you not fangirling all over me."

"It was hard not passing out; I'm glad I held myself together." He smirks.

The waiter drops off the check and without even skipping a beat, Jack scoops it up and places his credit card in the billfold.

"Thank you." He just nods and waits for my answer.

I play with the condensation on my copper mug when I answer. "It has good days and bad days. I'm lucky I get to do something I love, but it also comes with a lot of hard work, long days, and full schedules."

He nods. "I get that. It can be consuming. I feel that as well."

"Yeah?" I look him up and down. "And what do you wear your suit for day in and day out?"

Smiling playfully, he pulls on the sleeves of his button-up shirt, almost as if it's a nervous tick. "I'm in all kinds of business." Talk about an evasive answer.

"So you wake up every morning and tie your Windsor knot tight for 'all kinds of business'?" I ask, using air quotes.

"Something like that."

"Uh-uh." I place my elbows on the table and lean forward. "You're going to have to give me more than that or I'm going to assume you have no job at all."

"I have a job."

"Yeah." I lick my lips casually and lean a little bit more forward. "Prove it."

My challenge intrigues him, I can tell by the way he chews on the side of his mouth and studies me inquisitively. Keeping his eyes trained on me, he reaches into his suit jacket and pulls his phone from his pocket. Not even glancing at it, he hands it over to me. Nodding at the phone, he says, "Look at the notifications on the screen. I'm going to guess at least fifty emails and twenty texts have come in since we've sat down."

Squinting and quirking my lips to the side, I contemplate how serious he really is. Can one person really have that many texts and emails in an hour and a half? Only one way to find out. I make his phone come to life by pressing the home button and it immediately lights up with an endless amount of notifications. He has the privacy setting on so I can't see what any of them say, but they're all there, multiple emails and texts. *Did I just uncover why he is still single? A workaholic?* I glance at him and hand him back his phone. "Okay, so you do business things."

He laughs and pockets his phone back into his suit. "I own a few properties around town, stuff like that. Boring stuff that we don't need to go into detail about."

The waiter takes the check from Jack and leaves us at an impasse. Why is he so secretive? Is he hiding something? Should I be concerned?

Instead of wondering, I speak my mind. "Are you hiding something like some secret kink club I don't know about? Or are you selling weird things like teddy bears dressed in mermaid costumes and you don't want me to know about it?"

In the matter of seconds, Dennis brings back our check and Jack fills out the receipt and signs. Eyeing me, he puts his credit card in his wallet and says, "Just plain old property business, nothing too glamorous like mermaid teddy bears."

"And kink clubs?"

He grins at me. "No kink clubs; sorry to disappoint." He glances around the restaurant and then back at me. "I don't want this evening to end. Would you care to join me for a walk? The beach is only two blocks away."

"Are you asking for a late-night beach stroll, Jack?"

"I am." Standing, he buttons his suit jacket and offers his hand to me. For a brief moment, I stare at his hand, wondering if I should take it. Despite his intentional avoidance to talk about his job, he's amazing. He's an important man, that's obvious, but it makes me wonder, just how important? Important enough to not tell me his last name or go into detail about his business? Maybe that's okay though. It gives me something to find out about him. It gives me something to talk about on our second date and from the way this evening is continuing, seems like there'll be a second date.

Taking a step forward in my dating life, I put my hand in his and allow him to guide me out of the restaurant and toward the beach. For some reason, this seems like the beginning of something special, something that will stay with me for a very long time.

You're wondering how could that possibly be, right? How could I have that feeling so soon?

Easy.

The strong and powerful yet kind and funny man standing next to me is holding my hand without a second thought, as if he's been meant to hold my hand his entire life.

That's how.

CHAPTER SIX

NOELY

"How can you walk in those things?" Jack asks while staring at my feet. We're a block from the ocean, his hand still holds mine, and I can already smell the fresh sea salt in the air. The smell is comforting, reminds me of my childhood, of all the days I looked forward to hanging out on the beach with my family.

"You get used to them after a while. Just seems like second nature now. I almost feel weird when I have to wear flats." I have on my five-inch red pumps that match my dress perfectly. It was a no-brainer as to what shoes and lipstick to pair with the outfit. I'm killing it in red tonight.

"Well, they're sexy."

I glance at him and a grin spreads across his face. "Jack, are you trying to hit on me?" I ask in mock surprise.

"Nah, just telling you the truth."

When we reach the beach, Jack lets go of my hand, squats, and unties his shoes. "Care to join me for some bare feet in the sand?"

Don't mind if I do.

I kick off my heels and when I bend down to pick them up, Jack snags them from me and tosses them in the bushes along with his shoes and socks. I open my mouth to protest when he says, "I'll buy you a new pair if someone steals them, but I promise, they'll be fine."

"But . . . shoes." I reach out to them, as if they're Jack from Titanic and I'm Rose. I want to call out, "I'll never let go" but my impatient date tugs my hand toward the beach. Mentally, I tell them not to talk to strangers and to keep their heels sharp.

"You grew up in Escondido, so does that mean you went to Oceanside a lot?" Jack's question pulls me away from my abandoned shoes and toward the ocean in front of me.

I think back to my childhood, my brother and I boogie-boarding along the waves, my parents in their horizontally striped lawn chairs, both reading books, with a cooler between them serving as a mini coffee table. Almost every weekend in the summer we were out on the beach. It's where I grew up, and honestly, it's where my heart is—within the wake of the tumultuous waves.

"Oceanside was our beach of choice. We spent many summers along the shoreline, soaking in the sun and the water."

"We?" We're walking side by side, strolling slowly over the ground beneath us, making our way to where the tide has wet the sand.

"My family. I have an older brother, and we would spend hours in the ocean on our boogie boards, trying to catch waves and seeing who could ride onto shore the farthest. I never won." I chuckle.

"Ah. Your big brother never let you win?"

"Never." I shake my head and push a lock of hair out of my face. The breeze grows stronger as we approach the water, so I'm glad I have my hair pulled back in a low bun or else it would be flying everywhere. "What about you? Where did you grow up?"

"Not too far from you, actually. San Diego."

"Wow, we were pretty close. Did your elusive business practices bring you to Malibu?"

He chuckles softly to himself and grabs my hand, entwining my fingers with his. "Yes, my business brought me to Malibu. But I also love it here. Always have. My parents used to bring me here to visit my grandparents while they would hit up all the nightclubs in LA. I would spend quiet nights, listening to the waves and eating s'mores while my parents did their thing. They were all about dating each other, even when they were married."

"That's sweet."

He nods. "They are a beautiful example of true love."

True love, huh. I might just have to add romantic to Jack's growing list of why he's so great.

We reach the water's edge and Jack spins me in place, shocking me until his hand lands on my hip and he pulls me in close. Heat vibrates through my body from how close he is, how his scent is surrounding me, how his hand grips my side with such strength, as if he's trying to claim me as his, right here in the middle of the beach.

I'm about to ask him what he's doing when he begins shifting us side to side, leading me to a romantic dance under the glittering stars. The tide rolls in, splashing our bare feet as the sand molds and melts around our toes.

As if what we're doing isn't on the top five most romantic things ever, Jack casually asks, "Was it fun growing up with a brother? I'm an only child, and even though I had cousins, my grandparents and my parents gave me their undivided attention. I always wondered what it would have been like to have siblings."

Loving this moment, this natural and almost raw moment between us, I move my hand so it's gripping the back of his neck, pulling me in a little closer. "It was nice having someone to commiserate with when our parents were driving us nuts, and when I was younger, it was great to have someone to play with. But our teenage years? Yikes. There were too many hormones flinging around our house. It hasn't been until recently that we've gotten along and a lot of it has to do with my brother's wife. Alex married someone I adore, so getting together is a lot easier. I guess there are pros and cons, but I know when my parents get older, it's going to be nice to have someone to lean on, you know?"

"Completely." When was the last time I simply walked along the beach? As he tells me more about his family, I start to relax even more. He was reticent about business, but thankfully, not about his family. Maybe I don't have anything to worry about, after all. The hand on my hip moves farther down where it splays out across the width of my lower back, coming close to my rear. And once again, my body heats from my wet toes to my wind-blown low bun.

We dance for what seems like forever until I break the silence. "Can I ask you a question?"

"Shoot."

Is it weird how attractive I find it when he's so direct? Seems like an odd thing to find attractive, but it makes me think he's a shark when it comes to business—probably ruthless—and for some reason, that's exciting.

"How old are you?"

His chin runs along my hair as he chuckles close to my ear. "Isn't that a dating faux pas? Asking someone to reveal their age?"

Pushing away slightly, I look at him and smile softly. "I think that's only with women, so men don't count." Leaning in close again, I continue, "I'm just curious. You don't look old, but you seem so refined, so put together and important, unlike other men I've dated."

"Is that right?" I shiver and I'm not sure if it was from the way his voice sounds so smooth, so sexy, or from the breeze whipping off the ocean. Either way, Jack notices and breaks our contact. Before I can ask what he's doing, he removes his jacket and places it over my shoulders, encasing me in his toe-curling scent.

Taking my hand again, he leads me toward the top of the beach where the vegetation meets the sand, and to my surprise sits down, pulling on my hand to join him. Shoulder to shoulder, we sit together, my hand still wrapped around Jack's with his thumb slowly making lazy circles along my knuckles.

God, that feels so good. So good that it's raising goosebumps along my skin.

"I'm thirty-one. Not geezer status, but old enough to have experienced some things."

"Thirty-one, huh?" I bump my shoulder with him. "Man, that's getting up there."

He scoffs. "Yeah, might as well start digging my grave now, huh?" He buries his wet feet into the ground and I do the same, feeling the warm sand beneath my toes. "Let me guess, you're twenty-seven."

Right on the money. Although I *think* I should be insulted.

"You know, it's rude to be spot on about a women's age. You should always guess five years younger than what you actually think they are."

"Nah, you're definitely too sophisticated to be twenty-two. You're smart, beautiful, and have a great job, so there had to be some wisdom behind your years. Twenty-seven suits you."

Once again, I'm blushing. How is it possible that this man has made me turn red multiple times in one night? *God, what else could he make me do multiple times in one night?* From the size of his hands, I'm going to guess some pretty amazing things.

"You're quite the charmer, Jack. You're making it hard on me to try to find a flaw."

"Believe me, they're there." He brings the back of my hand to his lips and places a gentle kiss on my knuckles. His lips are soft, warm, and I desperately want him to press them against my lips.

I'm not a kiss on the first date kind of girl but for Jack, for this man who's swept me into his little world, I can easily make an exception.

Standing, he helps me up and brings me to where we dropped off our shoes, which causes a pang of disappointment. It hits me harder than expected. I'm really not ready for this night to end. It seems so strange. I only met this man a little over two hours ago, and yet I want more time with him. I want to talk more, to have more time holding his hand, taking in his scent, to listen to the deep rumble of his chuckle.

"Told you your shoes would be fine." Letting go of my hand, he leans down and picks up our discarded footwear. He sets my shoes upright on the ground in front of me, making it quite easy to slip my feet inside of them after brushing off the sand. Beside me, on the curb, Jack brushes his feet off, ridding the sand between his toes.

Oddly, I take in his feet, how long they are and devoid of hair. His toes are actually nice to look at as well, unlike other men's feet I've seen. I swear I've seen some with green toenails, no joke. Jack's feet are a far cry from gross, they're actually pleasing . . . sexy.

Hmm . . .

Okay, I might be a little far gone when it comes to this man, because thinking his feet are sexy, that might be going a little far. Although, in my head, I can see him wearing a pair of jeans, unbuckled, no shirt, and barefoot. Can I get an AMEN to that image? Irresistible, right?

I have to see him again, no doubt in my mind. There is something special about him, something I haven't seen in another man before, something I don't want to let go.

When Jack stands, I feel myself gravitate toward him, but not wanting to look needy, I let him make the next move, wanting to see where the night takes us.

He puts his hands in his pockets and smirks at me. "Feel like a late-night coffee? There's a place around the corner that's quaint and still open. Unless you're tired—"

"I'm not tired."

A lazy smile stretches over Jack's face. I think he feels it too, this connection between us, this electric energy. There's no denying it. We were meant to meet each other.

"Good, come with me."

He takes my hand in his and once again, I'm swept away by my very first blind date.

"There is no way you did that."

Jack's head falls back as his laugh takes over his body, his hand on my thigh in disbelief.

So many things are running through me right now: the intimate setting, a loveseat in the back of the coffee house, Jack's body almost flush against mine, his hand on my thigh with his thumb stroking my skin. His gorgeous laugh echoes against the small space we've taken over in the back of the coffee shop, filling me with such warmth that I feel like my body is about to combust from heat.

"I did," I confirm. "I wanted to see if Nomar Guirerra was all talk or not, so I accidentally walked in on him in his dressing room."

"Oh shit." Jack wipes at his eyes. It's the first time he's sworn all night and for some reason, it makes him that much sexier.

Nomar Guirerra is a famous surfer in Malibu who claims to be well endowed. I've seen him in a Speedo before, and unless he rolls his ding-a-ling up like a sushi roll, there is no way he's packing penis. No freaking way. And when I walked in on him in his dressing room, my suspicions were confirmed.

"All I can say is he must be a grower, not a shower."

Jack's laugh starts to subside but there is still humor in his eyes. We both finished our coffees twenty minutes ago but we've made no attempt to leave. Instead, Jack has moved closer and closer, hence the hand on the thigh.

"Do you gossip much? About celebrities, that is?"

"Not really." His question kind of throws me off. Am I gossiping? *Am* I a gossip? With Dylan, yes, but anyone else, usually not. I don't want word getting around that I tell celebrity secrets, or else I'll never get anyone on the show. "I have to be confidential with information I learn, because no one likes to talk to a morning show host who likes to gossip."

"Makes sense." He nods, still contemplating my answer. "Privacy is important, especially for me. I've been burned in the past about my private life being shared and exposed to the wrong people."

Huh, I wonder if that's why he's been so secretive about his business. That would make sense. Does he not trust me? Of course he doesn't. He barely knows me. For all he knows, I could be some psycho creep waiting to expose him. Wanting to put him at ease, I say, "Don't get me wrong, Nomar had it coming."

"The dude is a total tool, I get it," he answers, sounding a bit off.

"What about you?" I turn a little bit more so we're facing each other. His hand slides off my thigh, and I miss his warmth instantly. "Are you an office gossip?"

"Not even a little, but that's probably because I'm so far removed from all the gossip, I have nothing to share." He chews on his lip for a second and then says, "But if I heard Jimmy John got Peggy Leggy impregnated on the third floor copier, you can bet that beautiful ass of yours, I very well might spread that little tidbit around."

Beautiful ass? I like that compliment.

But back to what he really said. I scrunch my nose. "Do you really have someone at your office named Peggy Leggy and Jimmy John?"

He chuckles and shakes his head. "No. Jimmy John, Johnny Jim, and Peggy Leggy are names my grandpa used when telling me stories before I went to bed."

"When you would stay with him in Malibu?"

He nods his head. "Yeah, he used to open up the window in the bedroom they had specifically for me, so I could hear the waves crash onto the shore, and he would tell me a bedtime story. It was something he always used to make up on the spot and it was always about those three characters fighting a potato with red eyes."

"A potato with red eyes?"

He nods, his lips turned up in humor. "Yeah, my grandpa was very punny and very Irish. So everything was always potatoes and cabbage, even villains in made-up stories. But they were the best stories. I begged him when I was in middle school to write down his stories, to make a potato with red eyes book, something I could read when I wasn't at their house visiting, but he said it wasn't something he could write. What made the stories so great were their spontaneity." Jack sighs and shakes his head. "I wish back then, we had the technology we have today, because I would have recorded him, anything to hear those stories once again."

Immediately I reach out to him and place my hand on his leg, stroking it softly, my heart breaking from the sadness in his voice. "From the way you're talking, I take it your grandpa has passed."

Nodding, Jack takes a deep breath. "When I was a junior in high school. It really messed with my head. He was my best friend, and it about destroyed me. There isn't a day that goes by that I don't think about him. I just hope one day I'll be able to retell his stories to my kids while they listen to the waves crash, or at least attempt to."

"I'm sure you will."

Jack's hand covers mine, and he gives me a sad smile. I'm tempted to kiss the sadness right off his face, to make the light come back into his eyes, but I don't think that's my place. We've had an amazing night, but we're still brand new to each other, so I refrain.

Taking a look at his watch, Jack's eyes fill with regret. "I should get you home. You have a morning show to put on in a few hours, and I'm sure you're going to want to get at least a couple hours of sleep." Rising from the couch, he takes my hand in his, and we walk past the tables and chairs in the coffee house and out onto the streets.

"Did you take a taxi?"

"Uber actually."

He nods. "My driver is around the corner. I'm happy to take you home, but I'll understand if you want to keep that side of your life private still."

Should I let him take me home? That is kind of a big step, but I also want to spend just a little more time with him. Just a few more minutes.

"I'm pretty close, I don't mind walking actually," I say, feeling silly about driving. The only reason I took an Uber was because I didn't want to sweat in the sun while walking to the restaurant before my date.

Growing tense, Jack shakes his head. "No way am I letting you walk home alone at this hour. I don't care if it's Malibu. Can I walk you home if you're close?"

"I'd like that. It's really only about five blocks down the street."

"Five blocks? And here I thought I was showing you around the area." We start walking in the direction of my house.

"I thought it was cute. I liked it."

"I like you," he counters, his eyes trained on me as we continue forward.

Feeling suddenly shy, I keep my gaze forward, as Jack's jacket is still draped over my shoulders. "I like you, Jack," I answer on almost a whisper.

God, I want to bury my head in my hands. No matter how old I get, I think this will always be hard, to express yourself in such a vulnerable way. I always think making friends as an adult is hard, but finding someone to spend the rest of your life with, now that's the ultimate challenge. There's so much vulnerability. You have to be strong and confident, but when that's not your personality, when you embarrass easily, it almost feels like torture, trying to communicate with another adult about your feelings.

I just wish it wasn't such an awkward situation. Hell, even if I watch a fake sitcom couple try to express themselves romantically, I feel uncomfortable.

"You like me, huh? That's good to know. Does that mean when the app asks you later if you want to go on a second date, you're going to say yes?" Jack doesn't skip a beat, and I like that about him.

"Depends."

"Depends on what?" Jack squeezes my hand, sending a bolt of pleasure up my arm.

"Depends on if you're going to say yes."

For a moment, Jack is silent, as if he's really trying to decide if he's going to say yes. "There's no way in hell I would be able to say goodbye to you forever tonight. I not only want to see you again, but I *need* to see you again."

A long exhale escapes me. I swear I feel like I'm living in a movie right now. I never really thought men like Jack existed. I always thought they were a fictional character made up in someone's head. But here he is, in real life, asking to see me again. I can't say yes fast enough.

"I would love to see you again," I tell him sincerely.

We exchange a quick glance, both our smiles stretching across our faces. The rest of the walk, we're silent, and it surprises me how much I like the simplicity of enjoying each other's company and the feel of our tandem steps and clasped hands.

When we reach the gate to my house, I turn toward Jack and say, "This is it." I release his hand and hand him his jacket back. The loss of his smell surrounding me, hugging me, sends a bone-jarring disappointment through my body. *How creepy would be to ask to keep the jacket?*

Creepy.

You've known him for a few hours; don't try to claim his clothing just yet.

Taking in my quaint cottage house, Jack cutely smiles. "It's beautiful just like you." When he turns back toward me, he steps forward and cups my cheek, his eyes searching mine.

My breath hitches in my chest from his proximity, from the anticipation of his lips pressing against mine, sealing our night with a kiss.

What I wouldn't give for that picture-perfect ending. I feel like I've experienced his mind, his humor, his spontaneity, now I want to experience him physically, and not just little touches, but something more.

I want to know what he tastes like. What the scruff on his jaw feels like under my fingers, caressing the soft skin on my cheek. I want to tangle my fingers into his short hair, to grip tightly onto his neck, and not release him until I'm fully sated by his mouth.

"I had an amazing time tonight, Noely. One of the best nights I've had in a long time."

I press my palm over the hand that's cupping my cheek and rub the back of it with my thumb. "This has been one of my best nights in a long time as well," I tell him honestly. "I actually can't remember having this much fun before."

"I'm glad." Moving in even closer, Jack leans forward and gently presses a kiss against my cheek and then pulls away, deflating my hopes in the matter of seconds. "Thank you for tonight, Noely. Sleep well."

Stepping away, Jack puts his hands in his pockets and keeps his eyes fixed on mine as I try to comprehend what just happened. *No kiss?* Did he just kiss me on the cheek, something a friend or mere acquaintance would do?

Stunned, I press my hand against my cheek where he kissed me, and no doubt, look as confused as I am. Hands still in his pockets, he shrugs his shoulders. "All in good time, beautiful. Now get in your house before I do something I regret."

"What if I want you to do something you'll regret?" I ask, feeling a little foolish for being so brazen, but also wishing he wasn't so far away, that he would give me a tiny taste of what I know would most likely be one of the most soul-searing kisses I'll ever experience.

He takes another step back, as if he doesn't trust himself. The man must have some strong willpower because right about now, I'm two seconds away from flinging my body at him.

"If I start, I won't stop. I know myself too well. You've consumed me tonight, Noely, and I know if I kiss you, if I feel your lips against mine, there is no way I'd be able to say good night like a gentleman. So, from a distance I will say, thank you for an amazing night. I look forward to our second date." With a wink, he pulls his phone from his pocket, dials a number, and says, "I'm ready."

Like magic, a car appears and Jack hops in, his lip print on my cheek the only thing he's left behind.

Good God, that man is dangerous. Dangerous for all the right reasons.

Our second date can't come soon enough.

CHAPTER SEVEN

NOELY

"There you are!" Dylan says, flopping down in the makeup chair next to me. She hands me a paper cup full of coffee and takes a sip from her own cup, which I know is half coffee, half chocolate milk. She can't stand the bitter taste of coffee but is a beast without the caffeine. So I introduced her to chocolate milk in her coffee, and it seems what works for me works for her. I also like to put hot cocoa in my coffee too; that's a special nugget of info just for you.

"What happened to our morning breakfast together?" Dylan asks, pulling a muffin from her pocket and handing it to me. She likes to mother me—a lot—and I enjoy it on occasion, but I don't enjoy it when she starts lecturing me about safe sex and STDs, or when she takes out a napkin, dabs it on her tongue, and tries to wipe something off my face. I can go without those motherly moments.

Natasha, the queen behind my hair and makeup, is trying to tame the wet mess of hair on my head. I turn toward Dylan and point to my eyes. "See these bags? They need some attention, and it's going to take a lot of makeup to cover them up."

THREE BLIND DATES

A horrified expression passes over Dylan when she takes in my face. "Ew, your eyes look like they oozed under your skin and gathered into little pockets below your lashes." She goes to poke them but I swat her hand away. "Why are they—?" She pauses and then a giant smile crosses her face. "Oh my God, you had your date last night. Please tell me it went well. It did, right? Did you invite him back to your place? You did, didn't you? You invited him back to your place. Oh my God, you slept with him on your first date. You little hussy, you."

Thank God Natasha signed an NDA before she started working with us, or she'd have some pretty juicy material to sell to the tabloids on a daily basis.

"I didn't sleep with him; you know me better than that."

"You're right, you wouldn't sleep with someone on the first date, but it went well, right?" Dylan pokes my shoulder with a knowing smile.

I can't help but grin over my coffee. I've had a permanent grin on my face all morning. Yes, I was a little disappointed I didn't get my good-night kiss—well, good-night kiss on the lips—but his reasoning for not kissing me satisfied me. Hell, it more than satisfied me. It made me feel special, sexy, absolutely irresistible, and that's one of the best qualities a man can give a woman. Jack did it with a simple look and his devastatingly charming words.

Taking a sip of coffee, I rejoice as the hot liquid cascades down my throat. "It went really well."

"Ah, I knew it." Dylan bounces in her chair, excitement billowing over. "I'm ten years deep in my marriage, and don't get me wrong, I wouldn't trade it for anything, but I need to know everything. I want to know what dating is like today. Did he woo you? Was he funny? Oh God, is he hot? Please tell me he's hot."

"He's hot." I nod, trying not to giggle. God, I feel like a teenager. "He was impeccably dressed, first of all. He was dressed in a suit that expertly wrapped around his body in all the right ways. He's tall with brown hair and deep, deep brown eyes, making him seem all kinds of mysterious. But he's funny, outgoing, and his laugh—God, Dylan, his laugh. It's deep and rumbly and so freaking sexy."

"I love a good laugh." Dylan sighs. "Chad has a good laugh. I can appreciate a man who doesn't mind bellowing out a loud chortle. What did you guys—?"

"Excuse me, Miss, Clark, these were sent to you this morning." From the reflection in the mirror, I see a beautiful bouquet covering the person holding them.

Turning in my seat, I take them as Dylan squeals next to me, saying, "He must have pulled some serious strings to get those delivered this early."

She's right, he had to have paid a lot of money to have someone deliver flowers this morning, which makes them that much more special. I thank the PA and inwardly squeal. Pulling the card from the flowers, I read the handwritten note from Jack.

Good morning, Noely.

Last night, I got absolutely zero sleep because I couldn't stop thinking about you. I should have kissed you, and I'm regretting my decision now. Please forgive me and if you accept our second date, you are being warned now, I'm claiming that kiss I so stupidly forgot to capture last night.

Jack

I press the card to my chest and sigh. Yes, I freaking sigh. I sigh so hard because there's no denying it ladies, Jack is sigh-worthy.

Dylan nudges my shoulder. "What does it say? You're killing me here."

Smelling the flowers, I hand Dylan the note, not wanting to read it out loud. While she reads, I take in the bouquet Jack sent. It's unlike any bouquet I've ever seen. There is a beautiful balance of greenery with pops of purple and pink flowers. Absolutely stunning.

"He didn't kiss you last night?" Dylan hands me the card back, which I put in my pocket.

"He kissed me on the cheek." My answer causes Dylan to roll her eyes. "He had his reasons." I don't share why, seems weird to say if he kissed me he would have boned me, so I keep that to myself.

"So does this mean you're going to go on a second date?"

Bringing the flowers to my nose, I take a deep breath and let their calming scent ease my racing heart. "Without a doubt."

～

"Great show, ladies." Kevin calls out while pulling off his headset and hanging it on a monitor.

Feeling a little cramped from sitting for so long, I stand and straighten out my dress while stretching my arms out. "I'm going to head to the gym. Care to join me?"

Dylan shakes her head. "I have a million cupcakes to make for the kidlet's bake sale this weekend."

I would suggest Dylan just buys them, but I know better. She likes to be involved in everything when it comes to her kids, even if it means she's shackled to the kitchen, mixing multiple cupcake batters from scratch. She's supermom, and I admire her for it.

"What flavors are you making?" Dylan makes the best cupcakes. If she wasn't so good at her job, I would suggest she open her own bakery.

Looking to the ceiling, she recalls her chosen flavors by ticking off on her fingers. "Let's see. Orange creamsicle, lemon blueberry, and strawberry shortcake."

"Going fruity this go around."

Dylan shrugs. "I went chocolate last time, so thought I'd switch it up. Lift some extra weights for me. I'll be thinking of you when I'm taste testing."

I point at Dylan while walking away. "Bring me a lemon blueberry tomorrow and I won't tell our trainer you're eating cupcakes instead of working out at the gym."

"Deal."

I head to my dressing room, ready to get out of the tight confines of my dress. I have a shred of self-respect when it comes to disrobing after our show, and *unlike* Dylan, I wait to take my bra off until I'm in a private setting. *Like at home.*

Before I went on air, I received a notification via the *Going in Blind* app asking if I wanted to go on a second date with Jack, and I couldn't say yes fast enough. And to my utter delight, the big heart appeared on the screen. Jack said yes to a second date as well and suggested option B for our date. I fumbled quickly to read all about option B. Westward Beach Sunset Picnic this Saturday.

I don't think I could have picked something more perfect for our second date. We both love the beach, and if I had it my way last night, I would have spent a lot more time with my toes in the sand and Jack's body flush against mine, so to have another opportunity to replicate last night has me counting down the minutes until Saturday.

In my dressing room, I shut the door and pull out my phone. Before I went on air, I sent a message to Jack—or WindsorKnot—to thank him for the flowers. I've been dying to see if he messaged me back.

When I open the app, I'm rewarded with a little inbox notification.

My mind drifts to *You've Got Mail* and one of Meg Ryan's early emails in the movie where she talks about the excitement of hearing those three little words, "You've got Mail." I feel it. I understand it. The anticipation of waiting for that special person to connect with you again. In an age where instant gratification is the norm, it's a beautiful thing to have to wait for a little mailbox to light up.

Having zero patience, I open his message.

. . .

THREE BLIND DATES

*S*hopGirl,
 You're more than welcome for the flowers.
 I have a confession: I've done absolutely nothing at work this morning and you're to blame. Not only did I get zero sleep, but I wound up watching your show, unable to take my eyes off you, off those lips I didn't get to taste. It wasn't until my assistant snapped at me that I turned the TV off and tried to get some work done. You've ruined me, ShopGirl.
 Jack

Normally, I would find his response a little cheesy, but after spending a decent amount of time with Jack last night, I know cheesiness is the furthest thing from the truth when it comes to him. So far, he seems genuine and calculated. He wouldn't say something to garner a reaction. He truly means it and that's what's making my heart flutter a mile a minute.

I sit on the couch in my dressing room and type out a response.

*W*indsorKnot,
 I would like to take the blame for your lack of productivity this morning but I'm afraid I'm going to have to place the blame on you. Maybe if you actually kissed me last night, you wouldn't have to daydream about what my lips taste like.
 My suggestion: next time you see me, kiss me.
 Noely

~

I flick a piece of lettuce to the side and scrunch my nose at the salad bowl on my lap. Last night's steak put a little dent in the calories for the week, so the bland salad I ate for dinner has me wishing I listened to my stomach while picking up my takeout and grabbed the giant Rice Krispies Treat that was calling my name.

It doesn't help that Dylan has been sending me pictures of her cupcakes all evening either.

Setting my salad bowl to the side, I pull my blanketed legs to my chest and rest my arms on top of my knees while I look at the ocean. I don't have a beachfront property, but my home is on a cliff overlooking the ocean, so it's close enough for me.

I have yet to hear from Jack since my last message, and I worry if maybe I was a little too upfront . . . No, it was perfect. I refuse to second-guess myself during this process. I've been second-guessing my entire dating life. It's time I say what I want to say and do what I want to do. If I want to find a true partner in life, then I need to act myself. And Noely Clark would have easily given Jack a hard time for not kissing her.

Smiling to myself, I take in the waves crashing into the rocks just as my phone rings.

Kevin.

Ugh, what does he want?

"Kevin, what do I owe the pleasure?" Do you hear the sarcasm in my voice?

"Hope I didn't interrupt your beauty sleep. Lord knows you need it."

I breathe out heavily with my nostrils flaring. I know he's joking, but the man's taunts are touching my last nerve lately.

"Just enjoying a crappy salad for dinner. What's up?"

Kevin clears his throat and says, "Got a call from The Earthquakes."

My ears perk up. The Earthquakes, or Quakes for short, is LA's professional hockey team and whenever we get a call from them it means they want an interview. These are my favorite kinds of calls because outside my job, I'm a huge hockey and baseball fan, so when I can combine my career with what I love, it's always a plus.

"Oh? Do they have a player they want us to interview?"

"Not just a player, but Hayden Holmes."

THREE BLIND DATES

Be cool. Be cool. Oh my God . . . be cool!
But *gahhhhhhhh!*

Hayden Holmes. I get to interview Hayden Holmes. He's the up-and-coming rookie traded to the Quakes over the off season from Philadelphia. It was a huge gain for the Quakes because he has so much promise. He already rocked his rookie season, so with a year under his belt, I know he's going to kill it next season and thankfully, he will be with the Quakes killing it.

"Hayden, wow. That's really exciting." I play it cool even though my nerves are dancing around in my belly. I don't usually fangirl much, but this is a big deal. *He is a big deal.*

"Yes, since they called last minute, we're going to put him on as a surprise guest tomorrow. Their publicists have already sent over a basic outline of what to talk about with him, so I'll email that over. Give it a glance but it's like every other athlete interview we've done."

"Okay, so he's on tomorrow. What segment are we cutting then?"

"Fritattas with Dylan. We're moving that to Friday, turning it into Fritatta Friday."

"Oh, I'm sure she'll love that. All right, so then we should be good to go. I'll check the email and do a little research on Hayden before tomorrow morning."

"No need. I had Duncan put together a quick rundown for you, and I'm emailing that." Kevin pauses for a second before he says, "And for Friday, I also have a little ten-minute segment worked in while you're eating fritattas to talk about your little dating adventure."

"Come on, Kevin," I huff. He has to be over that by now.

"You're not going to get out of this, Noely. I've talked with Lynn at *Going in Blind*. She's working on a special segment with her team, but in the meantime, it will be a great personal piece for our viewers. If anything, you can encourage other singles out there to join the program. I mean, you did have your first date, didn't you? You can talk about that."

"And if I don't?"

Kevin sharply exhales, irritation seeping into my ear. "Noely, don't make me act like an ass to you, okay?" *Been there, Kevin. Been there.*

"Fine, but I'm not going to like it."

"Should have thought about that before you used company equipment. See you in the morning."

He hangs up before I can respond. Typical Kevin. Maybe it won't be so bad. If anything, I owe it to *Going in Blind* for matching me with Jack. Who knows, maybe my story could help others. Searching for love is a daunting task, so maybe a little added encouragement from someone who's been through the program is just what some of our viewers need.

Speaking of *Going in Blind* . . .

Eager to see if Jack messaged back, I open the app and am rewarded with a notification in my inbox. Once again, my stomach starts to do somersaults.

Jack wrote back.

ShopGirl,

Your boldness doesn't go unnoticed. Being a gentleman was my number-one priority but now I know who I'm dealing with, I'm prepared to drop the gentleman act and take what I want. This Saturday, it's going to be you, me, the open waves, and my lips on yours. Until then, put me out of my misery and tell me something about yourself I don't know. Spare me and give me a detail about you to help me get through these next few mundane days.

Jack

Leaning back in my lounge chair, the sky around me falling to a midnight blue, I snuggle under my blanket and type out a response, my smile never fading.

. . .

WindsorKnot,
    Have you ever wondered what it would look like if you took a hockey puck and split it in half? What you would see inside? I was convinced there was some kind of lucky charm inside one, so like the genius I was at twelve, I decided to find out for myself. With bravado and stupidity coursing through me, I placed a hockey puck on the back deck, roared my dad's chainsaw to life, and cut a line right through . . . the back porch, missing the puck completely. That was the moment I thought, if my parents really love me, like truly love me, they won't kill me over this.

    Thank God for unconditional love, right? Your turn.
    Noely

CHAPTER EIGHT

NOELY

"The lips, the teeth, the tip of the tongue, the tip of the tongue, the teeth, the lips," Dylan repeats over and over again, exaggerating her mouth movements. Every other break, she spends time keeping her vocals warm and her frontal placements crisp.

Her vocals usually wash right over me, but today, they're grating on my nerves. Maybe because I'm incredibly nervous. I'm going to be honest: professional athletes are a weakness of mine. For some reason, whenever I'm around one, I turn into a pile of mush and act like a complete ass. Ask Kevin, I'm sure he has a reel of me somewhere fawning over every professional athlete we've had on the show.

"Any noise annoys the oyster. Any noise annoys—"

"Me," I cut in. "Any noise annoys me. Dylan, you're warmed up, can you cool it on the tongue twisters for now?" I ask while looking over my notes for our segment with Hayden.

"Why do men who play with balls make you nervous every time?"

"Technically, Hayden plays with a puck, and I don't know. I

think it's the forearms; they're intimidating. You see them on TV and they seem so normal, but when you see them in person it's like, 'where did you get all those muscles?' It's just not fair to be that beefy—"

"Noely, Dylan, I would like you to meet Hayden Holmes," Kevin says, and because he interrupted my rant, no doubt I look just as mortified as I feel.

God, I hope Hayden didn't hear any of that.

Gathering myself, trying not to look all shaky and nervous, I stand and see a very tall, very built man smiling at me. His honey-colored hair is hidden under an LA Quakes cap, but his blue eyes are more vivid than in photos I've seen. His strong jaw is covered by a light scruff, and his lips are fuller than I would expect on a man. His white long-sleeved shirt stretches across his brawny chest, and the sleeves are pushed up, showing off his well-defined forearms. Figures! They had to make an appearance, didn't they? Damn you, forearms, damn all the forearms!

Taking a step forward, I reach out my shaky hand. "Hayden, it's a pleasure to meet you. Welcome to California. I'm sure it's a big change from Philly."

He smiles sweetly, causing a little dimple on the right side of his cheek to peek out. "I would say a big change is an accurate description." He chuckles. "Pine trees to palm trees is a huge leap." His large, calloused hand releases mine, and he turns to Dylan. "It's nice to meet you both. Thanks for having me on the show."

Ignoring Hayden completely, hand still in his, Dylan nudges my shoulder with hers and says, "Oh, the grip on this guy, makes you wonder what else he can tightly grip."

Rolling my eyes, I clear my throat and try to be the professional one between us. "Do you have any questions about your interview? Are you feeling good about it?"

Releasing Dylan's hand, he loops his thumbs in his belt loops and says, "I'm feeling good. My agent went over everything."

"Perfect."

"Noely, on in twenty."

"Okay." I nod at Hayden. "You might want to scoot out of camera shot until we call you."

Chuckling to himself, he backs away while giving me a wink, which only sends a heat of awareness up my spine.

Leaning toward me, her lips practically inside my ear, Dylan says, "Oh my God, he totally winked at you." I ignore her, not wanting to make a big scene in front of the man who is standing ten feet away. "Did you hear me?" Dylan repeats.

"Yes," I whisper shout at her. "I heard you hissing in my ear, now drop it."

"He wants in your pants—"

"Three, two . . ." Our director points at me.

Feeling a little flustered, I try to put on my professional Good Morning, Malibu face and read off the teleprompter. "Welcome back. Like we said at the top of the hour, we have a special surprise guest with us today."

"That's right," Dylan cuts in. "And he's a treat for both men and women. Isn't that right, Noely?"

A flush creeps up my face, and I just pray the lights wash it out. I don't know if it's Dylan's ribbing, or Hayden's gaze from the sidelines, or knowledge that Jack might be watching, but man oh man, my tongue feels swollen and my words sound garbled in my ears.

"Uh, yes, sure." I clear my throat and tap my cue cards on my legs. Looking around, Kevin gives me the universal signal for *keep going,* so I quickly turn to the prompter again. "If you haven't been paying attention this summer, you might have missed one of the biggest steals LA made, and we have our very own LA Quakes signed, star-studded hockey rookie from last season, Hayden Holmes joining us this morning." I stand with Dylan and start clapping along with the rest of production. "Please welcome, the newest LA Quakes forward, Hayden Holmes."

Stepping onto set, Hayden waves at the camera, that boyish smile probably melting the hearts of every Good Morning, Malibu viewer. Leaning in, Hayden presses a kiss against my cheek while his hand grips my side, sending my nerves into overdrive. Dylan reaches for a light peck as well and then we take our seats.

Shifting uncomfortably since Hayden's long legs are bumping against my knees, I sweep my hair behind my shoulders and look at my cards. *Good God, why am I so nervous?*

"Hayden, we're so glad you could join us today," I say, smiling brightly for the camera.

"Oh, I'm glad I could surprise everyone, and the warm welcome has made the move from Philly so much easier."

"After a season like last year's, you're just what our team needs, so we're grateful you're here."

Shyly, he chuckles and runs his hand through his thick hair. I've seen Hayden interviewed, and he's never seemed to be the overly confident asshole some athletes are. He's always seemed more down to earth, and right now, I'm getting that vibe.

For the next five minutes, we talk about his upcoming training, the guys on the team, and his transition from snow to sun. He laughs with Dylan, speaks dearly about the fans, and charms everyone in the studio.

"And we're out," Kevin calls while looking down at his clipboard.

I let out a long breath, as if someone was pulling on an imaginary corset wrapped around me and let go of the strings.

"Thank you so much, ladies." Hayden stands and looks at his phone. When he sees the time, he cringes. "I have a radio interview to get to. I hate to interview and run, but I don't want to be late."

"Not a problem at all," I answer. "Thanks for stopping by."

"Thanks for having me. I'll have promotions send over some tickets for you guys." With a brief hug, he bids us a goodbye and takes off, one hand stuffed in one of his jeans pocket, the other making a call on his phone.

"He's dreamy." Dylan pathetically sighs next to me. "Did you see his muscles flex under his shirt? I'm pretty sure his pecs were sending out some kind of Morse code to me during that entire interview. *Lick me, lick me.* I just wish my boobs were more adept in communicating, because I would have signaled to Chad through the camera that Hayden was my new hall pass."

"You didn't have to ask him if he was single," I chastise. "That was a little personal."

"Are you kidding? Of course I had to ask if he was single. That's our duty on Good Morning, Malibu, to ask the questions no other news channel will. Why do you think we sit here on these light pink couches, mimosas in front of us, and tissues popping up from the back of the couch? Because we're the show that brings you tears, laughs, and hunks. All the hunks." She pats my leg. "Now, do you want me to ask for his number for you?"

I dramatically roll my eyes. "No, Dylan. I have a date with Jack this Saturday, a date I'm really looking forward to. I want to see where that goes with The Suit."

"Oh, is that what you're calling him? The Suit? I like that."

Exasperated, I pat Dylan on the head and leave for my dressing room before she starts taking her bra off. I'm not in the mood to witness *and hear* her struggle.

The minute I reach my dressing room, my phone rings.

Checking out the caller ID, I smile to myself.

"Alex, how are you?" I put the phone on speaker and sit in my vanity chair to take off my earrings and makeup.

"Hey sis, I'm doing good."

I love my brother dearly, but he doesn't call often. He's more of a texter, so there is only one reason he's calling.

"So, I caught the show this morning." The smile I'm sporting grows even wider. Yep, I know exactly why he's calling.

"Oh yeah? What did you think? Did you like the music segment about the best tunes to use in the bedroom? Are you going to try those out with Lauren?"

"Uh . . . didn't catch that segment, thank God, but I did catch the last." Shocking.

"With Hayden Holmes?"

"Yeah. Hell, sis, you have the best job ever. How were you not worshipping at his feet while doing that interview? I would have easily started bowing in front of him if I were you."

Chuckling, I shake my head and wipe the makeup from my right eye. "I tend to stay away from bowing at my guests when doing interviews."

"You're missing out." Alex pauses and then asks, "So tell me, is he cool? I mean, I'm assuming he is, he looks pretty chill in his interviews. Is that all an act?"

I roll my eyes. My brother is so predictable. "He's chill, Alex. And before you ask, he already said he'd send over some tickets for the season."

"For the love of God, please tell me you're going to take me to a game."

"You're the first on my list."

"Fuck, yes!" I laugh. He sounds beyond ridiculous. "Do you think you could get me into the locker room? All I want is to be snapped in the ass by one of the players with a towel. I swear, I'll pull my pants down and give them the best kind of towel-snapping canvas, all white and creamy. That's one hell of an offer." *And Lauren loves him because . . .*

"Your gross ass, hanging in the air waiting for someone to snap a towel at it, is not an offer, Alex. That's a punishment." *A nightmare. I should know. I've been subjected to it before.*

"I'll pay them." Desperation drips from his voice.

Laughing, I say, "You need to get a life. I have to go to my spin class. Give Lauren a hug for me."

"Wait," Alex desperately calls out. "Do I still get first dibs on tickets?"

Exhausted, I say, "Yes, Alex. You get first dibs."

"Can I get that in writing?"

Without an answer, I hang up. Brothers, why are they so annoying?

I have much better things to do than assign tickets I don't have to my desperate brother. It's not like he doesn't have money to buy his own, but he thrives off free things. He always has.

I don't want to worry about him right now; not only do I have to prepare my little segment about my dating attempt before Friday, I have a message to respond to . . .

∼

Dearest ShopGirl,
    Have you ever thought about why a man gives a woman flowers? Why not a bag of groceries? Or a box of light bulbs, you know, something practical. Instead, we spend—or at least I do—an hour picking out the perfect bouquet, one that I not only think will make you deeply appreciate the gesture, but one that represents your beauty. I look for a bouquet that reminds me of your sweet smell, one that has the same pink blush as your cheeks, with a touch of your fiery red outfit. Sending a bouquet of flowers is a carefully mapped-out equation to gain your likeness, and yet, they die in a few days. So why not a carton of eggs instead?
    P.S. Did you get the flowers?
    Jack

Dear Bouquet Aficionado,
    A carton of eggs? A box of lightbulbs? Practical yes, romantic, not so much. I can go out and get myself a carton of eggs anytime I want, but flowers, those are special. There is something about receiving a bouquet from a man that sends a thrill of excitement through my body. It tells me I was on his mind, it shows me he cares, it gives me the impression that not only did I make my mark, but he wants to woo me.
    So is that what you're doing, Jack? Are you wooing me?
    P.S. I got the flowers and they were gorgeous. Thank you.
    Noely

. . .

Dear Woo-ee,
      There is something you need to know about me. I'm a ruthless businessman. In the boardroom, I'm a brilliant shark who makes split-second decisions about multi-million-dollar deals. I've made grown men cry using only words, and I don't take no for an answer. I get what I want, when I want it...
      Why am I telling you this? Because I know this is not the man I presented to you. You have seen the other side of me, the side of me that spends his time enjoying the gentle waves of the beach, who reminisces about potatoes with red eyes, and who will spend an hour analyzing every bouquet in a flower shop.
      Yes, Noely. I'm wooing you.
      Jack

Dear Ruthless Businessman,
      You get what you want, when you want it? Is that outside of the boardroom as well? Because I'm going to let you in on a little secret: I don't fold easily. Even with your big-bad-wolf businessman attitude, I will challenge you. I will be sure to make you work for what you want; it won't be handed to you. Do you think you're ready for that? Are you up for my defiance?
      Noely

Dear Defiant One,
      What's wooing without a little challenge?
      I do have a question though. That kiss I so stupidly skipped out on, the one that's up for grabs on Saturday, will that be a kiss I have to work to get, or will it be something that's easily handed to me? I ask so I can prepare myself for

the amount of wooing required.

On a scale from one to ten, ten being the highest amount of wooing, what are we talking here? A box of lightbulbs and a single daisy? Will that guarantee that kiss I so desperately need?

Jack

Dear Desperate for a Smooch,

Despite my inkling to say yes to a box of lightbulbs due to my lack of bulbs in my house, I'm afraid you're going to have to bring your A-game. Why, you might ask? Because I need to make sure you're not just all talk.

Actions, Jack. The best wooers, woo with action.

Noely

Dearest ShopGirl,

Happy Thursday. Actions speak louder than words, I'm well aware. Tell me, did a little brightness enter your life today?

Jack

Dear Expert Wooer,

Funny thing happened to me. I was getting ready for my show, and one of the production assistants brought me a purple box. There was no name attached to the parcel so I was unsure what it was, until I opened the lid and found a dozen, beautiful energy-efficient lightbulbs.

I might have snorted, but I'm neither confirming nor denying such a response.

All I have to say is, my house is brightly lit this evening and when I look around, light cascading and bouncing off my walls, all I can think about is you.

THREE BLIND DATES

You're bringing your A-game, and I think I might be in trouble.
Noely.

D*earest Noely,*
I pride myself in being honest, so I'll tell you this. You're in trouble. I have my eyes set on one thing and one thing alone. You.
This Saturday, you, me, and a kiss that needs to be claimed. I'm coming for you, Noely.
Jack

Jack is out for blood and I can't help but be giddy about it. What will his A-game be like? Is he going to turn up the heat? God, I hope so. Some people might have scoffed at a box of lightbulbs, but for some reason it was so fitting for him, and now I feel a little intimidated. What's Saturday going to bring? Is he going to kiss me when he first sees me? Or is he going to prolong it, make me wait?

I don't think I can wait, which means, I'm going to have to bring my A-game as well.

Seems like there is some primping in order. Time to make myself irresistibly hot, and I know just where to start.

CHAPTER NINE

NOELY

"Dylan!" I scream through the phone. "Dylan get over here now. Like stat. This is an emergency. Do not doddle, don't pick up donuts from the corner shop, and don't even think about bringing any kind of recording devices. Just get over here now!"

"Uh, I'm kind of naked."

"Then put some clothes on. For the love of God, just get over here now."

"But . . . I put the bath salts in my bath already."

"Oh my God! I'll buy you more, just get over here as fast as you can."

I hang up my phone and try to calm my racing heart. I close my eyes briefly, then open them and squint to look in the mirror. Squint because squinting makes it all better. At least that's what I try to tell myself. What was I thinking?

When I take in the squinted image in front of me, I try to tell myself it's not that bad, what I did wasn't a giant mistake, I'm making a statement, but . . . OH MY GOD!

There's a knock at my door, and I whip my head around to see who it is, as if I can see through my wooden door. Dylan's not that fast. We live pretty close, but it takes her at least ten minutes to put on underpants so that can't be her. *Unless she came naked* . . .

Is it Alex? I called him in a desperate panic because Dylan wasn't answering her phone. I left him a concerning voicemail about how my life is over with no explanation why. I probably scared the crap out of him.

Knowing he's going to kill me if I don't open the door, I take one last look in the mirror—a full-eyed look—send prayers to the heavens above for any kind of transformation, and open my front door.

"I don't need your ribbing—"

My voice falls from my lips as I stare at a perfectly executed Windsor knot. Horrified, utter mortification eclipsing me, and the need to hide myself, I screech like a hyena and slam the door shut, right on Jack's beautifully handsome face.

"Oh God, oh God, oh God." I start twirling in circles, holding the top of my head, trying to figure out what to do.

He can't see me like this . . .

Gah! He probably already saw me. Even though I like to believe I was lightning fast in closing the door, I know I wasn't. I stared at that damn Windsor knot for far too long.

There's another light knock on the door. "Noely."

Oh GOD! He's still here.

What am I talking about, of course he's still here. He probably wants a picture of the freak show he just saw. He probably wants to make sure it really is me who answered the door, and not some creepy stalker looking to murder innocent victims.

This is not the A-game I wanted to bring to the table, not even close. Unless he's interested in dating a psychotic clown.

Yes, you read that correctly. A psychotic clown.

Well, psychotic clown or maybe little orphan Annie, or . . . maybe Rose Nylund from The Golden Girls. Any of those will do, but I'm leaning more toward psychotic clown due to the crazed look in my eyes.

What did I do, you ask?

I tried to bring my A-game to the table, but instead I brought a lady version of a cotton ball.

I permed my hair, okay? I decided to do an at-home perm to give myself luscious waves. But instead, I'm staring down an uglier version of Justin Timberlake's Top Ramen noodle-head days.

Giant mistake, huge, like colossal . . . like my shoulder blade-length hair is now bouncing buoyantly at my chin. And my bangs . . . oh hell, note to all women out there, don't try to perm your bangs. You think they're going to turn into pretty waves. No, they are Tootsie Rolls curled straight to my forehead.

It looks like I stuck my finger in a light socket for a good two minutes until I thought my hair was styled.

There's another knock at the door. "Noely, open up."

He's not going away. Jogging in place, looking around, I try to find a solution. A baseball cap is going to make the ends stick out more, and I don't feel like channeling my inner Monica Gellar when she was in Barbados.

Think, think, think.

I scan my entryway and see one of my scarves hanging on a hook. A scarf! Yes, perfect. I snag the fabric, look in my entryway mirror, and start wrapping the scarf around my head, scooping up the curls and trying to tame them. Somehow, through all the twists and turns and rush to get the scarf tied and the combination of fluff protruding from my head, I manage to form a scarf cone on top of my head and with each attempt to down the point at the top, it pops back up.

"Noely, come on, open the door."

Christ, he's persistent.

Knowing this isn't going to get any better and he most likely isn't going to go away, I resign to scarf conehead and open the door, hand on hip, chest puffed. Maybe my confidence will distract him.

Wrong.

His eyes immediately go to my white and pink flower scarf wrapped around my head. Way to be subtle.

THREE BLIND DATES

With his eyes pinned on my "accessory" I take in his impeccable suit. The fabric looks so soft, yet pressed to perfection, crisp and tailored to his every muscle. And that tie . . . When we went on our date, he was sans tie with two buttons undone, but for some reason, seeing him in a tie, cinched to his powerful neck, it does all kind of things in my belly.

The suit . . .

If I learned one thing from spending time with this man and writing messages back and forth, it's this: confidence is key, so instead of slamming the door on his face once again, I tilt my chin up, hand on my front door, and say, "Jack, what a pleasant surprise. What do I owe the pleasure of this visit?"

Eyeing me skeptically, he points to my head and asks, "What's going on there?"

Well, he isn't very gentlemanly. Didn't his mom ever teach him to not point out someone's flaws?

"Oh this?" I chuckle and press my hand against my scarf cone. "Trying something new for the show. I think it might be too tall for getting a good shot with the camera, but we'll see."

Stepping forward, invading my space, his eyes trained on my head, he reaches and undoes my scarf with one flick of his fingers. While my hair bounces around my head, I'm unable to deny the euphorically clean smell permeating from the man in front of me, or the way his roaming eyes sexily take me in.

Lifting his hand, he wraps one of the curls around his finger and lets it spring back. He's not laughing, he's not even smiling. He's just observant, studying me. It's making me squirm, squirm to the point that I start to ramble.

"So, as you can see, I did a thing." I touch my bouffant hairdo. "Not sure if it's really me or reads morning show host." I shrug. "But you know, Jack, what's life without trying something new, right?" He still studies me, his eyes rotating between my face and my hair. What the hell is he thinking? Speak up, man! "What do you think?" I fluff the bottom of my curls with my palm. "Should I dye it red and learn to juggle?"

Taking another step forward, Jack laces his hand with mine, the one that's fluffing my hair, and brings it to his chest as his other hand floats to the back of my neck, pulling me in close.

My breath catches in my chest, my body stiffens, as he leans his head forward and slowly lowers his lips to mine.

He's going to kiss me . . . even with this hair.

Inches from my lips, his minty breath tickles me when he says, "I couldn't wait until Saturday. Forgive me." And in seconds, his lips are slowly nipping across mine, gentle and soft.

I melt, right here in my entryway with my light-socket hair, I melt into a giant puddle of swoon.

One hand clasped to his chest, I trail my other hand to his lapel and grip tightly, not wanting him to go anywhere.

At first he's slow, methodically learning the way around my lips. But I can sense the minute he's familiar from the way his tongue enticingly runs along my lips, parting them automatically. A low growl erupts from him as he pulls me even closer and his tongue dives into my mouth, seductively sending chills up and down my body, capturing me into a wave of bliss.

My veins heat up, my skin prickles with awareness, my muscles turn into liquid, barely holding up my body. Never in my life have I been kissed like this, with such passion, with such assertiveness, with such an all-consuming effect I can't remember where I am.

Pulling slightly away, his forehead resting on mine, his lips lightly press kisses against mine until he says, "Fuck, you taste good."

The somersaults in my stomach are on overdrive and the mishap of my hair is far from my mind until I hear from the doorway, "Holy hell, what did you do to your hair?"

I squeeze my eyes shut as Jack turns around, his hands still wrapped around me, bringing me with him.

"Oh hell . . ." Dylan pauses and when I peek over at her, she's taking Jack in, starting from his polished shoes, to his tie, to his perfectly styled hair. "Forget your hair, who is this stunning piece of man you have in your entryway?" Leaning forward, hand blocking her mouth from Jack and whispering loudly, she asks, "Is this WindsorKnot?"

Lips pursed, I nod.

"Oooooo, he is handsome." She sets down a canvas bag and grips Jack's tie, invading all his personal space. I whack her hand away but not before she can give it a bit of a tug. "Look at that, cinched up real nice."

"Can you not touch him?" I chastise.

"Don't you sass me." Dylan points a finger at me and that's when I realize she's wearing her pink terrycloth robe and slippers. Jesus. "I flew over here to help you, ignoring my peaceful bath, thinking you might have tried to pierce your own nipple or something ridiculous. So if I want to touch WindsorKnot, I can."

Tightening the knot on her robe, she faces off with me, urging me to pick a fight. *Not* wanting to get into it with Dylan, I capitulate. "Jack, this is Dylan, my co-host. Dylan, this is Jack."

Curtseying like an idiot, Dylan bows her head and says, "Pleasure to meet you. I've heard nothing but sexy things about you."

"Is that right?" Jack looks at me, and of course, I am blushing. *Again.* "Well, it's a pleasure meeting you, Dylan. I'm not used to seeing you in such . . . casual clothing."

She winks at him. "You're getting a real behind-the-scenes look at the Good Morning, Malibu cast, lucky you." Directing her attention to me, Dylan tsks. "What did you get yourself into this time, Noely?"

Not wanting to have this conversation in front of Jack, I turn toward him and say, "Um, I don't want to kick you out, but there are some pressing matters Dylan and I have to tend to."

"She's talking about her hair, Jack."

I take a deep breath, reminding myself Dylan is here to help.

Smiling brightly, Jack gently pinches my chin, his touch soft and sweet. "Not a problem," he whispers. "I'll see you Saturday." Leaning down, he presses the sweetest of kisses on my lips, lingering longer than expected then pulls away. With a sexy wink, he adjusts the cuffs on his button-up shirt and gives a curt nod to Dylan before taking off, leaving me in a sexually aware stupor.

Not even sure if he's out of earshot, Dylan says, "That was freaking hot. The way he kissed you like that. God, he's fine."

He sure is.

Smiling, I shut the door and face the mockery of Dylan. There is no doubt in my mind. She's not going to let me live this one down.

"Home perm?" she asks. I nod. She rolls her eyes and shakes her head before bringing her canvas bag to my couch where she dumps it out. A plethora of towels and Neosporin fall out along with a bottle of cherry vodka, a nail file, saran wrap, and olive oil. No idea what she thought she was getting into, but I'm glad she's here. "This was stupid, you know that, right?"

"Well aware."

"Okay, as long as we're on the same page. Do you have coconut oil and a leave-in conditioner? We have a leave-in mask to make."

We spend the next twenty minutes creating a mask, saran-wrapping my head, and blow-drying the wrap. Dylan eventually leaves, telling me to leave the mask on for an extra ten minutes before washing it out just to make sure the curls dissipate.

Please let this work, because even though Jack didn't seem to mind, I don't want to go to our date on Saturday with this hair . . . or hell, I don't want to go on air looking like this. Although, knowing Kevin, he would turn it into a segment of warning women about home hair treatments.

Yeah, I'm going to keep this mishap on the down-low.

After washing my hair five times and conditioning it once again, I rest on my bed, playing with my wet, yet relaxed hair. God bless, Dylan.

Curious, I open up the *Going in Blind* app and see a message in the corner . . . as well as a new match. Huh, that's odd. I didn't think I'd still be offered matches. Not interested, wanting to focus completely on Jack, I open his message.

. . .

Dearest Noely,
    That hair . . . it's very becoming of you. :)
Jack

Cheeky, cheeky man.
    Smiling to myself, I type him back.

Dear Jack,
    If you know what's good for you, you're going to ignore what you saw tonight and remember me as the girl in the red dress with the red shoes and red lipstick . . . and straight hair.
Noely

It doesn't take him very long to write back, which makes me think he's been waiting for a reply.

Dear Lady in Red,
    So on Saturday, if I ask you for tips on giving myself a perm, your answer is going to be . . .

Snorting, I type back.

Dearest Jack,
    Pushing your luck, Mr. Suit. I'd be careful if I were you, especially if you want a second kiss.
Noely

. . .

Dear Noely,
    Cancelling my order for my at-home perm kit as we speak. Don't want to jeopardize that second kiss.
    Jack

Clever, clever man.

CHAPTER TEN

NOELY

"You know, Kevin, I was thinking, maybe we can fill the next segment with viewer questions. I've been stockpiling some and thought it would be fun to—"

"We're doing the dating segment." His harsh tone and stern look shut me up. Walking away, he checks something off on his clipboard, and I'm frustrated.

Why can't we talk about Dylan's personal life? She has two kids, let's talk about her mom struggles, because that seems way more fascinating than my dating life . . . right?

"Let me guess, he shut you down?" Dylan asks, looking over her cards and sucking on a mint. It's her interview ritual.

"Didn't even let me finish your suggestion."

"I don't blame him. Viewer Q and A is a total bore. No one wants to watch that." Dylan shuffles through her cards and taps them on her legs. "Don't worry, this will be painless and hey, there's one thing to be happy about. Your hair doesn't look like a curly bush on your head anymore." She gives me a thumbs up, and I'm tempted to swat it away.

"We're on in ten, ladies. Take your places."

Ugh, here we go.

Kevin counts down and points at Dylan as a cue to begin.

"Do we have any single viewers out there? Anyone looking for love? Well, you're not alone. Our very own Noely Clark is in the market for a mate but has had a hard time dating due to her busy schedule. Luckily, she was recently approached by a brand-new restaurant in town called *Going in Blind*, a dining spot dedicated to blind dates and making the perfect match for you. Take a look." Dylan points to the screen as a short one-minute clip rolls talking about the restaurant and the process of joining.

Nerves flutter in my belly as I wring my hands on my lap. I've always been open and honest about my life on TV, and I think it's what makes me a great morning host. Opening up to viewers is important because once you're in the spotlight, they become curious. They want to know how you live, and I've been okay with that. Hell, I let the cameras in my exam room when I had to get my annual lady check. Cameras have been in my house, at a family dinner, watching me get waxed . . . they've seen it all. Well, not ALL, I've always stayed modest, especially when getting waxed, but you know what I mean.

This little snippet into my life shouldn't bother me, but it does. I don't want to share this part of me, and I'm wondering if it's because my love life has been non-existent ever since I can remember. It's always something I've been sensitive about, never finding love in this crazy world. And now that I have a chance at it, I don't want to lose it. *But it also involves someone else this time. Someone even more private than I am.*

The music dies down on the pre-recorded clip they just ran. Dylan turns to me, an understanding smile on her face and says, "Fascinating program. Tell us about it, Noely."

Plastering a fake smile on my face and laying my hands flat on my legs, I say, "I was a little skeptical at first, going on a blind date setup through an app, but I have to admit, it's a novel idea. It gives you the experience of a blind date without having to let down your friend or mother or relative because the date didn't work out."

THREE BLIND DATES

"Because we always think we have the perfect person for you, right?" Dylan chuckles.

"The worst words to hear from a friend in a relationship are *oh I have the perfect guy I want you to meet.*" I roll my eyes and shake my head. "Nine times out of ten, they are not perfect, not even close. I've been on my fair share of setups and not once has a friend, brother, mom, or neighbor been right, but with *Going in Blind*, there's a lot of promise."

"Does that mean you've been on a blind date already?"

Dylan clearly knows the answer to that question already but the viewers don't. Therefore, I must answer. "I have been on a date. It was flawless from the initial process of being matched on the app, to going to the restaurant, and then to the actual date."

Leaning forward, Dylan presses her hand against her crossed legs and says, "Tell us more about your date. Was he cute?" She wiggles her eyebrows at me, and I stop myself from rolling my eyes.

"He was . . ." I look to the ceiling, trying to recount Jack. "He was everything I was looking for in a man. I was kind of surprised actually. When I met Jack, I was a little worried we wouldn't have anything to talk about, but the minute we met, conversation was never at a lull. I believe a lot of that has to do with the restaurant as well, because they give you games to play to get to know each other better. Their sole purpose is to help you find your one and only."

"And did you find that in your blind date?"

I shrug. "Only time will tell. What I do know though is that I have a date with The Suit tomorrow, and I can't wait to see where it takes us."

"The Suit." Dylan nods and smiles. "I like that. Well, we hope your date with The Suit goes well tomorrow." Turning toward the camera, Dylan reads from the teleprompter. "This is only the beginning for Noely and her dating adventure. We can't wait to hear more and tell you more about the *Going in Blind* program. Until then, have a beautiful weekend." Dylan and I both wave at the camera until the red light turns off and Kevin tells us it's a wrap.

Exhaling, I lie back on the couch and look at the intricate set lights. That wasn't as painful as I thought it was going to be.

"You said his name," Dylan says, causing me to turn my head toward her.

"What?"

"Jack, you said his name."

"I called him The Suit."

Dylan shakes her head, "Not at first, at first you said Jack."

Did I?

It was such a blur. I can't remember what I said at all. It's all just morphing into one giant run-on sentence.

"Did I say his name?" Dylan nods, biting her lip. "I mean, I didn't say his last name. Hell, I don't even know his last name. Do you think it's going to be a problem?"

"I don't know, you're the one who has spent time with the guy. He watches the show, doesn't he?"

"On occasion . . . I think." Would he care if I said his name? It's not like anyone is going to know who I'm talking about. There have to be thousands of Jacks living in Malibu alone.

"Well, I would message him just in case, so he's not caught off guard."

"Yeah, maybe I will."

As I ponder my little slip-up, Dylan starts to take her bra off, once again making the entire production crew uncomfortable. It wouldn't be a Friday without Dylan tossing her bra to the side.

~

D*earest Noely,*
   Checking in, how's the hair? I know it's early, but I thought I would try to catch you before you went on air. I'm kind of hoping for your sake you were able to straighten out your hair situation . . . no pun intended.

For what it's worth, I still thought you were beautiful with your curly hair. It just made you that much more endearing.
Jack

D*ear Considerate,*
Thank you for checking in. You're so sweet. If you caught the show this morning, you would notice a lack of curls in my hair, because thankfully, all went well last night. Besides this one hair that keeps curling at the base of my neck no matter what I do. I just tuck that little defiant chunk of hair away.

Speaking of the show, I want to talk to you about a segment we went live on today. When you see the show, you'll know exactly what I'm talking about.
Noely

CHAPTER ELEVEN

NOELY

The breeze lifting off the ocean whips my hair in my face, temporarily covering my eyes. I push my hair out of the way and curse myself for not putting it up. I'm usually smarter than this, but because I went through hair drama yesterday, I wanted to show off my straight locks.

Bad idea.

Very bad idea, because not only am I eating my hair with each passing gust of wind, I'm getting lipstick all over my face from my hair brushing against my lips and then onto my cheeks. It's not even the slightest bit attractive.

Holding my hair to one side, I look around the beach, wondering where Jack is. He doesn't seem like a guy who is normally late, not that two minutes is late, but still. From my general impression of the man, time is a precious commodity.

And he's the one bringing the food and wine, so it's not like I could start drinking if I wanted to, not that I need to drink right now.

Well . . . that's sort of a lie. I wouldn't mind a little booze to ease my nerves. I shouldn't be nervous when it comes to Jack, but for some reason, I have a bad feeling. A very bad feeling.

Since my last message yesterday, I haven't heard from him. And who knows, he might have been busy all day with whatever business he conducts, so I have to give him the benefit of the doubt . . . but it also seems uncharacteristic of him to not message me back. The man sent me a dozen lightbulbs for crying out loud.

I shift in my miniscule jean shorts and tight-fitting purple blouse. I wanted to wear something casual but also pretty, something that showed off my body but allowed me to be able to sit on a blanket in the sand without worrying about some passerby able to see straight up my skirt.

I rest the blanket on the fence and look at the parking lot just as a black BMW sedan pulls in. I have no idea what kind of car Jack drives, but my stomach flips from the thought of him stepping out of that car.

I watch intently as a black loafer appears from behind the car door, followed by an impeccably dressed Jack wearing black trousers, a black button-up shirt sans tie, and black sunglasses that cover those deliciously dark eyes of his.

I smile widely at him when he spots me. Taking off his sunglasses, he tosses them on the dashboard of his car and he locks up, carrying nothing with him.

Odd.

When he approaches, I push off the fence and wait for him to reach me. When he does, his gaze is cast down, his features not the jovial ones I'm used to.

"Hey," I say shyly, feeling more nervous than ever.

"Hi." He places his hands in his pockets, and his standoffish stance is rocking my equilibrium.

Shouldn't he be scooping me up into his arms and kissing me? Isn't that what he's been wanting to do since we kissed the other night. Hell, isn't that what he wanted since date one?

Unsure on how to read this man, I take another step forward and ask, "Is everything okay, Jack?"

His lips purse, and he shakes his head.

Yeah, I don't like the look of this at all.

"I'm going to be honest with you, Noely." He looks up at me and those mysterious eyes slice me in half. They're stern, unforgiving, almost scary. "Do you remember what we talked about on our first date?"

First date? How about only date?

"You're going to have to be more specific. We talked about a lot of things, Jack."

"I'm a private person, Noely."

Oh crap, he did watch the show from yesterday.

"On our first date, I told you privacy was important, that I was burned in the past from my private life being shared without my consent."

Stepping forward again, I say, "Ugh, Jack, I'm so sorry. It was a slip-up and I feel awful. I really meant to just call you The Suit, but I was so nervous, and when I'm nervous I don't think and things just fly out of my mouth. I hope you don't think I did this on purpose, because exposing you like that is the last thing I would want to do." His eyes are trained on the ground between us. "But at least it wasn't your last name, right? There must be thousands of Jacks in Malibu. I think you're safe." I tug on his shirt, trying to lighten his mood, but it doesn't work.

"Two people have already asked me if I was the Jack you were talking about."

"What?" My voice reaches decibels only dogs can hear. "How is that possible?"

"They both knew I was taking part in the dating program, so they put the two and two together."

Oh God.

"I'm so sorry, Jack. I didn't even want to do the segment. It was my producer who kept pushing and pushing. I'm really—"

"I can't do this, Noely." He shakes his head, and my body goes stiff from his words. Stroking his jaw, he lets out a frustrated breath. "I can't have my life in the public eye. I don't want it in the public eye. I've spent a great deal of time trying to step out of the spotlight, trying to make my investments the center of attention and not the man behind them. It's taken a long time, but I'm finally there." He continues to stroke his jaw, his eyes pinned on mine now. "I like you, Noely, a lot, but you're too high profile for me right now. I'm in the midst of something big, a business that is on the verge of exploding into something amazing. I can't jeopardize that . . . for anything. If it doesn't work out, I'm not the only one affected by it. I've hired fifty employees to keep everything in check, and I can't possibly hurt them, not after all the hard work they've put into this project."

Is he really breaking up before we get started?

"Jack, I'm sorry. I really am, and I will do whatever I can to help fix things. Just tell me what I can do." I bite my bottom lip and hate that I'm getting emotional over this. "I don't want to say goodbye to you. I really think there is something special between us. Can't you feel it?"

He nods, and a brief glimpse of hope springs inside me. "There is something special between us, but I can't pursue it." He shakes his head. "I won't jeopardize anything. I never should have gone on the first date to begin with." He sighs and runs a hand over his face. "I just couldn't stay away." Shaking his head, he steps away, causing my heart to slightly crack. "I have to go." Looking me up and down, he says, "Take care, Noely."

When he turns around and heads to his car, I'm almost too shocked to do anything, but before he can close his car door, I call out to him. "So that's it, Jack? You're going to be just as evasive in stopping this as you were in sharing anything about you? Because of privacy? Even if what we can both see between us seems so good?"

"It's much more than that." *Well, hell if I know how it can be after one date, one kiss, and a few messages.*

"Yeah, like what?" I fold my arms over my chest, growing angrier by the second.

"It would be a conflict of interest, Noely."

A conflict of interest? What the hell is he talking about?

Before I can ask, he's shutting his car door and starting the engine. I watch as he places his sunglasses over his eyes and backs out of the parking lot, kicking up dust in his wake.

I'm stunned. I stand there for a few minutes before I finally say to no one, "You've got to be freaking kidding me." Shaking my head in disbelief, I repeat a little louder. "You've got to be FREAKING kidding me." Throwing my arms to the sky, I stomp toward my blanket, snag it along with my keys and head to my car.

A conflict of interest?

Privacy?

Not wanting to be burned?

What in the ever-living hell is he talking about?

And what's even more frustrating is that the man refuses to talk about it. I don't need to know his social security number or anything, just a little explanation, something more than his evasive answer.

But noooooo, The Suit can't possibly share *that* side of him.

Well guess what, Jack? You're dead to me.

Once in my car, I pull out my phone from my back pocket and open up the *Going in Blind* app. Without even giving it a second thought, I look at the second match sent to me. I have no idea if they normally send daters second or third matches, whether this is normal or not. But it's as if they knew I'd be needing another attempt.

RebelWithACause.

I study the profile. It doesn't say much; he is adventurous, loves homemade brownies, and does a lot of philanthropic work.

Interesting and what's even more interesting is his profile emoji. It's a motorcycle, something that seems like the complete opposite from The Suit, just what I need. I'm still completely confused how someone who was very forthright with what they wanted to do *with* me, can so quickly turn off that passion. He sent flowers. Lightbulbs. *He gave me hope.*

THREE BLIND DATES

And now that hope has dulled, much like my apartment when I throw out all the stupid bulbs I didn't need in the first place. One down. Hopefully not too many more before I give up completely.

Looks like we're about to get cozy, rebel.

Part Two

THE REBEL

CHAPTER TWELVE

NOELY

Hmm... I might have gone a little overboard.

I catch a glimpse of myself in the reflection of *Going in Blind's* front door and cringe. When I dressed for my blind date tonight, I might have *angrily* dressed. Meaning, I put on the sluttiest thing I owned, sexi-fied my hair, and donned the tallest heels I possess. I read like a classy hooker looking for a good time. Notice how I said classy and not trashy? Huge difference. Even though my boobs are spilling out of my tight black dress that ends mid-thigh, my makeup isn't smeared, and I'm wearing underwear... full-butt underwear.

See the difference?

Knowing there is no time to go home and change into something less "rebel" like—that's the theme I was going for—and more nun from the convent, I push through the door and I'm greeted by Veronica, the hostess.

"Miss Clark, it's lovely to see you tonight."

"Hi," I say shyly, feeling a little uneasy that I'm here again. They obviously know the first date didn't work out, the first date that's supposed to be THE match. It's kind of embarrassing, but when I look at Veronica, there is no judgment in her eyes. If there had been, I would have wanted to turn around and leave. Instead, I take a deep breath and say, "I have a date with RebelWithACause tonight."

"Yes, I have you right here. He hasn't arrived yet. Can I show you to the bar?"

"Please." Pulling on the hem of my skirt, trying to magically elongate it, I follow Veronica to the bar where there is another woman waiting on the far end. She's dressed far more conservatively than I am in a pretty royal-blue turtleneck dress. Unlike my curled and teased hair—yes, teased—hers is brushed crisply against her head into a high ballerina bun pinned at the top. She went classy sexy. Good for her. I tried that last time and look where I ended up. Right back where I started. Who knows, maybe her approach will work for her.

I take a seat across from her at the bar, the length putting enough distance between us so we don't have to make awkward conversation, which normally wouldn't be an issue for me. For some reason, I'm feeling slightly bitter tonight, a sensitivity I need to drop before my date gets here because no one likes sharing a delicious dinner with a bitter human.

"Miss Clark, it's a pleasure to see you," Danny, the bartender, says while placing a napkin in front of me. "Can I get you another Moscow Mule?"

I don't know if I should be impressed he remembers me or depressed. I wonder how many second timers he sees in here.

Trying to give him a smile, but failing, I say, "Maybe just a glass of rosé for me this evening."

Sensing my humdrum attitude, Danny leans forward and tips my chin up. Smiling brightly, he says, "You're not the only one in here on their second date. About half of the daters here are on their second, some on their third and fourth. It takes time to find the right match. It doesn't happen magically. On paper or in our data system, you might seem like a good match with someone else, but computers and graphs can't calculate the human emotion. So give yourself some credit, okay?" *I needed that. I have to trust he's telling me the truth.*

Perking up, I return Danny's enigmatic smile. "Thank you."

"Anytime. Now"—he looks me up and down—"how about I fix you one of my special Tom Collins?"

Perching up on the bar, I ask, "What makes it special?"

"The way I shake it." He winks at me and gets to work.

Danny would be quite the catch. I wonder if he's taken. Is *he* married? I want to be part of that breed. Yes, *the married* are their own breed. I want to swim around in that breed. I want to be the freaking HOA president of that breed.

"So, do you know anything about your date tonight?" Danny asks as he pours my drink into a tumbler from the shaker he was shaking vigorously.

I play with the napkin in front of me. "Um, not too much. He is adventurous and does a lot of philanthropic work. He also makes me believe he—"

"Hello."

I feel like I'm living in a déjà vu moment. Once again, a deep voice pulls me away from Danny to the man behind me.

Turning slightly as Danny sets my drink in front of me, I come eye to eye with a man who I can only describe accurately as a rebel. From his thick hair—pushed to the side on the top of his head—to his harsh scruff on his jaw, to the leather jacket draped tightly over his shoulders, and the motorcycle helmet under his arm, he has rebel written all over him. *Gorgeous* rebel.

"RebelWithACause?" I ask, hoping this extremely attractive man *is* my next date.

"ShopGirl?" The way he asks, his voice scratchy, yet sexy.

"That's me, but you can call me Noely." I hold out my hand for a shake, which he takes but doesn't let go right away.

"I'm Beck. Beck Wilder, it's a pleasure to meet you, Noely."

Beck Wilder, why does that name make my toes instantly curl?

"I believe our table is ready, if you would like to follow me. Veronica showed me the way."

"I'd love to." Turning to grab my drink, Danny gives me a quick wink, which helps settle my nerves, and I allow Beck to take my hand and help me off my bar stool.

"Right over here." He weaves me past a few high-tops until we're at a table next to a wall, giving us a small amount of privacy.

As I sit, I watch Beck take off his leather jacket, revealing a white button-up shirt with the sleeves rolled and at least three of the buttons undone, showing off a necklace strung together by a leather band. It's hot, like really hot, especially bouncing off his tan skin.

And now Beck has removed his jacket, I take him all in. My question to *Going in Blind:* What's with all of the hot muscular men in this program? Is that a requirement? Must have man pecs to apply? Not that I'm complaining, it's just slightly intimidating.

Letting out a short breath, Beck picks up the menu in front of him and gives it a once-over. "Oh damn, I love lobster and mashed potatoes; those are my weakness. What about you?" Looking over his menu, he eyes me with a devilish look, one that speaks of pure charm and trouble.

"I don't think I've ever had lobster. I've had tons of crab, but lobster not so much. Is it good?"

"Amazing. You should give it a go and if you don't like it, I'll eat your portion." Smiling wickedly, he takes my menu and stacks it on his.

"Well, if you take my lobster, I get your mashed potatoes."

As if I just slapped him across the face, Beck sits back in his chair and holds his hands up. "Whoa, whoa, whoa, let's not get too hasty here, okay? Taking a man's treasured mashed potatoes is a huge dating faux pas, and I don't think you want to commit a dating faux pas, do you?"

Enjoying his humor, I cross my arms over my chest and ask, "I don't know, what kind of offense is that? Is it like a slap on the wrist? Or is it like a giant curse that will hover over me, destroying any kind of chance I have at dating someone again?"

He rubs his chin and studies my question. "The pretty spectrum you just painted is kind of extreme, but if I had to choose, I would say it falls along the line of a slap on the wrist."

"Ah, okay . . ." I bite on my cheek, trying to hold back my smile but failing. "I think I'll take my chances then."

"Risk taker, I like it." He tips his water glass in my direction and takes a sip as the waiter takes our order, two lobsters with extra mashed potatoes, just in case.

Eyeing the cards to the side, I wonder if I should offer to play, the same way I played with Jack, but before I can ask, Beck dives right into our date. "Noely, tell me, what brought you here? To this program?"

The way he's leaning forward, his eyes set on mine, ready to listen intently, makes me feel comfortable, as if he's truly here for the right reasons: to get to know me.

The tension I've held in my shoulders eases and I play with the straw in my drink, starting to feel less anxiety ridden and more flirty. But because of how open I was with Jack, I'm also a little cautious. I won't lie to Beck, but should I be less forthcoming? Even after all I shared with Jack, it hadn't been enough for him to want to stay. *Okay. Knock it off, Noely.* Deep breath. Here goes nothing.

"Honestly?" He nods. "I haven't had the best of luck when it comes to dating. And with my busy schedule and my inability to pick the right guys, I thought I would give blind dating a try. It's nice how they run this program. It makes you feel comfortable, giving you a safe place to meet for the first time."

"I agree."

"What about you? Why are you blind dating?"

Leaning back in his chair, Beck scratches the side of his jaw as he studies me. "Honestly?"

"I gave you honesty." I smile at him.

"Fair enough." He takes a sip of his water, puts it on the table and continues to lean back in his chair, striking a very casual pose. "I'm recently divorced, but it's been over for a long time, eight years actually since we've been together."

Eight years? How old was he when he got married because his eyes may look weathered, but his face is still young.

Chuckling, he points at my head and says, "I can see your pretty little head trying to do the math. Let me help you. I married my high school sweetheart at eighteen. We were married for two years before we decided to get a divorce. It's taken eight years to finalize it all, for reasons I won't bore you with, but now that I'm out in the dating world again, I have no idea where to start. My buddy works behind the scenes here and suggested I give it a try." Looking me up and down, his heated eyes taking me in, he says, "I have to admit, I'm glad he suggested it."

That look, that dark, sultry look, is detrimental to any woman's libido. There is an unmistakable bad-boy quality about him with a side of alpha that's hard to miss. It's evident in the way he sits, in the way he's confident, yet casual. *Is that what I want? I had thought Jack was my ideal man, but I was so wrong. How can I be matched to two completely different men?*

But he's a twenty-eight-year-old divorcee, and it makes me wonder what went wrong. Were they too young? Or was there something else that split them up? It's obviously way too early to dive deep into the failures of his marriage, so I try to keep the topic light.

"Were you apprehensive at first about joining the program?"

"Hell yeah. When I was dating in high school, dating apps weren't really a thing. I mean, that was over ten years ago. Back then, I saw I girl I liked and I let her know. Now it's like . . ." He sighs. "There's a million rules we have to follow to not look like some kind of stalker. Like don't text too soon, don't respond right away, don't tell the person how you feel. Hell, who came up with all these misconceptions of dating?"

"Ugh, you're so right. It's like people don't want to look too desperate, they want to play it cool. But who cares? If you like someone, then you like them. Let it be known, right?"

"Exactly." Studying me for a second, Beck leans forward and pins me with those sexy, sultry eyes of his. "Let's make a deal, right here. By the end of the night, if we think this could go somewhere, if we enjoyed our time together, we let it be known. None of this running around the rules bullshit."

"I like that idea." I take a sip of my Tom Collins. "I like that idea very much."

∼

"It's so . . . thick."

"Get used to that, sweetheart," Beck answers with a wink, making me blush immediately. I don't think with that wink he's talking about the lobster tail.

Clearing my throat, obviously flush from his comment, I ask, "How do I eat this?"

"Easy. Just take the lobster meat off the top and set the tail to the side, cut up the meat, and dip it in that delicious little bucket of butter to your right."

"That's it?"

"That's it." Looking over at my lobster, he asks, "Want me to taste test yours for you, make sure it's not poisonous?"

"Nice try." I wave at him with my fork. "Stick to your own plate there, mister, or I might take it upon myself to dive into your mashed potatoes."

With a stern look, he points his knife at me and says, "Listen, do you see this plate between us?" He motions to the extra pile of mashed potatoes we asked for, a plate so large I don't know if two people would be able to eat it on their own. "This right here is the communal plate, okay? If you're feeling frisky and the need to eat off any other plate besides your own, this is where you want to go." He points to his plate. "See this pile of goodness? This is my plate, so I suggest you stick to your side, Noely, or else you won't know what might happen."

"Is that right?" I challenge him with a grin. "And what might you do if I cross into your territory? Stab me with your fork?"

Without even taking a second to answer, he says, "Yes. Yes, I will. I will stab that dainty little hand of yours with no regrets."

"Savage."

"Damn right." He plops a butter-dripping piece of lobster in his mouth and smiles. Oh dear, that smile, that look right there, it's going to get me into some trouble, I just know it.

"So, tell me about your job. You're a morning show host; what's that like?" Beck asks, shoveling a pile of mashed potatoes in his mouth. For how fit he is, he eats like a ravenous man-child, butter and mashed potatoes all over his face. And for some odd reason, I find it endearing.

Another thing I like about Beck, he doesn't know who I am, or what the show is about. It almost seems like he's been living under a rock for the past eight years. I wonder if that has to do with the divorce.

I dip a small chunk of lobster in my mouth and chew before I answer. "It's fun . . . some days, there are other days where I'm so tired it takes all the effort in the world to put on a good face, smile for the camera, and be engaging."

"Yeah, I can imagine. Having to be 'on' for a long period of time is hard. But don't you get to meet cool people?"

"I do." I smile shyly. "We do a lot of interviews with celebrities and athletes. I actually just did an interview with Hayden Holmes."

With fork midway to his mouth, Beck tilts his head to the side and asks, "Who's that?"

What?

WHAT?

Did he just ask who Hayden Holmes is?

I can't . . .

"Uh, what's happening to your face right now?" Beck asks, pointing at me.

"This right here?" I motion with my hand over my face. "This is called the look of someone in shock. How in the world do you not know who Hayden Holmes is?"

"I don't have cable." He shrugs. "I live off Netflix and HULU. Who is Hayden Holmes? Is he in a new movie or something?"

I nearly choke on my delicious lobster. In a movie? Is he kidding me?

"Oh boy, this might be the crutch in our blossoming relationship. I don't know if we're going to be able to get through this."

"Uh-oh." Beck places his silverware on his plate and levels with me. "Did I just screw up everything?" I playfully nod, to which he holds up a finger to me. "Give me one second." From his back pocket, he pulls out his phone and starts typing away. His finger scrolls over the screen where he stops to read something. Once he's done, he places his phone back in his pocket and says, "You know, I thought you said Hunter Holmes not Hayden Holmes. My mistake. Man, you got to interview Hayden Holmes? Holy shit! He's like the most promising player for the LA Earthquakes this coming season. Word on the street is, he's going to help turn the team around."

A snort bubbles out of me and I cover my nose in embarrassment, which only causes Beck to smile endearingly. Can I also point out that it's making me giggle for far too long that he called the Quakes by their full name? A non hockey fan wouldn't know any better. Earthquakes . . . see, more giggling.

"Don't you just love Google?" He takes another bite of his lobster, looking cockier than ever.

"It's a real life saver . . . or should I say date saver."

⁓

"You have to be quick, okay? First thing that comes to mind."

"That's why you called it rapid fire," I add with a cheeky grin.

"Cute." Beck leans over the empty dessert plate we shared and pokes the corner of my lip. "Are you ready, smartass?"

I love how he holds nothing back, how he's very honest and upfront and isn't trying to put on a façade to win me over. From the very beginning, I feel like I've gotten the real Beck, the no-holds-barred Beck, the sarcastic and button-pushing Beck. I like it. I like it a lot.

Preparing myself for his rapid questions, I say, "Okay, go."

Gripping the sides of the table, he levels his gaze with mine and starts shooting off questions. "Middle name."

"Jane."

"Real hair color."

I chuckle. "Dirty blonde."

"Third grade teacher."

"Mrs. Dole and she was a rotten ho bag."

He raises an eyebrow at me but continues his questions.

"Waffles or pancakes?"

"Waffles."

"Book or movie?"

"Movie."

"Ah, come on." He shakes his head at me, a smile stretching across his lips. "First pet's name."

"Denise. Denise the cat."

"Denise?" Beck mouths to me, his brow pinched together. He shakes my answer away and says, "Favorite movie."

"Easy, *You've Got Mail*."

Beck pauses. "Really?"

"If you say it's a crap movie, we're ending this date right now, going our separate ways, and we shall never speak of his night again."

"You know"—Beck runs his hand along his jaw—"I like your passion. There aren't many people out there who would end a blind date and erase it from their memory from the possibility of disagreeing over a movie."

"Call me high-maintenance, say I'm the worst blind date ever, I don't care, but don't you dare throw my favorite movie into the trash can."

"Wouldn't dream of it. I like *You've Got Mail* actually. I would say it's in my top five romantic comedies."

"Really? I thought you were a book guy, at least that's what you made it seem like."

"I am, but I also binge on Netflix."

"Oh, my kind of man. So if you have a top five list of romantic comedies, what else is on there?"

He twirls his glass of water in front of him, his face morphing into humor. "I don't know, Noely, I'm not sure if you're ready for that kind of knowledge. Top five romcoms, that tells a lot about a man. You might have to earn that answer."

"Is that so? All right, how would I go about earning it?"

He stands from his seat and snags his leather jacket from the back of his chair as well as his helmet. "I have just the idea."

CHAPTER THIRTEEN

NOELY

I stand on the sidewalk, fidgeting in place as I stare at the piece of machinery in front of me, straddled by the one and only Beck Wilder.

"Come on." He holds out a little helmet he pulled from under the seat in his motorcycle.

I eye his bike, feeling slightly intimidated but also intrigued.

He must notice my hesitancy because he asks, "Are you nervous?"

I hold up my fingers. "Just a little. I've never been on a motorcycle before."

"There's nothing to it." Popping the kickstand and standing tall, he pulls me toward him and places the helmet on my head. Snapping the ends to secure the helmet, he checks the fit and gives me a sexy smile when he takes me in. "Have to admit, you look hot in a helmet, Noely." Giving my dress a once-over, he shakes his head. "That dress, though. It's dangerous, girl. You know you can get into some trouble with that?"

Feeling friskier, I say, "I was kind of hoping I would."

Beck's eyes narrow as he bites on his bottom lip. "Hop on the back and hold on tight. Don't try to move with the motorcycle, leave that to me." Eyeing me one last time, he takes off his coat and wraps it around me, helping my arms into the sleeves. "Don't want you getting cold."

Caught off guard by his gesture, I give him a quick thank you and hop on the bike, hoping I kept all my lady bits covered while doing so. When I sit down, my dress rides up to dangerous levels. Luckily my pelvis is pressed against Beck's back.

Taking my arms, he wraps them around his waist and starts the bike all in one fluid movement.

Well, that's hot.

Do you know what's even hotter? The obvious set of abs this man is sporting. I can feel them under my arms, rippling and tight. Given he ate a pile of mashed potatoes tonight, I'm going to guess he must workout a crazy amount, especially from how his back muscles flex under his white shirt with the start of his bike.

I wanted something different. I wanted something adventurous. I might just be getting that right now with Beck Wilder.

Like a bullet out of a gun, we shoot off into the street, causing me to grip even tighter onto Beck's waist and press my cheek against his back as the wind whips past us. A carefree laugh pops out of me from the exhilaration of riding on the back of a bike with a sexy stranger. This is so not me, but I'm liking it. I'm enjoying the change in pace from my normal.

Lifting my head, feeling a little more comfortable, I take in the streetlights passing us by in a blur. I'm tempted to throw my arms in the air, as if I was riding a roller coaster but think better of it. I want to have fun, not severely injure myself.

Instead, I soak in the moment, the way my laugh vibrates my body, the way the bike feels rumbling beneath me, the way Beck's body feels pressed against mine. It's new, intoxicating . . . addicting.

After what seems like an hour but more like twenty minutes, Beck slows down and pulls into a parking spot on the side of the street. He backs up against the sidewalk and cuts the engine.

Removing his helmet, he looks behind him and says, "Wait right there." He kicks out the kickstand and dismounts from the bike. He rests his helmet on the handles and then takes me in, a large smile spreading over his lips. *Thank God I wore the granny panties.*

"Fuck, you look hot on my bike. And I was right, that dress is about to get you into some trouble tonight." He removes my helmet and holds out his hand. "Careful of the pipes on the side, they're really hot."

Not wanting to show too much off, I bring my leg over the bike and hop off with Beck's assistance. I run my hand through my hair, making sure I don't have helmet head, and then take off Beck's jacket, revealing, once again, the tiny little dress I wore tonight.

Nodding appreciatively, Beck takes his jacket, stuffs it in the seat with my helmet, and takes my hand in his while tucking his helmet under his other arm. "Come on, Sassy."

"Where are we going?" I try to keep up with his pace, ignoring the way his palm feels pressed against mine.

"You'll see."

My heart rate picks up as he leads me down a dark alley, barely lit by the street lamps behind us. Nervous, a bit scared, and certainly questioning my sanity, I shake in place as Beck knocks on a black door. As if in a movie, a slot in the door opens and two dark eyes with heavy eyebrows hovering over them appear. "Password."

"Puedo bailar," Beck responds in a Spanish accent, turning my insides into mush, but for only a second, because where the hell is he taking me that requires a password to enter?

All I can think is, this is it, tomorrow morning, they're going to find my half-harvested body along the beaches of Malibu with a note attached to me that says, "She didn't blind date well."

The heavy clinking sound of a dungeon lock echoes through the alley and Beck ushers me in.

I know, I should be stopping the progress down this dark tunnel with blind date number two and eyebrow security guard, but curiosity wins me over and instead of being the intelligent human being who thinks rationally, I'm that girl you scream at while watching a horror flick. You know, the one who's a complete idiot and winds up getting killed off in the first ten minutes. The one you yell at and throw your hands up in the air out of pure frustration.

She deserved to have her head chopped off by that chainsaw, she should have "saw" it coming. We've all said it one time or another.

So go ahead, say that about me and when you do, please say a prayer as well that my organs are the only things harvested from my body, none of that Jack the Ripper kind of harvesting...

As Beck easily glides me through the dark hallway, I can feel my palm starting to sweat against his, my resistance growing stronger and stronger the closer we get to a loud booming door.

Organ harvesting party, yep, sitting right behind that door, the one where the zombie apocalypse is collectively starting, that's the end of me.

Beck reaches for the door and I close my eyes, saying a mental goodbye to everyone in my life, wishing I'd texted Dylan before I came on this date.

When the door opens, I barely open my eyes to find a brightly lit room in red, orange, and gold hues with salsa music blaring through this underground room while a gaggle of different types of people move and shake their bodies on a lit-up dance floor.

Smirking back at me, Beck asks, "Ready to get a little dirty, Noely?"

Without waiting for an answer, he pulls me into the room, the beat of the music instantly sparking a wave of interest inside me. Beck starts shaking hands with patrons as we make our way down the stairs onto the main floor. This is not his first time, clearly, given how comfortable he is in the space. We reach a coat check and he hands the man behind the counter his helmet as well as my purse.

"Want something to drink?" he asks, leaning down to my ear so his scruff brushes against my cheek.

"Yes," I answer, nerves heightening every move and press of his body against mine.

"This way."

As we make our way past the dance floor, I can't help but watch the couples grinding, twisting, and turning together. Can Beck dance like *that*? I give him a once-over and try to envision him grinding against me, his hips pressed against mine. My face flushes from the mere thought of our bodies touching so intimately. I have no idea if he can dance, but I'm kind of hoping he can, because I wouldn't mind being held closely against him on the dance floor.

"What would you like to drink?" he asks me.

Taking in the scene before me, I smile and say, "A margarita please."

"Smart choice." Speaking fluently in Spanish, he orders drinks for both of us. He sounds so freaking sexy.

When he turns back around, I ask, "You speak Spanish?"

Looking out at the crowd, he nods. "Studied it for the past seven years." He answers so casually, as if studying a foreign language is just natural, something everyone does. I wonder if his studying Spanish had anything to do with how long it took him to get a divorce? Was he traveling the world? To say this man confuses me is an understatement, but I'm also intrigued. I'm thinking that's why I keep following him, and why I'm about to lose all inhibition on the dance floor.

"Here." He hands me a salt-rimmed glass. Winking, he cheers his drink with me and takes a sip, watching my lips intently slip around the rim of my glass. He licks his lips when my mouth pulls away from my glass, his hand snagging around my hip, pulling me a little closer to him. The attention is heady and causing a yearning within me that is quite unexpected. *Who is he? How am I reacting so strongly to this man?*

I swallow the lime-flavored liquid, allowing the alcohol to heat up my body. Feeling a little nervous, I ask him, "What did you get to drink?"

"Water." He takes another sip.

"Water?" My brow creases. "No margarita for you?"

"No alcohol." Moving me closer, he asks, "Want to find a table, we can talk a little, get you warmed up to the music?"

"That sounds good." From the look in his eyes, the hungry look, I'm going to need to drink a little bit more before heading out on the dance floor.

While we walk the perimeter of the dance floor, looking for a booth, I wonder why he doesn't drink. Now that I think about it, he had water at dinner too. Interesting.

Chalk it up to the things I want to know about him.

Doesn't drink alcohol.

Studied Spanish for several years.

Married at eighteen.

Broke up at twenty.

His divorce took eight years.

There are so many interesting puzzle pieces about this man that I'm actually kind of excited to fit all together.

Beck takes me to a half-moon shaped booth in the corner across from the live band. Secluded from other patrons around us, gaining an ounce of privacy just between us. Beck helps me slip into the booth first, then he comes up next to me and drapes his hand over the back of the seat, encasing me in his woodsy scent.

Mmm . . . he smells divine. How come I'm only noticing that now?

"This place is amazing, where did you find it?" I ask, taking a big gulp of my drink when Beck's hand behind me starts drawing small circles on my exposed shoulder.

"A friend told me about it a year ago. I try to come once or twice a month."

"Big dancer?"

He shrugs. "I'm all right. I just like the atmosphere. I'm all about living in the moment, Noely, and places like this, where you can let loose and experience life, these are the places I enjoy the most."

"How could you not? The music alone makes you want to throw caution to the wind and shake your body."

"I sure hope you're feeling the same way once you finish that drink, because I have plans for you on that dance floor." Looking over his drink, his eyes pinned on mine, I hear his silent message: things are about to get naughty.

Even though I'm slightly terrified, I think, bring it on.

∾

"There is no way that's what that line means."

"It sure as hell does."

"That's ridiculous. What, did you study palm reading as well as Spanish?"

He chuckles and says, "I just know things. And that line right there means you're allergic to coffee."

I shake my head and laugh. "You're such a liar."

He strokes my palm with his finger, running it along every line, making my insides flutter and my breathing pick up with each stroke. He's so close, his body practically on top of mine, his breath pressed against my ear, his scruff rubbing my skin ever so gently. And me, well, see my hips? Yeah, they're slowly gyrating in his direction. I would like to blame the margarita, or even the music, but I know that's not the case. It's my libido skyrocketing into dangerous territories from the way this man lightly strokes me in just the right way.

"Not a liar, just telling you what I see."

"Is that so?" I lean in closer and ask, "Then how come I have coffee every morning and I'm fine? Seems to me like you just wanted an excuse to touch me so you pretended to be a palm reader."

I hold my breath, waiting for his answer.

"You're right. I did. Now give me a chance to touch you even more." He retreats from the booth and holds out his hand for me to follow.

I take it without even giving it a second thought. Smiling devilishly, he guides me to the dance floor and immediately spins me into his arms where he takes my hands and links them behind his neck. Pulling me into his body, he places his hands on my hips and presses his forehead against mine.

As if it's second nature to him, he starts moving us back and forth along the dance floor, his feet effortlessly gliding us. Intimidated at first, after a few passes across the floor, I start to feel the music and my muscles begin to loosen up.

"That's it," he whispers just loud enough so I can hear him over the music. "Loosen those hips, Sassy."

A distinct trumpet and cowbell echo through the room, setting the pace and tone to the dance. It's fast, yet commanding, encouraging us to grind together, and that's what Beck does. His hands slide from my hips to my butt where he grips tightly and pulls me flush against his crotch. With my legs entwined with his, we stay in place as our hips gyrate together.

Breathless and turned on, I match his gaze with mine, his seductive eyes penetrating any last wall I might have had before this date, and for once in a long time, I let loose . . . completely.

"Just like that. God, you look so sexy."

Leaning my head back, I let my hair fall behind me and give it a little shake before lifting my head back up and meeting his lust-filled, greedy eyes. His hands grip my butt tighter and I'm greeted by a noticeable hard-on.

I did that to him, and if that isn't a turn-on, I don't know what is.

My fingers start to play with his hair, twisting and turning the short strands, causing his eyes to haze over. Is it weird I want more? That even though our pelvises are pressed against each other, I want to be closer?

The music now flowing through me, controlling my every movement, I glide my hands down to his shirt where my fingers dexterously undo two more of his buttons, exposing more of his tan skin, his necklace in full view now. It's a medallion I can't quite make out, but it doesn't matter right now, because all I care about is the muscular expanse of chest in front of me.

I slip my fingers inside his shirt and dance them across his chest, feeling the sinew of muscles flex with every move we make together.

When one of my fingers accidentally caresses one of his nipples, he growls into my ear and turns me around in his arms, causing me to temporarily lose my breath, that's until his hands find mine again, securing my butt right against his crotch. I sigh and loop my hand around me to the back of his neck, anchoring me in place while he swivels our hips together, his lips pressed against my ear.

"Fuck, you feel good against me," he whispers. His breath sends chills up and down my entire body as the music continues to guide me.

I push my butt even harder against his erection, heavy and obvious, swiveling my hips, loving the way I can feel his excitement so easily. I love that I affect him like this.

I've never been with a man so comfortable in his own skin that he doesn't care about how I affect him. It's like he's proud of it. *Of us.*

It's extremely rewarding.

Feeling the music, we dance slowly in tandem, letting the beat guide us. Still hanging on to him, my other hand now on top of one of his, he starts to feel the length of my leg, his body bending just slightly to reach the hem of my dress. When he moves his hand under the fabric, my breath stills for a second before he pulls away and lifts his hand back up my body until both of his hands reach my ribcage.

Oh God.

His head peers over my shoulder, his eyes trained down the valley of my cleavage. "I told you this dress was going to get you into trouble tonight and the way you're moving against me, my self-control is slipping, Sassy."

Taking a deep breath, I move his hand farther up my body and say, "Then let your will slip."

"Fuck," he growls into my ear, letting his hand move to just below my breasts. I suck in a breath from the contact and wait for him to move a little higher, but he doesn't. Instead, he swivels his hips with mine and moves his hands down my sides until they're resting on my thighs, his thumbs closing in on the juncture between my legs.

The heat level between us rises to inferno in the matter of seconds and my skin starts to prickle with need, a yearning I haven't felt since . . . well since Jack, but before that, since I can't remember.

"I don't know how much more dancing I can do with you," he says into my ear. "I'm about to combust here."

I turn in his arms and look straight at him. "Then let's get out of here."

The way the words fall off my tongue sound so foreign to me, but then again, there's not a chance in hell I want to take them back.

CHAPTER FOURTEEN

NOELY

Beck parks his bike and takes off his helmet as I do the same, letting the ocean breeze whip my hair around. The sweet smell of the salty sea makes me feel at ease as Beck turns toward me and in one swift movement, picks me up and swivels me around his hips so we're facing each other and I'm sitting on his lap, the front of his bike propping me up.

Tossing our helmets to the side, he gives me a once-over and then pushes down on the sleeves of his jacket until it falls off my body.

When I suggested we leave the club, I was unsure where we would go next . . . or what we would do next, so I'm a little surprised that we are parked on a cliff just off the Pacific Coast Highway. Call me a little slutty, but a part of me thought we would be going back to my place or even his place.

Although, from the look in his eyes right now, he doesn't necessarily care about the *where*.

Holding on to my waist with his strong hands, he looks me in the eyes and asks, "Have you had fun tonight, Noely?"

I nod and hold on to his white shirt, still loving how it's open just enough that I can see the definition of his pecs.

"A good enough time that if I call you tomorrow, you're not going to judge me for being so eager to talk to you again?"

"Honestly?" I move my hands a little higher on his shirt. "I would be insulted if you didn't call me tomorrow morning."

"Good, because I'm feeling this vibe between us, and there is no way in hell I'll be able to keep my distance after I kiss you."

"Kiss me?" I ask coyly, my body heating up before he even leans forward.

Biting on his bottom lip, he nods. "Yeah, kiss you."

Keeping one of his hands firmly planted on my hip so I don't move away from him, he trails the other one up my side until it grips my head and pulls me closer.

His lips are inches from mine when he says, "If you don't want this, you have three seconds to tell me no. I can't resist the pull between us. So tell me, Noely, do you want me to stop?"

"Not even a little," I answer, my hands pressed against his exposed skin.

Closing in on those last few inches, he pauses right before his lips connect with mine, and the need to explode from the pent-up tension inside me is overwhelming until he leaves no room between us and kisses me. *Oh God, does he kiss me.* He kisses me with passion, with yearning, with a grip so tight on the back of my neck I can feel with the push of his thumb into my skin how domineering he would be in the bedroom. *And I want that. More than I've ever wanted before.*

I melt into his touch, into the way his mouth glides across mine, as if our lips are old friends, reacquainting one another. Leaning into me, he pushes me against the front of his bike, stretching me out and moving his mouth deliciously across mine and then down my neck. My eyes open in shock from his nipping, but before I can really focus on what he's doing, I'm caught up in the stars shining above me, and the ocean that splashes below me, and the way this man makes me feel warm, a little bold, and a whole lot of needy. *For him.*

The hand on my hip slips farther down my side until it meets the hem of my dress. While his lips kiss along my neck, to my ear, and back again, he slips his fingers under the fabric and drives them forward to my hip where he plays with the thin strap of my underwear. My breath catches in my chest from the way his fingers expertly caress my skin, making chills spread across my skin with one flick of his thumb.

And as I stare at the glittering sky, I keep repeating over and over in my head I'm not this girl, I'm not the girl who gets this physical on the first date. But there is no way I can stop him. I'm desperate for it. *For him.* I want more.

Sensing how relaxed he's made me, he moves his head to my chest where he starts to kiss along my collarbone. Very slowly, as if he's testing the waters, his hips start to mindlessly rock into mine, his hard-on evident with each tiny and gentle push forward.

God, it feels good.

"So good," I whisper, loving how hot his mouth feels on my burning skin.

"You taste so good," he mutters, his mouth moving lower until he's kissing the swell of my breasts.

Yes...

More...

Lower...

"Hell," he mutters, stilling my hips that started to rock on their own accord. He lifts his head from my chest and takes a deep breath. His hand lifts from my hips and runs over his mouth in disbelief. "I need to stop."

"What? Why?" I ask, shocking myself. I should have stopped this the minute he twirled me around on his lap.

"Because if I don't, we might get caught for indecent exposure, and I'm sure your morning show producers wouldn't appreciate that."

Ah! I didn't even think about the morning show. *Hmm. Why*

didn't I think about that? Sitting up straight, I try to push down my tight skirt and shimmy away from the rebel himself before I allow him to stick his hand all the way up my dress to feel me up. And when I say feel me up, I mean squeeze my nipples. I want all the nipple squeezing right now. That's how turned on I am.

I press my hand against my forehead. "I didn't think about my morning show." Giving him a once-over, I playfully smack his chest. "Look at what you made me do. You with your yummy chest and sex appeal, you made me become a harlot in public." Leaning in close, I whisper, "You made me dry-hump you."

"And moan." He wiggles his eyebrows.

"I didn't moan." Did I? At this point, I wouldn't put it past me.

"You moaned, and it was hot as hell."

"I blame you." I shift farther away from him, as far as I can get in the tight space I'm caught up in.

Laughing, he grips my chin with his finger and thumb. "I'll take all the blame, Sassy." Pressing forward, he places a soft kiss on my lips and before I can deepen it—because apparently I have no self-control tonight—he puts some distance between us and says, "I think it's time I get you home before things get more out of control than they are."

I know he's right, he's being sensible, but the giddy, turned-on woman inside me doesn't want to say good night.

"Come on." Picking me up in one swoop, he dismounts and turns me on the bike so I'm facing the right way. Picking up our helmets, he places his on the handlebars and gently places mine on my head. Shaking his head, he says, "It's time to say goodnight."

CHAPTER FIFTEEN

NOELY

"Where is she?" Dylan shouts down the hallway as she approaches. When she turns the corner into hair and makeup, looking like a complete disaster who just rolled out of bed, she screeches when she sees me. "How did it go? Did the ho-fit work?"

"Ho-fit?" I ask, a raise in my eyebrow.

Natasha is once again working her magic while I sit in my makeup chair, reading over my morning notes and sipping my coffee, trying to infuse some caffeine into my system, begging for a jolt to get me through the day after a very long, sleepless night thinking about Beck Wilder.

"You know." Dylan addresses her body. "Our ho-ish outfit. Did it work? Was your date all over you?"

Huh, you could say that.

I smirk over the edge of my coffee cup making Dylan squeal and clap her hands. "Oh, you sly old dog." She places her elbows on her armrest, her body facing me completely, and rests her head in her palms. "Tell me all about it. Did you, you know . . . do a little P and V action?"

"What constitutes as P and V action?"

Dylan sits back, clearly not anticipating such a question from me. "Oh my God, your V touched his P, didn't it?"

"Depends."

"Depends on what? It's a simple question, did your V touch is P? Did privates collide?"

I shrug. "It depends."

Confused now, and slightly irritated, she says, "There is no depends, it either did or it didn't."

"Not true. A P and V can touch without getting down and dirty. Like for instance . . ." I stand and use Natasha as an example. "May I borrow your body for a second?"

"Of course," she answers. She loves that she gets to be part of every conversation she overhears between Dylan and me.

"Look," I press my pelvis against Natasha's and pull away. "My V just touched Natasha's V, but did we share a sweaty night together? No it was just a little V tap."

"A vag high five."

"Exactly." I point at Natasha. "A little chest bump but with our lady bits."

"Okay, you're annoying me." Now sitting in her chair like a normal person, she adds, "So you didn't do it?"

"No." I shake my head just as Natasha begins curling it again.

"So what happened—"

My phone beeps with a notification, a rather obnoxious notification. Last night, when Beck was dropping me off, we both got notifications from our *Going in Blind* apps asking if we wanted to go on a second date. We said yes, and then Beck forced me to change my notification sound to an old-fashioned horn. Aaaawoooo-ga! It is obnoxious as hell, but he said whenever I hear it, I'll know it's him.

Hearing that horn this morning puts a giant smile on my face. Once we reached my place, we made out for a little bit longer on his bike before he walked me to my door and reluctantly said good night. Even though I was ready to invite him in, he must have sensed my nervousness because he backed away, hand in his hair, looking utterly provocative with his undone shirt and rebel-ish ways.

"Uh, are you ignoring me?"

I hold my finger up to Dylan as I open up the app and read a message from RebelWithACause.

Sassy,
Told you I wouldn't be dicking around with the "rules." I want to see you again. The app suggested we go to a cooking class. I'm not much of a cook, but all I can envision is you in an apron. Now, this is something I have to see. There's a class this coming Friday. Come cook dinner with me.
Your rebel.

Smiling like a fool, I type him back as Dylan pokes me in the arm. "What did he say? You can't just smile like that and not let me know what's going on. Come on, share with the married woman. If you share, I'll tell you what Chad and I did last night, and I promise it's not a riveting story about folding laundry together."

Ignoring her, I write back.

Rebel,
Me in an apron? That's what you've been envisioning? Clearly I didn't tempt you enough last night. I must do better next time.
Sassy
P.S. Count me in for Friday.

. . .

THREE BLIND DATES

I press send and turn to Dylan. "What do you want to know?"
"Everything. Don't hold anything back. Start with the P and V."

Rolling my eyes, I sip my coffee and say, "His name is Beck. He's the epitome of a rebel with his motorcycle, dark look, and tempting alpha attitude. His past is mysterious, divorced at twenty, had some kind of eight-year hiatus on life, and doesn't drink alcohol."

"Doesn't drink alcohol? Why?"

I shrug. "No idea. I didn't get into it, thought it was too heavy of a question for a first date."

My phone honks and I giggle to myself.

"Is that him?"

I nod.

Sassy,

Did I forget to mention you weren't wearing anything under the apron when I was daydreaming? That makes a huge difference. My mistake. I'll be sure to remember to include such vital details next time.

Your rebel

P.S. I can't wait to kiss those delicious lips of yours again.

Rebel,

Your mistake has been forgiven but hasn't gone unnoticed. Please be more specific next time . . . very specific.

Sassy

P.S. You never told me your top five romantic comedies like you promised.

. . .

Turning back to Dylan, I say, "After we left the restaurant, Beck took me for a ride on his motorcycle."

"Really? That's hot. Where did you go, did you make out?" She laughs at her question.

"We did, but before that we went to some underground salsa club where he ground up against me for a good half hour."

"No, he didn't." Dylan slaps the armrest of her chair and bounces in her seat. "He danced with you? Ugh. The only kind of dancing I can get Chad to participate in is *Just Dance* on the Wii, and let me tell you, he's far too good at the Spice Girl song *Wannabe*. The man beats me every time." She sighs. "So you dry-humped on the dance floor, that must have been nice."

My phone honks again, causing Dylan to groan in frustration.

Sassy,
Don't you worry. I'll be very specific next time. By the way, for our Friday date, can I request you wear the dress you wore last night? I didn't get a good enough look at it.
Your rebel
P.S. In no particular order; You've Got Mail, Overboard, When Harry Met Sally, My Big Fat Greek Wedding—that family is crazy, and Sixteen Candles.

Rebel,
Unfortunately I need to inform you that said dress was retired last night after nearly showing off my lady areas far too many times. If you want, I can allow you to say goodbye to it on the hanger, but that's the best I can do.
Sassy
P.S. Your selection not only pleases me, but makes me think you actually watched these movies. I would have pegged you for a Bruce Willis, Die Hard fanatic.

THREE BLIND DATES

• • •

Turning back to Dylan, I say, "There was dry-humping on the dance floor, a lot of wandering hands, and heightened senses. It got to the point that when we left, electricity was bouncing between us. He then took me to a cliff overlooking the ocean, practically laid me across his bike, and made out with me."

Dylan starts to fan herself. "Oh Christ, I think I'm starting to climax just thinking about that. He made out with you on his bike? That's so hot."

"And he almost sucked on my breasts. I mean, he kissed the top of them and gently thrust his hard-on into me."

Natasha above me sighs as she finishes up the last piece of my hair that needs to be curled, her eyes all dreamy.

"I know, right? Natasha, it was like a freaking movie. A dirty one, but a movie with the way he took charge, the way he spoke to me, the setting of the night with the stars and the ocean and the light breeze that puckered my nipples." I hug my phone as if it's him. "It was . . . perfect."

"I'm not going to lie, your dating life is turning me on, and I don't know if I should be worried," Dylan says, pulling a nail file from the counter in front of her. She starts to go to work on her thumb when she asks, "So I'm going to assume it's a go for the next date."

"I said yes."

My phone honks, which causes Dylan to roll her eyes. "I'm going to go pick out my outfit before I turn into a raving bitch full of jealousy." Getting up from her chair, she says, "I'm probably going to wear royal blue." She takes off and I start to mentally assess what dresses I have in my dressing room that would complement her royal-blue choice.

"Are you going to check your phone?" Natasha asks as she starts assessing eye shadows for me.

Smiling, I nod.

• • •

Sassy,
    Retired before being able to experience being slowly peeled off your body by me? Is there any way we can remedy that?
Your rebel
P.S. Bruce Willis? It's the leather jacket and motorcycle, isn't it?

Rebel,
    Like I said, the dress has been retired, but I'm sure the black lingerie that accompanied the dress last night wouldn't mind being peeled off.
Sassy
P.S. It's the accumulation of the jacket, the bike, the alpha, the demeanor... everything.

I spend the next twenty minutes talking to Natasha about the program and encouraging her to give it a try while she applies my makeup. She laughs my suggestion off but from the curious look in her eyes, I can tell she'll look into it later.

While in my dressing room, minutes away from going on set, my phone honks at me. This honking was a good idea because every time I hear the sound, a huge smile spreads across my face.

Sassy,
    Consider it peeled... by my teeth.
Your rebel
P.S. Just admit it, you're attracted to me.

. . .

Taking a second to catch my racing breath, I sit down on the vanity in my dressing room and type him back.

Rebel,
I'm about to go on air, turned on . . . by you. I think you owe me something for the torture I'm about to go through.
Sassy
P.S. Yes. I'm attracted to you. Now you admit it, you want me.

He writes back almost immediately.

Sassy,
It's cute how you think you make the rules between us. I think it's best that you know early on, I'm the one who takes charge. The only thing I owe you is my tongue in your mouth and a whole lot of my hands on your tits.
Your rebel
P.S. I want you . . . fucking bad.

I might not know much about this man, like what he does for a job, where he lives, or what his story is, but what I do know about him, I like, and what I don't know, I look forward to finding out. At least for now, there is one thing I'm certain of: he keeps me on my toes, puts a smile on my face, *and* causes significant heat in my veins.

CHAPTER SIXTEEN

NOELY

"Toss me another biscuit," I call out to my niece who has a glint in her eye and the determined look of a major league baseball pitcher.

Plucking a biscuit from the basket in front of her, she cocks her arm back and a little part of me sweats, because I can foresee where this is going . . .

"Wammeee." Before I can decipher the incriminating sound coming from my niece, Chloe, I'm pegged between the eyes with a buttery, flaky biscuit.

"Chloe Michelle," my sister-in-law squawks as she walks into the dining room carrying two glasses of milk, one for me—I like milk, sue me—and one for the walloper herself. "When someone asks you for a biscuit, you do not chuck it at their head."

"But Daddy—"

"Daddy isn't a good example for anything. In fact, he's been grounded ever since we've been married. So unless you want to be grounded for life, I suggest you take cues from me, your mother, rather than your immature father."

Chloe turns to Alex and asks, "Daddy, you're grounded?"

Leaning back in his chair, casual and unaffected by the fastball biscuit his daughter just knocked me with, he tosses a piece of broccoli in his mouth and nods. "Yep. And do you know what happens when you're grounded for as long as me?"

"What?" Chloe leans in, her glass of milk halfway to her mouth.

"You lose your hair." He points to his early balding head.

Chloe's eyes go wide, and her lip starts to tremble as she spins toward her mom. "I don't want to lose my hair." Tears immediately follow the dramatic, shrill voice of my niece from her father's blatant lie.

Lauren, my sister-in-law, gives Alex a *you're dead* face and scoops Chloe into her arms and carries her out into the living room, away from her father. Smart move.

"Yeah"—Alex plays with the leftover food on his plate with his fork—"I'm going to pay for that one later."

"I look forward to seeing the wrath Lauren has in store for you."

"You'll be long gone by then." He glances at his watch. "Hell, it's already seven thirty, don't you start melting when the clock strikes eight?"

Tearing apart my biscuit, I stick a piece in my mouth and revel in the homemade, gluten-filled, delicacy. Lauren is a master in the kitchen, and if I don't leave five pounds heavier, I'm virtually insulting her. I've been trying to convince her to do some cooking segments on our show but she has yet to agree. Keeps saying she's camera shy. If I were honest, I think it's because she doesn't want to share her recipes. She's one of *those* people.

"Don't get salty at me, bro. You're the one in trouble, not me, and don't even think about dragging me down with you."

"Why are you here again?"

I'm about to answer when Lauren comes back into the dining room, minus child, sits in her seat, and downs the rest of her beer. Without looking at her husband she says, "Your daughter wants to start using your Rogaine so she can still do naughty things but keep her hair. I hope you're happy."

"You use Rogaine?" I quirk an eyebrow at him.

"It's not Rogaine. Lauren, stop calling it that." Alex huffs his displeasure, and it makes me giggle. "It's an Aveda product. Has some natural crap in it to help my hair follicles become more active."

"It's easier to say Rogaine." Lauren shrugs and turns toward me. "Did you enjoy dinner?"

"Meatloaf is my favorite, you know that. Plus these biscuits? My trainer is going to kill me, but it was so worth it. Thanks for having me over."

"Of course, we love when you eat with us, especially when you have juicy stories to tell us when children are distracted by Bubble Guppies."

"Juicy stories?" There is a crinkle in my brow. I don't have any gossip, at least none they don't already know. And I know what you're thinking. *You said you don't gossip, Noely.* Well, I don't, besides my family. I tell them things, and I'm okay with it.

"Don't hold out on me." Gesturing with her thumb over at Alex, she says, "I'm married to this guy; I need some dirt on your new dating life. Tell me all about this blind date venture you're on."

"Ah, I see where you're going with this." I shift in my seat and cross one leg over the other. "You want to grill me, don't you?"

"As your sister-in-law, I think I've earned the right, especially after giving you such an adorable niece. That little hellion came straight out of my vagina, just for you."

So true, well . . . sort of. I wanted a little baby to cuddle and play with and I wasn't about to have one of my own, so I hounded Alex and Lauren until they got pregnant. Granted, they wanted Chloe as well, but I might have been a little too invested when it came to her ovulation schedule.

"So because you gave me a niece I have to tell you everything?" I fold my arms over my chest—defensive stance 101.

Giving me a pointed look, Lauren says, "Did you not hear me? I pushed a child, a living, breathing thing out of my VAGINA for you. That means, you tell me everything." She takes a biscuit and plops a piece in her mouth. "And don't leave out the good stuff just because your brother is here."

"Yes, please tell me all the sexual things you're doing," Alex deadpans.

"My pleasure." I wink. *It's moments like these that I see the heavens open with beautiful payback for all the horrible things Alex did to me when I was a teenager.* "So I dry-humped a man on a motorcycle."

"I'm out." Alex stands quickly from his seat, hands in the air. "No way am I going to sit here and listen to that. Bubble Guppies here I come."

Lauren pats him on the side and nods toward the kitchen. "Be a dear and start on the dishes." She blows him an air kiss. "Love you, beefcake."

He shakes his finger at Lauren. "Don't be getting any ideas from her. I don't want you coming up to me tonight asking me to dry-hump on Chloe's rocking horse because you felt like trying something new."

"Please, dry-humping on the rocking horse is never going to happen. Now her bean bag chair, that's a viable option."

Rolling his eyes, Alex takes off but not before gathering some plates to take to the kitchen. He's a good husband.

When he's out of earshot, Lauren twists toward me with dreamy eyes. "So you dry-humped on a motorcycle. God, that sounds hot. Tell me all about it."

I spend the next few minutes recalling my date with Beck, blushing when I speak of all the . . . uh, touching we did. I'm still a little shocked I let loose that much. There were multiple times that night I felt Beck's "excitement" on me. And you know what, it only spurred me on to beg for more.

Harlot, that's what I was, an absolute harlot, and I have zero regrets. Hell, I'm ready to grind up on him on our next date while we cook dinner.

"Beck Wilder." Lauren leans back and pretends to smoke a cigarette while looking at the ceiling. "God, just his name makes my toes tingle, but knowing he's a motorcycle-driving, salsa-dancing, Spanish-speaking, erotic-humping rebel? Well, I very well might be in lust for you." She takes a pretend puff and blows her "smoke" toward the sky. "And he's a good kisser?"

"So good."

"Damn, that's some excellent stuff. And what about The Suit? That's completely done? Or are you dating two guys right now? Is that even allowed within this app?"

"I have no clue, probably not, but I'm done with The Suit."

"Oh?" She raises an eyebrow at me. "What happened there?"

I'm still bitter about the whole thing—clearly—by the way I slightly snapped when I said I was done with him. But can you blame a girl? We had this great connection and then out of nowhere, without a second chance, he breaks everything off. I mean, I get it, we were only going to go on a second date, but it was the way he was wooing me, our messages, our date, his kiss. It was . . . intentional. It just seemed like there was something special there. Something really special, but because I said his FIRST NAME on TV he couldn't go any further with me.

Uh . . . get over yourself.

Immature response? Maybe, but that's where I am right now when it comes to Jack. Riding the express train down Immature Lane.

"He wasn't the one," I answer vaguely, not wanting to dive into the Jack situation.

"I would say that's unfortunate since it looked like you really liked him on your show, but now that Beck Wilder is in your life, I mean, did The Suit dry-hump you on a motorcycle?"

"Not even a little." *But we did dance by the water at the beach.*

"Then in my opinion"—Lauren puts a hand to her chest, looking like the wiser one—"it's his loss, your gain. So what's next with the rebel?"

"Cooking class on Friday and then who knows what."

"Maybe he'll take you to a sex club. I've always wanted to go to one of those."

THREE BLIND DATES

Alex takes that moment to walk through the dining room, wearing an apron with a picture of Chloe on the front, and rubber gloves up to his elbows covering his hands. He stumbles over Lauren's confession and his jaw drops open.

"Oh hey, sweetie. Looking hot." Lauren sends him a wink and instead of questioning her confession, he gathers more dishes and quickly retreats into the kitchen.

"I think you just made his penis shrivel."

Lauren flings her head back and laughs. "Yeah, he's going to be a little shaken up, nothing a blow job won't cure."

"And it's time for me to go." I stand from my chair and call out to the family room. "Hey pretty girl. Auntie is leaving, come give me a hug."

The pitter-patter of Chloe's bare feet against the hardwood floor grows louder as she approaches. When she makes it to the dining room, she flings her string-bean body against mine and gives me a giant hug.

"Love you, Auntie."

"Love you, too, sweetie. Be good for your parents, okay?"

Nodding, she takes off toward the family room while yelling Bubble Guppies at the top of her lungs. And that right there is the reason I'm waiting a tad longer to have kids. Maybe until I'm thirty . . . well, thirty and married. I have to get married first. *I want to get married first.*

The thought of marrying Beck passes through my mind briefly. Is he marrying material? Would he think he's done the marriage thing and doesn't want to go there again? He's humping material, that's for sure, and for now, that's good enough. We have plenty of time to dive deeper.

Giving Lauren a hug, I say, "Thanks for dinner."

"Anytime. Keep me updated on the humper."

"I will."

Calling out to the kitchen, I say bye to my brother just as Lauren comes up behind him and grips two handfuls of his ass. He grunts and spins on his heels, capturing her in his wet, gloved hands. Eh, things are about to get a little frisky in there.

"Wait until the kid's asleep," I call out, waving a hand behind me.

They may be an "old" married couple, but they're what I strive to be.

What I want so desperately.

The kind of camaraderie my soul craves. They're one of the main reasons I'm testing out this *Going in Blind* program, because whenever I see them, I get jealous.

Being single is fun . . . for a little bit. But I've realized that there comes a time in a person's life when they just want to be able to have a partner in crime, someone you come home to every night, and wake up with every morning. Someone who cheers during your triumphs and carries you when you fall. And when you see that kind of relationship in real life, playing out in front of you? It's impossible not to want the same thing for yourself.

It's why, after the debacle with Jack, I pushed forward, well that and pure animosity. But it's why I will continue to push forward, because right now, I have all the materialistic things people *think* makes them happy: the house, the car, the successful career. But what I really want, what I truly, desperately want is romance. I want to hold my husband's hand in a movie or when we walk to the store. I want to yell at him one minute over something stupid, then be making passionate love the next, simply because we can't stay mad at each other. I want to be cherished, for someone to call me his own. And I want to give myself to that someone for as long as we both shall live.

I want to be in love.

CHAPTER SEVENTEEN

NOELY

S*assy,*
    Thong, granny panty, G-string, or boy cut? Inquiring minds want to know.
    Your rebel

R*ebel,*
    Isn't it a little presumptuous of you to be asking such personal questions about my undergarments?
    Sassy

S*assy,*
    No. Answer the question.
    Your rebel

. . .

R*ebel,*
   Well, when you put it that way, thong. Grannies when I feel like it. I don't own any boy-cut underwear, and the G-string? That's for special occasions.
Sassy
   P.S. What about you? What kind of underwear do you wear?

S*assy,*
   Our next date better be considered a special occasion where your underwear is concerned.
Your rebel
P.S. What's underwear?

R*ebel,*
   I guess you're just going to have to wait and see what's considered a special occasion where my underwear is concerned, aren't you?
Sassy
P.S. Are you telling me you go commando?

S*assy,*
   That's exactly what I'm saying. See you Friday, G-string and all.
Rebel

∽

"Thank you, have a good night."
   "Give me five stars and I'll give you five stars, deal?" My Uber driver calls out just as I'm about to shut the door.

"Uh, sure."

He places his hands on the headrest and twists completely toward me. "I mean it, lady. Give me five stars. I've been dinged too many times with a one star."

"Okay, well maybe it's because you seem to be assaulting me with this five-star business."

"I'm desperate."

"It shows." I give him a courteous smile and put some distance between the car and me. What has the world come to where we're begging each other for five stars on a driving service app? Just be a decent human and you'll score well. What's with all this pressure?

A notification on my phone pops up.

Bobby Michael rated you a three-star rider.

"What the hell?" I look up to see him peel away like a dickhole, waving his hand in the rearview window.

Three stars my ass. Mumbling to myself, I give him three stars as well. I'm not vindictive, but I'm not going to give him five stars after that stunt.

"Ohhh nooo, Bobby Michael, you're three stars at best." I close my app and say, "That'll teach him, give me three—"

"Talking to yourself now?"

Startled, I fumble with my phone and drop it on the pavement in front of me. When I go to pick it up, a perfectly polished wingtip shoe is in front of me. Looking up, I come face to face with those deep chocolate eyes I only got to stare into for a brief moment in time.

"Here." He hands me my phone and helps me to a standing position by lifting me at the elbow.

Stammering, showing zero sophistication, I snag my phone and stuff it in my purse. "Thanks. Excuse me." I try to walk past him but once again, he grips my elbow.

"It's good to see you, Noely."

It's good to see me?

IT'S GOOD TO SEE ME?

Jack, *The Suit*, the man who told me rather ineloquently at the beginning of our second date that he wanted nothing to do with me is now telling me that it's "good to see me"? He must have sniffed some of his shoe polish this evening.

But not wanting to come off as a bitter wench, because let's be honest, we only went on one date—a beautiful one—but one date, I tamper the crazy and smile politely.

"Nice to see you too, Jack."

Trying to get a move on again, I attempt to walk away but his grip stays firm on my elbow.

"Where are you going? Can I escort you?"

First of all, who says escort these days? Second of all, NO, YOU CAN'T ESCORT ME. Why on earth would he think it would be okay to "escort" me? Does he not remember the beach? Does he not remember the way he so easily discarded me? Does he not have any clue how embarrassed I was when he drove off without a backward glance?

Looks like he forgot and might need a little reminder.

A gentle one.

Extracting my elbow from his firm grip, I turn so I'm facing him directly, a position as a businessman I know he will appreciate. "Jack, it is lovely to see you, but as I hope you can remember, you made it quite clear you want nothing to do with me given my 'loud mouth.' So I'll say thank you for picking up my phone and be on my way."

"I never said you had a loud mouth." His shoulders are set back, his position stoic—unapologetic—seeing him, his broad chest and dark eyes captivate me, I still want to drive my foot between his legs. That'll teach him a lesson. *It's not like I'll need what's between there anytime soon. I mean, anytime* ever.

"Well whatever you said, you made it clear you didn't want to have anything to do with me. So, it was nice to see you, but—"

"Where are you going?" He pulls on the sleeves of his button-up shirt under his unblemished suit jacket.

Caught off guard from his abrupt question, I take a step back. "I don't think that's any of your business, sir."

"Didn't say it was. I was just wondering why you're dressed like that, walking along these dark streets by yourself."

I scan my outfit. I'm wearing black heels, black high-waisted trouser pants, and a long-sleeved, lace-covered, black crop top. I think I look rather stunning, especially with my hair curled and pinned to the side, showing off the expanse of my neck.

"What's wrong with my outfit?"

"Nothing." His heated gaze scans my body, searing me with every inch he consumes. *How is that possible? I don't like this man.*

Feeling exposed, I tilt my chin up and decide to deliver a blow I'm hoping will get Mr. WindsorKnot to move on.

"If you must know, I'm on my way to a second date, one I know will actually happen because unlike you, this man has no qualms in dating *me*. So if you'll excuse me, Jack, I must be on my way."

I take a step toward the direction of the cooking class, waiting for him to grab my elbow one more time, but when he doesn't, I take a look over my shoulder to see Jack piercing me with a stare I can't quite read. Adjusting his Windsor knot, he nods and says, "Have a good time, Noely."

And with that, he walks in the other direction, leaving me in a rather confused and bewildered state.

"Yeah, I will have a good time," I mumble, walking away as well. "You . . . you infuriating man."

What the hell was that?

∼

I need to go back into my Uber app and give that driver a one-star review. No wonder he's desperate for stars. He dropped me off three blocks away from my destination, so by the time I make it to the cooking class, I'm sweaty, slightly out of breath, but at least on time.

I might have booked it quicker than I wanted in heels, but I'm on time, and that's important because I didn't want Beck to think I'd stand him up. I know the kind of nerves a second date in this blind-date situation can bring, and I don't want Beck to feel any doubt. I want this date. With him.

I open the big metal door to the warehouse where cooking classes take place, and I'm greeted by black jeans, black boots, a black button-up shirt with the sleeves rolled up and top few buttons undone, and a wickedly gorgeous man. *God, Beck is attractive.* His hand is pulling on the ends of his hair, making him look nervous, but when he turns to see me, his eyes meet mine, the worry etching his brow disappears, and a slow, sexy smile spreads across his handsome face.

"Hey there, Sassy." He comes up to me, places his hands on my hips, and presses a brief kiss on my lips. It's been far too many days since I've been kissed. "You look gorgeous."

"Thank you. You look handsome yourself." I slip my hand in his and say, "I'm sorry about the wait; my Uber driver was a real ass and dropped me off at the wrong spot."

I don't mention my little encounter with Jack, because honestly, that's inconsequential in the grand scheme of things. And he'd have no idea who Jack was, and I am not going to explain that.

"No problem. They're just getting started. I reserved the fifties kitchen for us."

"The fifties kitchen?" I raise a quizzical eyebrow at him as he guides me into the giant warehouse full of tiny little blocks of kitchens, all with their own theme. There's the futuristic kitchen that looks entirely too foreign to me. The farmhouse kitchen with its multitude of roosters, the Christmas kitchen full of red and green plaid, and the Hobbit kitchen that looks more like a woodland diorama than anything. There are more kitchens scattered along the wide-open space, but before I can really take them all in, Beck takes me to our kitchen.

I feel like I've been transported back in time to when June Cleaver was the primetime mom rather than Gloria from Modern Family.

"Is that a pink fridge?"

"It is." Beck chuckles next to me. "And before you start asking, yes, those are blue and white cabinets."

I place my purse on a hook at the entrance of the kitchen and pull down the two frilly white aprons hanging up. "I assume these are for us."

"Looks like it." Without even a second thought, Beck puts on the apron and cinches it around his tapered waist. I give myself a moment to take him all in, his scruffy jaw, dark hair, hazel eyes, and carefree attitude. It isn't even his looks that makes him sexy. It's the way he carries himself, with such unabashed confidence, as if nothing can rock him. And when I think about the fact he's divorced, it amazes me. I know it's been a while, and perhaps he hasn't been celibate throughout the past eight years like I originally thought, but how can he be so upbeat? I am trying to be patient, but I dearly want to know him better.

"Are you going to just stare at me all night or are you going to put on that apron and join me?"

"Uh, sorry." I shake my head and fumble with my apron. Beck walks up to me, takes the apron, and helps me put it on, his strong, masculine scent making me wobbly with each breath I take.

"Let me help you with that, Sassy." When he's done tying the strings around my waist, he pinches my chin with his thumb and forefinger and says in a husky tone, "You can stare at me all you want later, but right now, let's make some food." He leans forward and slowly presses a seductive kiss on my lips. Now that's a kiss full of promises of what's to come.

When he pulls away, he takes my hand and brings me to the counter where there is a recipe book propped up by a stand. The kitchens around us are already buzzing with couples cooking and instructors walking around.

We need to get to work.

"Everything okay over here? Do you have any questions?" a petite woman wearing a chef's coat and hat asks, her hands folded in front of her.

"Hi, I'm Beck." Beck leans forward and shakes the lady's hand. "I think we're good. Just follow the recipe, right?"

"Yep, and if you have any questions, there are instructors walking around at your disposal. There is wine in the fridge. Have a nice evening."

She takes off, hands still folded, wandering around to the other kitchens.

"Want me to pour you a glass of wine?" Beck asks, going to the fridge.

"What are you going to drink?"

He holds up a bottle of water and smirks at me. "I hope you like red wine, because that's what your option is."

Feeling slightly bad that Beck isn't going to have a drink, I say, "Just a small glass is fine."

"You got it." He looks around the cabinets until he finds where the glasses are and starts laughing. I'm studying the recipe for scalloped potatoes, baked chicken, and . . . Jell-O when I direct my attention at Beck to see what all the commotion is about. He holds up a cup to me that has a picture of a hairy-chested man in a bathing suit. "Oh hell. Sorry, Sassy, but you're skipping the wine glass and drinking out of this tonight."

He pours the cold wine into the glass and we both watch in fascination as the man's bathing suit starts to disappear and his penis begins to make a full-frontal appearance.

"Holy fuck." Beck laughs even louder and holds the cup up to both of us. "Sass, he's naked."

Chuckling from how excited Beck is, I point and say, "And his bush is as hairy as his chest."

"This one is all man." Laughing some more, he hands me the cup of wine and says, "Have fun sucking that down." I nearly choke. Probably would literally too . . .

Digging through the cabinet, he makes an "aha" sound and then holds a glass in front of me of a woman in a bathing suit.

"Are we about to see some nipples?" I ask him, drinking from my naked-man cup.

"I think we are. And here I thought I was only going to see one set of nipples tonight." He winks at me, sending a wave of heat up my spine.

Are we showing each other our nipples tonight? Beck's sexy laugh flits through me and I think, yeah, we very well might be showing each other our nipples tonight.

CHAPTER EIGHTEEN

NOELY

"You're a liar."

"That's bold," Beck replies, tossing a towel over his shoulder and sprinkling a dash of salt over the raw chicken, as if he's the Salt Man, drizzling seasoning with cooking swagger.

"It's true."

"Yeah? How so?" Spinning on his heel, he opens the oven with one foot, yes, his foot, and plops the chicken in the oven with the potatoes already baking.

Leaning against the cabinet, I wiggle my finger at him. "In your messages, you said you weren't much of a cook, and yet here you are, acting like a professional in the kitchen."

He gives me a seductive glance. "Turning you on?"

"What, no, I mean, yes, I mean . . . no, that's not the point. You said you can't cook."

Wiping his hands, he sets the towel on the counter and says, "No, I said I'm not *much* of a cook, meaning I don't cook often. But when I do, I do it well." Entwining his hand with mine, he pulls me closer where be blocks me in with his large body. Spinning me around, so my back is to his front, he whispers in my ear, "Now help me toss this salad."

His body is so delicious against mine, his heat enveloping me, causing my body to quake deep down in my toes. "Does tossing a salad really require two people?"

"It does." He slips his hands up my sides and down my arms where his hands cover mine. Together, we pick up the wooden spoons and dip them in the salad Beck put together. That's been pretty much the entire night—me sitting on the counter, legs crossed, sipping my wine slowly, watching while Beck works his way around the kitchen, making me laugh, and sending me heated looks every chance he gets. He's seducing me, and he's doing it in a fifties kitchen wearing an apron sported by grandmas around the world.

With his body pressed against mine, his head leaning over my shoulder, the scruff of his jaw caressing my cheek, he says, "Tell me, Noely, did you wear your special-occasion underwear?"

"Why, Mr. Wilder, I don't know if that's proper dinner conversation."

His lips graze deliciously against my ear, causing a light thrumming to pulse between my legs. "We're not having dinner at the moment, so my manners don't have to be censored yet." He kisses the spot just below my ear and says, "Answer me, Noely. Are you wearing your special-occasion underwear?"

"Depends. Are you wearing underwear?"

"I told you I don't," he practically growls in my ear right before his head moves to my neck where he peppers kisses along my skin. Wanting him to go farther, I tilt my head back and rest it on his strong shoulder, the salad completely forgotten. "Are you, Noely?"

"Yes," I whisper, loving the way his lips feel so soft, so gentle, but aggressive at the same time. It's a lethal combination that leaves me shaking in my heels.

"Did you dress naughty for me, Noely? If I were to take off your shirt right here, right now, would I find the same black lace that matches your shirt?"

"Maybe," I answer, feeling shy but invigorated. "It's not the same really. What's underneath is see-through."

And that's a fact. To add to my harlot streak, the kind of streak I'm starting to take to, I put on see-through lingerie tonight, with the intention of giving Beck a little peek. I wanted to give him something to think about, but nothing he gets to fully see, because well, I am a lady after all.

Ahem, motorcycle humping . . . I know, I know. That wasn't very ladylike, but hey, if you were in my position, you would have done the same exact thing. No doubt in my mind.

"See-through?" Still gripping the wooden spoons, Beck turns me, loops my arms around his neck and lifts my body onto the counter only to step between my legs and nestle himself closely against me.

Hands still on hips, eyes heady—eager—he leans in, putting only a breath between us.

"Give me a taste of your lips, Sassy. Remind me how good you taste."

"But the salad," I breathe out heavily. "It needs to be tossed."

"The salad isn't going anywhere." Beck cups the back of my neck and wets his lips. "But this need I have for you . . . it's burning strong. Kiss me, Noely."

Unable to focus with my brain turning into an abyss of fog, my body reaches out to the man in front of me. I feel hypnotized as my lips near his.

"Don't hold out on me now. Kiss me, Sassy. Kiss me like you fucking mean it."

The hand that isn't wrapped around my neck runs down my thigh where it plays with the crevice between my hip and leg. My entire center melts into a puddle and before I can tell what I'm doing, the wooden spoons fall to the ground, and I pull Beck the last few inches until our mouths slowly glide along each other's. At first I keep my kiss soft, exploratory, but when Beck steps closer and I feel the telltale sign of his erection, I hook my legs around his and open my mouth, giving him full access.

Grunting, his tongue strokes inside my mouth, long, languid strokes that send chills down my spine, the thrill of making out with this man in public, in a fifties-themed kitchen adding to the rush of this experience.

It's hot, it's risky, it's something I never thought I'd do, but with Beck, it's as though I allow him to push me to the threshold of my limits and then past them.

Slipping my tongue against his, I dive deeper, pressing, pushing, wanting and needing more as I claw at his hair, my heels digging into his legs, my breath becoming labored.

My tongue is stroking his, our mouths melding together, just as a distinct cough comes from behind us. Startled and embarrassed, I push Beck away and hop off the counter to find the chef who greeted us standing with her arms folded and a less-than amused look on her face.

Beck doesn't allow me to push him too far away. His hand snags around my waist and once again my back is pressed up against his chest . . . and his hard-on.

Good Christ, this man.

From the look the lady is giving us, I feel like I'm back in high school, caught making out under the bleachers, and I'm about to be sent to detention.

Clearing her throat, the chef says, "I know cooking can be very exciting, but please refrain from getting overly physical with each other in our kitchens. Save that for when you get home. Thank you."

She tips her head and walks away, authority in every step she makes.

"Oooo, you got us in trouble," Beck sing-songs in my ear.

"Me?" I turn to face him, my finger pointing at my chest. "I wasn't the one who lifted me on the counter and begged for kisses."

"Nah, that was all me, but you were the one who said you were wearing see-through lingerie. I'm a man, Sassy. You can't say shit like that and not get yourself in trouble." He tips my chin. "Keep that in mind."

With a smirk, he tends to our food, checking the oven and flitting around the kitchen as if we weren't just about to have a full-on grope session in a public kitchen.

How can he seem so casual when I'm burning up inside?

~

"Uh, let's see, something you don't know about me. Well, that's a lot," I point out, while a piece of chicken waits on my fork ready to be consumed. For the record, he's a good cook, like my stomach wants to eat all the food, even what's on his plate, that's how good he is. It's not very often I get a home-cooked meal, unless I'm at Alex and Lauren's house. So this is a treat, especially since an extremely hot man cooked it for me.

"That's why we're playing this game. Tell me something obscure, like you used to plant raisins in the summer hoping they would come back as grapes."

I tilt my head to the side. "That's an odd thing to say, unless . . ." I put my chicken in my mouth and then point at Beck. "Did you try to grow grapes from raisins?"

"Never worked, can you believe that?" His charming smile gets me everytime.

"Hard to." I chew the rest of my chicken and swallow. Holding his water glass to his lips, he waits for my response so I think about what to say. I don't have anything like trying to grow grapes but I do have something. "I'm in the Guinness Book of World Records."

"No, you're not . . . are you?" His playful interest makes me feel important, content, and also excited about our pairing. I really hope more single people give *Going in Blind* a try. Although such different men and dates, so far, I'm impressed with their ability to match like-minded people.

I nod. "I am. Go ahead, look me up. Noely Clark, right there in the book."

"For what?" He leans back in his chair. "Wait, let me guess." Stroking his chin, I can tell he's about to unleash some ridiculousness, and I can't wait to hear it. "Okay, you beat the record for longest make-out session with a dog."

Chuckling, I shake my head. "Nope."

"Most deviled eggs eaten in a minute."

"No, that's puke-worthy though. I would never be able to eat more than two deviled eggs in a minute."

"Most wedgies given in a minute."

Laughing some more, I say, "No, but who would volunteer to help break that record?"

"Not me, since I don't wear underwear." I roll my eyes. "Oh I know, you hold the record for most four-leaf clovers found on St. Patrick's Day."

"I've never found one in my life."

"Damn. Looks like I'm striking out, Sassy. Give me a hint."

Peering over my glass of wine, the one I've been nursing all night, I say, "It has to do with dancing."

"Dancing?" His brow lifts in question. "Huh, okay, dancing, dancing . . ." He snaps his fingers at me and leans over the table. "You hold the longest time for hanging upside down on a stripper pole by only your thighs."

I quirk my lip to the side as my brow pulls together. "That's not dancing."

"To hell it's not. Strippers are dancers, they just do it naked. If you think about our first date, you dancing against me in that tiny dress of yours, you were practically naked."

"Practically? That's a far stretch. All my parts were covered so don't you try to turn your little nonsensical logic on me."

He laughs, the sound rumbling through my chest, warming me up to a comfortable, relaxed state. "You never answered me. Was that the world record you broke?"

"No, nice try though."

"A guy can dream. Now tell me what it was."

"You give up? How is that possible, your guesses were so close." Sarcasm drips from my lips.

"Okay, Sass, lay it on me."

I spin the stem of my wine glass and say, "I was part of the biggest twerking dance group in college my senior year. We all got on the football field, played some Rhianna, and then twerked it out for the entire song."

"You're serious." I nod. "So you twerked for an attire song with a bunch of college students?"

"Yeah, there were a lot of flying butt cheeks that day. And let me tell you, twerking for an entire song is not easy. My back hurt for days after."

"I can imagine." He studies me for a second then asks, "Do I get to see this twerking at some point?"

Chuckling, I shake my head. "I think my twerking days are over."

"Never say never, Sassy."

"What about you?" I ask, wanting to know more about him. "I don't even know what you do for a job. How is that possible?"

He shrugs. "Eh, it's not that important in the grand scheme of getting to know someone but if you must know, I'm a muralist."

"A muralist. As in someone who paints murals?"

His grin is laced with humor. "Great definition."

"I'm sorry, I've never met a professional muralist before. Have I seen any of your work?"

"Depends." He shrugs, acting so casual it's almost annoying. For some reason, I think being a muralist is a big deal. That's a huge talent to hide. I mean, saying you're an artist is one thing, but being a muralist, someone who paints on the world's biggest canvases, that's a whole other league of artistry. "Have you ever been to the zoo or museums in San Diego or Los Angeles?"

"Many times. Why, do you have paintings there?"

"Just a few. You know when you're trying to look for an animal in an exhibit and in the background, there is a painted habitat behind them? I painted some of those."

"Really?" I don't know why this is so fascinating to me, but it is. "And at the museums . . ."

"I've painted and touched up a lot of the dioramas. I do some other random pieces of work, but a lot of my contract work comes from the zoos and museums."

"That's incredible." I sit back in my chair and cross my leg over the other. "I'm kind of in awe. When I thought about your profession, muralist never popped in my mind."

"Oh yeah? What did you think I did?"

"I don't know." I pin him with a questioning look. "You're kind of mystery. You like to talk more about me than yourself, or you like to just joke around, so I'm really shooting in the dark where you're concerned."

"You seem to be doing a good job so far."

"Yeah, but you have to know my little daytime-talk-show heart wants to know everything about you, right?"

For the first time since I met Beck, his back stiffens and the jovial look he once wore has morphed into a passive one, a facial expression I can't quite understand. To say that is unusual is an understatement. I am good at reading people, as it's one of my better skills that makes me good at my job. And Beck . . . well, it's as though he's just shut down on me. *Why?*

"Not much to know that actually matters."

"What does that mean? Clearly there is stuff to know, but you don't want to talk about it."

He tips his water glass in my direction. "Exactly."

"Well, you're going to have to open up at some point, you know. That's what dating is all about, getting to know one another."

"I'm well aware of how dating works there, Sassy. I'm also well aware that the night is coming to a close and the kitchens around us are starting to shut down. So how about we put these dishes in the sink and head out."

Caught off guard from his abrupt departure from our previously easygoing moment, I nod and say, "Sure, let me grab my phone and call an Uber for myself."

Standing from his chair, he rounds the little table and pulls me to a stand as well, with his hands resting on my lower back, he says, "No way am I done with you tonight. We're just done with the first half of our date."

"First half?" I swallow hard as his face inches closer to mine.

"First half," he whispers right before his mouth presses against mine, prying my lips apart, and kissing me until my toes curl right there in my heels. *Yeah. It's a thing. I know that now.*

CHAPTER NINETEEN

NOELY

"You've changed my life."

"That's not the first time I've heard that," Beck says, facing me as we sit on a lounge chair in my backyard, overlooking the ocean.

After we left the warehouse, Beck drove me around the city for a while, letting the wind whip through me, making me feel alive all over again. I've never felt so free, so daring, than when I'm on the back of Beck's motorcycle.

Then again, I'm feeling pretty alive right now with Beck's gaze directed at me, his back completely turned away from the ocean and its glittering splendor under the starry night sky.

"Seriously, how come I've never tried this place before?" I take another spoonful of the gelato we picked up on the way back to my place. Spumoni gelato is heaven. Never in my life have I tasted anything so smooth, so flavorsome. I very well might have to go to Maria's Ice Cream place every day on the way home from work. We bought a pint to share, and I'm pretty sure I've eaten more than half, but from the sexy gleam in Beck's eyes, I'm going to say he doesn't mind.

"You seem like a Baskin Robins kind of girl, am I right?"

Mouth full of ice cream, I answer, "Their ice cream cake is to die for. They have that crumbling crunch yum yum on the bottom that is so damn good."

"Crumbling crunch yum yum. You know, I think that's the real terminology they use."

"Is has to be." I take another scoop from the carton Beck is holding. "Thank you for tonight, Beck."

"Anytime, Sassy. I'm glad you decided to go on a second date with me. It's been fun. And hey, the view isn't so bad either." He eyes me up and down.

"Oh please, is that the best you've got? A lame line and a once-over? You know, I expect more from you, rebel."

"I'm a little out of practice, but you can't hold that against me."

Setting my spoon to the side and crossing my legs, I ask, "Am I the first woman you've dated since your divorce?"

"Dated, yes. Other things . . . no."

"Other things?" I pause and then my mouth forms a knowing O. "Ohh, like sex."

"Yes, like sex." He laughs.

"So why start dating now?"

Setting the ice cream to the side, he brushes his hands on his pants and leans back on the lounge chair, his hands propping him up. "Not sure, really. My buddy thought I should try out the program, so I did."

"Well, that's convincing." *Not.* "Do you think you'll ever get married again?"

"You know, we don't have to talk about this right now." Moving forward, Beck leans over me and in one swift movement, he unlatches the back of the lounge and lays me down flat, crawling over my body until his weight is on top of me, making me feel warm and cozy.

I straighten out my legs, which settles his non-underwear-covered crotch right against mine. Am I really going to do this? Is he really going to do this? He hasn't been subtle about his intentions, but is he all talk? Or is he without a doubt all action?

From the way he's looking at me, pure sex dripping from him, I'm going to guess he's action and that makes me nervous. Not because I don't want him. Hell, I would be insane to not want him. But what makes me nervous is that I've never really done this before . . . launched so quickly into a sexual relationship with someone before an emotional one.

"Why the creased brow, Sassy?" His eyes bounce back and forth between mine.

"Nothing." I shake my head, trying to rid the constant questioning in my head. *You have a hot guy on top of you who wants you, Noely.* Enjoy the experience.

"Are you sure? Because you look worried. Are you nervous?"

"I'm not worried." Beck's thumb starts to stroke my cheek, easing my nerves. "Just a little . . . shy, I guess."

"Shy?" His head pulls back and he gives me another once-over. "You, shy? The girl who showed up to our first date in a dress no bigger than a handkerchief."

Sighing, I say, "That was a different outfit for me than my usual."

"And what about tonight?" His fingers graze along my side to the exposed skin of my crop top. A sizzling sensation bundles up in the pit of my stomach from that little touch, from the way he's looking at me with those sinister eyes. "This outfit, including what's underneath, doesn't say shy to me."

He's right, it doesn't, but maybe what it comes down to is this: I might be a tease with no follow-through. At least that's what it's feeling like right now. But is that really who I am or have I been burnt before, enough to not trust that I'm the girl who gets to keep the guy?

"Tell me, Noely, what would you like to do tonight?"

"Uh, what do you mean?" I wiggle under him, my G-string becoming wetter by the second with each pass of his fingers under the waistband of my high-waisted pants.

"You know exactly what I mean." His fingers play with the button of my pants and when he undoes them, I'm impressed. He did that with one freaking hand. And then he pulls down the zipper of my pants . . .

His hand slides inside, and slowly, he starts to bring the waistband of my pants down until they're resting at my hip. He spans his hand across my exposed stomach, his thumb stroking the skin below my belly button, igniting every nerve ending in my body.

"If you want me to stop, tell me, right now . . ."

"Stop," I answer, causing him to push up to look me directly in the eyes. Confused, he's about to say something when I cover his mouth with my hand. "Not out here, not where my neighbors can hear." His face morphs into something brazen and without saying a word, he scoops me into his arms and walks me into my house. "Down the hall, to the right," I say, knowing exactly what he's looking for.

When he tosses me on my bed and stands before me, his eyes pinned to mine, unbuttoning his shirt slowly, I wonder if this is really happening, if I'm about to go to bed with a man I've only hung out with one other time. Granted, we did do the humping, but this is different. This is entirely different than a little dry rubbing.

I bite my bottom lip, feeling my nerves start to blossom again, and Beck notices. His hands are still on his shirt. All the buttons are undone, exposing his tanned and toned skin. And look at those abs. Holy hell.

"What's wrong, Noely?"

Propping myself on my elbows, I take a quick peek at the little patch of hair leading below Beck's waistline and then move my gaze to his eyes where there is deep concern. Wanting to be truthful, I say, "I'm just nervous. You're, you know, this hot alpha-type rebel who can sear my panties off with one look. I've never done anything like this so soon, and it makes me nervous."

"But you want this?"

I nod. "I do."

I think I do, I mean I do. I really do, but then again, I have so many questions, like why did he get a divorce? Why did it take eight years? Why did he refrain from telling me what he did until tonight? Why are there so many secrets?

Is Beck someone I can see myself with for the long haul?

Shirt off now, his chest ripples as he lowers himself to my body and pulls on the waist of my pants until they're completely off. Tossing them to the floor, he keeps his eyes trained on what he just exposed: my lacey black G-string.

"Hot," he mumbles, moving his hands to my crop top, his fingers trailing a path of heat along with them. My skin prickles from his touch, my body reacting to every move he makes, while my head questions every little touch and sound. "Lift your arms, Sassy." Since my body and brain are currently not connected, my arms lift on their own accord, and in one swift movement, Beck has my black see-through bra exposed, my nipples poking against the fabric, looking for release.

Lowering his head, his lips hum against mine briefly before they glide to my collarbone, nipping and sucking, making their way to my bra. Through the fabric, his hot breath hovers above my nipple right before he grips my breast with one of his strong hands and brings it to his mouth. My chest rises from the bed, my eyes wide with shock, and my breath comes in erratic pants. His teeth graze my nipple and a lone cry escapes past my lips.

"So fucking responsive," he says before moving to my other breast, giving it the same treatment. My mind is now a fog, all inhibition thrown out the window as I allow myself to get lost in the moment, to lie back and enjoy rather than worry where this is going to take me.

Beck kisses his way back to my mouth and lifts me off the bed to a standing position. Unsure of his next move, I wait, my hands twining around his hair as he reaches behind me and undoes my bra. The cool night air puckers my nipples and my nerves are heightened with each pass Beck makes of his hands down my back until they reach my G-string. His hands slip under the waistband

and grip my ass, pulling me into his pelvis where I deliciously feel his erection knocking at the zipper of his jeans.

His lips press against the spot where my neck meets my shoulder and he sucks, he sucks hard, nibbling at the same time. All I can think about—other than how good that feels—is: I hope he doesn't leave a mark, or else Natasha is going to have a hell of a time in makeup.

"Lie down, Noely." The way his commanding voice directs me has my hands shaking in anticipation. *It's been so long since a man has brought me such ecstasy.*

When I'm splayed across the bed, I feel exposed, but sexy at the same time. It's the look in Beck's eyes as he runs his hand over his jaw, taking me all in.

"Beautiful." Bending at the foot of the bed, he grips the sides of my G-string and pulls it down, leaving me utterly naked. Not wasting any time, Beck yanks on my legs and hangs them over his shoulders so my heated center is right at his mouth.

"Wh-what are you doing?" I stammer.

"This," he answers right before he parts me and presses his tongue against my clit.

"Ohhh . . . God," I breathe out heavily as my body melts, molding to the mattress.

"Fuck, I knew you would taste good. So sweet, so addicting." His hands press on my inner thighs, his thumbs delicately spreading me open to him while his tongue makes long, languid strokes.

It's never been like this before. Ever. My body so aware, so on fire, ready to explode at any second. I've never had a man so invested in my pleasure before, so focused on me. It's always been about the act of sex, the end goal, the grand finale, but with Beck, it feels different. Is this what Dylan has been talking about all along?

This feeling, this all-consuming sense of euphoria with a man, a man who wants nothing more than to pleasure you? *How have I never experienced this before?*

I'm having a sexual awakening. *This* is what sex can be. This is what it should be.

I thread my fingers through his hair, my hips moving with each swipe of his tongue against my slit.

"Yes," I moan, the sound foreign to my ears. "Yes, Beck."

At the mention of his name, he presses his tongue harder and a wave of pleasure rockets through me, up and down my spine. Moving his entire mouth against my slit, his scruff rubs against my inner thighs. One of his hands grips my ass tightly, the other presses down on my stomach, keeping me in place. My clit starts to throb, the sensation rocking my body closer and closer to the precipice, as if each thrum climbs me higher and higher.

"Oh God, oh God, Beck."

His mouth lifts and he asks, "Are you going to come, Sassy?"

I nod, my eyes closed, my lips pressed together, my body floating, throbbing, waiting . . .

As if he's studying me, he takes his time lowering his head to my pussy, and when he does, he lightly blows on my arousal, causing my hips to buck right into his mouth where he devours my clit, sucking on it so hard I think I'm going to shoot off the bed.

Climbing and climbing and climbing, my heart racing a mile a minute, my legs numbing, my vision going black, my mind going blank . . . and then it hits me. My senses leap and my orgasm takes over, throwing my body into a pit of orgasmic bliss. I convulse, hips thrusting against Beck's tongue, greedy, riding out my orgasm until I can't take it anymore, until the pleasure is too much and I'm on the verge of tears.

Laying my arm over my eyes, I breathe out a heavy sigh and say, "Oh my God, Beck."

"Feel good?"

"So good." He kisses his way up my body, his fingers playing with my nipples, bringing me back to life and into the present. When I open my eyes, I see him hovering over me, the look of absolute joy spread across his face, as if he just accomplished one of his biggest goals.

I take a second to look him over, to take him in from his chestnut-brown hair, to his delicious scruff that graces his strong jaw, to his soft pliable lips, and all the way to his masculine and built chest. The way his jeans hang low on his hips, hinting at the lack of underwear underneath, makes my mouth water and pulls me out of my fog.

Lifting up, I reach for his jeans and pull him in closer. I undo the button, and I'm instantly fascinated by the way his abs flex from my initial touch. Wanting to see how else I can make this man react, I pull down the zipper, and then loop my hands inside his waistband and push his jeans down.

When I lift back up, I'm greeted by his erection. Wait, let me rephrase that. I'm greeted by his thick, pulsing erection. While I stare, Beck makes quick work of his shoes, socks, and pants and pushes me back onto the bed, his body hovering over mine, his erection hard and wet with pre-cum.

Oh God . . .

I press my hand against his chest and urge him to lie down. Taking direction well, even though he seems to be the one in charge, he lies across my bed, his head resting on my pillows, a smirk playing on his lips.

Smugly, but with a sexy confidence, Beck laces his hands behind his head and awaits my next move. There is something about the way Beck has given me the rights to his body—his confidence in my abilities—that has me moving on top of him, my hands grazing his thighs until they meet his erection. Settling into position, I grip his length and start to stroke leisurely, getting a feel for him. God, he feels so good. Beck relaxes into the mattress and watches me, his eyes heavy with lust . . . *lust for me.*

Keeping my gaze trained on the rise and fall of Beck's delectable abs, I lower my head while my hand strokes him and press my tongue along his stomach, licking each divot. Let it be known that I'm quite partial to what he has to offer.

"Fuck, you're making me so goddamn hard."

My hair falls over my face like a waterfall, hiding the blush caressing my cheeks from his confession. I use the curtain to my advantage and run the soft strands along his skin, sending goosebumps up and down his legs. Gripping him a little tighter, I bring my hand to the top of his dick and squeeze hard before releasing and going back down. I repeat the process over and over until Beck's composure is slipping.

Reading his cues, I squeeze my hand at the top again at the same time that I bring my mouth to his tip, licking it very lightly.

"Fuck." He squeezes his eyes shut, his response everything I could have hoped for, so I repeat the action.

Grip, lick, grip, lick.

Fascinated, I watch Beck grip the comforter beneath him, his knuckles turning white, his hands straining for control.

Needing more, wanting to see how far I can push him, I bring my lips to the tip of his cock and then suck him in while my hand squeezes his root.

I work him. Sucking hard, my mouth moving along the head of his cock, my tongue dragging along. With my free hand, I reach between his legs and grip his balls, lightly fondling them. Together, I work my hands and my mouth careening him to the edge of no return.

Beneath me he stiffens. His skin glistens with sweat, his grunts turn me on, and the strain in his neck, in his pecs—in every corded muscles running up and down his body—tells me he's on the edge, teetering, ready to fall over.

"I'm going to come, Sass. Pull away."

I don't.

Instead, I suck harder, I squeeze harder, and I flick my tongue on the underside of the head.

"Fuck," he roars as he comes, his breathing heavy, his chest rising and falling rapidly.

Pulling away, I watch as he falls and floats, the same reaction I had what seems like only minutes ago.

"Christ, Noely." He breaths a heavy sigh. "Get up here." Pulling on my hand, he brings me to his chest and snuggles me close. "Get in here, pretty girl." Nudging the comforter out from under us, he drapes the blanket over our bodies and wraps his arm around me. I rest my head on his shoulder as my hand goes to his chest. It feels oddly comforting to be held like this. I've always loved cuddling. I just never thought I'd be cuddling this early on. *Never thought my rebel would be my cuddler.*

We lie in silence for a few moments. Is he going to say something? Is he spending the night? Do I offer him a drink and a high five? Yay, orgasms!

I'm about to ask Beck if he really does want a drink but he interrupts the battle in my head. "Hope you don't mind me spending the night; you wore me out." Kissing the top of my head, he pulls me in a little closer and holds on tight. *Feels so good, if not unusual and unexpected.*

I guess that answered my questions.

CHAPTER TWENTY

NOELY

A low groan vibrates in my ear, waking me to the bright sunlight filtering through my window. In a bit of a haze, I shift on my bed and still when my hand comes in contact with another body. *A warm body.*

Beck.

God, last night . . .

Slipping out from under the covers, from the warm little cocoon we created, I snag the robe on the back of my door, wrap it around my body, and tiptoe out of my bedroom to the kitchen where coffee is already brewing. Thank you, automatic timer. I pour myself a cup and head to my back deck where all the debauchery started last night.

Not bothering to sit up the lounge chair from last night, I take a seat in the other lounge, bring my knees to my chest, and sip my coffee while looking over the crashing waves of the ocean.

Last night was . . . Ugh, last night was eye-opening.

It isn't because I was with Beck, a domineering, sexy rebel, but it's because I realize now, at the age of twenty-seven, that sex can be fun—well, oral sex for that matter. It's never been like that. I've never felt so alive in the bedroom.

Yes, I've had an orgasm before, but nothing that's taken over my body like last night. Nothing that had every nerve ending in my body standing on end begging for more.

From the very beginning with Beck, it's been physical. From the way he first devoured me with one look, to the little touches here and there, to our dancing, our first kiss and dry-humping, to last night. I simply couldn't take my hands off him.

He's showed me that men can be addicting, that the act of physically being with someone can be addicting, and to be honest, that scares me, because I want so much more than the physical.

"There you are." Beck's morning voice is deep, rumbly with a hint of scratch to it. Taking a seat in front of me, exactly like last night, he holds out his hand for my coffee, and I hand it to him.

While he sips, I take him in. His hair is disheveled, giving him boyish charm. His scruff is thicker, darker, and his exposed chest is looking mighty fine as well as the unbuttoned jeans covering his legs. How is it possible for someone to wake up looking that attractive?

Five bucks says I look like Medusa right now.

Feeling slightly self-conscious, I pat down my hair when Beck is looking out to the ocean. When he turns back to me, he hands me my coffee cup.

"That's good, thanks." He pulls my legs down and lays them across his lap, his fingers massaging my calf muscles. "How are you doing, Sassy?"

"Good." I smile over the rim of my coffee mug. "How about you?"

"Fantastic."

"Good." I nod my head awkwardly, unsure of what else to say.

"Morning afters not really your thing?"

"Just, never done one before I guess, not with someone so new. And we didn't really have sex-sex, so to me it even seems more awkward. I mean, I put my mouth on your dick, but our privates never actually touched. Don't you think that's weird?"

"No," he answers matter-of-factly. "Sometimes just engaging in the act of sex is all that's needed."

I nod, my lips pursed. "Did you not want to do it with me?" It's an odd question to ask, but I'm curious about the holdup.

"I did, but I knew you weren't ready. Honestly, I wanted to help you relax. I wasn't expecting anything in return, but when you started undoing my pants, I couldn't stop you. I wanted to feel those lips on my rock-hard cock."

"What do you mean you knew I wasn't ready?"

"I could see it on your eyes. You were unsure. I didn't want to pressure you into anything. So I kept it simple."

Thoughtful, sexy, and domineering, I should be head over heels in lust right now, but for some reason I'm not.

And I think I know why.

"Thank you, I was really nervous last night." I bite my bottom lip and say, "I usually have more of an emotional connection with men before I jump into bed with them."

Sitting back, Beck asks, "You don't feel an emotional connection with me?" The pull in his brow is telling me he's truly confused.

"I don't mean to insult you, Beck, because you are really amazing. I know dating isn't something I'm very experienced at, but we seem to be very physical with each other." *And it's great, but I think I should be expecting more.* I know I want more, but is that realistic?

"Nothing wrong with that, Sassy."

His hand goes up to my knee and a part of me wants to dissolve into the lounge and let him take over, but a larger part of me stops him before he can go further.

"Why won't you tell me about your divorce?"

That stops him.

Removing his hand from my knee, he rubs his jaw and sighs. "It's not something I want to talk about."

"Why? Are you still in love with her?"

He shakes his head. "Not even a little."

Okay, there goes that theory.

I set my coffee cup on the ground next to me and press my hands against Beck's. "Are you scared I'm going to judge you? I won't, if that's what you're worried about. Getting married at such a young age—"

"It wasn't that. We were ready when we got married. We just went our separate ways."

Feeling a little disheartened, but wanting to be honest since I'm in this dating program for a reason, I say, "Beck, are you ready to be dating someone? You say you are, and you want to get out there, but I don't think your heart is in it . . . or your mind."

He's silent for a second, his gaze cast toward the ocean. "I want to forget it all, the last eight years. I wish there was a way to wipe it from my memory."

"Wipe what?"

He shakes his head, and I realize right then and there, no matter how much I push, how much I question him, Beck isn't going to talk because he's not mentally ready. If there is one thing I know well, you can't force anyone to talk if they don't want to.

What's sad is, I don't know if he will ever talk, at least to me.

We sit in silence, both our minds wandering, our euphoric night a distant memory, and our impending future closing with each breath we take. At least, that's what I'm feeling.

"I like you," Beck finally says. That makes me smile. He really is a wonderful man.

"I like you too."

"But not enough, right?"

"It's not about liking you or not, Beck, or my attraction to you, because that's all there. In spades if I'm honest. It's about making a connection on another level, and I don't think you're mentally ready for that. You need to clear out the tainted headspace you're hanging on to."

Huffing out a long breath, Beck runs his hand through his hair. "Fuck," he mutters.

"Yeah, fuck," I repeat, feeling sad.

"You want more." *So much.*

"I want it all. The marriage, the husband, the children. I'm already there, looking for it, but I think you're just coming out of the fog you were in."

Laughing, he says, "Yeah, kind of not ready to be married again quite yet."

"Understandable." We smile at each other, a general understanding of one another passing between us.

For the next twenty minutes, we joke around, drink cold coffee, and talk about nonsense, never diving past the surface. When it's time, I help Beck gather his things and walk him to my front door.

Turning toward me, he pulls me into a hug and presses a kiss to the top of my head. "You're amazing, Sassy, you know that, right?"

"I do now." I squeeze his waist, already feeling the loss of his fresh, rebel-ish attitude.

Sighing heavily, he pulls away and tips my chin up. "If you don't find Prince Charming right away, message me, okay?"

"Deal."

He presses a light kiss against my lips, and with a sad, yet devastating smile, he leaves. Pressing my body against the doorjamb, my arms folded over my chest, I watch Beck mount his bike, put on his helmet, and roar the engine to life. After a tilt of his head in my direction, Beck takes off down the road and out of my life.

~

"Oh my God, Dylan, it was the cutest place I've ever been to. Every kitchen was different and there were professionals walking around, giving you privacy but also helping you out if you needed it. Perfect for any type of date."

"Especially for a second date with The Rebel, right?" She wiggles her eyebrows at me and takes a drink of her mimosa.

"It was the perfect date, recommended by *Going in Blind*. They must have gone around the city and found every possible dating excursion, and after experiencing it for themselves, mashed it up in their system to suggest it to the right couples who would enjoy it. Genius, really."

"So you had a good time?"

"I had an amazing time. The Rebel did most of the cooking, which was fun for me. I sat back and drank wine while he worked his way around a fifties-themed kitchen in a white frilly apron."

"Did you get pictures?"

I shake my head, really hating this conversation, but knowing I have to have it, thanks to Kevin. I smile into the camera and shake my head. "No pictures, unfortunately."

"That's a bit of a fail on your part." This makes me laugh. What I'm sharing now is most definitely the PG-13 version of what we talked about in hair and makeup. When I described what the photos would look like, because, yeah, Beck is hot, Dylan actually blushed. I'm amazed she's holding it together now.

"Even if I took pictures, and even though I love our viewers, I wouldn't be sharing those here. I'm sure my dating harem would like to keep their privacy." I learned that lesson pretty darn quickly, so that last comment is aimed at Kevin. *Thanks for ruining Mr. Suit's future.*

"Harem? Is that what you're calling it?"

"It's going to be a harem soon," I sigh, leaning back on the couch, temporarily forgetting I'm still on camera.

Looking a little uneasy, Dylan asks, "What does that mean?"

"Ugh, I had a great time with The Rebel, like the best time ever. We clicked on so many levels, but . . ."

"But what?" Dylan is sitting on the edge of her seat, waiting for my response.

"It just didn't work out. We're on different wavelengths right now. But it's okay. We ended things on a wonderful note, and I'm sure I'll see him again. Even if it's just as a friend. No doubt in my mind."

"So what does this mean?"

I shrug. "Going back to the drawing board I guess. I know the right man for me is out there and honestly, *Going in Blind* has brought me closer to happiness than I've experienced in a long time."

"So you're going to throw your name in the hat again?"

I bring the champagne flute to my mouth and take a sip. After I swallow, I say, "I am, because as they say, third time's the charm."

Part Three

THE JOCK

CHAPTER TWENTY-ONE

NOELY

"So you give the guy a blow job and then send him on his way? How does that work?"

"Can you keep your voice down?" I ask, lifting a ten-pound dumbbell overhead only to start counting out my tricep extensions.

"I'm sorry but you sprang this breakup on me this morning without any kind of background information. I thought Beck was it. He was charming, hot, domineering, had a motorcycle. What more could you want?" Dylan is still reeling over my "split" with Beck, can't you tell? I truly think she's living vicariously through me.

"He was very closed off. He wouldn't talk about anything that delved too deep into who he was or his past."

"So? He dry-humped you on a motorcycle, that should be reason enough to stick around."

I give Dylan a pointed look as our trainer makes a huffing sound next to us.

"I'm not using *Going in Blind* as a hookup app. If I wanted to find someone to have sex with, I would join Tinder. This is different for me, Dylan. I want to find someone I can spend the rest of my life with, someone who wants kids—a family—who can understand my work schedule but also demand some attention himself. I want what you and Chad have."

"Two demonic children and morning shower sex?"

Chuckling, I nod, "Yes."

"Do you want to borrow Chad and the kids, see if it's something you're really interested in?"

I pull up a BOSU ball and start doing pushups, my breath becoming labored. "Thank you for whoring out your husband to me, but I think I want to try to find my own."

"He's yours if you want him." Resting against the wall, not putting any effort into our workout like normal, Dylan asks, "So it's really over with The Rebel? Like really, truly over?"

"For now, yeah. I mean, he said if I don't find what I'm looking for, he wants me to message him."

"So he's waiting around?"

"I hope . . . not," I grunt, performing my last pushup. I roll to the side and sit on my butt, legs spread out, sweat dripping down my chest. "Honestly, he seems to have some demons. I hope he's trying to work through those, because until he does, he can't move forward, not just with me, but in life."

"Damn."

"Dylan, are you going to finish your workout today?" our trainer asks, looking less than pleased at my co-host.

Bending at the waist, Dylan grabs her calf and lamely says, "Charlie horse, ouch."

Our trainer rolls his eyes and I'm pretty sure if Dylan wasn't paying on a monthly basis, and paying well, he would have dumped her as a client. But the money keeps rolling in so he continues to pretend to train her, despite how frustrating it can be.

Throwing in the towel, our trainer gives us a quick rundown of the rest of the week's schedule and sends us off to the smoothie bar—Dylan's favorite part of her "workout"—so we can replenish our bodies with the right nutrients.

THREE BLIND DATES

I order the kale protein smoothie with Greek yogurt and chia seeds, the smoothie our trainer tells us to drink, while Dylan picks the berry bliss smoothie that is full of sugar. How she keeps her figure, I have no idea.

Taking a seat at a high-top table with smoothies in hand, Dylan sucks on her straw, eyes marveling in her flavorful drink. "God, this is so good, much better than that kale crap that gets caught in your straw."

"It's really good, actually." Sort of.

If you tell yourself it's good, then your taste buds follow suit, right?

"So what's next? Do you go on another date? Are you going to quit the program? From my view, it doesn't seem to be working. Two guys down, no promises of happily ever after in your future."

She sure knows how to make a girl feel good.

"I think I'm going to try again. I mean, why not? So far, the matches have been dead on, almost perfect. I've had so much in common with both guys in different ways, but the timing has just been . . . off."

"Is that what you're calling it? Timing? Couldn't it be that the men you keep being matched with have some kind of underlining issue?"

"Not issue, just . . . you know . . ." I trail off, not sure how to put my thoughts into words.

"An issue. That's what it's been and don't deny it. Jack *seemed* like the perfect catch. I was even rooting for him, but one little mention of his name on national television and he scurried away. And then Beck, my main humping man slips into our lives, and good Christ, was he ravenous—"

"And that's *all* he was. He didn't even give me a glimpse into his dark past, just the tip of the iceberg. Even when I asked for more."

"But the oral, that was good."

Sigh. It was. It was so damn good. And a little part of me wonders what it would have felt like if we went all the way. Would it have been unbelievable? Mind-blowing?

Maybe, but I've never been a *sex for the hell of it* kind of girl. There has always been emotion involved with my sexual encounters, and I wonder if going all the way would have left me feeling empty rather than fulfilled.

"It was, but I want more than sex."

"Yeah, yeah, yeah. But, you're young and should be having flings with irresistible men. You know, be all *Sex in the City*. Be a Samantha."

How do I put this without sounding ridiculous . . .

"Samantha isn't my style. I'm more of a Charlotte. I hate being lonely, especially with our grueling schedule. You get to go home to Chad and your kids and have people love on you and hold you and take care of you. You have a partnership, an ever-lasting friendship, someone to hold your hand when you're nervous or scared, or want to be cuddled." Taking a long pull from my straw, I swallow. "I don't want to be single. I've never enjoyed it; I don't have that type of personality in my blood. So, yes, I'll go back. I will look for another date, and who knows, third time might be the charm."

Dylan studies me, her chin propped up by her palm. "The Suit and The Rebel. Who will be next?"

I shrug, feeling nervous about another blind date. "Who knows, maybe it will be the nerd."

"Or the construction worker."

"Or the cop." I point at her.

"Or the single dad."

"Don't forget the Navy SEAL."

"Ah," Dylan sighs. "Any military man. We could be totally off. You might get the theater geek."

I tap my chin with my index finger. "Hmm, the theater geek. I could totally go for that. Maybe he was in Hamilton."

"Shooting for the stars, are we?"

"If I was shooting for the stars, I would have said someone like Chris Hemsworth."

Dylan stares at the ceiling, a sparkle in her eye. "If Chris Hemsworth is signed up on *Going in Blind*, I'm going to personally

THREE BLIND DATES

ask Chad to make me a profile, hoping he doesn't mind a little brother husband situation."

"For Chris, I'm sure Chad would jump on board."

~

"Any matches yet?" my sister-in-law asks while looking over my shoulder. I'm flopped on her couch, Chloe is decorating my legs with the Paw Patrol stickers I bought her, and Alex is watching a National Geographic show about elephants and their diminishing herds.

"Uh, let me check."

It's been two days since I put in a request for another date. With Beck, I didn't even have to put in a request; it just appeared, which makes me nervous now because what if there are no more matches out there for me? The app and restaurant are still new, so what if I barreled through my only two matches? What if there's a limit?

Is there a limit? Do I look like a serial dater according to the system? I know they specifically said this is not a hookup app. I really hope they don't think I'm doing this just for a hookup. Surely there are other people in the same boat as me. Hell, Danny at the bar said I wasn't the only one on a second or even third date.

Squinting, afraid there will be no matches, I carefully open the app and pray to the dating gods that there is someone else out there for me.

Dramatic, I know. But I'm feeling pretty low after the first two dates.

"You have a match."

Thank you, dating gods.

"Looks like I have a match." *Again.*

"Really?" Lauren asks, scooting in closer so she can take a look as well. "Who is it? What's his handle? What does it say about him? Did he message you?"

"No message, no name, remember? But it looks like his handle is . . ." I start giggling.

"What is it? Is it something stupid like CallMeDaddy? Or BlowiesRock?"

"Or ManHands?" Alex chimes in, eyes still fixed on the TV.

"Man hands?" I mouth to Lauren who rolls her eyes, looking completely exasperated over her husband's little addition.

"Why would man hands be bad?" I ask.

Alex flicks a few pieces of popcorn in his mouth. "Don't know, just seemed like a weird name."

"How about balloon butt? That's funny," Chloe chimes in.

I tickle her neck. "That would be funny. Should I call you balloon butt now?"

"Noooooooo. I'm Chlo-money."

"You're not Chlo-money." Lauren makes that known real quick. "Your father is in big trouble for letting you watch *Keeping Up with the Kardashians*."

"Hold on, repeat that." I sit up a little taller, all thoughts of my match out the window when Lauren drops a bomb. "Alex, you watch *Keeping Up with the Kardashians?*"

No shame emitting from the popcorn-eating fiend, he says, "Ever hear of a guilty pleasure? That's mine. Go ahead, ask Lauren what hers is; you will judge her even more."

"We don't need to talk about that." Lauren clears her throat and points at my phone. "What's his handle?"

"Uh-uh." I shake my head. "You get no information until you tell me what your guilty pleasure is."

"Not in front of my daughter, okay?"

Leaning closer, I whisper, "Is it porn?"

"What's porn?" Chloe asks, popping her head up from the floor.

"Go get a popsicle," Lauren says, directing Chloe to the kitchen with her arm.

As if the little girl never asked the question, she skips off to the kitchen gleefully.

THREE BLIND DATES

Shyly, I shrug my shoulders. "Sorry." A giggle escapes me. I can't help it. It's like the time I told Chloe to tell her dad he has a penis. I still laugh about it to this day. In front of his work colleagues, she went up to him, pointed at his crotch and in her cute little voice, she said, "Daddy, you have a penis." Oh God, I've never seen my brother's face turn that red in my entire life. He patted her on the head, said thank you, and sent her on her way. Later that night, when he asked Lauren about her little obvious pointing out of the genitals, Chloe ratted me out and said, "Aunt Noely told me to say it." Took a bit for Alex to get over that one.

Clearing my throat, I ask, "What's your guilty pleasure?"

Lauren picks at an imaginary piece of lint on her pants, defiance in her body language. She's not going to break, thankfully. I have Alex.

"Alex, what is it?"

Without taking a second to consider his wife's feelings, he says, "Cricket."

My brow pinches together from utter confusion. "Cricket? What show is that? Is it on Netflix or Amazon?" Since I'm in the entertainment business, I know every show out there, reality and sitcom, and I've never heard of Cricket. The only shows I'm not entirely familiar with are Netflix and Amazon originals.

"Not a show, Noely. The sport. Cricket . . . the sport."

"What?" I turn to my sister-in-law, laughing and unable to hide the huge smile on my face. "Your guilty pleasure is watching cricket?"

"Ask her about her little box she has in our upstairs closet."

"Hey Alex, why don't you shut your effing mouth?" Lauren says, shooting daggers in his direction.

"You have a box?" I'm bouncing up and down now, maybe a little too excited about this new revelation.

Folding her hands on her lap, Lauren pushes her shoulders back and says, "I suggest you move on from this moment, and I suggest you move on quickly—"

"We had to upgrade our cable package so we could get the

cricket channel." Alex clearly is digging his own grave over there and loving it from the look on his face.

"You think that's funny, Alex? Yeah, see how funny it is when you're looking for a little nighttime crawling and the gate is closed."

Eh?

That's a weird and disturbing way to tell him sex is off the menu.

Shaking the creepy image I've conjured up in my head, I turn to Lauren and say, "Please tell me if you have a favorite team."

Sighing, her eyes to the sky, she says, "Australia, mainly because their uniforms are green and yellow and yellow looks good on me. And before you ask, yes, I have jerseys and hats and pom-poms in my little box in the closet, okay? So let's move on, shall we? What the hell is the man's handle?" Her voice rises, sounding a little out of control, so before she flips out, I decide to give her a break.

But if you don't think I'm not going to store away this cricket information for my own personal use, you're sorely mistaken.

"It's IceBiscuit."

"Ice biscuit?" Lauren asks, a sneer in her lip. "What kind of name is that? Is he a baker?"

"What? No."

"Oh honey." Alex shakes his head, eyes still trained on the elephant show.

Holding back my laugh since Lauren is already feeling sensitive about her love for cricket being exposed, I say, "Ice biscuit is a term used in hockey. It basically means the puck."

"Well, that's stupid."

I let out a heavy sigh. "It really isn't, but that's besides the point. This guy loves hockey. His profile picture is a hockey stick, too."

"Is he a Quakes fan?" Alex asks, finally giving me some of his attention.

When the jingle for a local pizza joint comes on the TV, I realize it's a commercial. Of course he can pay attention now.

THREE BLIND DATES

I scan IceBiscuit's profile, looking for any kind of indication that he might be a Quakes fan. "Doesn't say. But it does say he likes hockey, pool, and can make a pretty mean cheesesteak."

"Hey, I like cheesesteak and hockey, maybe I should date this guy." Alex pops a few more pieces of popcorn in his mouth.

Lauren snags my phone from my hands and tosses it over to Alex. It hits his belly with a resounding plop. "Have at it, sweetie. Let him know you like your nipples to be played with when getting frisky."

Way too much information about my brother.

Alex picks up the phone and looks at the screen. "Eh, there is no mention of his love for animals on his profile. Deal-breaker." He tosses his phone back at me and returns his attention to his elephants.

"Well, thank God for that," I add sarcastically. "What do you think, should I accept the date?"

"I say go for it. Who knows, this very well might be the guy for you."

He very well might be . . .

CHAPTER TWENTY-TWO

NOELY

"Miss Clark, how lovely to see you." I fidget in my skinny jeans and heels as Veronica greets me . . . *once again.*

Okay, so I might have been gung-ho about date number three, but I'm not so excited about seeing *Going In Blind's* employees. Don't they want to take a night off? Maybe go run an errand while I check in? I glance over at the bar, and yep, Danny is over there, smiling at me.

Crap.

With a heavy sigh, I say, "Hi, Veronica. I have a date with IceBiscuit tonight."

"Yes, we have you right here." Veronica's annoyingly charming smile lights up the entryway of the restaurant. Is she judging me? Does she think I'm difficult? I sure as hell hope not.

I'm a pleasant lady with a sassy demeanor, adventurous spirit, and big mouth . . . on occasion.

"Your date hasn't arrived just yet, but if you'd like me to show you to the bar, I'm more than happy to."

"I'm good." I put up my hand. "I'm familiar with the bar

already, but thank you." For good humor, I give Veronica a wink and waltz myself toward the direction of the bar.

No surprise, I beat my date again. *The downside of always being early.*

What will I order this time? A margarita? I'm feeling a little spicy and bitter tonight, a little lackluster. Maybe not as desirable as usual.

Maybe it's because I dressed like a peasant tonight.

Well, not really a peasant, but I had no drive to make myself irresistible. Instead, I threw on a pair of grey skinny jeans, a black turtleneck—yes, turtleneck—graced my neck with a statement necklace, put my hair up in a tight knot on the top of my head, and called it a day. I didn't even shave my legs so you and I both know, there is no way in hell this date is going anywhere near humping surfaces.

The only thing that's really spicing up my outfit is the bright red lipstick I put on during my ride over. It was a last-minute decision I'm pleased with. I have to give the guy something after I donned a black turtleneck. Might has well come to this date dressed like a nun.

But for the record, it's a tight, fitted black turtleneck with three quarter length sleeves. it's stylish, not something Michelle Tanner from *Full House* wore.

Adjusting my purse on my shoulder, I continue to make my way to the bar when I come face to shoulder with a broad man.

"Oh, pardon me." I catch my balance on my heels, praying I don't topple over.

"Excuse me."

My ears pick up and when I catch *who's* standing in front of me, my nerves start to tingle and a little annoying flutter takes place in my stomach.

"Noely, lovely to see you." His hands grip my shoulders, steadying me from our bump.

Clearing my throat—wishing I looked like the hooker I was last time I was here—I say, "Jack, lovely to see you as well."

His eyes roam up and down my turtleneck, the corner of his lip tilting ever so slightly. That itty-bitty look right there has me itching to go Hulk on my clothes and sexify myself in zero-point-two seconds just to show him.

Shoulders pushed back, he adjusts his tie and gives me one more once-over, his eyes burning a wave of heat through my veins, making my turtleneck choice that much more worse. *What is his deal? He wanted nothing to do with me, so why does he bother with all the sizzling staring?*

Feeling uncomfortable, slightly bothered, and heated, I say, "Ya here on a date, pal?"

When did I start talking like *that*? Yikes. I have no idea. Chalk it up to being caught off guard.

"Indeed. Isn't that why we're all here?"

Arrogance; that's fun to deal with during small talk. *Not.*

"I guess so." Scanning the room, looking for an empty table, I ask, "Who is it?" I spot a girl to the right, hair in pigtails, a brown scarf wrapped up to her chin, and a rose in hand looking around. To the left, there is a gorgeous blonde wearing the lowest-cut shirt I've ever seen, showing off her ample cleavage, looking stunning. Let's face it . . . a little slutty. Please let it be pigtails, come on, pigtails.

"Why so interested?" Jack asks, stepping in a little closer.

"Uh . . ." Scanning his position up and down, I clear my throat. "Just being friendly."

"Friendly? Or Jealous?"

Jealous? *What?* Is he insane? Of course I'm not jealous. I don't even know what jealousy is. I don't have a jealous bone in my body. Not a single one . . .

Please let it be pigtails. *If he goes with the tramp, I know he'll more than just kiss her cheek tonight.*

He takes another step forward, crowding my personal space, and making me sweat even more in this damn top. I'm tempted to pull on the collar around my neck but refrain from showing any tells on how he affects me. *Still* affects me.

"Don't flatter yourself, Jack. Just being friendly."

Not saying a word, he keeps his eyes trained on me, his stature sophisticated, alpha in all the best ways. Putting both his hands in his pockets, he rocks back on his heels, eyes still trained on mine. "Have a good night, Noely."

And just like that, he pushes past me, leaving me in a wake of his delicious cologne. My nose soaks it up as if it's the only air left in the room.

Glancing back, because I like to torture myself, I watch as Jack unbuttons his suit jacket and takes a seat across from the blonde, who gently places her hand over Jack's as if they've known each other for ages. Chancing a quick look in my direction, Jack straightens his jacket and takes me in one last time, making me turn red from those mysterious eyes of his.

Damn him.

Flustered, I grip my purse tight to my side and turn away, pointing my body directly toward the bar. *Why? Of all the men I could run into tonight, why Jack? Freaking sexy, writer of schmexy messages of the wooing variety* . . . Don't think about him, Noely. You know he wants nothing to do with you.

I skip all pleasantries and flop myself on the bar top. "Danny. Whiskey, stat."

"Whiskey?" He raises an eyebrow at me. "Are you sure about that, Miss Clark?"

"You can either give me a glass, or pour it right down my gullet." I lean my head back and point to my mouth, losing all kinds of self-respect.

Chuckling, looking slightly nervous, Danny grabs a glass and pours me two fingers of amber liquid.

I snag the glass from him and open wide, letting the liquid slosh around in my mouth. I swallow hard and my entire body shakes as my face puckers and my throat burns.

"Oh hell." I squeeze my eyes shut, hating myself right now. "Oh crap, that's bad." Not even giving it a second thought, I gulp the rest of the glass down and shudder uncontrollably. I can only imagine what I look like right now: a turtleneck-wearing fish out of water, flapping around for dear life at the bar.

Cute.

Beyond attractive.

Eat your heart out, blonde with big boobs.

When I open my eyes, Danny is staring at me, concern etched in his features. "Give me another, bar tenda," I say with a weird accent.

Something is happening to me, and I fear for IceBiscuit. He's in for quite the ride, that's for damn sure.

"Maybe we slow down," Danny suggests. "How about for every whiskey, you drink a water? I think that's a good idea."

I lean over the bar and wiggle my finger at Danny in a "come hither" manner. When he's right in front of me, I lean forward even more and grab his shirt, bringing him in dangerously close, our foreheads touch.

"Danny . . . dearest man who serves me booze. Do you see the way my eyes are flitting back and forth? Can you feel the crazy exuding from them?" He nods, swallowing hard. "This is my third date here, okay? This is my third time trying to find somebody to love me after two failed attempts from this supposedly perfect matchmaking system. I'm feeling a little out of control, mildly psychotic, and you know what, I will just say it, slightly turned on." Shit, I didn't want to say that to Danny. Shaking that thought, I continue, "So please be a gent, and scamper behind your little bar and give me more whiskey. Got it?"

I push him back, releasing his shirt and like a perfect lady, fold my hands on the bar, waiting for my drink.

"You know there have been many people—"

"I'm going to stop you right there." I smile crazily at him. I can feel the devil trying to peek out. You know, the inner devil all women have, the one who turns us into a flame-throwing, fire-spitting she-dragon when people are least expecting it? I'm teetering the line right now, ready to burn this restaurant to the ground.

To the mother effing ground!

"Just bring me the booze." I tap the bar counter. "Right here, put the booze right here. Go on, *friend*. Booze me up. Give me all the riches of intoxication."

Sighing, Danny gives in to my demands and fills up another glass. When he sets it in front of me, I lean over and tap him on the cheek. "Such a good boy."

With both hands, I grip the tumbler and pour it back in my mouth like I'm trying to get the crumbs out of an almost-empty chip bag. The liquid burns my throat once again, but I welcome it. I welcome the shudders, loving how I can feel my body starting to float. I have one more glass, because why not? Yes, this was a good idea. A very good idea. I just need to loosen up, find my groove, feel the blind date—

"ShopGirl?"

I spin around in my chair, probably a little too fast, given I need to grip the back of my chair to steady myself.

"IceBiscuit?" My eyes don't meet his. Instead, I'm at nipple level, taking in his very broad and muscular chest. *Wow.* Heat rises to the back of my neck, and I know it's not the whiskey; it's the powerful chest right in front of me, and are those . . . are those his pecs? They're all defined and large and yummy and . . . sigh. Curiosity pops out of me before I can stop myself, and I poke his chest. When I'm greeted with a firm bounce, I giggle to myself. "Pecs," I mutter under my breath. Yep, yummy indeed. IceBiscuit is putting the work in at the gym and not shoving cheesesteaks down his throat. Hand on his chest, my fingers diddling his shirt, I look up to find a very confused but familiar face.

Shit.

Crap.

Oh God.

Have you ever felt all the blood in your face leech out of you, as if every last piece of color drains from your features and falls to the floor from total and utter embarrassment?

Try not only diddling your date's chest, but diddling the one and only Hayden Holmes's chest.

Shaking my hand away, as if he's burned me. I stand from my chair but stumble forward. Clearly, heels and whiskey don't mix. I fall to my knees and curse under my breath. I pop up quickly, my legs feeling like a newborn calf's, and throw my arms up in the air like a gymnast on her dismount. To add to the embarrassment, I say, "Nine point five, not a perfect ten, but I'll get there." I laugh nervously and right my shirt, while lowering my arms. "They don't score like that anymore, but who's really going to say fourteen-point-two-six-seven? I mean, especially when the viewers don't know the degree of difficulty. You know?" Hayden just stares at me, so to put that final nail in my coffin, I punch his arm and say, "Gymnastics, am I right?"

Exposed and embarrassed, I glance at Danny, who's watching from a distance with a look that says, *I told you so*. In my head, I shout back at him, "Shut up, Danny!"

Hayden reaches behind his neck and pulls on it, his large bicep flexing beneath his shirt. He's dressed casually in a dark pair of jeans and tight-fitting, long-sleeved shirt. "Uh, are you okay?"

"Yep, fit as a fiddle." I motion with a low fist pump across my body, as if to say, just dandy. Although I'm thinking just dandy would have been better than fit as a fiddle. Who can really know at this point? They're both something my grandpa would say with a hop and a click of his heels in the air.

"Good." He looks around, scanning the restaurant. "Never thought I'd run into you here. Are you ShopGirl?"

"I am but you can call me, Noely. Noely Clark." I awkwardly grab his hand from his hip and shake it. "Nice to meet you."

Puzzled, Hayden laughs. "I remember who you are, Noely."

"Oh yeah, of course." I pat my legs and say, "This is weird. I, uh, I didn't think I would be matched with you, so I'm feeling nervous and intimidated. Because, you know, you're all hot and whatnot with your hockey body and strong thighs and nice hair. And I'm sure if you turned around right now, I would see your high, tight ass." My hands cup together and my face scrunches as I form a tight ass for him.

Note to self.

Whiskey equals truth serum. *Shit. Shit and double shit. Why tonight? Why Hayden?*

"Thanks." He chuckles and looks over my shoulder. "Started early on the drinks?"

"Maybe." I bite my bottom lip. "Third blind date and rough day equals more drinks for me."

Hayden knowingly nods. "Got ya. Should we get some food in you so you don't pass out onto your dinner?"

"Good idea." I bop his nose, hating my inability to stop my hands from doing stupid things.

Hayden holds out his arm to me, which I take no time in grabbing. Ooo, so many muscles. I can feel his forearm rippling beneath my palm. Forearms are the new abs. I'm calling it now.

I snag my purse, throw a wink in Danny's direction, and follow Hayden.

"Veronica said we have the table in the back." He walks me into the dining room where I quickly make eye contact with Jack.

His gaze is pulled from titty mountain and focused on my wobbly legs. I shoot him a little wiggle of my fingers and then point to Hayden while mouthing, "My date." With a wink, I give him the okay sign with my fingers and walk past him, adding a little saunter in my hips. *I think it was a saunter. I just pray it wasn't a jostley sway.*

When I look over my shoulder, I notice the strong set in his jaw, the unhappy purse of his lips, and his dark, vexed eyes.

Yikes.

Titty mountain isn't as riveting as he thought she would be. Maybe I'll have a little fun with this.

Hayden pulls my chair out for me like a gentleman and helps me sit. The wobble in my heels is real. Thankful for a long tablecloth, I kick my heels off under the table and toss my purse to the ground.

In my head, I know my classiness is nowhere to be found, but for the life of me, I can't stop myself from not caring.

Hayden takes the seat from across me and says, "What are the odds we were setup with each other?"

"Great ones." I finger the rim of my water glass while I lick my lips a little too heavily, as if there's frosting on them and I'm a ravenous beast trying to get it off.

Hayden's eyes widen, and he coughs while covering his mouth, a smile tugging at his lips.

Does he think I'm sexy licking my lips . . .

Or does he think I'm certifiable?

I'm going to guess the latter.

Needing to pull my shit together, I sit tall and bring the menu to my face, close, too close. Trying to focus.

"Eh, these words look all jumbled to me." I set the menu down. "I've had the lobster and the steak on my other dates. What's left?"

Stumbling to look at the menu, he clears his throat and takes a second to answer. "Uh, the butternut squash gnocchi with brown butter sauce."

"Sign me up." I tap the table and lean back in my chair.

Head tilted to the side, Hayden studies me. "How many drinks did you have, Noely?"

I cringe and lean forward, shout whispering. "Is my booze showing?"

"Just a little."

With my hand blocking my mouth from the rest of the dining room, I say, "At least it isn't my nipple that's showing."

Chuckling, Hayden says, "Hey, you've definitely got that going for you."

I lift my water glass to Hayden and say, "To not showing nipples."

Mirth in his features, he lifts his glass as well. "To not showing nipples."

∼

"God, I'm ravenous." I shove more gnocchi in my mouth, body hunched over my plate, water glass in hand, fork in the other. I chug my drink and shove more gnocchi in my mouth. "This is so good, don't you think?"

Sitting back, eyes wide, fork halfway to his mouth, Hayden watches me tear into the dinner that was placed in front of us. "Uh, haven't had a chance to take a bite."

Pulling back from my shoveling fork, I lift his utensil to his mouth. "Eat, eat. Enjoy." I sound like Mrs. Clause telling Santa to get his fill of food.

Eat, Papa . . . eat!

A little scared—I don't blame him, if there was a mirror in front of me right now, I'd be scared too—Hayden takes a bite of his gnocchi and I watch as his eyes close, his taste buds savoring every nuance of flavor bursting on his tongue.

"That is good."

Mouth full, I reply, "Best dinner option I've had since I've been here. I mean, the steak was melt-in-your-mouth steak. The lobster with mashed potatoes? Boy, were those smooth on the tongue. But this gnocchi, talk about a myriad of flavors."

"It's pretty damn good." He chuckles. Eyeing me from behind those long black lashes of his, he asks, "So you keep saying this is your third time here. Am I really your third blind date?"

I point my fork at him and nod. "You are. You're the third guy I needed for my tripod of dating. Do you feel special?"

Did I mention that I guzzled down another whiskey before dinner was served? I wasn't going to have another drink, but when titty mountain moved her chair around to Jack's side and started playing with his hair, it was either throw up in the bathroom from how nauseating the scene was, or have another drink. I don't like gross puke mouth, so . . .

I can see why Jack wanted nothing to do with me now. That's his type. His messages to me were a load of crock. Why did he bother?

The whiskey went down the hatchet and infused my blood-alcohol level to a dangerous limit where rather than having a pleasant conversation with Hayden, I'm licking my fork and winking at him through my half-downed water glass.

Plopping some more gnocchi in his mouth, Hayden says, "I do feel lucky. From the looks of it, I get to experience the looser side of you."

"Eh, eh, eh." I wave my finger at him like he's a naughty boy. "You're not getting in my pants so don't even think about it. I didn't shave my legs, so not going to happen, fella."

Coughing abruptly, Hayden pats his chest and takes a sip of his water. "Didn't mean loose as in, sexually loose. Just, you know, personality loose."

"Oh." I ponder that for a second and take another bite of my gnocchi. "Misread that one, didn't I?"

"Just a little."

"Are you going to tell your hockey buddies you went on a date with Noely Clark from Good Morning, Malibu, and she told you she didn't shave her legs?"

"First thing tomorrow morning." His smile puts me at ease. Cheeky man. "So what happened with the first two dates?" Hayden pushes some gnocchi around on his plate.

"Are you asking me to provide a postpartum on my first two blind dates?"

"I mean . . . not really. Was wondering what went wrong. Did you not shave your legs for those dates as well?" The flash of those brilliant bright white teeth has my stomach churning, and in a good way. Not in a *you've had eight fingers of whiskey* way. Eight fingers, shit, that requires two hands.

"I shaved and wore a dress. Both times." I set my fork down and cross my arms over my chest.

"You wore a dress?" His eyes grow wide. "And you wore a turtleneck for me? That's some messed-up shit, Noely."

Laughing, a little too loudly—thank you, whiskey—I say, "With a statement necklace. I didn't wear a statement necklace on my other dates, so frankly, you're the real winner."

"Am I?" He cocks his head to the side. "I get turtleneck with unshaved legs and the other guys get dresses with no sight of hairy Mary anywhere?"

"Hey." I lean toward him, and whisper shout. "Don't make me pull my pant leg up right now. It's a light stubble. A stubble!"

"Keep the pant legs down there, lady. No need to disgust people in the middle of their dinners."

Lips pursed, feeling light with humor, I say, "You're a freaking smartass, you know that?"

"Well aware. So tell me about the dates. You shaved your legs and wore dresses, so that wasn't the problem. What happened? Fart by accident?"

"I will have you know, all flatulence was held in, thank you very much." I tilt my chin, showing off the layer of class I have . . . well, attempt to have. "It wasn't anything like that. The first dates actually went really well, like, super well. It was the dates after that kind of fell apart."

"Give me examples. I want to make sure I don't screw anything up this go around." *He does?*

His sincerity is sweet, but even though his words sound genuine, it almost seems like he's saying them on autopilot, as if someone pre-programmed him to say those words at this time. I'm drunk, but I can still tell when someone isn't speaking the truth.

There are underlying emotions he's not trying to show, that he's hiding away from me and thanks to the whiskey, I can't quite pinpoint them. *Having thought that, I did miss Jack and Beck's underlying issues. Kind of.*

Not wanting to dig too deep into his emotional status, I say, "Well, the first guy, man, was he . . ." I pause my head glancing in Jack's direction. I don't know what comes over me, but in a very loud whisper, I point behind my hand and say, "Right over there, the guy with the girl whose boobs are swallowing her neck whole, that was my first date."

Conspiratorially leaning forward, Hayden cutely follows my pointing finger. His curious eyes take in Jack and titty mountain, his gaze inquisitive but also calculating, as if he's measuring himself up to Jack.

It's hard to compare the two. Hayden is bulky with the muscles, a jock to the extreme with his calloused hands, thick arms, and swagger. Jack . . . he's stoic, sophisticated, mysterious, with his dark eyes and confusing conversations.

"He seems like a nice guy. I mean, his eyes are trained on that girl's face rather than the blatant display of cleavage. There's something to be said about that."

"Maybe he's scared of her boobs; maybe he's afraid they're going to pop out any minute and eat him alive."

"Possibly, but from his stand-offish body language, I think he's prepared to defend himself from an attack from man-eating tits." Hayden smiles at me. His lips looking soft and kissable. Hmm . . .

Straightening my napkin on my lap, I say, "Well, he has issues with privacy. I accidentally said his name on TV, his first name, mind you, and he broke a gasket. Lost his damn mind. Paraded around kicking trashcans and plucking weeds from the side of the street only to toss them in my general direction." Okay, the last part is a lie, but it almost felt like that. "The rage on that one. He was sweet at first. Boy ooo-ee," I say a little loudly. "Talk about LOSING.YOUR.SHIT." I shake my head. "Such a shame, you know?" I motion to my body, allowing Hayden time for a once-over. "He could have had all of this."

"Statement necklace and all."

I finger my necklace and wiggle my eyebrows. "It's growing on you now, isn't it? Aren't you glad I wore the turtleneck?"

"Couldn't be more pleased. What's cleavage when you can stare at a statement necklace all night?"

I slap the table, drawing attention from the other diners. "That's what I'm talking about." My voice rises, and I blame the whiskey once more. I look around the room as voices quiet to see what the commotion is. I smile politely and nod at diners, trying to reassure them everything is on the up and up at my table. When I make my rounds and my gaze settles on Jack, his jaw still firmly set, almost like he's grinding his teeth. *And he's looking straight at me.*

Just to have some fun. I twiddle my fingers at him and say, "Ahoy, Jackie Boy."

Hayden waves as well, joining in on my ridiculousness. I have to give the man credit. He doesn't mind embarrassing himself with me.

There is no return of our greeting, just a clearing of his throat when he turns his attention back to his date.

"Well," I huff.

"That was rude," Hayden finishes for me.

"You're telling me." I lean my chin into my propped-up palm. "God, technology has really desensitized us. If I sent him a text message with a waving emoji, I bet he would reply with a smiley face."

"He doesn't seem like a smiley face guy."

I think about it for a second. "Yeah, he doesn't, does he?"

"More like"—Hayden rubs a hand across his chin, and I truly enjoy the sound of his skin caressing his five o'clock shadow—"a dress shoe. That's what he would send. Two dress shoes because three is preposterous and one is inexcusable." *He's as crazy as me, and he's had nothing to drink tonight. Can we all say . . . match made in heaven!*

"God, you're so right. He would send me a freaking dress shoe as a hello. And here I am, sending him the cha-cha girl in her red dress freaking ole-ing around his ass and he sends me a dress shoe."

"Men." Hayden rolls his eyes and takes a sip of his water. "Not me though, I wouldn't send you a dress shoe."

"No? What would you send me? Wait." I hold up my hand. "Let me guess." I tap my chin with my finger, trying to think of all the emoji options. "Hmm . . . well, not knowing you all too well, I'm thinking you'd send me the dragon and cucumber."

"What?" He laughs, the sound hitting me straight in the sternum. Clearly I have a little something when it comes to men and their laughs. While I thought Jack's was sultry, and Beck's was sexy, Hayden's is . . . alluring. And from interviewing him the other week, I know he is a man who laughs often. And here I am getting a little turned on. *Yet again. Not sure if I can blame that on the whiskey as well.* "Dragon and cucumber, where did you even come up with those?"

I flit my hand about. "They just came to me. I'm right, aren't I? You would totally send me the dragon and cucumber emojis."

"What does that even mean if I sent those to you?"

I shrug. "Some hockey code I would figure out two months from now and then laugh my ass off."

Hayden shakes his head. "There is no dragon and cucumber hockey code, I can promise you that."

"Okay, then what would you send me?"

"I feel a little inferior after the dragon and cucumber mention, but I would send you the wilting rose."

"Wow." I sit back in my chair, arms crossed over my chest. "Well, that's freaking depressing. Uh, thanks for my wilting flower."

"And then I would follow it up with a candelabra, a clock, and a baguette."

"Eh?" I know my face is unattractive right now, the confused look not showing off my best features, but a baguette? What?

Hayden shakes his head. "Guess you're not one to communicate in emojis, because any pro would know I'm trying to say Beauty and the Beast, meaning, *hey come on over and snuggle with me while we watch the movie.*" Hayden shakes his head. "I thought you were better than that, Noely."

Shocked and disappointed, that's me. "Well, I hate myself now. Of course, baguette." I shake my fists to the air. "Baguette!"

CHAPTER TWENTY-THREE

NOELY

"So you never told me about the second guy."

The booze is starting to wear off—thanks to the three glasses of water Hayden forced me to drink, and the bread I've downed over the last hour and a half. The worst part of the booze wearing off is I'm very much aware of the ass I've made of myself this entire evening. So thumbs up to me.

"The Rebel? Not much to say there. He was a really good guy, one I got along really well with, but he was more . . . how do I put this? He was more into the physical aspects of the relationship and wasn't ready to dive deep into anything just yet. He had a ton of mystery behind him that he wasn't ready to talk about. It wasn't that I needed to know right away, but it would have been nice to see a future for finding out."

"Totally. It's hard to make a connection with someone when they're so closed off." Insightful. Hayden surprises me.

"Would you be insulted if I said I'm kind of surprised by you tonight?"

"Depends why you're surprised? If it's because you thought my hands would be much bigger outside of my hockey gloves, we're going to have a problem."

Chuckling, I regard his hands. They are huge. I don't think they could get any bigger without looking ridiculous. "No, this has nothing to do with your hands. I'm kind of surprised on how sweet and keen you are. I've met a fair share of athletes through events and interviews and none of them are like you. They're cocky assholes most of the time. But not you."

"They don't make them like me very often. I'm a golden egg, so be careful." Adorable, sexy, intelligent, thoughtful, and athletic all wrapped up into one large package. What more can a girl ask for?

"You really are." I play with the fork on my dessert plate, running it through the last bite of cheesecake I can't finish. "So is Beauty and the Beast your favorite movie? You mentioned it earlier so I'm assuming it is."

"It's one of them." He smiles sheepishly. "Along with Braveheart, of course." His attempt to recover his manhood is cute. Braveheart is good and all, Mel Gibson makes my knees quiver, but there is something to say about a man, a powerfully elite man, claiming a children's movie as his favorite. It gives him heart, and I'm honestly loving that right now.

"Of course, Braveheart is everything." Not really, but a little pump to his ego helps fuel that smile of his.

"What about you, what's your favorite movie?"

"Easy. *You've Got Mail.*"

"Huh, never seen it." The way he says that so casually, as if it wasn't the best romcom ever made makes my inner dragon growl . . . just slightly.

"What do you mean you've never seen it? Uh, hello! Meg Ryan, Tom Hanks, they send emails and love blooms behind a screen while in reality, they hate each other. How have you not watched such a riveting and heart-filled movie?"

Studying me and treading carefully, Hayden says, "I can see you're very passionate about this movie."

"Passionate is a timid way to describe my feelings for the

movie, but we don't need to go into detail about my feelings. What's more important is the fact that you've never seen the movie. And you were checking off all my boxes, Hayden. This is such a travesty." Dramatically I throw my head in my hands.

"Not a travesty. Shit, we can't have that." Scouring for a resolution, he continues, "How about this. For our second date, we watch *You've Got Mail,* and you school me on everything Tom Hanks, Meg Ryan, and the email sending. How does that sound?"

"You're thinking second date?" Holy crap, that's a little shocking given my drunken state and obvious attempt to stir Jack from across the dining room.

Full of confidence, *clearly* forgetting every drunken thing I did and said tonight, he nods. "Would love a second date."

Well, well, well, looks like the turtleneck was a winning choice after all.

"I guess it's a date then."

~

"I'm going to run to the bathroom real quick. Meet you outside?"

"Sounds good." Hayden helps me out of my chair, holding his hand out, acting like an absolute gentleman.

This date has been so different than the first two. Maybe it's because we already knew each other, so there wasn't the awkward moment of trying to get to know a complete stranger. I felt relaxed, more at ease, and before you start saying, "Noely, it's called booze," this wasn't from the booze.

It's as though I've known Hayden my whole life, like we were long-lost friends getting reacquainted. It was nice. Comfortable.

Looking over my shoulder, I catch Hayden checking out the light sway of my hips as I retreat, and a surge of feminine power electrifies my ego. After three dates, I've still got it. Smiling, I go to the bathroom and pee for what seems like five minutes causing me to chuckle to myself. Call me immature, but when I pee forever, it makes me giggle. It's like, are you going to stop anytime soon, down there?

Hmm . . . maybe I'm still a tad drunk.

Once I wash and dry my hands, I take a few moments to tend to my hair in front of the mirror, make sure my lipstick isn't on my teeth, and pop a mint in my mouth. I suck on it hard, trying to soak in all the minty flavor, infusing it on my tongue, because you know, just in case.

Do I want Hayden to kiss me?

Uh, yeah.

He's Hayden Freaking Holmes. I would kiss his toe if he asked me to.

Hell, I would still mint up for his toe.

Pleased with my appearance and happy with my mint mouth, I head out of the bathroom, purse tucked under my arm and one thing on my mind: Hayden Holmes.

I strut down the narrow hallway—you know, just in case Hayden is still watching—and inconveniently catch my heel on a crack, catapulting me forward into a dense and corded chest.

"Oh Lord, you saved me from a faceplant," I announce, grateful for not eating hardwood floor.

"Those heels are dangerous."

Oh hell.

Glancing up, I stare into *those* eyes, the ones that have followed me all night.

"Jack." Pushing off his chest, I try to put some distance between us but his hands catch my elbows, attempting to steady me.

"You seem to be stumbling a lot tonight."

"Keeping tabs on me?" I step away this time, shaking his grasp. I brush off my arms, trying to rid the burning feelings his hands imprinted on my skin.

"I'm an observant man, Noely. You should know this."

"Actually, I shouldn't, you know, since we only went on one date."

Jack's jaw very carefully shifts back and forth, the movements so small that it almost seems like he's not moving at all. "Are you going home with him tonight?"

Did he just ask that?

Where the hell does he get off?

"I don't believe that's any of your business. So if you'll excuse me, I have a date to get to. And just so you know, if he asked me to kiss his toe, I would."

Errr...

Not what I wanted to say, but this man makes me so goddamn flustered. Instead of cringing, I own my statement and push past him, our shoulders brushing. "Use protection when you kiss his toe. Athlete's foot is a real thing."

"You're infuriating," I call out, my voice echoing off the hallway. "Have fun with titty mountain."

"I will."

His answer stops my urgency to walk away. I turn on my heel to find him leaning against the wall, arms crossed, an impassive look on his face. The corner of his lip turns up, his eyes knowing he got me, and I hate it. I'm tempted to walk back and smack that smirk right off his face but then again, that's probably what he wants.

But why? Why is he doing this? He. Doesn't. Want. Me. He wants Miss Uncomplicated Sure Thing Titty Mountain.

Such a twisted man. Instead, I turn toward the dining room and head straight to Hayden, who's standing at the entryway of the restaurant, hands in pockets, rocking back on his heels.

When he spots me, his face lights up, and a boyish grin peeks past his lips. *He's happy to see me. Thank God.*

Sigh, just what I needed.

"All set?"

"Yeah, sorry, I peed a lot."

Probably information he didn't need but at this point, I don't think there is one thing I could say to Hayden that will deter him from going on a second date with me. Hell, I shouted the word baguette tonight. If we could get through that moment, I think we can get past anything.

"There is a little park two blocks down; want to go on a little walk?"

"I would love that."

∼

From behind, Hayden grips the chains on either side of my head, pulls back and then pushes his hand against my lower back, sending me forward. My heels and purse are in the sand next to me as I swing, bare feet in the cool night air, feeling young and free.

"I can't remember the last time I was on a swing."

"Me either," Hayden says, planting himself on the swing next to mine.

"Sex swing excluded."

"Obviously." He starts pumping his legs, not trying to get too high, just giving himself a bit of a lift.

When I'm casually swaying back and forth I ask, "What was it like, hearing the news you were traded?"

Hayden lets out a long breath. "Kind of sucked to be honest. I thought Philly was going to be my home. I grew to the player I am today because of the Brawlers, so when my agent called me to tell me the news, I almost felt let down, like my family was giving up on me."

"Ouch. I never thought about it that way. I mean, you get more money." I try to put a spin on his sour change in life plans.

"Money is money. But I grew up in the area and wasn't far from family and friends. Now I'm more than three thousand miles away. It's a change, an adjustment. I'm sure I'll get used to at some point."

"Did you have good friends on the team?"

"A few, but I was only there a year. It was more my friends and family . . . leaving people behind didn't feel too good."

People. Why do I feel like there's more to the "people" he speaks of? Possibly his long-term girl? I'm about to ask him who in particular, when he says, "The Quakes have been very welcoming though. The guys are awesome, training so far has been intense but rewarding, and I can feel myself getting stronger every day." Okay, what happened there? He was open and truthful initially, but that answer seemed like the media-approved answer. However, I'll let it slide. Keep things light. For now.

"Stronger than you are already?" My swing slows drastically. "Are you going to be one of those athletes with no neck because you're lifting an elephant every day over your head?"

"Is that what athletes with no necks do? Lift elephants?"

"Every morning." I chuckle, knowing how ridiculous I sound.

"No, that won't be me. But if I can build up my quads more, I wouldn't be mad about it. It's my legs that get me through a game and the stronger the better."

"Makes sense." My swing almost stops. Gripping the chains, I lightly push myself back and forth with my toe. "Did you always want to be a professional hockey player?"

"Since I was four." Hayden's eyes look so dreamy when he talks about his sport. You can tell he's one of those athletes who truly loves playing. He doesn't seem to do it for the paycheck or the fame, more for the thrill of the game. I like that about him. "But I never expected myself to be where I am today. I knew I had talent and with a lot of hard work, I could achieve my goal—"

"But not win rookie of the year."

"Not so much." He sheepishly chuckles. "It's humbling and rewarding to see all my late nights and early mornings in the gym pay off. I just hope there isn't a sophomore slump."

"Hayden Holmes, no way. He's going to take the LA Earthquakes to the championship."

"Ha, we will see. We have a long road ahead of us, especially after last season."

"Not our finest season." Not even by a long shot. The LA

Earthquakes were trash last year, embarrassing actually, so how they acquired Hayden, I have no idea.

"So you're truly a hockey fan, not just for the camera?" His question isn't mean at all. I like the sincerity in his voice, as if he's truly hoping I'm a hockey fan.

I tuck a stray hair behind my ear that the wind picked up. "Born and raised Quakes fan. My dad and brother were adamant about watching every game and, wanting to be part of their chanting, I started watching at a young age and got hooked. If there aren't at least two fights on the ice I'm disappointed."

Hayden laughs. "You know it isn't just about the fights, don't you? It's about how each team can handle the puck. The passing, the stamina, the goaltending, the cohesiveness of the team."

"And the fights." I smirk, causing Hayden to roll his eyes. "Have you ever gotten in one?"

"Plenty."

"But your face is so pretty."

He wiggles his eyebrows at me. "It's because I'm a good fighter."

"So if we went to a dark alley, you would be able to defend me from an assault?"

Hayden casually swings next to me, his feet guiding along the ground beneath him. "First, we wouldn't go into a dark alley; that seems like a bad idea. Second, yes, I would pummel ass for you."

I clasp my hand to my chest. "I think that's the nicest thing anyone has ever said to me on a date."

"Ah, so does this mean I'm beating your other two blind dates?"

"Easily."

Maybe . . .

Possibly . . .

It's a fun date, an easygoing date, carefree and fun. There is no pressure to look sexy, no pressure to be on my best behavior. Which is fortunate, given how appalling my behavior has been. I feel comfortable around Hayden, and to me, I think that puts him above The Suit and The Rebel.

THREE BLIND DATES

    Can I be cheesy for a second? I'm going to throw a cornball moment at you.
    Are you ready?
    Prepare yourself.
    But since I'm feeling all revved up on sports talk . . .
    Coming down the final straightaway, The Jock leads the way, trailing behind is The Rebel, and way behind is The Suit. Despite The Suit's attempt to throw a curveball in the pursuit for my heart, it looks like The Jock might be the one who scores the goal.
    See what I did there? So many sports analogies.

CHAPTER TWENTY-FOUR

NOELY

"You really didn't have to give me a ride home." I turn in the buttery-soft leather seat of Hayden's Porsche Cayenne so I'm facing him.

"It was no trouble at all. Plus, it would have been weird waiting for your Uber driver when I could easily give you a lift."

"So gentlemanly."

With the car in park, Hayden peers out his window and takes in my little cottage overlooking the ocean. "Nice place. If I didn't have to live close to LA for training, I would want a place like this. Something not too big but overlooking the ocean. Do you spend most of your time listening to the waves crash?"

"When I'm home, yes. It's comforting to me. Work can be demanding, so when I get a chance to hang at home, I'm out on my deck enjoying the fresh, sea-salted air."

"So when I'm breathing in the beautiful dirt-filled smog air of LA, I'll know you're out here, taking in the ocean."

"Pretty much." Quietly, we smile at each other; our banter is so light and free. "Do you want to come in? You can check out my deck."

THREE BLIND DATES

The lift of Hayden's questioning eye makes me laugh. "You can check out my deck. Is that code for something else?"

I snort and cover my nose, hating how unattractive that was. "Oh my God, no." I laugh with Hayden. "I really meant my deck."

He undoes his seatbelt and nods. Suggestively, he says, "I would love to check out your *deck*, Noely."

I follow suit. "I really mean deck. This isn't one of those moments where you're looking at a picture on my wall, turn around and there I am, standing tits a-blazing, nipples winking at you."

"Well, that's just disappointing." His smirk is completely adorable. In fact, everything about this man is adorable. When I met him before our interview on Good Morning, Malibu, it didn't take more than a minute to be charmed by him. In fact, had I not been a little wobbly and excited about my first date with Jack, I probably would have wondered if Dylan had been right about Hayden. Had he been interested in me then? What did he think tonight when he found out I was ShopGirl? Because, here I am, two weeks later, opening my door to this six-foot-four gentle giant with spades of sexy mixed in with charisma, charm, and intelligence. I'll admit it. He has my stomach in knots, and now that all the imbibed confidence has worn off, when he sends his smile my way, I'm feeling something. Is it because I've *seen action* in the last month? A little from Jack, a lot from Beck...

I take no time in unlocking my front door, switching on a few lights and leading him to the deck. The crest of the moon shines on the waves, glistening and sparkling, creating a romantic atmosphere. I toss my purse on one of the lounges and briefly think about the last guy I brought out here.

Beck.

How we made out on the lounge, his large, defined body pressing against mine. His arousal hard and thick between my legs, only thin pieces of clothing between us. My face heats up, my cheeks scorching with what we did next, where we ended up.

I peer at Hayden, who's gripping the rail, absorbing the light whisper of the wind and the rolling waves. He's been sweet, conversational, and interested in my drunken stories, but he's also been a little standoffish. He pressed his hand on my lower back when walking, but that's the extent of our contact.

Makes me wonder, is he shy? Is this larger-than-life jock shy? It's hard to believe a man of his size, of his brawny and muscular structure, could be timid. It's almost an oxymoron.

But then again, maybe this is what I need. Maybe I need to take this dating thing at a snail's pace. Because let's be honest. The Suit was assertive, told me what he wanted and took it when *he* wanted it, hence the most limb-melting kiss I've ever had. With The Rebel, hell, I think we all know what happened there. Little Noely boo-foo couldn't keep her pants buttoned and wound up doing wicked things with her mouth.

With Hayden, this feels like it could really go somewhere, like we're clicking on a different level. If I want to make this work, maybe I need to take a different approach, really establish a base before I start throwing my body at him.

"This is beautiful, Noely. God, how can you even leave your house? I would have one hell of a time trying to get my ass out to work if I lived here."

I giggle. "Work. It's funny hearing your profession referred to that. I mean, I know it's work for you, but to me, you're a freaking hockey player, not pushing pencils over at Al Schmenky's Accountant firm."

"Al Schmenky?" Hayden's confused face is adorable.

I shrug. "He makes sure I don't go to tax jail. Great man, a little too much by the book, doesn't let me write my hair stylist off as a work expense, and he really loves a good baklava."

"Who doesn't?"

"Weird people. There is something about the honey and nuts and the dough." I kiss my fingers and toss them in the air. "Perfection."

"Still drunk?" *He looks amused.*

"I wish I could say I was."

Looking back at the ocean, Hayden asks, "Can I ask you a personal question?"

"Why not? I practically outlined my nipple with my finger for you over dinner."

"That was a very candid moment for you."

"Candid or drunk?"

"Maybe both." He shakes his head. "Why did you join the *Going in Blind* program? You're beautiful, know a lot of people, and have a good head on your shoulders, you know, besides the nipple drawing and whatnot." *Shouldn't I be asking him that question? Why is he using Going in Blind?*

Instead of focusing my attention on Hayden when I answer, I lean on the ocean for solace. "Besides the fact that I've had horrible luck attempting to pick out men for myself, I wanted to try something new. I was in a rut. I wanted to meet someone who was equally interested in starting a relationship, with the aim of marriage. I don't want to just hookup, I want something real, something palpable with meaning."

"You want your forever."

"Yeah, I want my forever." Awkwardly, I stand a few feet from Hayden, wondering what he thinks of that answer. Is he looking for the same thing? Is my answer going to scare him off? Before I can torture myself with diving too deep into what his thoughts could possibly be, I ask, "Why did you join?"

"Camaraderie, the hope for something more, someone other than teammates to lean on. I'm kind of over the whole hookup scene." He bites on his bottom lip. "I kind of got a taste of what a relationship could be like and I want that." *Ah, he did have to leave someone special behind.*

"You know, Hayden. You surprise me. I keep saying that, but you do. You're grounded and real, and I like that about you."

"Humble upbringings. Growing up, I learned that when everything else seemed to disappear at the drop of a hat, family stuck around. I try to keep that in mind when the fame starts to become overwhelming. Play for the game, not for the fame. It was my dad's motto for me growing up. I write the saying in every helmet I wear so I carry it around with me."

"That's really sweet. And your family, are they all in Philadelphia?"

"Scranton, Pennsylvania, actually. I grew up a little north from there in a town called Binghamton in upstate New York, but my parents moved to be closer to family when I graduated from high school and went off to college."

"Oh man, they must have been so upset when you were traded."

"Yeah, you could say that, but now my mom is ready to spend her winter in California. My dad on the other hand, is a winter man through and through. He's the guy who will go up and down the neighborhood street, snowplowing everyone's driveway because he enjoys it."

"God, that sounds like my worst nightmare."

"It's my dad's dream." Hayden chuckles. "Especially after I bought him the cream-of-the-crop snowplow. You know how some guys wax their cars? My dad waxes his snowplow. It's ridiculous."

My voice grows bubbly when I say, "I think I would like your dad. He sounds like a dedicated fellow."

"You can say that. He's a good guy. Cried when I flew out here. We have a special bond."

"Was he the one who took you to all your hockey games?"

"Both my parents did, but my dad was the one who strapped pillows all around his body and stood in front of a goal so I could practice my shooting."

A giggle pops out of my mouth as I shake my head. "He did not."

Hayden nods. "He so did. My mom has so many pictures of my dad standing in the goal, pillows everywhere. He's a big guy so he blocked most of the goal. I had to try to get around him."

"And that's why your shot is so precise."

"Yep, all thanks to my dad."

I lean on the rail and turn toward him, a tilt to my head.

THREE BLIND DATES

"That's a really cute story. It's always a beautiful thing when someone has such a good relationship with their family."

"They're the best." His eyes wander to me, curiosity lacing his features. "What about you? Do you have a good relationship with your family?"

Good, yes. Annoying . . . at times, especially when . . .

"Oh my God," I say, realization hitting me.

"What?"

I press my hand against my head. "I have a good relationship with my family, especially my brother, Alex. My brother who's going to freak the eff out if I tell him I went out with you."

"Ah," Hayden answers knowingly.

"I mean freak OUT." I press my hand on Hayden's forearm, his sinewy tendons flexing beneath my palm. "Like, he might camp out in front of my house and follow me around, waiting for me to meet up with you. When I told him about our interview, he was practically bouncing his leg up and down like a dog. I'm afraid to say it, but he might be in love with you."

Hayden raises an eyebrow at me. "Is that so? Well"—he fluffs the collar of his shirt—"I might just have to meet him. Look out, Noely, seems like you have competition."

Chuckling, I say, "Have at it. But I must warn you, Alex is married, has a kid, a beer gut, and likes to spend Friday nights watching specials on the National Geographic channel."

"My kind of man," Hayden retorts wistfully.

~

I take another sip of my hot chocolate and snuggle into the blanket draped over my lap. We pulled two lounge chairs together, pushed them to the railing of the deck, made some hot chocolate, and are now sharing a blanket while staring at the stars and listening to the ocean crash into the cliffs below us.

"What was the one thing you wanted so badly for Christmas as a kid but never got?" Hayden asks, his foot brushing up against mine.

As I get to know him, it's clear that what makes him an assertive and aggressive forward on the ice, isn't part of his resting temperament. He's quite . . . calm, and even though I think he's attracted to me, he's subtle in how he shows it. A glance here and there, a light touch on occasion, yet that's all I need to become hot and bothered by this mammoth of a man. I feel like such a hussy. Three men have caused this type of reaction in me during the last few weeks. With Hayden, despite his indirect way of showing me he's interested, it's the way his body moves toward mine, the way his eyes rake over me from head to toe, and the way his voice turns sultry when we speak of anything sexual.

Trying not to be distracted by his cologne—why is it men's cologne smell so yummy—I take a moment to think about his question. "Besides the obvious real-life unicorn?"

"Obviously." He laughs.

"Hmm . . . honestly, I can't really think of anything. My parents were always pretty cool about getting us presents at Christmas. Although, when I was older, my brother, Alex, left for college and they decided to go all out. They bought him a brand new laptop and mattress. I got a comforter that Christmas. When I went to college, my new laptop—refurbished actually—was a birthday and graduation present. What kind of crap is that?"

"Wow, that is kind of crappy." He smirks. "It's one thing to give someone a mattress and computer for Christmas, but to make you combine presents, that's just outrageous."

"Tell me about it. Alex is a great accountant now, and he says it's because he slept well during college, and he had a trusty computer by his side. He never misses a chance to rub it in my face."

"Ha, sounds like my brothers."

"Ah yes, you have two younger brothers, right?"

"Yep, both play hockey, both annoying."

"Why do I feel like I should know this?"

"Your stalking abilities are slacking."

"They are." I turn in my lounge and curl my knees up to my chest. "So what about you? Was there anything you wanted for Christmas you never got?"

Casually, as if it's second nature, Hayden presses his head against the lounge and places his hand on my blanket-covered knee, his thumb very slowly running back and forth. Oh sweet Jesus, I wish there was no blanket right about now. Would it be weird if I yanked the blanket out from over me, like a tablecloth, hoping it doesn't disturb Hayden's fingers? Maybe if I held up my finger and said, "Would you mind doing the touching under the blanket?" Too upfront? A little brazen?

Possibly.

But for the love of tiny orgasms, Hayden Holmes is caressing my knee—albeit over a blanket—but he's touching me, sweetly touching me. I can hear the trumpets sound: he's making his first move.

Now, you're probably thinking I'm kind of a slut here. Three blind dates. Three hot men. Three different, yet incredible panty-melting moments where I've been ready to throw away my long-held boundary of only having sex within a relationship. But I can assure you, *this is not normally me.* And I'm not sure if it's because I have gone to these dates expecting they're my emotional match—as per the app and program—that's caused a more instant desire for a sexual match. It could be the fourteen-month dry spell, but I'm not convinced. However, whatever the reason, it's as though my girly parts have been buried below my subconscious and in the presence of three gorgeous specimens of men, she is popping up and saying, "Yes! I'm still here! Engage! Engage! Rid me of my cobwebs. Please!" Well, that's what I can hear, anyway . . .

Clearly, I need to contain my raging hormones and refrain from pelvic thrusting in his face while biting down on my lower lip.

"Are you ready for this, I think I'm about to blow your mind."

"Ooo, am I about to get some juicy dirt about your elementary years?"

"Yep and this goes in the vault, got it?"

"Sooooo no broadcasting this on my morning show about the hot new hockey player the Quakes just acquired?"

"Hot, huh?" I roll my eyes, causing him to laugh. "Yeah, this is not morning show material."

"Got it." I zip up my mouth. "Your secret is safe with me."

"All right, so do you remember when we were younger, how toe socks were all the rage?"

I squint my eyes, trying to understand where he's going with his. "Uh, I remember they were all the rage for girls."

He nods, his lips turn up, and his strong neck exposed to the midnight sky. "Well, I wanted a pair so bad, like it was all I asked for. I just wanted toe socks."

"Why on earth would that be something you wanted?"

"My cousin let me wear hers one day and I couldn't get over how they made my feet look. I mean, they were socks conformed to each individual toe. Hell, it was blissful wearing those things."

"Oh my God." I snicker.

"Laugh all you want, but those were the shit back then. Unfortunately, they didn't make them in colors I could pull off—"

"Like pink?"

He shakes his head. "Not at such a young age. Plus, my feet were too big at that point. I nearly tore my cousin's socks."

"What a sad, self-deprecating story you chose to tell me."

Turning toward me, his eyes bounce between mine as he pushes a stray hair behind my ear, his fingers lingering on my face, grazing my jaw. My breathing immediately starts to pick up from his simple touch, from the way he's looking at me, so steady, so heavy with curiosity.

Slowly, his thumb pads across my bottom lip, pulling on it ever so slowly and releasing before I can think much of the touch. When his hand starts to glide down the small column of my neck, he says, "Thought I should tell you a story that shows you I'm not perfect, even though I like to think I am."

Gaining a little courage, wanting to push him further since he turned the heat up between us, I say, "I knew you weren't perfect, or else you would have kissed me by now."

A slow, lazy smirk spreads across his mouth. There goes taking things slow . . .

"Not because I didn't want to." He leans in and kisses my forehead. "I'm going to get going. Mind if I use your bathroom before I go?"

"No. Of course not. Second door on the left down the hallway."

"Okay. Thanks." He then pops up, well, as much as someone as hulky as Hayden Holmes can *pop up*, and heads inside. It's not really what I expected, but weirdly, I think I'm okay with that.

After folding the blanket and collecting our cups, I head to the kitchen.

"Sorry, Noely, I should have done that," he says as he points to the cups. *His momma raised him well.*

"It's all good."

He grabs his jacket off the couch and I meet him at the front door. Turning toward me, he keeps my hand in one of his and cups my cheek with the other. "You're beautiful, Noely, and I have really enjoyed our date. Here's what I'm thinking. You are someone I'm very comfortable with. In fact, I'm surprised how in sync we are. That could be the success of the *Going in Blind* app, or it could be just us. I'm going with the latter." I am trying so hard to concentrate on his words, but the look in his eyes is mesmerizing. Sincerity. When he strokes my cheek again, it almost brings tears to my eyes. He is so tender with me, and I actually feel . . . cherished. I want to agree with him. I think it is us, but he hasn't finished.

"I am looking for someone in my life long-term, like you are, and from how good tonight has felt, I want to give us a go. You mentioned how things were too physical, too fast with your date before me, so I want you to know I'm conscious of that. I want to build a base with you, Noely."

My eyes search his, true sincerity ringing through them. Never in a million years would I have thought Hayden was such a sensitive man. I thought an alpha male takes what he wants all the way, kind of like Jack, but instead, he's sweet, charming, and considerate.

Slow is what I wanted; so slow is what I'll take.

Reaching around me, Hayden pulls me into his chest, his chin resting on the top of my head. "When I was in Pennsylvania, I was in a brief relationship. I saw what it was like, the handholding, late-night phone calls, and early morning texts. It was nice, especially after feeling so lonely on the road. It was so fucking nice. You asked me why I joined the program, and there is my answer. I want long-term, the family like the one I came from. I want to build something strong, something to last forever, just like you. So what do you think?"

Even though I desperately want him to kiss me, to maybe stick his hand up my shirt and do a little fondling—thank you, hormones—what I want *more* is a forever, so I nod into his chest. "That sounds perfect to me."

CHAPTER TWENTY-FIVE

NOELY

Noely,
I swiped yes to a second date. Your pretty little ass better say yes also. I didn't like any of their second date options, so I clicked on other. I have an idea, if you're up for it.
#1 Rookie of your Heart < - - Was that lame?

Hayden,
Oh God, I snorted so hard. #1 Rookie of my heart is very cornball, but I also love it. Sometimes a little cornball in a man is what wins me over. But don't go overboard. *Points finger at you*
Of course I swiped yes for a second date. And you didn't like the options? Bowling not your thing? What's your idea? I'm up for anything.
Noely

. . .

Noely,
I've got plenty of cornball to win you over. Remember toe socks? But I will be sure to even it out so you're not bombarded.

As for the date, I remember having a little conversation with you about You've Got Mail. If the offer still stands, I'd be willing to watch it with you, but I have some conditions.

#1 Cornball

Hayden,
Spreading the cornball out is a very good idea. Don't lay it on too thick, but throw some my way every now and then.

And you want to watch You've Got Mail? *Jumps up and down, flails arms* You just made my night. I'm game, but I have to ask, what are your conditions?

Noely

Noely,
I kind of wish I got to see your little excited jig. Maybe I can get a replay on our next date?

And my conditions are simple. I demand the following: a good blanket, a quality cuddle, and cheddar/caramel popcorn. Do you think you can deliver?

#1 Cuddler

Hayden,
Number one cuddler, huh? That's kind of bold of you, don't you think? You better live up to the hype, mister.

Cheddar/caramel popcorn, done. And I'm the queen of

comfortable blankets. Your conditions are barely conditions. How about I add one? Tacos from Mehi's Taco Shop. Pick them up on your way over. Ten should do.
   And that jig . . . only if you're lucky.
   Noely

N*oely,*
   Ten tacos? Are you insane? Twenty at least for two people, but since I'm supposed to be eating healthily, I'm going to go with fifteen. I'm going to assume you're not a savage and you're implying the original taco and that's it.
   #1 Taco Consumer

H*ayden,*
   *Oh boy, are you in for a show. *Cracks knuckles* I'm going to show you how to eat tacos. Get twenty, I will house you and your popcorn. And of course original. Mehi shouldn't even have any other options other than that.*
   I'll grab the popcorn and supply the venue and blankets. You bring the tacos. Can't wait.
   Noely

∼

"I've got to go."
   "Why won't you just tell me? Come on, Noely."
   I let out a long, frustrated breath and count to ten . . . slowly.
   The one time my brother catches the morning show, he tunes in just at the time I start talking about my date with The Jock, aka Hayden. It was the first time I told Dylan about the news too, so on air of course, she was drilling me with questions, as if we were in the makeup room together. It was rather uncomfortable, slightly

invasive, but luckily I held my own, kept Hayden's identity a secret, and didn't divulge too many details, including the night's whiskey consumption.

When the show was over, oh boy, did I hear it from Dylan. Apparently she doesn't like to be surprised on air, and hearing about my date while the cameras were on was unacceptable to her. I spent the next two hours, even during our training session, apologizing and catching her up on everything . . . in great detail.

And just when I thought the questioning was done, Alex called.

"I won't be able to sleep. Is that what you want? For me not to sleep? Don't think about me. Think about what the lack of sleep in me will do to Lauren and Chloe. You know I'm a beast when it comes to sleep. Don't make me be a beast to my wife and child, my innocent child."

"Alex, this is a new low for you, you know that?" I light a few candles around my living room. Nothing extravagant just a few to set the mood.

"You're being unfair and nasty. So nasty to me. I . . . I"—he starts to stutter, his words sounding heavy—"I just might"—sniff —"cry."

"Don't be an idiot, Alex. I know when you're fake crying."

"Come onnnnnnnn. Noely, please for the love of God just tell me who the athlete is. Be a pal, a true sibling, do a guy a favor."

"What have you ever done for me?" I flop myself on my couch, enjoying torturing my brother way too much.

"Uh, it's called the five-year-old that likes to walk in on me while I'm doing my morning business. That's what I did for you. I gave you a niece."

"Nuh-uh, don't give me that crap. You made your deposit in Lauren and *she* gave me my niece. You can't jump on her guilt trip and call it your own."

He huffs. "Fine. Uh . . ." I hear a snap of his fingers. "Oh, I know."

"You don't know."

"Ohhh"—he laughs—"I so fucking know." Pausing, most likely for suspense—such a tool—he clears his throat. "Your freshman year, first semester, Alpha Nu's frat party—"

"Fine!" I will not allow him to go into the details of that drunken night and how he had to rescue me from a balcony half-naked . . . not my finest moment.

"Ha, knew I could get you to spill the beans."

"Yeah, whatever, but that's the last time you can use that against me. Do you understand?"

"Consider it used, now tell me who it is." I swear Alex could be a teenage girl right now, pigtails bouncing in the air as he excitedly waits for the details about my date. There are times in his life when he has absolutely no self-respect . . . or no nut sac for that matter.

"You have to PROMISE you won't tell anyone. I mean it, Alex. You can't brag to your other accountant friends, or tell the checkout person at the grocery store, and you absolutely can't tell your neighbors by putting a billboard out in your front yard."

"I did that as a joke, once, settle down. I won't make any billboards."

"And you won't tell anyone."

"Promise, I won't tell anyone."

Squeezing my eyes shut, I take a deep breath and quickly say, "It's Hayden Holmes."

There's silence on the other end of the line right before Alex screams at the top of his lungs. "Lauren, LAUREN!!!" His voice cracks while screaming. "For the love of God, LAUREN! Noely is going out with Hayden Fucking Holmes."

"What happened to not telling anyone?"

"Lauren doesn't count." He takes a deep breath and then . . . "Lauren, did you hear me? Hayden Fucking Holmes. Noely is banging him. LAUREN!"

"I am not," I say over his yelling. "We had one date." Soon to be two.

"Jesus Christ, your face is red. What's happening?" I hear Lauren say off in the distance.

"Noely is dating Hayden Fucking Holmes."

"It's actually just Hayden Holmes," I try to correct over Lauren's screaming.

"Put it on speaker, put it on speaker."

"I don't know how to."

"Liar."

There is fumbling of the phone and then Lauren's very-loud, ear-piercing scream projects into my living room.

"You're dating Hayden Holmes? Is that the jock you were talking about on the show? I mean, I thought you might be dating someone who was a professional athlete but not the most sought-after hockey player."

"It's not a big deal," I respond, trying to tamp down their excitement. "He's just a normal guy."

"No way, nope, not even close," Alex chimes in. "Hayden Fucking Holmes is not a normal guy. No normal guy can handle a puck like he can. He's a god, a fucking *god* on ice."

Oh Jesus. Can you see why I didn't want to tell my brother, or Lauren for that matter? Maybe subconsciously that's why I didn't tell Dylan right away either.

"Okay, well I'm going to go now."

"Why?" Lauren questions with curiosity in her voice, excited curiosity. "Is he coming over?"

"Ehh—"

"Oh my GOD! He's coming over to your house, isn't he? I can smell it. I can smell the promise of sweaty, hot hockey sex in the air."

"What's hockey sex?" Alex asks.

"You know . . . the kind where he rips her clothes off, lifts her above his head, and eats her out while spinning around the room like he's on the ice."

"That's not fucking hockey sex. That's figure-skating sex.

THREE BLIND DATES

Hockey sex is more like she holds pucks over her nipples while he fucks her on the bench in the locker room," Alex counters.

"No way, it has to be on the ice. He's going to take her to the rink tonight, flip on the scoreboard and play porn while he fucks her over the goal. They're both wearing skates of course, porn everywhere, blaring through the speakers, there's a hockey stick involved somehow, and he's all veiny and sweaty and says things like my semen are scoring tonight."

And that's my cue . . .

I hang up and toss my phone on the coffee table. That got out of control and quickly. I knew I shouldn't have said anything. They're going to make this a living hell for me. Their obsession with hockey, let alone Hayden Holmes, is unhealthy and now that they know I'm possibly dating him, I can foresee some unscheduled visits . . .

Oh shit.

I pick up my phone and quickly type out a group text.

Noely: *I swear on your lives, if you show up here tonight, I will: 1. Never speak to you again, and 2. Make sure you are banned from all LA Quakes games. I have the powers; don't make me do it.*

I don't really have the powers, but they don't know that.

Noely: *P.S. We're not having wild hockey sex, whatever the hell that is. Leave us alone.*

Their responses come in at rapid fire.

Alex: *I thought you needed your toilet fixed. I can come fix it right now. I will be right over.*

Lauren: *I made you muffins. Don't you want my apple cinnamon muffins fresh out of the oven?*

Alex: *All my clothes are dirty, so I'll be wearing an LA Quakes jersey, hope that isn't a problem.*

Lauren: *All my clothes are dirty too. I'll be coming topless, hope that's okay.*

Alex: *Is it weird that I want to watch the hockey sex?*

Lauren: *Is it weird that I want to watch it and replicate it right there on the spot, move for move?*

Count to ten, count to freaking ten. I take deep breaths, letting the air slowly release through my nose, eyes shut, yet tension is consuming me. They're not going to mess this up for me; they're not . . .

Please, God. Don't let them mess this up. This is the second date. I am not *dating* Hayden Holmes yet, but I do want the chance to.

. . .

Noely: *Remember those season tickets I promised? Consider them sold to someone else if you show up here tonight. I will not even feel bad about it. And don't call me. I swear on Martha, I will sell those tickets so fast. Got it?*

Martha, Chloe's doll. *She's* the reason Alex and Lauren have been able to lead a somewhat *normal* life with a five-year-old. Martha is the savior of their lives. Martha is Chloe's best friend and they will do anything and I mean, ANYTHING, to keep Martha happy. Oh, Martha wants a tea party? Lauren makes three different kinds of scones and lays out an entire spread with her nice china. Martha wants to watch Bubble Guppies? Alex switches the channel. Martha is the boss, and I know this, and to hell if I'm NOT going to use that to my advantage.

Alex: *Leave Martha out of this, for Christ's sake!*

Lauren: *Don't you dare bring Martha into this hockey-sex world.*

Noely: *Don't force me to do so. I have no qualms with unbraiding Martha's hair.*

Alex: *You BEAST!*

. . .

Lauren: *For the love of all boners, don't touch her hair. I swear to God, don't touch her hair. We will stay away. Okay? But promise us one thing...*

Noely: *What?*

Lauren: *Tell him we said hi.*

I huff and roll my eyes, hard, like the most exaggerated eye-roll you'll ever see.

Noely: *Fine, I'll tell him you said hi. I will even send you a message of me doing it.*

Alex: *Oh God, I have a boner.*

Lauren: *Excuse me while I go twiddle my husband and myself.*

Those two. Way too much information. I toss my phone back on the coffee table and go to my bathroom, wanting to make sure that conversation didn't make me pull all my hair out subconsciously. I mean . . . Hayden Fucking Holmes is going to be here any minute. I have to make sure everything is in place.

THREE BLIND DATES

Yes, I said Hayden Fucking Holmes, because guess what, he is a GOD!

∽

"Oh shiiiiiit," Hayden says while covering his mouth. His large frame is taking up a good percentage of my couch, feet up on the coffee table—after he asked of course, such good manners—and one of his long arms is around my shoulders, pulling me close to his side. "Tell me he's not trying to woo her, not after he put her out of business."

"He's wooing," I say with a big smile, loving how Hayden is so into the movie.

"Damn, Joe Fox has some big balls." Hayden shakes his head. "I mean, he's insulted her, stood her up, and took away her last memory of her mom, and he thinks he can turn around and woo her with some flowers and promises of wanting to be friends? Wow, I need some Joe Fox swagger." *Um no. Your swagger works just fine.*

"He's pretty convincing, isn't he?"

"Hell, after his little speech, I think I would be having the same thoughts as Meg Ryan right now. Look at the wheels turning in her head." Hayden laughs. "Fuck, this movie is good."

A laugh trickles up from the depths of my stomach and lights up Hayden's face. I try desperately *not* to react when his eyes —*seductively*—cast a serious glance in my direction.

Take it slow.

Become friends, pull a Joe Fox. Don't rush into things. That's what happened with the last two dates. There is time to have wild hockey sex—yes, I thought it—but let's focus on the bond we're sharing right now. Just because he's staring at your lips doesn't mean you should thrust your tongue in his direction.

But, he's licking his lips . . .

My phone buzzes next to me for the hundredth time, at least that's what it feels like.

Whatever thoughts were running through Hayden's head pause as he clears his throat and nods at my phone. "Uh, is everything okay? Your phone has been buzzing all night."

I know exactly who it is. Of course they wouldn't let me get away with not messaging them.

I sigh and pause the movie. "It's my brother and sister-in-law. They, uh, saw the show where I talked about dating a jock, and they battered me into telling them who it was. I'm sorry, I know it's probably—"

"It's okay," Hayden says with a smile. "My brothers were hounding me too. I told them I was going out with a hot morning show host."

Cue a huge blush in my cheeks.

"Oh." Feeling shy, but also incredible—thank you, Hayden—I say, "Well, they threatened to come over here because they're huge fans of The Quakes and you. I told them to leave us alone and said I would message them telling you they said hi."

"Ah." Hayden knowingly nods. "Let's FaceTime them."

"Oh my God, no. I'll just text them really quick."

"Where's the fun in that?" Nodding at my phone again, he says, "Hand me your phone."

"Hayden, you don't have to do this."

"I want to. Honestly, I kind of want to see if your brother screams like a girl." A giant laugh rumbles from the pit of my stomach. *Oh my God. He is my people.*

Now that he says it, I kind of want to see if Alex screams as well. Alex will legit soil himself. Wanting to see my brother cry on FaceTime, because I know that's also what will happen, I hand Hayden my phone after I scroll past the fifty texts from him and Lauren and call them on FaceTime.

We both prop each other up but instead of holding the phone so we're both in the picture, Hayden only has the camera on him. Oh God, Alex is going to lose his mind.

The phone stops chiming and connects so the picture we're

seeing is of the ceiling. Chloe must have Alex's phone. I giggle . . . hard.

"Uh." Hayden looks at me.

I whisper, "Chloe, their five-year-old must have the phone. Tell her hi."

"Hello?"

"Who's this? Why do you have my aunt's phone?" She's still not good at pointing the camera at her face, so all we see is the top of her head.

"I'm your aunt's friend. Is your, uh, dad there?"

"He's in the kitchen eating his feelings."

Both Hayden and I snort. That is so something Alex would say. What an idiot.

"Do you think you could take him the phone?"

"Yeah. Hold on, Martha. We'll take pictures in a second."

With a confused pinch in his brow, Hayden mouths, "Martha?"

I giggle some more and whisper, "Her doll. They're best friends."

"Daddy!" Chloe shouts, causing Hayden and I to jump from how loud she is. For a little girl, she has some pipes. "Daddy, a man wants to talk to you."

"What?" You can hear Alex ask in the background.

"I told him you're eating your feelings but he still wants to talk to you."

"Don't . . ." Alex pauses. "Christ, don't tell people that."

"I'm not gonna lie, Daddy. Can I have a donut?" The phone that's been jostled around is now tossed so all we can see is black. She must have put it face down. "Please, Daddy?"

"Yes, but don't tell your mom."

Hayden snorts, and I watch in fascination as his neck muscles bounce when he chuckles. So sexy.

"Don't run with it in your mouth. Christ!" Sighing, Alex picks up his phone and brings it to his ear. "Hello?"

"FaceTime, dude," Hayden says in a deep voice, deeper than usual. I clamp my hand over my mouth, holding back my laughter.

"What?" Alex pulls the phone away and when his eyes take in the screen, they shoot wide open and he jostles it in his hand until it crashes to the ground. "Fuck. Fucking hell. Fuck, fuck, fuck. Holy Fuck!" Clambering for the phone, he jostles with it some more until he finally brings it to his face. The picture is shaky. He's a blubbering mess right now. "Oh fuck. Oh FUCK!" His hand goes to his forehead. "Oh shit, it's . . . it's . . ." His eyes start to water and I don't think I've ever been more happy in my entire life.

"Hey man."

Stunned, speechless, jaw wide open, Alex stares at the phone and then before Hayden can say anything else, Alex yells at the top of his lungs and starts running. "Lauren. LAUREN!" His voice cracks.

He pushes through a door and you can hear Lauren say, "What the hell, Alex? Did you—?"

"It's Hayden Fucking Holmes. Look, he's on the FaceTime. Look!"

"What?" Lauren twists the phone so she's looking at the screen and . . . cue the screaming. "Oh my GOD!!! It's Hayden Fucking Holmes!"

There is nothing to really do but laugh, and laugh hard. Hayden and I sit there, our chests falling up and down, chuckling together as Lauren and Alex freak out.

"I need to show him my boobs," Lauren says. "Unzip my dress, Alex, undo my bra."

"On it," he calls out, as if his wife showing Hayden her boobs is the most natural thing ever.

Hayden looks at me and mouths, "He's okay if she shows me her boobs?" I snort and roll my eyes. There really are no words to explain the insanity that is my brother and sister-in-law.

I snag the phone from Hayden and sternly say, "All articles of clothing are to stay on. Now, calm down, take deep breaths, and try to act like normal adults or else I will hang up and turn my phone off for the night."

"Don't hang up," they say at the same time in a panic.

THREE BLIND DATES

"Okay, then get yourselves together. I'm going to hand the phone back to Hayden and you're going to act like adults, right?"

"Yes."

"All clothes are on."

"I'm going to piss myself," Alex whispers to Lauren, but we both hear it . . . clear as day.

Shaking my head at my family, I hand Hayden the phone and say, "You asked for this."

Relaxing into the couch, casual as ever, Hayden brings the phone in front of him. "Hey, you guys. Noely has spoken very highly of the both of you."

Gobsmacked, mouths hanging open, they just stare at the phone.

"Uh, so I heard you were big fans of the LA Quakes."

"Fans," Alex mutters. Is that . . . drool coming out of his mouth?

"Okay, uh, so I was wondering, we have a little exhibition coming up on Thursday. Thought maybe you guys might want to attend with Noely. I can get you some good seats and some of my jerseys. How does that sound?"

"I like hockey," Lauren says, her hand falling to the cleavage of her dress, her finger starting to tug on the fabric. Oh Jesus.

Nodding, and feeling a little awkward, Hayden says, "Okay. Well, I'll set everything up with Noely. Nice meeting you two." He hands the phone back to me and chuckles.

When I come back into view, Alex and Lauren lose their minds, speaking at rapid pace over each other, to the point that I can't understand a damn word they're saying. All I hear is fucking god, nip slip, hockey sex, and something about being hit in the head by a puck.

Not wanting to put up with this, I hang up and tuck the phone under my leg. Turning toward one another, Hayden and I lose it completely, buckling over in laughter. "You realize what you just did, right? You invited two crazies to your game."

He shrugs. "Nothing I haven't seen before. It's funny and looks like I made their day."

"Year, Hayden. You made their year."

"All the better." Slipping his arm back around my shoulder, he says, "Let's get back to this movie. I want to learn more about this Joe Fox swagger." *And so we do.* What a night.

~

"Keep the bags. If I take them home, I will eat them in one day. Can't afford all the sugar."

"But you brought over five bags of popcorn. We ate one. What am I supposed to do with all of this? Especially since I provided a bag myself, like we talked about."

Hayden shrugs unapologetically. "Take it to work, be the girl that everyone likes because she brings in the best popcorn ever."

"Hmm." I tap my chin. "Being that girl *does* sound like fun."

"Everyone likes that girl."

"They do. And if I say it's from my jock, they will like me even more."

He taps my nose, almost brotherly. "Now there's an idea."

The last few hours have been fun and very . . . platonic. I mean, yeah, we snuggled, but there was no inappropriate touching, there was no making out, and there sure as hell wasn't any hands in pants.

I know, I know, take it slow, build a relationship, blah, blah, blah. But would it hurt him to make a teensy tiny move? Like an accidental nipple graze? Maybe an *oops, is my hand down your pants?* Didn't mean to do that? Hell, at this point, I would settle for an accidental linking of our pinky fingers. But nothing.

Just a bop to the nose, an arm around my shoulder, and a possible heated look here and there. And to be honest, I'm not sure if it was a heated look, or if it was my horny self wearing sexified goggles making me believe there is something going on when in fact, there is nothing.

Feeling slightly frustrated, I step forward and put very little space between Hayden and me. "So, is there going to be a third date?"

He smiles sweetly and pulls me into a hug, his arms overlapping over my shoulders. It's comforting, sweet, gentle . . . *friendly*.

"Of course. How about Thursday, after the game. We can go out for a drink with Alex and Lauren."

Uhh, not the kind of third date I was thinking about. I'm about to protest when he unleashes me from his hold and steps back, putting both his hands in his pockets. *Hands. In. His. Pockets.* Is it me? Or would anyone else think he seems . . . put off right now?

I take a second to study him. His posture seems stiff, his eyes almost look guilty, and there is an air about him that seems like he's on the verge of running, like a skittish cat waiting to flee.

The last thing I want to do is go on a third date with Hayden with my brother and his wife tagging along, but at this point, I don't think there is much hope for anything else.

Swallowing hard, mimicking his stance, I nod. "Thursday sounds great. You really didn't have to give us tickets. That was really sweet of you."

"Ah, it's nothing. It will be nice to have someone cheering me on."

A bubble of humor pops out of me. "Hayden, you do realize that probably more than half of the arena will be cheering you on, right?"

He chuckles, his shoulders flexing as he shyly looks up at me. "I know that, but I mean, you know, someone I actually know. My family and friends tried to make it to as many games as possible, so I almost always had someone I knew watching me. Being traded out here, it's been one of my worries, not having someone in my seats, cheering me on."

It wouldn't surprise me if he toed the ground and said, "Aw shucks," at this point, that's how adorably sweet he looks. *Just like a little kid. How old is he again?*

"I kind of want to put you in my pocket right now, you're so cute."

"Ah hell." Hayden runs his hands over his face. "Just what every guy likes to hear."

"It's cute though. I don't know, but for some reason, I have this preconceived notion about athletes being assholes, hot assholes, but assholes nonetheless. You're throwing me for a loop."

"Where did you get that notion from?"

I lean against the wall of my entryway and cross my arms over my chest. "I've interviewed a few athletes, and they were boring, full of themselves, and after the cameras were turned off, they had no problem making a pass at me and my co-host. It was just . . . icky. I feel like that's a good way to describe it."

"Those guys don't make up the majority of professional athletes. I promise, there are a lot of good guys out there."

"I'm starting to understand that." My lips turn up, and for some reason, I feel shy. Hayden is a genuinely nice guy. He doesn't put on a front; he doesn't act like someone he's not. He's honest and true, which in my eyes is very alluring.

"Well, I should get going. Thanks for having me over, Noely. I had an awesome time, and I might have a new favorite movie."

I point my finger at him, growing serious. "Don't you dare tease me."

He holds his hands up in defense. "I would never. *You've Got Mail* is a good movie. Talk about the perfect way to get a girl. I mean, that dude was romantic as hell."

"Something you would emulate?"

Hayden shrugs, hands back in his pockets. "Who knows? Maybe. Wooing a girl anonymously, winning her over by just learning about her through her mind. That's sexy. There's something beautiful about learning about a person through their brain rather than their looks."

"Yeah?" I bite my bottom lip. "Is that why you're standing over there, avoiding any kind of physical connection with me?"

He chuckles, bending his head slightly only to look up at me through his impossibly long eyelashes. "I'm standing over here because a heated relationship, well, if that's what you want to call it, consumed me."

"Is this the relationship you've brought up a few times?"

He nods, taking a deep breath. "Yeah, it was like we didn't take a damn second to enjoy each other. From the beginning it was zero to sixty, but I feel like we also had an alarm clock counting down our days until I left for California. Doomed from the beginning."

I study him. There's something in his eyes telling me there's more to this story than he's saying. I start connecting the dots in my head. He wants a relationship like the one he used to have. He wants to hold hands, he wants to develop a friendship, but he doesn't want to take things too fast. *With me.*

Is he still reeling from his last relationship? Did this girl actually mean something to him?

"Did you really like her? Like . . . like her, like her?"

His strong hand grips the back of his neck, his palm and fingers really pulling on his skin. "It doesn't matter anymore. It's over, and I'm starting a new chapter in my life."

That's a solid answer full of avoidance. I think I might have just struck a nerve and come to a conclusion as to why he's been a little standoffish and friendly, rather than passionate. He's scarred, and a little bent from his previous relationship. But is he actually over her or still trying to find his way?

If I didn't know Hayden's intention behind joining the program, I would throw in the towel right now. But he needs time and maybe someone new, someone refreshing.

I don't want to be feeling hurt by this, because Hayden hasn't been deliberately playing with my feelings, but part of me wonders whether Lynne vetted the men as much as she did me. I had to prove to her that I *was* looking for long-term, not just a show gimmick. And yet, the three men I've spent time with haven't actually been ready to move toward a long-term relationship.

And with Hayden? I haven't had the same warm fuzzies and butterflies, but there have been moments of spine tingles. I'm thoroughly enjoying getting to know him and can see an awesome friendship developing.

But, and sadly, I think it is a *big* but. Does he want someone else to own his heart yet? Is he ready for someone like me?

CHAPTER TWENTY-SIX

NOELY

Noely,
Tickets are being held at will call for you, your brother, and your sister-in-law. There are also jerseys waiting for you as well with your preferred sizes. If they don't fit, I've already informed the merch store to let you switch sizes. I really hope you guys have fun, and don't forget to cheer me on.
#1 At Being Prepared

Hayden,
Uh, talk about organized. Thank you so much. You really didn't have to do all this. You're seriously making my brother's year. I don't think he will ever stop talking about this game. It hasn't even happened and he's already talked my ear off about it.
I owe you.
Noely

. . .

N oely,
  You owe me nothing, just your cheering, and maybe a congratulatory hug after.
  As for your brother, is he one of those guys who would dive around in the stands, begging to be hit in the head by a puck? Why do I think he might have this passionate need to be branded by an ice biscuit to the skull?
  Also, how did your coworkers like the popcorn? Were you the popular girl that morning?
  #1 Popcorn Supplier

H ayden,
  If Alex had a chance to be whipped, kicked, slapped, and branded by a puck, he would take it, no questions asked. Pretty sure he would close his eyes and point to his head, marking a bullseye for the person shooting at him. He has zero self-respect.
  As for the popcorn, gone in a day. My coworkers were savages and actually fought over the bags, it was . . . embarrassing and also comical to watch. I saw someone use a computer mouse as a weapon. You caused a riot with that popcorn, but I will tell you, I was very popular that day. So thank you.
  Have you told any of your teammates about You've Got Mail? Are you all going to watch it on your first away trip of the season?
  Noely

N oely,
  I knew the popcorn was going to make you friends, not that you have to make friends. Just from getting to know you, I can tell you're a people person.

THREE BLIND DATES

And you'll be happy to know, I brought You've Got Mail up in the weight room and I've not only gained interest from my teammates in the Joe Fox swagger, but I also gained interest from the training staff. A few of the guys have said they've seen the movie but haven't seen it in a long time. Looks like we might have a movie to watch on our first away trip. I'm almost tempted to create a Joe Fox workbook, something we can all take notes in, because that man has no qualms in owning up to his faults and mistakes. Hell, he made a woman fall in love with him who truly and utterly hated him, to the core. Seriously . . . *stands and claps*

#1 Fan of Joe Fox

Hayden,
I'm glad to hear you're spreading the news about You've Got Mail, really expanding the love for the movie. But I must say, I'm a little nervous. Your passion for Joe Fox is becoming borderline unhealthy. Yes, he won Meg Ryan over with his charm, unexpected drop-ins, and jokes, but I think Tom Hanks was a rarity in this movie. I'm not sure how realistic his character is.

I don't want you to be misled. So before you go and try to put me out of my morning show job and try to do a reverse act of love, I suggest you study the movie a few more times before you start applying your "Joe Fox" swagger in real life.

Also, can't wait for the game!
Noely

Noely,
So I detect a little jealousy? You're warning me off using Joe Fox techniques because maybe you want me all to yourself? Could that be the case? Don't worry, Noely, you're

the apple of my eye right now. (said in cheesy voice with hands to heart while bent on one knee) <- - Dramatic but charming.

And I can't wait for the game either. The guys have been dope here. I think we could have a shot at the cup. I know every team says that, but we have a lot of young, hungry men on this team. They want a championship and I want to help get us there.

And in case you were wondering, the snow cones are shit, the pretzels sub par, but the nachos, they'll win you over. Choose right, Noely.

#1 Concession Stand Know It All

Hayden,

Jealousy? Pffft, what's that? I don't think I've ever been jealous of anything in my life. But if you use your Joe Fox moves on anyone else but me I will cut you! < - - See what happens when you spark the crazy? :)

Seriously, you made my girly bits all tingly with your confidence for a championship win this year. The Quakes need a break and if you say this might be the year, I will hand out all kinds of sexual favors to your teammates to make sure it happens. I want to go to a play-off game so bad!

And . . . snow cones are trash, the pretzels need more salt, and the nachos are heaven in my mouth, extra jalapenos. Thursday, I'll be the girl in the stands, raising hell with the officials while nacho cheese drips down my face. I have no respect for myself while at hockey games.

Just a heads-up.

Noely

. . .

N*oely,*
Tingling girly bits, sexual favors to my teammates (this is unacceptable), and a nacho-cheese dripping, yelling banshee? What did Going in Blind get me into?"
#*1 Fan of Your Brand of Crazy*

~

"I really think I'm going to faint." Alex waves his hand in front of his face, clutching his jersey from Hayden to his chest while he looks over the rink. The players are warming up, the stands are filling, and the concession stands are humming with greasy, overpriced goodness.

"Please don't faint. That would be utterly humiliating," Lauren says, not paying attention to her husband, but rather ogling the men on the ice.

"Yeah, no fainting allowed. Why don't you go take our seats and watch warm-ups? I'm going to grab a beer and some nachos for myself."

"Want to grab some beer for us?" Lauren asks with a hopeful look in her eye.

Leveling with her, I ask, "What did I tell you on the way over?"

"You brought us to the game, but you're not here to spoil us. You're in your own element and to not embarrass you."

"Exactly." I tug on my Hayden Holmes jersey that's a little snug around my chest. "Now, if you don't mind, I'm going to go get some nachos and a beer. Please don't act like fawning idiots."

I start to walk away when Alex calls out to me. "I love you, Noely. You've made my year."

I let out a heavy sigh and pinch the bridge of my nose. "What kind of beer do you want?"

"Sam Adams," they both say in unison, as if they were planning this entire time. I wouldn't put it past them.

Slightly irritated but also happy for Alex and Lauren, who are gingerly moving down the arena steps to our designated seats, I make my way to my favorite nachos stand. I know this stadium inside and out. I know where all the draft beer is, where the bottles are, where the trash snow cones reside, and where the best nachos on the planet exist.

It took me a few games to figure it all out, but I've got it down now. The best nachos are right by the merch store and the best draft beer is diagonal from the nachos. It's a quick one, two pick-up. And if you walk yourself behind the kiosk vendors, you run into less people, which means less people to crash into your precious nachos. I learned that the hard way one game where a kid ran into me, slamming my nachos into my chest and giving me cheese boob for the rest of the game. Of course, his parents were nowhere to be found so it wasn't like I could wring their pockets for more nacho money. Frugal, no. I wanted justice for my spilled nachos and that's not too much to ask for.

Making my way past rowdy fans, children wearing oversized jerseys—some Hayden Holmes jerseys, how cute—and the myriad of promotional games, I spot my nachos bar . . . with a long line.

Not surprised. Looks like my secret might be out.

Resigning to a wait, I take my place in line and pull out my phone to text Hayden good luck just as someone bumps into me from behind.

"Fancy seeing you here?"

I know that voice . . .

Spinning around, I turn to face a pair of eyes I've stared into in the most intimate ways.

"Beck, oh my God, hi." He scoops me into a hug and squeezes me tightly. It's been a couple weeks since I've seen him and he still has the same effect on me.

"Sassy, how are you?"

When I pull away, my hands skim down his arms, my gaze fixed on his scruff-filled jaw and transfixing eyes. God, I forgot how attractive he is. How that's possible, I have no idea, but for a brief second, I wonder if breaking things off with Beck was a smart move.

He looks so fresh, so free, so demon free. Then again, he was good at having a good time, of pushing his past behind him and focusing on the here and now.

"I'm good, how are you?" I give his arm a squeeze before putting my hands in my pockets. No need to get too handsy with this man. "You look good."

He winks. "Thanks, Sass." He takes me in, my skinny jeans and tight-fitting top. "You look damn good yourself." I love how he still calls me Sassy. It's *our* thing, and I like that we have a thing. But should I? Is that wrong? Looking at him, being enveloped by his scent, the words he rumbled at me before we parted come back loud and strong. *"If you don't find Prince Charming right away, message me, okay?"* Does that offer actually still stand? *Noely. Why would you want to know that?* He nibbles on the corner of his lip and my body immediately heats up, the urge to have him touch me, to lean into me, to press his lips against my skin is entirely too overwhelming.

And we stare, the energy between us sparking, igniting a flame that never really died, only simmered.

This is not good.

You're with Hayden right now. You're here to support him. You're having drinks with him later . . . with your brother. God.

Clearing my throat, I try to diffuse the sexual chemistry between us with conversation. "What are you doing here? I didn't think you were a huge hockey fan."

"My buddy got tickets, dragged me along. Nachos are my jam, so figured I'd at least get my filling in cheese and chips while I'm here. What about you?" His eyes knowingly light up. "Happen to be here for a certain jock you might be seeing?" The way he wiggles his eyebrows, that smirk on his handsome face, I just want to reach up and kiss him.

"So you've seen the morning show?"

"Watch it every morning." He rocks back on his heels. "I have to see who my sassy ends up with."

Okay, my heart is beating a mile a minute. It almost feels like I've been running an endless marathon. I'm breathless, my body heated, electrified... horny. Having Beck Wilder standing in front of me, hands in his pockets, looking sexier than ever with his five o'clock shadow, devastating smirk, and broad, confident posture, I'm concerned by how much I want him. I shouldn't still want him, but I can feel myself weakening.

"I got to tell you, you've moved from The Suit, to The Rebel, to The Jock, all very different. Who are you feeling the most?"

Well, the one I've FELT the most is The Rebel, but I'm not about to tell him that, not with the way he's unabashedly looking at me. He knows, I can see it in his eyes. He knows he's the one who's held me the most, the one who's been the most intimate.

Trying to play coy, I say, "I don't think that is any of your business. My time with The Rebel came to an end."

"I wouldn't be too sure of that, Sassy." He nods at the line for me to move forward.

Overtly confident and tempting as hell, he stares at me, boring a hole deep in my bones, reminding me just how much this man so easily consumed me. He's dangerous for sure. Need I remind everyone of the humping on a motorcycle? See, dangerous. He's bad news, a troublemaker, an excellent deliverer of orgasms... I mean, no, he's... he's... God, he's so hot.

Chuckling to myself, maybe from the way I'm staring like a carp with its mouth open, he asks, "What do you get on your nachos?"

"Cheese," I say.

Like an idiot.

I watch as his shoulders pull on his tight-fitting plain shirt as he chuckles, his muscles straining against the fabric. Sweet Jesus. "Cheese is a given, what else are you putting on your nachos?"

Nachos, what are nachos? All I can think about is how the program has put me through the gauntlet of hot guys.

"Noely?" Beck bends down a little. "Are you okay?"

"What?" I shake my head. "Yeah, sorry. Just thought of a

segment for the morning show." Utter lie. "My mind starts spinning with ideas when that happens. Um nachos, I like cheese and jalapenos. I keep it simple, what about you?"

Suspiciously he eyes me but answers without questioning me. "I like onions and jalapenos."

"So you like breathing fire?"

"How else am I supposed to stay warm in this ice box? Unless . . . want to go make out in a hallway? I'm sure that will warm us up quickly."

"Ha!" I'm feeling extremely uncomfortable. "You wish." I take a small step back, praying I don't bump into the person behind me just as Beck takes a step forward.

"Yeah, I do wish." His teeth skim over his bottom lip and a deep urge to pull his lip with my teeth consumes me.

NO!

There will be no lip pulling. Think about Hayden, sweet, caring, Hayden. Sexy hockey player Hayden. Hayden, with the funny personality and bulging biceps.

"Ma'am, can I help you?"

"What?" I whip around and lose my balance over my tangled legs. Before I can faceplant it into the packages of Skittles in front of the cashier, Beck's strong arm wraps around my waist and catches me, pulling me close to his chest.

"Watch it there, Sassy. Your face almost tasted the rainbow."

His hand splays across my stomach and for a brief moment his thumb rubs along my skin where my tight shirt has inched up.

"Uh, thanks." I straighten and pull my shirt down, but not before Beck gets one more rub of the pad of his thumb over my stomach. *Does he want me? Did his attraction not cease either?*

This is wrong. This is so beyond wrong. *But it feels so good.*

"What can I get you?" the cashier asks crossly, losing her patience.

"A Coors Light and nachos with extra jalapenos," I order, nixing the Sam Adams. I can't deal with that right now.

"And I'll take the same but add some onions on my nachos," Beck says, stepping beside me and handing his card. When I go to protest, he says, "For old time's sake, let me treat you."

As if we're the best of friends. Out of all people to run into, why Beck, why now?

I look over my shoulder. Is Jack milling about somewhere in a dark hallway, waiting to spring out on me as well? That would be just my luck. Only with him, he would drive me insane with his incessantly proud candor and evasive comments. At least with Beck, I know exactly what he wants and his hand was mere inches above it a few seconds ago.

"Thank you," I say as I step aside and wait for my nachos and beer. We stand there in uncomfortable silence for what seems like forever when in fact it's a few seconds. The concession lady hands me my beer and nachos, which is covered in jalapenos—I love this stand so much—and Beck snags his as well.

"Where are you sitting?"

I point with my beer in hand toward our seats. "Five rows up from center ice."

Beck nods with a smile. "The Jock is treating you well. Good, he better be. You're a rare find, Noely. You deserve the best." Leaning forward, he places a soft kiss on my cheek. "Good seeing you, Sass. You take care and if things don't work out with The Jock, you know how to get in touch with me." *Does he really mean that? Did I misunderstand him?* Should I have been more accepting that perhaps it does take time to talk through the dark, long-term issues? Maybe I expected too much of him too soon. *What am I doing?* Deep breath, Noely. You're here because of Hayden, the man who wants to give long-term a shot. *With me.* I think.

With a wink, he takes off in the opposite direction from where I'm sitting, and I sigh with relief. Focusing my attention back to the game, I walk toward the back row of the ground-level seating, taking in the men on the ice.

From afar, they seem so small, consumed by their padding. I know that's not the case, especially Hayden. He's tall, built, and a machine on the ice. His thick thighs look even thicker under his padding, and his shoulders, much broader than normal.

Wanting to be there for him, I make my way to my seat where Lauren and Alex are sitting on the edge, their eyes focused on the players in front of them. I take a seat and they don't even say anything to me. They're in the zone, so I don't bother mentioning their lack of beers.

I pluck at my nachos and stare out onto the ice, mesmerized with how fluid Hayden is on his skates, weaving in and out, his stick gliding along with him. He's powerful, a force so strong I would be nervous if I was his opponent.

I never pull my eyes away from Hayden. I'm trained on him, watching every little move he makes, and when he saddles up next to a trainer and takes his helmet off, I'm infatuated. The screams of girls making themselves known are drowned out, and the buzz surrounding me fades. All I can see is Hayden, hair wet and tousled, beautiful blue eyes shining with excitement, and a smirk spreading across his face when he looks up to find me sitting in *his* seats. With a nod of his stick in my direction, he acknowledges me, and then takes off toward his bench.

Oh my heart . . .

CHAPTER TWENTY-SEVEN

NOELY

"I think you might have killed my brother."

Hayden laughs next to me, arm draped over my shoulder, his fresh soapy scent consuming me. "I liked him. He's a good guy."

"He practically humped your leg from afar."

"Is that what he was doing? I just thought he had a nervous twitch."

"No, he was humping you from afar. Don't hold it against him. I'm pretty sure it was involuntary. I wouldn't expect anything less from him."

Hayden chuckles and holds the door open to his car, helping me in. "He's my favorite kind of fan. So passionate. They're the best. They could have come out with us. They didn't have to go home."

"Yes, they did." I take a seat. Hayden is gripping the top of my passenger side door and casually staring at me. "They were overwhelming at the game, and I don't think I could have taken any more time with them tonight."

"Ah, I see." Head tilted, he grips the door tightly and asks, "If you're tired, I can take you home."

"Just tired of them, not of you. Let's go get that drink."

With a nod, he shuts my door and rounds the front of his car. I put my seatbelt on and marvel in the woodsy, yet fresh smell of his car.

When Hayden hops in the car, he says, "Uh, I'm kind of new here, where should we go?"

Laughing, I say, "You live on the outskirts of LA, right?"

"Yeah, close to Santa Monica."

"Okay, perfect, an Uber from there won't be too far." I caught a ride with Alex and Lauren here. Wanting more time with Hayden is why I didn't go home with them.

"I can take you home."

"Don't even think about it. That's an hour drive from Santa Monica. No way. That's sweet though, thank you." I can see he doesn't like my response so before he can counter, I add, "Don't even think about taking me right now."

He chuckles. "Damn, you're good at reading minds."

"I could see it in the way your brow creased. You were just going to start driving to Malibu now."

He shrugs. "I don't have to be at the weight room until eight in the morning, I'm good with driving."

I shake my head. "Not going to happen. Let's drive to Santa Monica. There's a cute little bar that will be quiet, not very crowded and hopefully, you won't be recognized too much, although your larger-than-life stature might be a dead giveaway."

"Can't help how I grew."

His response makes me laugh. I've never heard anyone put it like that.

For the next half hour, we make our way toward the small bar in Santa Monica, listening to the GPS on my phone and talking about the game.

Hayden was amazing, no surprise there. He looked fresh and agile on the ice, skating skillfully and easily around the veterans.

His two goals brought the Quakes to their first pre-season victory. I praised his game but all he could say was they wouldn't have won if it wasn't for their goalie, Brett Vento. Granted, he did make some impeccable saves tonight, but you can't win without scoring goals either, and Hayden was the one who did that tonight.

"How sweaty do you get in all that gear?" I ask as Hayden parallel parks on the side of the road, a block from the bar.

He shifts the gear to park and presses the button to cut the ignition. Pocketing his keys, he slightly tilts his head toward me and says, "Really fucking sweaty. Like, you wouldn't want to be going out on a date with me right now if I hadn't taken a shower."

"Ew, really?"

He chuckles and climbs out of the car. Reaching my door in no time, he opens it for me and holds out his hand. "I know the ice is cold, but we are skating three twenty-minute periods with about fifteen pounds of equipment. We get hot as balls."

"Makes sense. I mean, I get that you sweat, I just wasn't aware about how much."

"Too much to make it even the least bit sexy."

He takes my hand and leads me to the bar. I revel in the way he takes charge, the way his hand is calloused and so large around mine. Even though his hands are gloved when he plays hockey, I can still feel the roughness of his palms from his countless years of handling a stick. And even though his hands are a little coarse, I love them. Reminds me that Hayden is very much all man.

Hayden places his hand on my lower back and guides me into the deserted bar, which is exactly what I was hoping for. I point to the back corner and say over my shoulder, "There is a booth back there, want to snag it and I can grab us a few drinks?"

"Why don't you grab the booth and I'll order the drinks. What would you like?"

Smiling from his gallantry, I say, "Extra dirty martini, three olives."

"Extra dirty?" Hayden lifts an eyebrow at me. "You're an olive juice girl?"

"Guilty." I take off toward the booth. Sitting on the side that allows me to take in the entire room will ensure Hayden has his back to the bar, so hopefully, if someone walks in, they won't recognize him.

I know what you're thinking: but Noely, you're one of the hosts for Good Morning, Malibu. You would be surprised by how many people really don't care. I'm not idolized like Hayden is. I'm more the person you point at from afar and say, "Hey, isn't she that girl who drinks mimosas on television?"

Yep, that's me and damn proud of it.

Hayden walks over with my dirty martini and a beer for him. From the dark color of it, I'm going to assume it's a beer I won't like. I prefer light beer with fruity accents. Blueberry beer, put that in my mouth. Grapefruit? Shoot it down the gullet. Pumpkin beer, pretty much pumpkin anything, truck it on over to my beer hole.

"Thank you." I take my drink and then nod at his. "What did you end up getting?"

"Don't judge me, okay?"

"No promises."

"Brutal." He shakes his head with mirth. "It's a peanut butter porter. The bartender swears it tastes like a Reese's Peanut Butter Cup."

"Are you serious? Does it?"

"Only one way to find out?" He brings the glass to his lips, his dark pink lips that look so soft, so freaking kissable. If only I knew what it felt like to have those lips pressed against mine, pressed against the spot that rests just below my ear, or the spot that rests below my belly button . . .

God, for the first time in my life, I'm jealous of a beer glass.

Like a voyeur, I stare at Hayden, his lips against the glass, his thick throat as he swallows the beer, and the way his eyes close when the flavor comes alive in his mouth. Hot, so freaking hot.

"What do you think?"

He takes a moment to assess. "You know"—he twists the glass

in his hand—"I think I would rather be drinking your olive juice right now." His giant body shivers as he pushes the drink away. "Reese's my ass."

"Let me taste." He easily offers up his glass and I take a small sip, letting the rich and very strong flavor wash over my taste buds. And just as expected, I shiver violently while swallowing, avoiding a spit take. "Oh hell, that's bad."

"Like, it tastes like rotten-ass bad."

"I have no idea what rotten ass tastes like, but if I had to choose, I would say that's pretty close."

Laughing, Hayden stands from the booth and takes his glass to the bartender who understandably pours something new and lighter. I'm assuming it's his go-to by the way he drinks it on the way to our booth.

"Did you have fun tonight?" he asks when he's settled in the booth across from me.

"I did, thank you so much for inviting us. And before you even ask, I had the nachos, extra jalapenos."

"My kind of girl." He tilts his beer in my direction and takes a sip.

The entire way over here, we talked, joked, and enjoyed each other's company. It was a wonderful drive, but lacking one major thing: sexual chemistry. And it's not from not trying. We have our moments here and there, like when he holds my hand, or presses his hand against my lower back, or when I catch him checking me out. But those moments are few and far between.

There is something holding him back and I want to know what it is. Now the question is, how do I go about talking about it without being too direct?

Mulling over my options, I ask, "Do you like me?"

Okay, maybe I could have been a little more subtle.

"What?" He chuckles. "Do I like you? That's an odd question to ask. Of course I like you, or else I wouldn't be here with you. Why do you ask?"

THREE BLIND DATES

Yeah, that was a weird question, an uncomfortable one for sure. But leave it to me to make things awkward.

I spin the stem of my martini glass, staring at the olives, a little too embarrassed to look Hayden in the eyes. "I don't know. I know you wanted to take things slow, but it almost feels like we're more like friends than a new couple. You've been to my place twice now, at night, and not even a little kiss."

His lips press together and his brow creases, looking slightly upset over my assessment. Running a hand over his face, he says, "It's not you—"

"Oh God, the classic *it's not you, it's me* line." I lean back in my seat, waiting to hear the reason why he's been so slow on the old intimacy. Even worse? I know. In the back of my mind, even though I really like Hayden, he's about to call things off.

"I don't mean for it to sound cliché."

"I know you don't, but man, does it still sting." I take a large gulp of my martini and stick all three olives in my mouth. Snapping in the air, I get the bartender's attention and press my palms together, praying he brings me another. With a curt nod, he gets to work. Such a good man.

"Let me explain, Noely, before you get upset, or get drunk. I mean, I do like drunk Noely, but I'd rather you be present for this conversation."

Should I tell him I've already checked out?

Trying to act like an adult, I sit back again. "What's going on, Hayden?"

Sucking a deep breath, he stares into his glass and takes a moment before he answers. "During the off-season, I spent the last few months on the East Coast in my hometown. I spent a lot of time with my good friend who introduced me to this girl." Ugh, I knew there was someone else. It's so obvious he's hung up on another girl. I should have pinpointed it the first night. But thanks to too many drinks, I couldn't read Hayden very well. But now, it's clear.

"You don't need to say anything else. I get it."

Trying to tamp down the crazy that's starting to pop out of me, Hayden places his hand over mine and squeezes it. "Please let me talk."

Why does he have to sound so sweet? I almost wish he was an asshole, because what he's about to tell me would be so much easier to swallow if I could blame it on that. *But once again, I can't. This is on me not being the one.* "I'm sorry, go ahead."

Keeping his hand firmly planted over mine, he continues, "I met this girl, and she was different. A little outlandish, spoke what was on her mind, and she kind of captured me. She was different than anyone I've ever met."

"She sounds lovely," I grit out, hating every second of this. *Please, Hayden, please continue to tell me how great this girl was.*

A little heavy on the sarcasm there.

"She was. We had a bit of a fling and went all-in, both knowing what we were doing was going to end since I'd been traded to LA. But knowing this, we were still all-in, spent almost every waking hour with each other when she wasn't working or I wasn't training. And then the time came to say goodbye." He shakes his head, pain etching his features and even though I don't really enjoy listening to the guy I'm dating talk about another girl, I feel sad for Hayden. It's so clear this girl has a hold on him. *And yet, she might not even know.*

"She walked away easily, a reaction I wasn't prepared for. I was kind of hoping, after our months together, that maybe she'd consider moving to LA."

"But she didn't . . ." I finish for him.

Lips pressed together, he shakes his head. "She didn't. I told myself it was okay, that what we had was just a fling. But I know deep down, the feelings I had for her that were going to take a long time to shed."

"Is that why you joined the *Going in Blind* program? To get over her?" I am starting to get a little pissed here. But I will try to hear him out. *Why the hell did I have to be matched with three men who weren't in any way ready to settle down?* My role for Hayden Holmes was to help him get over someone else. Yay, me.

"That and to meet new people, to maybe find someone to take my mind off her." He sighs. "And then I met you." Well, be still my racing heart. Even though his words are sweet, I can still see the trepidation in his eyes.

"It's going to sound lame, but I didn't think going out with someone else was going to be so much fun. I really enjoy your company, Noely."

Want the sure-fire way to slap a girl in the face without actually slapping her? Tell her you enjoy her company because she's *fun*. Yep, nothing like being put in the friend-zone to rev up the sexual engines.

Trying not to grind my teeth too hard, I say, "I really enjoy your company too, Hayden." I would enjoy it more if there wasn't a mystery girl sitting between us, blocking any kind of interest Hayden might show toward me. "But . . ." I egg him on, wanting to hear the words come from his mouth.

Leaning back in his booth, his hand lifts from mine and runs down his face as he blows out a loud breath. "Fuck, I don't know, Noely. I want to move on, I want to start something up with you, because you make me happy. You make me laugh, and we have so much in common, plus you're fuck hot. I couldn't have asked for a better match when it comes to the *Going in Blind* program." *Tell me about it.* "But I don't know, there is just something from stopping me. Rather, someone, I should say."

Three men. Three perfectly matched men. Three perfectly matched, handsome, amazing men and here I am, being told I'm not the one they really want . . . again. I'm angry now, but I can't take that out on Hayden. At least he's being honest. What's the use of being *fuck hot?* That only makes me someone a man wants to bang, not love. That's certainly how Jack saw me, until he decided I wasn't even worth that. Beck nearly took advantage of that, but *managed to* restrain himself.

What the hell is wrong with me . . .

Why don't they want me?

Resigning to my single-dom fate, I sigh and say, "I get it, Hadyen. I really do. I like you a lot, but I'm not going to come second to someone who's still on your mind, you know? It's not fair to me."

"I know, it isn't at all. Shit, I feel like a total dick." His fingers run through his dirty blond hair. "This is not how I wanted this to go. I thought I could push through, but I think I need some closure." *Yeah, I'd rather he didn't have to* push through *to like me enough.*

"Closure is helpful." Seems like I've been getting a lot of closure lately.

"Yeah, I guess. I think I need to make a phone call."

"Sounds like it." Feeling resolved, I say, "For what it's worth, I really appreciate you being honest, because being strung along when your heart and mind are somewhere else is not something I like to participate in."

"I thought I owed you that much." His head is cast down, arms folded now. When he looks up, he rubs his hands over his thighs, looking like he needs to expel a bunch of energy. "Can I ask you something?"

"Of course."

"If I can . . . you know, find closure, do you think it's possible you'd be open to trying this again?"

I shift my jaw back and forth. "You mean try dating again?"

He nods. "I know I haven't made the best impression so far, but I really like you. I just need to clear my head, you know?"

I would like to say, "Do you really think I'm going to wait around for you to get your head on straight?" But after this third failing attempt to find *my one*, I'm going to put my search on hold for now. Even though it looks like I'm a strong person, on the inside, I'm taking a brutal beating to the heart.

"I would like that," I answer with a sad smile.

And another one bites the dust.

"You look like hell."

"Thank you," I answer, shoving another sour gummy worm in my mouth. I bought the five-pound bag last night. I made my Uber driver stop at the grocery store while I filled my cart with gummy worms, Cheese Balls, and a six-pack of grape soda. It's the perfect cure for self-loathing, or at least I thought.

Calling in sick to the morning show is something I've never done before, but after last night's disappointing departure from Hayden, where he gave me a sweet hug and a kiss on the head goodbye, I knew there was no way I would be able to put on a happy face for the viewers. So, I called in sick and watched Dylan manage the show with our fill-in, Krystal, while I threw tiny Cheese Balls at the screen, nailing Dylan between the eyes on multiple occasions. It felt nice.

That was until Dylan showed up at my house unannounced.

"I knew you weren't sick. You're such a liar."

"I am too sick." I wrap my arm around my lower half. "Ouch, cramps. Oweee, being a lady sucks. Fuck you, moon!" I shake my fist to the sky.

Dylan's brows cinch together in confusion. "What does the moon have anything to do with your period, which I know you're not on because we get them at the same time, and we had our period two weeks ago."

God, fucking uteruses wanting to rip their linings out together. Be original, stop doing the deed with every other uterus around you, and get your own time slot! I'm tempted to whack my uterus out of spite but refrain.

"The moon," Dylan eggs on.

I wave my hand as dismissal. "It's something my brother told me about. I can't quite remember the details, just that the moon decides our periods, something like that."

"If that's the truth, the moon can go straight to hell." Plopping on the couch next to me, Dylan picks up a few loose Cheese Balls on the coffee table and plops them in her mouth. How she's married, I will never know. "What's the real reason you called in sick and left me with Krystal? It better be good, because her incessant need to poke my shoulder when she tells a joke has me itching to punch you in the face."

Krystal, although a very lovely weather girl for the station, is not the best co-host. She laughs too loud, pokes too hard, and loves interrupting you mid-sentence.

"Hayden and I called it quits last night. I don't want to get into it, but let's just say there's another girl he needs closure with. Oh, but don't worry, when he finds closure, he *might* want to try dating me again."

"And how long could that take?"

I roll my eyes. "My point exactly." I shove three worms in my mouth and chew while talking. "You know, I thought joining this program was going to be it for me. I really thought I was going to find my match, my forever, but all I've met are three incredible men at the wrong time. It's as if the moon isn't satisfied already fucking with my period; it's messing with my cosmic dating life too."

"Cosmic dating life?"

"You know, the greater force that controls the universe. The moon is part of that and fucking with me. It's like it got together with the stars and planets and said, 'Let's mess with Noely. Let's pretend like we're aligning, that we're bringing her this great man, and when she starts to think this is it, this is the man for her, let's say just kidding and unalign ourselves.'"

"I don't think stars and planets and moons talk to each other."

Feeling a little crazed, I sit up on the couch cross-legged, the bag of gummy worms in my lap. "That's what they *want* you to think, but they talk, Dylan, oh BOY, do they talk. Those motherfucking gaseous orbs. They talk, and not only did they formulate this plan against me, they thought, *why not hit her up with this plan three times, really make her feel bad about herself.*" And as much as I tried to hear the words about how great I was, fuck hot, and whatever, it did nothing to seal the small tear in my heart. I'm tired of trying, to be honest. And probably the worst thing is my boss made my un-love life into a feature on our show. So, not only do I have to feel like shit about myself privately, the whole world—okay, just our viewers—will know even after three tries, no one wants Noely Clark.

Dylan is silent for a second, her head now resting against the back of the couch, eyes cast to the ceiling. She snags a worm from my lap and plops it in her mouth, and then I do the same. For a few minutes it's silent until Dylan finally says, "If that's the case, I'm going to have to heavily consider reneging on the star I sponsor every year. To hell if I'm going to have it fucking with my best friend." She makes a slitting motion over her neck. "You're dead to me, star!"

And that's why we're friends.

One star down, a trillion to go . . .

Part Four

THE MYSTERY MAN

CHAPTER TWENTY-EIGHT

NOELY

"Did you check out the new lineup for today's show? Kevin switched up the ending segment."

"Why doesn't that surprise me?" I say while snagging the schedule from Dylan to study it. "I swear he does this to make sure we can adapt easily. It's annoying. When is he going to—?"

I pause, my eyes fixated on the last segment: Noely and Dylan —interview *Going in Blind* owner.

It's been two weeks since things with Hayden stopped, and when *GiB* app asked me if I was happy with my results, I might have written in the comments section to go fuck itself. Maybe I was drinking that night. Maybe I wasn't. Can't be too sure.

But all I can think is . . . was my rather brash comment sent straight to the top? Oh hell.

"From your silence, I'm going to assume you see what's changed."

We were supposed to do a segment about puppies on surfboards—riveting, I know—but now it looks like we're diving into my life once again.

"Why on earth do we have to interview the owner? That won't

be awkward. I already announced to the world that I called it quits with The Jock. What the hell am I supposed to ask the owner? Why am I still single?"

"That might be a fun question." Dylan smirks into the mirror from behind me.

Yanking the tissues from my collar so I don't get makeup on the white of my shirt, I toss them in the trash and head out of the hair and makeup room.

"This is ridiculous. I'm going to go talk to Kevin. Enough is enough. I think I've paid my penance for using his stupid camera equipment. I shouldn't have to be subjected to this crap."

Dylan trails behind me, walking fast in her heels, which is difficult, given she lives in sensible flats most of the time. Hell if I care though. I'm on a rampage, blood is boiling in my veins, and the stir of my inner dragon is ready to be exposed. I can feel it, smoke is snorting out of my nose, horns are starting to sprout from my head, and I'm shaking my behind as if a hundred-pound tail trails behind me. Snorting, huffing, and puffing, I pump my arms down the hallway, ass shaking, determined on one thing and one thing alone: it's time to give Kevin a piece of my mind.

When I reach his door, I don't even bother knocking. Dragons don't knock. They charge forward, break the shit out of drawbridges, and take baths in moats. Throwing the door open, exaggerating my movements, I stand in the doorway, hands on hips, chest puffed, eyes crazy and say, "Kevin, how dare—?"

The man sitting in front of Kevin's desk stands, and his dark hair and finely tailored suit stretches across his expansive back, snagging my attention. When he turns around, my breath catches in my throat.

"Miss Clark." That voice, those eyes, the way he addresses me. I want to punch him and then kiss him all at the same time.

"Jack, wh-what are you doing here?"

Kevin stands as well, his eyes blazing. All semblance of my inner dragon lady completely vanishes the moment I make eye contact with Jack . . . again.

"Noely," Kevin grits out. Yep, he's not pleased with my little barge in. "If you don't mind, Mr. Valentine and I were just finishing our conversation. It would behoove you to remove yourself from the room and try knocking next time."

Mr. Valentine?

Jack Valentine?

As in the billionaire of Malibu?

"It's all right, we were finishing anyway." While buttoning his jacket, Jack gives my attire a long, languid perusal until his eyes meet mine. "Noely, always a pleasure seeing you."

Walking past me, his cologne taking a permanent residence in my senses, I wait for him to shut the door before I turn to Kevin . . . whose little vein on his forehead is throbbing rather aggressively.

"What the hell is he doing here?" I ask, not caring about the vein. I've seen it throb more at worse times.

"You can't just barge into my office—"

"Yeah, yeah. I'm sorry." I wave him off. "Now tell me what he's going here."

Raking a beefy and frustrated hand over his face, Kevin slouches in his chair. "Jack Valentine is here for the last segment. He's the owner of *Going in Blind*, the one you'll be interviewing."

Have you ever been sucker punched? I haven't. I've never been punched actually, but for the first time in my life, it actually feels like Kevin plowed his fist through my stomach and took all the air in my lungs along with him.

"He's . . . he's the owner?"

"Yes, and he was going to give me a free membership, but because you so rudely interrupted, I wasn't able to seal the deal."

I throw my hands in the air. I hate my producer. "Heaven forbid you should pay for anything, Kevin. You frugal bastard!"

Storming off, I try to find Dylan. *I need my friend.* But, instead, I'm ushered to the stage where they mic me up. Thirty seconds until we're on air, and I feel like going savage on our set, tearing through the couch and table like a beast on a rampage.

Can you hear the snarl? See the fangs? That fire in my pupils?

Yeah, it's real. And it's going to have to come out somehow, someway. *Oh shit. This isn't going to be pretty. Viewers, beware. The dragon lady is back, and someone is about to be burned.*

~

Dylan nudges my arm. "Dude, you've been horrific this entire show. Can you stop fake smiling like that? It's creepy."

"This is how I smile now." I cross my arms over my chest while Dylan tries to talk to me during a commercial break.

"We have one segment left, can you please look alive?"

"Alive? You want me to look alive?" I ask, pointing to my chest. "I've never been more alive in my entire life." I never thought I'd be one of those celebrities capable of a mental breakdown on camera, but by golly, can I feel it happening. A maniacal laugh escapes me, my teeth showing entirely way too much. My mouth won't settle out of its creepy smile. It's like horse teeth neighing in every direction, begging for a carrot.

"Uh, why are you bucking your leg against the floor like that?"

"Horses do that," I answer.

"Sweet Jesus," Dylan says on a whisper. "You're cracking, aren't you? You're losing your cool."

Hunkering down, I get inches from Dylan's face, our foreheads practically touching when I say sarcastically, "Do you think?"

Dylan searches my eyes and is about to say something when, "Hello, ladies."

Son of a bitch.

Our heads whip to the side to see Jack sit on the couch across from ours, unbuttoning his suit jacket with an over-confident smirk on his face.

"Mr. Valentine, what a pleasure." Dylan reaches her hand out and shakes it. "I've enjoyed living vicariously through Noely and her dating adventure."

"Don't be nice to him," I whisper through the side of my mouth, arms crossed over my chest.

"What?" Dylan turns toward me, completely confused.

Jack leans forward and sips from the mug provided for him. "I believe she told you to not be nice to me."

"Uh, she didn't say that." Dylan laughs nervously.

"That's exactly what I said."

"I know, I heard you," Jack says, looking so damn casual that it makes me want to choke him with his stupid, perfectly tied Windsor knot.

"Umm, what's going on here?" Dylan looks between us as the thirty-second countdown starts.

"Why don't you tell her, Mr. Valentine?" I seethe.

"My pleasure." Jack crosses his leg and holds his ankle over his knee. "Miss Clark doesn't want you to be nice to me because I was the first man she dated in the program. Apparently she has sore feelings about it."

"I knew you looked familiar," Dylan says, snapping her finger, remembering the time she met Jack when she tried to rescue me from my at-home perm.

"Sore feel—" I start to shout but catch myself. Calming my voice, I say, "I don't have sore feelings. I couldn't care less that it didn't work out between us. What I do care about is people lying to me."

"I didn't lie to you," Jack answers, looking so pompous.

"Yes, you did."

"No, I didn't."

"Yes, you did," I say with more force.

He shakes his head. "No, I didn't."

"Yes—"

"Okay, this is fun," Dylan says. "But I'm going to have to cut you two off. We have a show to finish in ten seconds, so, Noely, put on your professional pants. You can argue who lied to whom after the show is over. Okay?"

Twisting my mouth to the side, I turn away from Jack, take a sip of my drink, and plaster a smile on my face just in time for the red light to come on.

I read from the teleprompter, introducing Jack, recapping my dating experience—*barf*—and then to the man who's made me so hot and cold the last few months that it's hard to even look him in those dark brown eyes. "Jack, it's a pleasure to have you here." I nearly choke on the word pleasure, which garners an elbow to the rib from Dylan.

"Thanks for having me, ladies." If only he was a little closer, I could flick him in the head with my index finger. That would teach him.

"Where did you get the idea for *Going in Blind?*" Dylan asks.

"Well, if you're anything like me, you've had a hard time actually finding the time to meet someone. My schedule is quite hectic, so I thought why not create a safe zone for those with busy schedules, for those wanting to meet someone of substance. I thought that something other than an app could be viable, a place for couples to meet up. A safe haven for that initial meeting."

"Such a great idea, so different, and as you know, our Noely gave it a shot. Would you say it was how Jack described it? A safe haven for dating?"

"Oh yeah, yep. Uh-huh, the safest. So safe, the greatest of the safe, couldn't have been more pleased with the safety, because that's what I wanted, safety, not love or anything."

Cue the hysteria.

The side of Jack's jaw twitches, but that's the only sign I see of his displeasure from my answer.

Laughing nervously, Dylan says, "If you've been watching the show, Mr. Valentine, you would know Noely has gone out with three very different men from the program. She referred to them as The Suit, The Rebel, and The Jock."

"Yeah, none of them worked out." I cross my arms over my chest, cutting Dylan off. From the corner of my eye, I can see Kevin's face starting to turn purple, so I add, "Timing was off with all the guys. Great program though." I give Jack an over-exaggerated, sarcastic-on-my-end, thumbs up.

"Timing is important when you're are trying to meet someone.

Everyone is in different stages of their lives and even though you might be a good match, sometimes, if the timing is off, it might not work out."

"Yeah, timing is *precious*." I drown the rest of my mimosa and twirl the stem of the glass in my hand. "Tell me, Jack, would you ever participate in your own program?"

He eyes me suspiciously, so does Dylan, who I can see is panicking from my ad-libbed question. "I would. I have confidence it would find who I'm looking for."

"And what about timing? What if that got in the way? Would you do it again? Look for another date?"

Dylan's head bounces back and forth between us, as if she's watching a tennis match, her mouth slightly agape, her leg bouncing nervously.

"No," Jacks answers with conviction.

"Oh, why is that?"

Casually running his thumb over the brown leather of his shoe, he says, "Because, I trust the program would be right about the first match it gave me. If I have to wait and pursue someone at a later time, then I would. Because as our program states, your first match is usually the person you're most compatible with."

My nostrils flair, and before I can lash out on him, Dylan says, "Oh, it looks like we're all out of time. Jack, thank you so much for spending part of your morning with us."

"It was a pleasure."

Oh . . . suuuuuure it was.

My mind fades as Dylan singlehandedly wraps up the show, and as I wait impatiently for that red light to . . .

"Finally." I stand just as the red light goes out. I storm off toward my dressing room, getting rid of my microphone along the way. I can't be in the same room as him for one more second.

"Noely, my office," Kevin says as I walk past him.

Ignoring his request, I shout back, "Not now, Kevin. Not fucking now."

I'm not much of a swearer, or a rule breaker, or someone to

ignore a boss for that matter, but right now, with Jack Valentine a few feet away from me, I need space. I need the space an ocean can only really provide.

The thought of my balcony, calling to me, has me pushing forward to my dressing room, passing every nice and considerate coworker I have who is praising the show this morning. Ignoring all of them, I make a mental note to bring donuts on Monday morning for the entire crew. That will make up for my rudeness.

Not bothering to show any grace, I fling my dressing room door open and close it quickly. Standing in front of my vanity mirror, I place my hands on the counter and bow my head. With my eyes squeezed shut, I try to take a few deep breaths.

Jack Valentine, the owner of *Going in Blind*, my first blind date, the man who likes to keep his private life private, just blew my mind and not in a good way.

Why didn't I put two and two together?

Hmm . . . maybe because he lied to me. *The bastard.*

In a very immature and bitter voice, I say, "Hi, I'm Jack, and I'm a handsomely attractive liar and manipulator. I want love. *Not.* But I do really want to mess around with people's minds. Come join my program, you'll find the love of your life and live happily ever." I roll my eyes just as my door opens. Not in the mood to talk to Dylan, I say, "Dylan, please, not now."

The door shuts and the lock clicks. Looking into the mirror, I catch Jack's intense gaze in the reflection. Standing ramrod straight, I turn around just in time to catch him adjust his tie and step forward.

"Not Dylan."

Feeling slightly breathless, a little caught off guard, and a whole lot of angry, I say, "Have you ever heard of knocking?"

"I have. Chose not to."

"I could have been naked."

"And that's a problem, because . . ."

Looking stoic as ever, Jack casually sticks one of his hands in his pants pockets and studies me, heat blazing in his hungry pupils.

Why me? Why didn't he find someone else to write nonsense to? Give false hope to?

Caught off guard from his statement and his roaming eyes, I ask, "Wh-what are you doing here?"

He takes another step forward, his body inching closer to mine, giving me no place to retreat, thanks to my vanity counter.

"Kevin asked if I wanted a promotional spot on the show and after all the dates you went on, I thought it would be a good idea, give the program a boost."

"Your program sucks," I spit out. "And I didn't mean what you were doing at the show, but what are you doing here, in my dressing room, with the door locked?"

Keeping his eyes fixed on mine, he says, "I have a disgruntled member. I want to address the issue personally. My goal is to make all my members happy."

I fold my arms over my chest, drawing Jack's attention to the swell of my breasts for a brief second before his eyes travel to mine. "Have you been keeping tabs on me this whole time? Playing matchmaker from behind the scenes? Laughing as you set me up with men who seemed attainable but were in fact, actually not?"

"No."

I don't believe him. And he can tell.

He steps even closer. "As much as you think otherwise, I didn't get my jollies from watching you date man after man, Noely." *Only two. Only two men.*

As we're toe to toe, and his dark eyes are searing me in half, I say, "You make it sound like you're angry I gave the program two more shots. That you would rather be the man I dated, which is rubbish." Why I said that, I don't know. Maybe because I wanted to push his buttons, maybe because he's been pushing mine since the day we met, and every unfortunate meeting after that.

"Maybe I do want to date you."

"Pah!" But the minute Jack takes another step forward and places his hand on my hip, I clam up. "What, uh, what are you doing?" His tall, toned body presses against mine, towering over me with a sense of power I've never felt from a man before. I've heard of men walking in a room and owning it, but I've never experienced a man walking up to me and owning the air around me. *Owning... me.*

That's exactly what Jack is doing.

"Your hand is on me," I point out when he doesn't answer my question. "Do you realize that?" Leaning back slightly, I point at his hand that's on my hip. "See that? That's your hand, and it's on my hip." His thumb starts to stroke my hipbone and a wave of chills roll up my back and down my legs.

"I'm aware." He takes one last step forward, and in one swift movement, lifts me onto the counter of my vanity, spreads my legs, and nestles himself into me.

The mirror lights shine furiously on Jack, and even though when I look in the mirror they don't mask my flaws, and when I stare at Jack, I can't find one flaw. Not one hair out of place, not one blemish or wrinkle. He's flawless and utterly handsome.

The counter height means I'm almost eye to eye with Jack as his dark irises stare into mine. "Have you missed me, Noely?"

"Uh . . ." *Is he drunk?* I don't smell alcohol on him. Maybe he's lost is damn mind. I've heard of businessmen losing it from stress, so maybe this is a cry out for help. "Have you failed to remember why we didn't have our second date?"

"No."

"Oh, okay." I nod when both his hands circle my hips. "So, you remember breaking things off with me, having a little hissy fit about me mentioning your *first* name, and then taking off, leaving me high and dry *before* our second date? You remember that?"

"Yes."

"Okay, because from the way you're holding me, looking at me as if you're about to kiss me, it almost seems like you've forgotten that little tidbit."

"Nope, I remember." His hands roam up my arms to my shoulders, then to my back where he finds the zipper of my dress.

My breath catches in my chest, and my hands, once pressed

against the top of the counter I'm sitting on, seek and find the lapels of his jacket for support.

His fingers play with the zipper, never unzipping it, just tempting me as his legs spread mine wider, causing the skirt of my dress to rise higher up my thighs.

"Jack, wh-what are you doing?" I ask, breathlessly.

"I think you know what I'm doing, Noely."

"But why? We hate each other." *I do. I hate this man. I truly hate him.*

Don't I?

Leaning forehead, his beard scrapes my cheek when he whispers in my ear. "I don't hate you, Noely. Do you hate me?"

"Yes." The sigh in my voice reveals my lie as his scruff grazes my cheek again.

"I don't believe you." His voice is low, full of sexy promises I know he can fulfill from the way his fingers play with the little flyaway hairs on the back of my neck. While one hand plays with my hair, causing me to tilt my head back ever so slightly, exposing my neck to him, Jack's other hand presses against one of my exposed thighs, causing my legs to quiver. His nose slowly runs up the column of my neck, his hand on my thigh stroking higher until he reaches the top of my leg. His finger grazes under my lifted skirt, barely skimming the backside of my butt.

Within a few seconds and very little touching, this man has my body humming and yearning for more of his addictive touch.

"Tell me you don't want this, Noely. Tell me you want me to stop, that you don't want me to unzip your dress and suck on your gorgeous tits."

"I . . . I . . ."

Knock. Knock. "Noely, let me in."

Dylan.

My body goes stiff under Jack's assault.

Not skipping a beat, Jack presses his lips to my ear and says, "Tell her you're busy but will call her later."

"But . . ."

Gripping the back of my neck, Jack bites my earlobe and then repeats himself while his thumb caresses my skin. "Tell her you're busy and will call her later."

Well, if he insists.

Trying not to sound as breathless as I feel, I answer, "I . . . I'm busy. Call later."

"What?" Dylan asks, sounding annoyed. "I want to talk about Jack. Come on, let me in." She knocks again.

Nose running along my cheek, his body heated against mine, lips millimeters away, he says, "Tell her you'll call her later." Fingers pressed against my ass, he squeezes, hard, and then moves to the front of my dress, running his fingers along the hem until he reaches . . .

"Call you! I'll call you," I blurt, my thighs clenching together. "C-call you later."

"You're being weird."

Jacks fingers draw a line along the edge of my thong.

"For the love of God, I'll call you later."

There is a harrumph from the other side of the door and then the distinct sound of her footsteps retreating away. Thank God.

"Mmm, good job," Jack hums in my ear, causing my entire body to quake with need. His hand once again plays with the zipper of my dress, but this time, his fingers start to pull it down so slowly I might die if he doesn't go faster. "Now tell me, Noely. Tell me you don't want this, tell me to stop."

For the life of me, I can't. I want to have all the morals in the world that say, "Hey, you were mean to me, therefore you don't get to have me." But I'd be lying if a little piece of me didn't think about what this might feel like, being under Jack's strong command, feeling his body rub against mine, enter me, please me . . . *satisfy me*.

I'd be lying if I said I didn't think about it every time I've run into him, every time I studied him from afar. Seeing his unflappable stature, the way he draws attention from everyone around him, it's hard not to think about what it would feel like to be commanded by him. Because of that, I lean into his touch instead of away.

"I can't," I answer.

"You can't what? I want to hear it from those fuckable lips of yours."

While he awaits my answer, he slowly continues to drag the zipper of my dress, one tooth at a time. Goosebumps erupt all over my skin in anticipation of what this man will do to me.

I know he can ravage me. And even though he drives me crazy, that he made me feel stupid for saying his first name on TV, and that I want nothing to do with him anymore out of pride, I slip into his little world, into his arms, into the press of his mouth against my neck.

"Say it, Noely..."

CHAPTER TWENTY-NINE

NOELY

Knowing this might be a mistake I'll most likely regret, I push forward anyway, because I'm past the timeframe of saying no. My body wants this and my brain is too fogged with lust to stop my body from calling all the shots.

"I can't tell you no."

"Exactly what I wanted to hear," he rumbles into my ear as his hand slides down the rest of my zipper, exposing my back to the mirror behind me.

The zipper ends just at the waistband of my thong where his fingers are sensually caressing my lower back, teasing my skin, lighting my nerves up, and giving me a prelude of the kind of magic his fingers possess.

The heat of his mouth feels magnificent as his lips lower to my neck. For support, I grip his shoulders and lean into his kiss, reveling in this moment of total abandonment. I'm not this girl, the one who has sex in a dressing room with a man she should hate. But there's a little part of me, a naughty part, who wants to live in this fantasy, who wants to experience him. Despite how much Jack drives me crazy—and not in a good way—I can't say no to this.

Nibbling his way up my neck, his hand works its way underneath the thin strap of my thong only to scoot me closer to his body, causing my legs to spread even wider. When his mouth reaches my jaw, my lips part, a gasp rolling off my tongue when he licks the spot below my ear. Body on fire, mind dazed, I lean into his touch and allow myself to feel his fingers, the heat coming from him, the way his hands are working up my thigh and down to my ass. He's assaulting my senses and making me almost feel love-stupid, unable to process anything but the pounding between my legs, and the burning need I have for his next move.

"More," I whisper.

Not responding, he works his hands to my shoulders as his mouth finds mine, pressing, sealing our connection with his soft, pliable lips. I sigh and open my mouth to his demanding tongue that takes no time searching out mine. We connect, our mouths working each other, our tongues wrestling, tangling, licking. *God, I've wanted his kiss.*

With his mouth pressed hard against mine, he slips the top of my dress down my arms, exposing my purple lace bra. Keeping his mouth on mine, his eyes closed, he pushes my dress to my stomach. For a brief swipe, his thumbs caress my stomach and then move to my breasts where he cups them softly. I gasp into his mouth when he squeezes, my hips fling forward, connecting with his large and prominent erection.

He's so hard, so determined with his tongue, demanding more, edging me to meet his every stroke, tempting me to want more . . . and hell, do I want more. I want it all.

He moves his mouth to my jaw, then my neck, and finally my collarbone where he licks, suckles, and flicks his tongue, causing a steady thrumming to take place between my thighs. His every touch makes me wetter than before; his kisses singe me, his scent entices me, urging me to move faster and faster.

Pulling away, Jack brings his gaze to my breasts. A small, dark smirk crosses his lips as his fingers rub over my nipple through the fabric.

"Yes," I quietly moan.

"So hot," he responds, flipping the cups of my bra down and pulling out my breasts in one swift movement. Before I can say anything, his mouth sucks on one of my nipples and my hands instinctively go to his head where I grip his hair, holding him against my chest.

Wet and hot, Jack works his tongue over my nipple, flicking it and then sucking on it, hard. He repeats the process over and over, causing me to writhe beneath him until he bites down on my nipple, his teeth making their mark.

"Ah," I cry out, thrusting my hips into his, and my chest deeper into his mouth. "Yes, more."

Growling, he tends to my other breast, making the same wave of torture—biting and sucking, biting and sucking, over and over—creating a light sheen of sweat over my body. I don't think I can take the pleasure anymore, the build up, the tension.

The bundle of nerves between my legs is tightening, throbbing, thrumming for attention.

Unable to control myself, wanting so much more, I begin to undo his shirt, leaving the top few buttons clasped with his tie. My hands stumble along the buttons, fumbling horribly as I blindly try to undo his shirt while his sinful mouth continues to do naughty—*delicious*—things to my breasts.

Once I have his shirt undone except for the top button, I undo his belt buckle and pants, leaving them open but untouched. Instead, I run my hands up his stomach, surprised by every divot and tight muscle I feel beneath my fingertips. This suit, this businessman, this closed-off and prickly human has a toned and cut body, something you see on Men's Health, not underneath a starched suit.

I'm shocked, but even more turned on from the surprise.

My fingers tickle along his skin, soaking in the soft feeling and memorizing every sinew and corded muscle rippling under my touch, urging me to his pecs where I flick his nipples with my fingertips.

"Fuck," he groans against my breast, disengaging briefly to catch his breath. When he lifts his head, the stormy look in his eyes I'm so used to disappears, and I'm captured by the look of unrestrained lust. His hands go to the hem of my dress, reach up and pull down my thong, which he then tosses to the ground.

"Back pocket," he grunts. "Condom in my wallet."

Not even taking a second to think about what he's demanding —because Jack doesn't ask—I reach around him, remove the condom from his wallet, and rip the foil open. Hands still on my thighs, Jack looks at me through his lashes and says, "Put it on, slowly."

My breathing picks up as every nerve ending in my body is on fire. Mouth watering, hands shaky, I lower his black Calvin Klein boxer briefs and expose his impressive erection.

Sweet Jesus, he's huge. I glance at him and catch the small smile that plays across his lips. He's satisfied with my reaction. Prideful. Hell, I'll give him this cocky moment, because the man is packing something large. *Hallelujah*.

I roll the top of the condom over the crown of his penis and like he asked, slowly roll it down, inch by very long and thick inch until it's at the root of his cock. When I look for more direction, he spreads my legs even wider and nestles the head at my entrance.

"So fucking wet," he whispers. I'll admit I love seeing his neck muscles contract as he strains for self-control. Gripping his length, he runs the head up and down my wet slit. I prop my hands behind me, pressing my chest forward and bracing myself as my head falls back, loving the feeling of his sheathed cock running up and down my arousal, feeling how turned on I am.

"God, you're beautiful, Noely," Jack mumbles right before inserting himself inside me in one hard thrust. My eyes shoot open and a gasp falls out of my wide-open mouth. My breasts begin to bounce as Jack starts to thrust in and out, his hands gripping my thighs, pulling me in with every thrust.

There is nothing I can do but brace myself against this powerful man who seems to have lost all control as he slams into me, his balls bouncing off my ass, his fingers pressing deeply into my muscles, his sweat-coated hands never letting up on their grip.

"God, yes," I moan when he starts to bottom out, widening my legs even more.

The girth of his cock, the length of it, the way he swivels his hips in and out has me aching for more, quaking for a finish, bursting to scream his name at the top of my lungs.

"So tight, so perfect," he grunts, picking the pace up, sliding in and out with such force that my toes start to tingle and my vision starts to tunnel.

The prickling of my skin, the throb my of clit, the hammering, my stomach clenching with each thrust . . .

So hard.

So forceful.

So freaking good.

"Oh God," I whisper, my teeth biting down on my lip as my inner walls start to contract. Jack growls and swivels his hips even more. And *that* does it. My orgasm finally consumes me as everything around me fades and the euphoric feeling ripping through me takes over. Jack stills inside me. He grunts as his head falls to my shoulder, his breathing erratic, just like mine.

I don't think I've ever come that hard, and from the look in Jack's eyes when he lifts from my shoulder, neither has he.

His chest heaving, his hair disheveled from his thrusting, and his clothes out of place, he pulls out of me, disposes his condom, and quickly cleans up. Feeling shy, I put my breasts back in my bra and scoot the hem of my skirt down. But before I can pull my dress back up, Jack cups my neck and pulls me close to him for a searing kiss that reaches my toes.

Barely pulling away, he speaks softly, "Go out with me."

I must be in a serious post-coitus fog because I swear he just told me to go out with him.

"What?" I ask, leaning back to study his features.

THREE BLIND DATES

"Go out with me, Noely."

Yep, okay, I heard him correctly.

Snapping my legs shut, I push past him, right my dress, and try to zip it up with my back turned to him. When he sees me struggling, he steps behind me. His body heat hits me hard as his fingers graze across my exposed skin when he helps me with my zipper. Holding me in place, he kisses my neck gently, sending my mind into a tailspin.

Did he just *tell* me to go out with him?

But better yet, did I just have sex with him?

From the gleeful way my body is feeling, I'm going to say that's a yes. *And not just sex. Oh Lord, not just sex.* I didn't believe sex could actually be so . . . salacious. *Erotic.*

Carnal.

What the hell was I thinking?

Oh God, I look like such a slut. And don't try to tell me I don't. I know what you're thinking: look at that Noely chick. She just had sex with a guy who dropped her like a pelican with no wings—ignore the reference, I have no idea where that came from—giving in to him the minute he stuck her breast in his mouth.

Yes, this is true. I let the nipple sucking happen, but . . .

But . . .

God, there is no excuse. I'm slut-zilla, climbing dicks like skyscrapers.

Be disgusted, because I am.

"What the hell was that?" I ask, stepping away and crossing my arms over my chest.

Looking a little confused, Jack fixes his clothes and says, "Uh, from what I know, that was sex."

"I know what it . . ." I take a deep breath. "I know that was sex. I'm asking what the hell it was for?"

"Well, usually sex is for pleasure and for procreating. Since we used a condom and are not in a position to be raising a child together at the moment, I'm going to say it was for pleasure. But then again, if you thought we were procreating, I'm going to have to—"

"I know we weren't making a child. Jesus, Jack!" I fling my arms in the air. "Why the hell did you come in here? To get what you didn't get on our second date? Well, congratulations, you got it, now you can leave."

To say I'm upset with myself is an understatement. I got caught up in the moment, in the feel of his body, in the way he made me tingle from head to toe. And I'd be lying if I denied wanting that to happen. But now?

I feel stupid. *Used.*

Cheap.

"Noely," he says sternly, taking a step toward me.

I hold my hand out to stop him. "Don't, Jack. Just don't, okay?" I shake my head. *Why, Noely? Why didn't you have an ounce of self-control? Why?* "Please just leave. This was a mistake, a giant one."

"Why was it a mistake? Your body didn't think so. Neither did mine." He takes another step forward, causing me to back into the wall.

Growing angrier with him and myself by the second, I answer, "Do you not remember how we ended things? You shut me out. You were the one to call it quits over something so asinine. I said your first name, that was it, it wasn't like I said I dated Jack Valentine, the owner of *Going in Blind.*" I shake my head. "Gain a little perspective, Jack. We had a connection, something I thought could grow into a beautiful relationship, but you threw it away."

Threw me away.

Blowing out a heavy breath, I walk past him to retrieve my purse. I need to get out of this room. I need to get away from him. From this shitty, shitty day.

But before I can make my way to the couch for my purse, Jack stops me with his hand on my wrist. Eyes cast forward, head bent down, he says, "I got scared."

Not giving in, I say, "Scared isn't my problem. You should have been a man and talked to me rather than running away." Yanking my hand away from him, I say, "This was a mistake. Please don't consider it an open window to a relationship we *could* have had. Because as far as I'm concerned, the chapter about us is closed."

I hate him.

I hate myself.

I hate this.

With that, I grab my purse, fling my dressing room door open, and take off toward my car, face probably red, and a little stumble in my step from my wobbly yet angry legs.

∼

"This biscotti is to die for. Want a bite?" Dylan asks from her side of the little bistro table we're sitting at outside one of my favorite coffee shops in Malibu.

"I'm good." I spin my coffee cup in my hand, staring at the lipstick-stained opening of the to-go top. Yep, grabbed the wrong lipstick today. Not surprised since I can tell I'm wearing my underwear backwards and have my left contact lens in my right eye.

Pay attention, ladies, this is what happens to you when you let yourself get fucked senseless by someone you should stay as far away from as possible.

And you know, it's not that Jack isn't a great guy, or we don't have a lot in common, because we do. Hell, we know how to have one hell of a good time together, but it comes down to morals. And I had none yesterday. Zero.

He hurt me, made me feel so stupid, and yet when he claimed me, I couldn't resist. That's called lust, uncontrollable lust, and now, on the day after, I'm suffering with the biggest regret hangover one could ever imagine.

"Ugh, you're starting to annoy me with your *woe is me* attitude. Are you still mad about this Jack thing? I mean, it sucks, yeah, he didn't tell you he owned *Going in Blind*, and yet, that might have been deceitful, but at this point, who cares? You've moved past him."

Oh, if she only knew.

"Which reminds me, are you really not going to ask for another date?"

I shake my head. "No, not after knowing Jack owns the place. I'm sure he's keeping tabs on me. Also, the first date is a given, the second is acceptable, because not everyone hits it off on their first blind date. The third date is pushing my luck, and the fourth would be downright desperate. I can't show my face there again. It would be completely humiliating."

"They see so many people every day. I don't think they'd remember you." *She is so wrong.* Danny saw the mess I was on my date with Hayden. Veronica probably did too. I have lost every ounce of respect for myself, so I can't expect it from them.

"They know me by name there." Dylan snorts, which should piss me off, but at this point, I've given up caring. "I know this is going to sound cliché from a scorned woman in my position, but I'm done with men."

Dylan grandiosely rolls her eyes, making a giant spectacle out of her response. "Oh please, you're not done with men. You say that, and just watch, you're going to fall for a man who accidentally is plopped on your lap. Happens in all the movies. The heroine swears off men, and then all of a sudden, BAM, she's married."

"That's not going to happen here. I promise. I think I'm cursed. I had three wonderful men I could have dated and none of them worked out." *None of them wanted me. For the long-term.*

"Maybe you didn't brush your teeth enough." Dylan shrugs her shoulder and sticks the rest of her biscotti in her mouth.

"What?" My brow creases. "What does that have to do with anything we're talking about?"

Dylan flicks her front tooth with her fingernail. "You have a poppy seed stuck in your tooth." In an instant, I'm running my tongue over my tooth. "Maybe you had food in your teeth while eating your fancy meals with these men. That could have been a real turn off."

I shake my head. "I don't know why I talk to you." I press my palm to my forehead, my elbow leaning on the table. "It wasn't because of something in my teeth. Believe me, I didn't have anything in my teeth."

"How do you know? You didn't know about the poppy seed. Could have been food in the teeth."

"It wasn't food in the teeth," I shout, drawing attention from the people around us. "Everything just seemed so off when I was with each guy. Like with Jack, something so benign threw him for a loop. Beck, he was so amazing—"

"So hot," Dylan points out with a smile.

"Yes, so hot, but his reserve put a huge line in the road between us. And then Hayden."

"Ugh, that poor bastard."

"Still hung up on an old relationship." I take a sip of my coffee. "And what sucks is that honestly, they all seemed so perfect for me, but not ready for what I wanted."

Dylan wistfully shakes her head. "The Suit, The Rebel, and The Jock. *If* you had to choose, given they were free of all demons, who would you choose?"

I press my lips together, trying to compare them in my head, which I'm learning is an impossible feat.

"I have no idea, honestly. They were different in their own way but could fit easily into my life . . . into my heart."

Could they, though? Fit into my heart and life?

Would I really have been able to fit into theirs?

Jack's? No. He made that clear. Case closed. Beck's? No. He was so reticent to offer anything of substance to know if I'd fit. And Hayden's? With my schedule and his traveling, would we have fit together? If I add up how much time I actually spent with each guy, did I really have enough information to believe in a happily ever after with any of them? Yes, the blind date idea can work wonders when you're matched with someone. But it takes intentional time to work out the glitches, to see the future, to believe in long-wanted possibilities. I sigh and press my head against the table. "This is stupid."

In her absentmindedly motherly way, Dylan pats my head and strokes my hair. "There, there. If you want, Chad has a few accountant buddies who rock the numbers well, know Excel formulas by heart, and have a steady collection of calculators, something rather riveting to see in person. The evolution of the little counting machines is fascinating. We can set you up with one of them. Who knows? Short-sleeved plaid shirts might be exactly what you're looking for."

Yeah, that's a big fat no.

I shake my head, no, unable to stomach the thought of going out with one other man at this point. Playing the get-to-know-you game, asking the same damn questions over and over again? No, thank you. I'll pass. It's time to accept my reality.

I'm joining the ranks of the single ladies, by far the safest choice for my heart.

CHAPTER THIRTY

NOELY

"Press the button! Press the button!" I shout at the TV, my mouth full of popcorn, my feet dressed in fluffy socks, and my body draped in an oversized T-shirt that covers my knees and elbows. "Come on!" I bounce on my sofa, praying one of the coaches from *The Voice* presses their button for the girl who's singing her heart out on stage.

I don't get to watch much TV during the weekdays, so I make sure to record my favorite shows and binge watch on Sundays. It's the perfect way to be lazy and forget about the world around me. It's been a little over a week since my dressing room mishap, and I'm still trying to find ways to distract myself.

Just as the beautiful-voiced girl finishes her song, Adam Levine presses his button. The crowd goes wild, the girl starts to cry, and I feel myself getting choked up.

"That's right, Adam, you sexy beast. You press that button." I toss a piece of popcorn at the TV when they show Blake Shelton. "Moron," I mutter just as my phone beeps at me with a notification.

I glance over at my phone on the arm of my navy-blue sofa and see a notification from the *GiB* app; I have a message.

What?

Picking up my phone, I study the notification for a few seconds, as if I'm waiting for it to telepathically tell me what it says.

Surely I wasn't set up with another date? Is Jack messing around with me? Did Hayden change his mind? Can you tell I might be still holding out for him? Just a little?

Feeling curious and a little self-destructive, I open the app. Expecting to see a handle I know like WindsorKnot or even RebelWithACause, I'm surprised when there is a completely new message waiting for me from a VERY familiar handle.

NY152.

I know this handle. I know it very well, and I know the story it belongs to, or movie per se.

Noely,
Don't you love Malibu in the fall? It makes me want to buy a bouquet of newly sharpened pencils. Don't you agree?

Me

Errr . . .

What kind of message is that? Who loves Malibu in the—

And then it clicks.

Duh.

It's the first email Tom Hanks sends in *You've Got Mail.*

Joe Fox writes Kathleen Kelly and says, "Don't you love New York in the fall? It makes me want to buy a bouquet of newly sharpened pencils."

NY152 is Joe Fox's handle in the movie . . .

Confused, intrigued, and shamelessly giddy, I cautiously write back.

. . .

THREE BLIND DATES

NY152,
Charming, but confusing. Who are you?
Noely

I sit back on my sofa, wishing this app worked more like a text, so I could see if they were typing back. The only thing that indicates they might be reading my note is the green circle next to their name, which shows that they're logged into the app.

I turn my attention to *The Voice* just when my phone beeps with another message. Pausing the show, I open the app again and read,

Noely,
What if I were to tell you I could possibly be The Suit, The Rebel, or The Jock? Would you be interested in seeing one of them again? Maybe give one of them a second chance? Or have you written them all off?
Me

Stunned, I lean back on my sofa, staring at the message in front of me. Is this a joke? Or is this real? Could this just be a viewer? No, because they wouldn't have my handle. The only ones who have my *Going in Blind* handle would be the three men I dated. And they're the ones who know about my *You've Got Mail* obsession. I shared my obsession with all of them, and I watched the movie with Hayden.

Twisting my lips to the side, I contemplate my answer. Could I give any of them a second chance? Well, I know who I won't want to give a second chance to. But Hayden and Beck? Hell, possibly. Beck told me to call him if things didn't work out. Did he catch the show when I said nothing happened with The Jock? He was very intense and handsy at the hockey game.

What about Hayden? He was always very gentle and slow when it came to our relationship because another girl still owned his heart. If they're out of the picture now, why wouldn't he simply message me that? Say he is ready? He did talk a lot about Joe Fox and his swagger. Thinking back to our conversations, hell, he said he'd woo me Joe Fox style. Is it Hayden? And would I want to give him a second chance?

I *think* I would . . .

But, what if it isn't Hayden?

What if it's Jack? The alpha suit that thinks he can get what he wants. I've endured a lifetime of Jack Valentine already. Could I risk putting myself out there one more time in the off chance it's neither Hayden or Beck, but Jack?

I gnaw on the side of my cheek, thinking over my options. Is the possibility of finding my forever worth the heartache of things not working out again?

My little romantic heart is saying yes. *What is love without risk?* I know I was just swearing off men, but maybe, just maybe this could be it. I've admitted to having an intimate connection with each man, it wouldn't be like I was starting from ground zero, but more like picking up where we left off.

Gaining more and more confidence with each internal thought, I type a message back.

NY152,
A second chance? Hmm . . . could be possible, but first I need to ask you, who are you? The Suit, The Rebel, or The Jock?
Noely

. . .

THREE BLIND DATES

It doesn't take him long to reply back.

Noely,
    Where's the fun in that? I couldn't possibly give away my identity just yet. All in good time, beautiful.
Me

Y152,
    Are you . . . You've Got Mail-ing me?
Noely

Noely,
    Indeed I am. Until tomorrow, have a good night, beautiful.
Me

Staring at my phone, feeling slightly breathless and definitely restless, I'm amazed. Which man is *now* determined to . . . woo me?
  But for the life of me, I can't pinpoint the *who*, so instead of trying to solve the puzzle, for the first time, I'm going to go along for the ride.

CHAPTER THIRTY-ONE

NOELY

N*oely,*
Confession: I spent an entire weekend watching random documentaries on Netflix. From Blackfish to Twinsters, to The Propaganda Game. But in all honesty, my favorite documentary was easily I Know That Voice. There's something about voice acting that intrigued me, something I always thought I could possibly be good at. A dream come true would be to have a cameo on The Simpsons or in some Seth McFarlan production. Bonus dream points if the character looks like me.
Me

N*Y152,*
Since I don't really know who this is, you've thrown me for a loop, because between the three men I went out with, I can't imagine any of them wanting to be a voice actor, let alone it being their dream to have a cameo on an animated

298

show. As I sit here, trying to determine who you might be, not one of you is coming to mind.
  Color me confused.
  Noely

Noely,
  Maybe stop trying to guess who I am. Instead, get to know me on a different level. This is your chance to learn to love my soul rather than the person you've perceived me to be.
  And for what it's worth, I think with your voice inflections and charisma, you could rock it as a voice actor.
  Me

NY152,
  Learn to love your soul, huh? Those are some strong words, dropping the L word so early on in the game, but I'll take you up on your challenge.
  Voice acting would never be my thing. I think I would feel silly trying to act into a microphone, but if I was offered a cameo on Days of Our Lives, now that's something I would jump on before they could finish offering me the gig. But one requirement I have would be a good drink toss to someone's face. I've always wanted to throw a drink in someone's face out of pure anger.
  Noely

Noely,
  I'm currently taking notes to never truly piss you off. Drink up the nose isn't something I'm fond of. Believe it or not, I've had a drink tossed in my direction and with the right angle and liquid, you can do some real nostril damage.

Maybe I can show you one day. I can throw a Bloody Mary up your nose, see if you like it.
   Me

NY152,
   A Bloody Mary? That's what you want to toss at me? A chunky, peppery, hot-saucy Bloody Mary? Why on earth is that the drink you would choose when trying to woo me? Believe it or not, I'm not looking for a celery stick to nail me between the eyes.
   Noely

Noely,
   Be glad I didn't suggest one of those fruity drinks with an umbrella. The result of that kind of drink toss would probably land you in the hospital with an eye patch dangling in your future. A Bloody Mary is tame compared to pineapple umbrella drink in the face. Trust me, you're getting off easy.
   Me

NY152,
   It's greatly concerning how much you know about drinks to faces. I'm starting to question your vast knowledge on the topic. Do I need to worry? Should I have a Bloody Mary on hand whenever I'm around you, just in case I need to be ready for a good dousing to your face?
   Noely

Noely,
   I would like to say leave the Bloody Mary at home, but then again, who am I to deny someone's request of a

conceal and carry Bloody Mary? I'll be honest, load that purse up, you never know when you need to douse someone's nostrils with a vodka-soaked nutritional breakfast. I just hope I'm not on the receiving end of your tomato cocktail.
Me

∽

"Ughhhh, this one is too heavy. Aunt Noely, please help me." Turning toward Chloe, I eye the pumpkin she's trying to pick up. "Sweetie, first of all, that's a fake pumpkin. Second of all, it's nailed into the concrete, so you can't have that one."

"But you said any pumpkin."

"I did, but I meant any real pumpkin."

Chloe eyes the nailed-down pumpkin then puts her hand on her hip. "Semantics!" she yells, flinging her arms in the air and storming off toward the array of already-picked pumpkins next to a grandstand where an old folk singer is strumming his guitar, singing a country-esque tune into a microphone. What I'm confused about is how a five-year-old knows how to use the word semantics.

"Got to love that ocean breeze," Alex says next to me, taking a deep breath. A pumpkin patch on the beach doesn't really scream fall, but that's Malibu for you.

"Your daughter just tried to take the fake pumpkin over there that belongs to the giant Cinderella carriage."

Alex takes in the pumpkin and brings his cup of hot apple cider to his mouth. Mind you, it's eighty degrees out with a light breeze. "Glad she's thinking big. And you should have encouraged her. I would have loved to tire her out a little more, trying to unhinge that pumpkin from the cement."

"You're pathetic." I look around. "Where's Lauren?"

Alex nods to the side. "Playing giant chess with that old man over there. She's in the zone and asked not to be bothered."

Why am I not surprised? Propping my feet on the bench of the picnic table I'm sitting on, I rest my arms on my legs and take in the families milling about the beach, picking at pumpkins, playing yard games, building sand castles—so weird—and enjoying a nice hot cup of apple cider.

Don't you love Malibu in the fall?

I chuckle to myself; there is no difference from summer Malibu to fall Malibu except for the abundance of pumpkin-spice-flavored everything.

Which reminds me . . .

"I'm going to get a pumpkin-spice muffin. Do you want anything?"

"Oh, grab half a dozen, we can all partake in a little fall delight," Alex chimes like a douche.

Patting my brother on the shoulder, I start to walk away and say, "Maybe lay off on waxing your balls for a bit; you're starting to sound like a lady."

"Bare balls are just as enjoyable as a bare vagina."

Why do I even bother? I take off before he can go into detail about his . . . bare balls.

Making my way toward the food truck, I dig my sandal-covered feet through the sand, past Lauren who seems to be trash-talking an old man, and right in line where I consider my muffin options. Should I go with six pumpkin-spice, or a variety—

"Why hello there, Noely."

My eyes squeeze shut and for the life of me, I can't figure out why I keep running into this man, why the universe insists upon him continuing to show up in my life. I'd never seen him before our first date.

Coincidental? Or are the dating gods drunk and having way too much inebriated fun?

Turning around, trying to be polite, I say, "Jack, good to see you."

When I look into his eyes, they are full of humor, and what seems like adoration. Odd.

But what is even more odd is, this is the first time I'm seeing

Jack Valentine in anything but a suit. Instead of his classic three-piece set with accompanied Windsor knot, he's sporting a pair of dark wash jeans, and a very simple white polo that clings sexily to his built and broad chest. *I've touched that chest. That gorgeous, muscled . . . STOP.* He's wearing sandals, SANDALS, and his beard almost looks scraggly, like he decided to not trim the sides this morning, giving him an infinite amount of sex appeal.

Damn men and they're irresistible facial hair.

Smiling, those beautiful dark eyes sparkling with mirth, he nods at the truck and asks, "Whatcha getting?"

Whatcha? Did The Suit, Mr. Fancy Pants, just say "whatcha getting?" What happened to being prim and proper?

"Muffins," I almost shout, trying to check my voice level to a normal pitch. Looking around, I ask, "What are you doing here? Don't you think a single man at a family pumpkin patch full of children looks weird?"

Chuckling, looking lighter than ever, he says, "I'm here with my sister and her two munchkins. What about you? Single lady in a pumpkin patch doesn't scream normal either."

"My brother and sister-in-law invited me. Their five-year-old is kind of obsessed with me," I joke.

"I don't blame her." Jack's lips turn into one of his gorgeous smirks.

Feeling uneasy, I skid my foot on the ground. "Well, I guess I'll get back to my muffins." Turning around, I face the line that's five people deep in front of me. Out of all the times for the line to be super slow and long, it has to be now, with Jack's eyes burning a hole in my back.

Standing still, eyes fixated on everything BUT the man behind me, I bite on the side of my lip, skin prickling with awareness. Could this be anymore awkward?

"You know, you can talk to me," Jack whispers, his head inches from mine. My spine straightens from his proximity, and my shoulders tense.

"I'm okay waiting in silence," I answer without turning toward him.

Stepping up next to me, Jack says, "Still mad?" I should have known I couldn't get away with that question.

My nostrils flare and I allow him to bait me. Facing him, I say, "Not mad, just not interested. You had your chance, Jack."

"Who says I want another chance? I only want to be friends."

He wants to be friends? Is he trying to get on my good graces? Could he be NY152? Thinking over my conversations with NY152, I decide to test him. If I'm going to have to stand in line with him, then I can make the most of it at least.

"Why do you want to be friends?" I ask skeptically.

He shrugs, hands in pockets, his triceps flexing with each movement he makes. "I like you, Noely. You make me smile and are easy to talk to. I can see my chance at being with you has slipped past me, but maybe we could be friends."

Is he for real right now? I feel like I don't even recognize this man, this subdued, sweet, and very casual man. He's a far cry from the domineering alpha in a dark suit. I'm caught off guard to be honest.

Mulling it over, I decide not to answer him. "What's your favorite brunch drink?"

Confused, brow pinched together, Jack asks, "What?"

"Let's say you're out to brunch with your fancy folk, you know, the other suits in your life—"

"Businessmen don't do brunch."

Exasperated, I say, "Fine, you're on a date—"

"Is it with you?"

"What?" I shake my head. "No, stop interrupting me."

"Well, if the date is with you, that changes things. I'd want to impress you so my brunch choices wouldn't be the same."

Hand on hip, I answer, "You're frustrating, you know that?" He shrugs and gives me a boyish smile. "You are not on a date with me. How about with your sister? That should be easy to answer."

He nods for me to continue, thank God. "Okay, so you're sitting down for brunch with your sister and you think, hey, wouldn't it be great if we got drinks? She agrees, so you pick your favorite breakfast drink . . . alcoholic breakfast drink. What do you choose?"

Looking more confused than ever, he asks, "What does this have to do with anything? Is this an initiation question you ask anyone who wants to be friends with you?"

"Just answer the damn question."

"Umm . . ." He pauses, still looking at me as if I'm crazy. Come on, just say it, just say Bloody Mary. If he says Bloody Mary, I know it's him, I'll know he's NY152. "I guess it's never too early for a tequila sunrise."

Blowing out a frustrated breath, I fold my arms over my chest and turn away from him.

"Was that not the right answer? Does this mean we're not friends now? Was the right answer mimosa since that's what you drink on the show? Okay, I change my answer to mimosa."

"You can't change your answer; you've already put it out there." Frustrated and confused by the change in Jack, his more easygoing attitude, I say, "Can we just get our muffins and part ways? I don't—"

Before I can finish my sentence, Jack is hauling me out of line —I was three people away from the front, damn it—and taking me behind a storage unit.

"Hey, they're not going to give me my spot in line back." I look behind me right before he closes me off to the public.

"I'll get you muffins after this, I just . . ." He blows out a frustrated breath as he runs his hand down his face. "I just need to get something off my chest, okay?"

"Demanding. There's the Jack Valentine I know."

Not taking my goading, he says, "I was burned by a girlfriend in the past. My fiancée actually." I straighten up once Jack's face blanches. "When I told you I was scared the other day, I meant it. I'm very protective of my personal life and my family because it was once dragged through the mud by my ex, selling out to my competitors, giving them personal information and key business decisions that hurt not only me, but also my family. We've recovered but I was scarred by that." He grips the back of his neck and I watch his bicep bulge against the tight sleeve of his polo. "When you said my name on TV, I freaked out. Am I proud of what I did? No, not in the slightest. I truly regret what I did, because every time I run into you, I see the beautifully intelligent and dynamic woman I foolishly let slip from my grasp." My breathing hitches in my chest, and my mouth goes dry. "I know maybe in a different world, another chapter, we could have shared the kind of relationship I'm striving for, but I'm not blind to see I've burned my bridge where you're concerned."

"Th-then what are you looking for?" I ask, feeling breathless, a little unsure, and regretful for what could have been.

Smiling sadly, Jack grips my hand in his and plays with my fingers. "I guess I want to try to build that bridge with friendship. I know that's asking a lot, but I want us to be civil when we see each other. Even though you pissed off is hot, I would rather have a conversation with you than watch your fine ass stomp away in frustration."

This man can't be real. He's so up and down, so hot and cold, and now he wants to be friends. Legit friends. Is that something I can do?

The man before me is gorgeous. Knowing how attracted to him I am, I don't think I can be friends. But from the desperate look in his eyes, the pleading coming from the chocolate pools, I find myself nodding.

"We can be friends."

And then it happens. That devastating smile comes to life, causing my heart to skip a beat.

"Yeah?" I nod while swallowing hard. "Sounds good." Looking over my shoulder, he nods and says, "Line is almost gone, I'll get us some muffins."

With a tip of my chin, he takes off, just like that, as if we're in elementary school, confirming friendship and then taking off. I don't know, but for some reason I expected more, like rules, or what to anticipate when it comes to being his friend, but instead, I'm left wondering what the hell this is all about.

When I finally gather my thoughts together, Jack is walking toward me, two bakery boxes in hand. "Here, I got you six pumpkin-spice muffins and a variety for the other six. Try the cheesecake, it's my favorite." With a wink, he hands me the box and says, "See you around, *friend*."

Uhh . . . what the hell?

CHAPTER THIRTY-TWO

NOELY

"It's totally Jack." Dylan tips a bag of Fritos into her mouth and talks while chewing. "It's obvious." She rolls her eyes. "He wants to be your friend? Yeah, right. He's totally Joe Fox-ing you right now. Remember in *You've Got Mail* when Joe Fox decides to turn a new leaf after he breaks up with that horrid woman? Where he has a serious talk with his dad, and realizes he wants to be happy and the only one who can do that is Kathleen Kelly?" Dylan points at me and then licks her fingers. "You're sooooo Kathleen Kelly, and he's trying to make things right again. Hello, Captain Obvious."

The thought has crossed my mind, but when I mentioned breakfast drinks there was not even the slightest hint of recognition. He's either a really good actor, or he's not NY152.

"I don't know, Dylan. Yes, Jack's actions are rather weird and suspicious, but I'm not convinced he's NY152."

"Oh come on, who do you think it is? Beck? He's too busy humping girls on heavy machinery to spend his time wooing you over a dating app. Hayden, well . . . hell, I kind of wish it was him, but I have an inkling it isn't."

THREE BLIND DATES

"Yeah, is that the same inkling that told you to eat a bag of Fritos after our workout or you might have a bad rest of your day?"

"As a matter of fact, it is." Dylan crumbles her chip bag and tosses it into the trash can next to her. "I know you want it to be Beck or Hayden, but I really think it's Jack." She takes a sip of her orange soda and wiggles her fingers at me. "Let me see the messages once more."

"No." I stand and toss my empty kale smoothie in the trash. "I don't want to listen to you dissect the messages again. You make no sense when you do that. Blood Mary isn't code word for something else."

"You never know until you fully dissect everything."

I roll my eyes and wave to my friend. "See you tomorrow morning." When I walk away, I pull my phone from my bag and light up the screen to see there is a new notification. Giddy, I go to open it when I run right into a wall . . . a muscular wall.

Flying backward, my phone dropping to the ground, my ass joining it, I look up a little dazed to see Hayden hovering over me.

"Shit, I'm sorry, Noely. I didn't see you there." He fumbles around, pocketing his phone quickly and helping me to my feet while picking up my phone as well.

Once standing, he hands me my phone and squats to look me in the eyes. "Are you okay? I'm so sorry, I guess we were both kind of buried in our phones."

"I guess so." I laugh nervously. "What are you doing here? Don't the Quakes have their own gym?"

"They do." Hayden chuckles. "But there is an acupuncturist here that came highly recommended. Normally she would come to the sports training facility but she has a commitment tonight and I need treatment like yesterday, so she said if I could make the drive, she could get me in."

"Is it Patricia?"

"That's her. Have you worked with her before?"

I shake my head. "No, but Dylan swears by her. What's bothering you?"

"Right shoulder blade and rotator cuff. It's been stiff for days, and I haven't been able to shake the pain. I'm hoping this gets me on the right track." Hayden grips his shoulder as he speaks.

"Me too. We need you out there on the ice." I smile at him, which in return makes him smile. So damn sweet.

"I've missed you, Noely. That smile of yours is addictive."

Turning my phone over and over in my hand, I'm tempted to ask him. The question is on the tip of my tongue but the fear of being disappointed makes me hesitate.

"I've missed you, too. Seems like you're doing well though, a winning record and holding the most goals on the team so far. I would say you're killing it."

"They guys have been awesome to work with, that's for sure."

"Haydeeeeeen!" Dylan says, walking toward us with her gym bag in hand, phone in the other. "Look at you, all meaty and muscley. What are you doing here?"

"He has an appointment with Patricia for acupuncture," I answer for him, my nerves spiking with the presence of Dylan. She has a loose tongue and will say anything without thinking. I can only imagine—

"Do you like Bloody Marys, Hayden?" Dylan asks, leaning against the wall of the hallway, twirling her hair, looking innocent. *I know* her intentions are the least bit innocent.

Politely, Hayden smirks at Dylan and nods. "Love them." Facing me, he checks his watch. "I hate to be rude, but I better get going. Ladies, it's been great seeing you again." He presses his hand on my arm and softly says, "Take care, Noely."

With a parting look, he heads toward the acupuncture room, leaving me with a pounding heart, a tingling sensation on my arm, and a wandering mind.

Is it him?

"Doesn't he have a game tonight?" Dylan asks, completely ignoring the Bloody Mary comment along with the little glances he shot my way.

"Not until seven."

"Wow, he must really need the acupuncture." Twisting off the wall, she walks toward the exit. I chase after her and yank on her shoulder so she has to face me.

"Are you just going to ignore his Bloody Mary comment, or the way his body language was clearly angled and interested in me?"

"It's not him," Dylan says, brushing me off.

"Why would he say Bloody Mary then?"

"Maybe because he has horrible taste buds and really likes them."

"Dylan, that can't just be a coincidence."

Placing her hands on my shoulders, she levels with me. "Think what you want, but it's not him, I know it's not."

"Just like when you KNEW Tom Brady was going to break his leg last season, and he never did. That was the biggest upset you could have predicted."

"Break a leg has many meanings. I don't have to defend myself here. I know it's not him."

"Think what you want, but I think it's Hayden. NY152 fits the bill for Hayden. Sweet, funny, and super hot with his words. Plus . . . Bloody Marys."

Dylan rolls her eyes and shifts the strap of her bag on her shoulder. "Okay, but when it's not him, don't make me tell you I told you so."

~

I'm finally home after the gym, Dylan's predictions, running errands, and the grocery store where I might have gotten myself a gallon of strawberry ice cream and chocolate shell syrup. It goes against everything my trainer has put on my food chart for the week, but now I don't care. I need ice cream. I need ALL the ice cream.

Settled on my couch, I flip the TV to the Quakes game, bring my bowl of ice cream to one of my knees, and hold my phone in the other. I haven't had a chance to look at my message yet, so I'm dying to see what's waiting for me.

There are two messages.

Noely,
I just settled into my new house and I need to make an announcement; decorating isn't my strong suit. What's with all the patterns, textures, colors, and matching but not matching? I went to the store today to get some curtains and wound up buying a spatula, wicker basket, and a candle that smells like leather. Weird thing is, I don't like wicker.

Do you think I can get away with decorating with the basket, spatula, and candle and call it a day?

Desperately awaiting your opinion.

Me

New home . . . hmm. Hayden was looking for a place. Did he finally find a place? That would make the most sense.

Opening up the next message, I read that one as well.

Noely,
I read something today about wasp spray and how every household should carry a bottle in their nightstand in case someone breaks into their house. Compared to Mace, wasp spray has a farther, more accurate stream for attacking purposes. And clearly, wasp spray to the face doesn't seem like a walk in the park to me. Do you have wasp spray in your nightstand . . . among other things?

Don't worry if you don't. I had five cans sent to the studio for you. When you spray someone in the face with it, think of

me. But let's hope you don't ever have to spray someone, unless they're annoying, then spray the shit out of them.
Me

Chuckling to myself, I type out a response.

NY152,
First of all, congratulations on the house. That's amazing and I'm pretty sure decorating with a spatula, wicker basket, and candle is the new style. So, rock it.
As for the wasp spray, I can't say that I've been so lucky to have such a weapon at my disposal, or have I had it in my nightstand for that matter, but there are other things in there . . .
It's a shame you're having the wasp spray delivered—which won't be hard to explain at all when it shows up—because it would have been nice to see you deliver it to me personally. See what I'm trying to say here?
Noely

Noely,
Getting impatient I see. All in good time. I have to make sure you're truly, madly in love with me before I show myself. What if we meet up, like in *You've Got Mail*, in the middle of a garden, and you see me turn a corner and think, oh crap . . . him. That's not a risk I'm willing to take. I want you to be like Kathleen Kelly when she cries and says, "I wanted it to be you. I wanted it to be you so badly."
Until I think you're truly ready, I'm going to wait patiently and read your words.

Me

NY152,
    Trying to make my heart pitter-patter? Well, you're doing a good job at it. Now if only you would do it in person, but I can see where you want to be utterly confident. You know there was always something wrong with each date I went on. Sorry to say but The Suit, The Rebel, and The Jock were not perfect, despite what they might think.
Noely

I send my message, smiling to myself. I'm totally goading him, wanting to see his reaction. If it were Jack or Beck, I could see them countering their response with an over confident "yeah, right," but Hayden, he's more sensitive, so I could see him answering...

Wait a minute.

I focus on the game in front of me and turn up the volume. Leaning forward, I search for...

"Son of a bitch," I whisper just as my phone dings with a message from NY152.

Hayden skates across the ice, handling the puck with ease past defenders and passing it off to Sven who takes a shot but misses, the puck reflected off the shoulder pad of the goalie.

And then there were two...

I open up the message from NY152

Noely,
    Something wrong with each date? Doubtful when it comes to ours. Hell, I keep thinking about our first date and how you so easily captivated me. You're thinking about three

dates. *I have some competition. Don't worry. I'm up for the challenge.*
   Me

I twist my lips to the side. "Nice try, NY152," I say in a smarmy voice. Unless Hayden is messaging me and skating at the same time, which doesn't seem to be the case since both hands are on his stick right now, I'm going to rule out him being a possibility.

Huh, and I really thought it could have been him.

And what's weird is, I'm not devastated it isn't. I never felt he was really mine to start with. Not his heart, anyway.

That leaves The Suit and The Rebel, Jack and Beck. I have no idea or even small inkling who NY152 is, but I might as well point out his slip-up.

NY152,
   I would say I'm thinking more about two dates right now. I applaud your attempt to keep your identity hidden, but I must say, you've made a mistake. You see, I said on the show I was dating a jock, I didn't say what sport, but I will tell you this, as I talk to you, I'm watching him skate around on the ice right now . . . on TV.

So your little mystery is down to two. It's just between The Suit and The Rebel now. Are you getting nervous?
   Noely

Not even trying to hide it, he responds within minutes.

Noely,
   Well, damn. I guess I'm losing my touch. I've gotten

too relaxed. You're keeping me on my toes. I promise, I won't have another slip-up.

Me

NY152,
Another slip-up would actually make my day.

Noely

CHAPTER THIRTY-THREE

NOELY

Me
Noely,
Coffee, how do you take it?

NY152,
With lots of chocolate. I can't stand the bitter taste of coffee but I crave the caffeine. Dunkin' Donuts makes a chocolate donut-flavored coffee that I dump half a packet of sugar-free hot cocoa into. I give it a good stir and voila, delicious coffee. You should try it.
Noely

Noely,
(Attached: picture of Dunkin' Donuts Chocolate Glazed Donut coffee mix and sugar-free hot cocoa mix)
I'm going in this morning. This better be good. Have a good day, beautiful. I'll be catching the show this morning.

Me

I smirk to myself just in time for Dylan to walk into my dressing room with a basket under her arm and an annoyed look on her face.

"Honestly, first it's wasp spray—which I still don't get—and now it's coffee and hot cocoa. What's it going to be next? If he's taking requests, can you please request some of that delicious biscotti, or maybe some fudge? Oooooo, how about a pie? Mama wants some pie. Pumpkin, mmm, no." She shakes her head, finger to chin. "Apple, ask for some apple pie." The basket she carried into my dressing room is full to the brim of my favorite morning drink. This guy . . . he's wooing, he's wooing hard.

"I'm not going to ask for pie."

"Oh come on, I should get something out of this. Chad burped in my face this morning, reminding me how much romance I really need."

"Maybe you need to take that up with Chad." I take one last glance in the mirror, fluff my hair, and go to my door. "Come on, we have a show to do."

Walking through the hallway, Dylan following behind me, I accept a line-up from one of the production assistants and look it over. We have a cooking segment today, we're making apple fritters —to say I'm excited about that is an understatement. I've been smelling those all morning—and we'll also be talking about ways to decorate your house for fall on a budget. Looks like we're going to have a good show.

"Hey, wait up." Dylan hobbles behind me. I can hear her clunking about, her shoes echoing in the hallway. "If you don't ask for pie, how about some gummy worms?"

"I'm not asking for gummy—"

I stop mid-sentence, my hands at my side, my body stiffening from the sight in front of me.

Beck is standing next to Kevin, and they're shaking hands.

THREE BLIND DATES

When Beck turns in my direction, a huge, devastating smile crosses his face.

Dylan rams into my back and she muffles behind me. "What the hell are you doing?"

Speaking from the side of my mouth, watching Beck carefully say his goodbye, his body pointing toward me, I say, "Dylan, where did you get that basket? Did someone drop it off?"

"Uh, a production assistant gave it to me to give to you. I have no idea who dropped it off. Why?"

"The Rebel is here, and he's walking in my direction."

"What?" Dylan starts hopping up and down, head looking over my shoulder, trying to get a better look. "The humper is here? Oh my God, is he that gorgeous guy in the leather jacket?"

"That would be him."

His smirk lights up the path toward me, and I can do nothing but stare when he stands before me, bright-eyed and happy to see me.

"Hey, Sassy. You look beautiful as always." He leans forward and kisses my cheek. His hand lingers on my arm, even when he puts a little distance between us.

"Beck, hey." I'm having a hard time disguising my surprise. "What are you doing here?"

"One of the charities I work on is Feast for Families and with Thanksgiving coming up, I wanted to make sure we secured some promotional spots to spread the word. Last year we served over one hundred fifty families, so I'm gunning for two hundred this year."

"Wow, that's amazing."

"There's a lot you don't know about me." *Maybe because you never opened up to me.*

Dylan takes that moment to butt in. Sticking her hand out, she says, "Hi, I'm Dylan, Noely's co-host and best friend. I think it was very brave of you to put yourself out there and hump my friend on the first date." She gives him a small clap. "Well done, well done."

Eyebrow raised and a cocky smile on his face, Beck nods at me.

"Told her about our first date? Don't blame you. I haven't been able to stop thinking about it either."

Assessing him, Dylan points her finger up and down Beck's body. "This is dangerous right here. No wonder you called him The Rebel. He has trouble written all over him."

"Only the best kind of trouble," Beck responds

"Dylan, Noely, on set, please. We're on in thirty."

Smiling and slightly nervous, I scoot past Beck and say, "Nice seeing you."

I attempt to walk past him, but his hand grips my elbow. Facing the other direction, he speaks softly. "I'm sticking around. I'll see you after the show."

"Oh wonderful. Maybe you can take your shirt off for us during commercial break." Dylan does a little jig toward the couches while I roll my eyes.

"No need to take your shirt off during commercial break," I reassure him.

"It's not something I'm opposed to." With a parting wink, he releases my elbow.

Oh Christ, I don't know how much more of this I can take.

~

That was the longest show of my life. Not only did it feel like it droned on forever, but every time I looked at camera one, which was almost the entire show, I could see Beck, standing right behind, his eyes relentless with their pursuit. The perspiring that happened, the stumbles I made while reading the teleprompter, the fumbling I did when handling the Thanksgiving decorations we played around with, it was all because of one man who didn't stop staring at me.

"Great show," Dylan says, removing her mic. "I really liked it when you spilled that orange glitter everywhere, I'll be picking that out of my nostrils for weeks. So, thank you."

There was a lot of fumbling . . . unfortunately.

"Sorry. I was a little off today."

"A little off? You said cornuco-cupine two times before you realized you were trying to say cornucopia."

"It's a hard word to say," I answer, sheepishly.

"Do you think it's him? Is that why you're nervous?"

I let out a long breath. My eyes catch Beck's quickly before he turns back to his phone, his fingers typing away. "I still don't know. Is it a coincidence that I received a basket of coffee and cocoa this morning, the same day Beck shows up to talk about a spot with Kevin? I mean, it's all too coincidental, you know?"

"It does seem awfully convenient. Why don't you just ask him?"

"What?" I shake my head. "No way. What if he isn't NY152? That would be humiliating."

Dylan sighs and leans back on the couch. "Yeah, that would be pretty humiliating."

"Hey, good show," Beck says, stepping onto the set, looking around, taking in the low-hanging set lights and fake Malibu background behind us.

"You're only saying that to be nice." I brush the skirt of my dress over my legs, trying to busy myself. "I was a train wreck today."

Beck shrugs. "My favorite was when you took a bite of the fritter and a huge piece came off, so you decided to shove the whole thing in your mouth and continued to ask interview questions. I don't think I've ever seen someone pull off talking with their mouth full and look so pretty at the same time. It was impressive."

My ears heat up and I can feel my cheeks turn red. "Yeah, not one of my finest moments."

"But hilarious." Gesturing with his head, he says, "Want to grab a coffee?"

"Uh, sure, that would be nice," I answer nervously. "Just let me wrap up a few things, and I'll meet you in the lobby."

"Sounds good."

He takes off toward the lobby while I stand from the couch.

When I turn to Dylan, she has one hand on her hip, the other behind her head, her teeth biting down on her bottom lip and she's thrusting her pelvis in the air.

I don't even bother to stick around. I make my way to my dressing room and grab my purse. I check my phone to find a notification. I have a message from NY152.

Curious, I open it up.

Noely,
    Cornuco-cupine? I need two of those for Thanksgiving. Can I pick those up at any store, or is that something I need to order from you?

Also, that dress . . . Fuck, you looked hot in it.
Me

Smiling like a fool, I type back.

NY152,
    Cornuco-cupines are available at every major retailer starting next week. Be sure to get yours as soon as possible. I heard they're a hot commodity.

Also, I would say you're looking hot as well, but then again, I have no idea who you are or what you're wearing, so I'm afraid I can't return the compliment.
Noely

I shut my dressing room door and head to the lobby just as I receive another message.

. . .

N oely,
   All in good time.
Me

Shaking my head at his reluctance to give in, I put my phone in my purse and walk to Beck. Looking up from his phone, he pockets it and smiles brightly.

"I have just the place for us, Sassy." He holds his arm out to me, which I link with mine and allow him to guide me out of the studio.

~

"Wow, I had no idea you were part of such a great program," I say, sipping my coffee.

"I'm very proud of it," Beck answers somberly, his demeanor changing from teasing to serious.

For the past half hour, I've listened to Beck speak passionately about his involvement with Feasts for Families. He not only helps, but he founded it. I knew from his dating profile he was passionate about philanthropy, but I had no idea the extent of it. And that's a shame, because it shows we didn't really take the time to talk about things.

"So your handle RebelWithACause rings true."

He nods, leaning back in his chair. "It does." Stroking his jaw, he studies me and says, "Eight years ago, I flipped my world upside down with one wrong decision and since then, I've spent every day trying to change the man I once was. Trying to be better, trying to wash away the thoughts of the lives I changed."

Curious, I place my hand on his and ask, "What did you do?"

Pained and clearly uncomfortable, he lets out a long breath. "Let's just say, I don't drink for a reason." He's silent as he stares at his coffee and I realize that whatever happened, whatever he went through, has truly affected him to the core. It's branded him, imprinted on his soul. Now his purpose is to serve for others. *He's a good man.*

Not wanting to push him too far and also happy for how he opened up to me, I say, "Do you only work with families during Thanksgiving?"

He shakes his head. "No, I volunteer with a lot of different organizations. I also do some public speaking, but my favorite thing is teaching the kids at the museum. We have a discovery zone and every Tuesday we paint murals on paper for future exhibits. I give them an animal, we educate the kids on their natural habitat, and then they paint their own diorama mural. It's fun to see what they come up with."

"That's kind of awesome. I mean . . . I want to come paint a habitat."

Beck chuckles. "Kids only. Sorry there, Sassy."

I snap my fingers in disappointment. "Darn."

Looking more relaxed than ever, Beck asks, "So how's it going? Go on any other blind dates after the jock?"

"No." I shake my head. "I've kind of taken a break on the whole dating scene."

"Yeah?" Beck plays with an unused napkin that's on the table, fidgeting with the corners. "Why's that?"

I shrug my shoulders even though I know the answer. "Just thought I should focus on me a little bit."

"Or are you worried that the next date won't work out as well?"

Twisting my lips, I stare at him, hating that he hit the nail on the head. "Maybe," I answer shyly.

"No need to be self-conscious, Noely. You're a catch." He fidgets with the napkin. "Any guy would be lucky to date you." Slowly, he lifts his eyes. His eyelashes are full and black, making the hues of his irises pop.

"Yeah?" I ask, feeling uncomfortable from the way he's looking at me, as if any moment he's about to tip our table over and devour me. From the beginning, Beck has been easy to read, his body language is quite clear. Right now? He still wants me.

"Yeah." He shifts in his seat and gives me a once-over, luring me into his lustful ways.

Physical. It's been so physical with him. Maybe it's his aura or the kind of vibe he gives off. Whatever it is, once again, it's pulling me.

Clearing my throat, trying to tamp down my hormones, I say, "I should probably go, I have some things . . . I have some errands to run."

"Yeah, I better get back to the museum. I have some wall touch-ups to make." Beck stands and collects our trash. Tossing it in the garbage can behind him, he turns to face me, and watches intently as I stand, lending a hand that I take. It's warm, and large, and rough, everything I expect him to be. Maybe everything I want him to be?

Guiding me out of the coffee house, hand still attached to mine, he spins me to face him when we reach the front. He places his hands on my hips and smiles at me, causing my breath to catch in my throat.

"Thank you for spending some time with me today. It was fun catching up." He reaches up and brushes a strand of hair behind my ear, his hand lingering against my cheek.

"It was," I say, my voice feeling heavy with lust. "I loved hearing about your different charities. It will be good to get you on the morning show to talk about them, especially Feasts for Families."

"I would love that." Scanning my eyes, his bouncing back and forth, he smirks and leans forward, placing a light kiss on my forehead. "I'll be in touch, Sassy." With one parting glance, he releases me from his tight grasp and takes off toward his motorcycle. I watch him hop on and secure his helmet, his leg straddling the powerful piece of machinery between them. He gives me a chaste wave, roars the bike to life, and in one swift move, drives off, the rumble of his bike echoing in his wake.

Clutching my purse to my side, I stare into the distance.

I'll be in touch, Sassy.

What did he mean by that? Could he possibly be alluding to NY152? I know he wants me physically, and in sharing that small morsel of information about himself, I can almost believe he's wanting to open up emotionally.

Thinking about the program more intelligently, Hayden really couldn't have been NY152 because how would he have been able to make a new profile? Beck has a friend behind the scenes and Jack owns the whole program, they both have access to creating a new profile. The question is, which man is it? Is Beck the one who wants me to desperately fall in love with him? Hmm . . . now I'll be obsessing even more over this.

~

N*oely,*
Have you ever had a day where you find yourself in a daze? The kind of daze that is neither happy nor sad, but just contemplative? I had one of those today. I found myself walking along the country market, looking for nothing, but taking in everything. I stood in front of a toy store window. I stared for what seemed like forever, observing all the bright colors, the flimsy objects that are supposed to entertain kids, and I kept thinking, where has the time gone?

I can remember like it was yesterday, playing in my room with my Teenage Mutant Ninja Turtle action figures, not a worry in the world besides the new shoes I was dying to have. It seems so close, yet so distant.

Life was simple back then, now everything has its challenges . . . like you.

I walked around aimlessly, trying to figure you out, trying to think of ways I could help you understand the pull I have toward you, but it almost seems impossible to put a gravitational pull into words.

How do you explain to someone that deep in your soul, you

know you're meant to be with someone? Like our meeting was kismet? Like the roller coaster of our lives came to a conversion point, at a time we weren't ready for, but a time we needed the most.
 Does that make any sense? Am I making any sense at all?
 Me

NY152,
 Maybe it's hard to write out because it's so much easier to show. If you feel so strongly about us, about what we share, why don't you SHOW me. Go out on another date with me. I'm getting stir crazy. I want to know who you are.
 Noely

Noely,
 Let me ask you this. If you could choose between The Suit and The Rebel, is it a clear-cut choice? Would you be disappointed if the one you wanted to show up turned out to be the other? Do you have your heart set on one particular man?
 Me

NY152,
 At this point, I have my heart set on you.
 Noely

CHAPTER THIRTY-FOUR

NOELY

"Mommy doesn't exist for the next few hours, but she loves you, don't forget that. She loves you so much she wants you to leave her alone. Bye, bye." Dylan hangs up her phone and plops it in the cup holder of her chair. Leaning her head back, she soaks up the sun.

Fall in Malibu doesn't necessarily scream pumpkins and apple cider; it's maybe a few degrees cooler, but that's about it. That's why Dylan and I are hanging out on the beach, toes in the sand, faces pointed toward the sun, soaking in the sun's rays. The breeze makes it a little chilly for a bathing suit, so instead I'm wearing a pair of small denim shorts and a red V-neck shirt, perfect for the seventy-five-degree weather.

Huffing next to me, Dylan says, "God, I love those kids, but if they call me one more time while I'm trying to bury the sun into my pores, I'm going to go home as a bitter woman and pee all over their toys."

"That's horrifying, but for some odd reason, I'm envisioning it in my head."

THREE BLIND DATES

"Am I wearing a carpet vest? As a bitter, peeing mom, I feel like I would wear a carpet vest."

"Uhh . . ." I pause from the odd question. "I never thought about clothes for you."

"You want me to be naked? Typical. You're such a pervert." I can't even with her.

"Fine, you have a vest." I roll my eyes and sip my water.

We sit in silence, our feet warming from the sand, the waves crashing, echoing through the quiet beach. We chose a deserted location, intentionally staying away from tourists. In all honesty, we chose a private residence beach. Dylan's friend owns a beach house and is out of town right now, so we might have jumped their fence with our chairs and cooler, then hiked it down the steps along the cliff that brought us down to their private beach.

I'm not proud of it, but I'm very happy about it, especially since I don't have to listen to random tourists yell at their kids to be careful.

Dylan pops open her e-reader and starts reading, her sunglasses helping protect her eyes from the brightness of the sun. Seeing she's distracted by her latest historical romance infatuation, I pull out my phone. Since my last message, I haven't heard anything from NY152 and it's making me slightly apprehensive. Did I scare him away? Does he not believe me?

What I've come to realize over the last few weeks while messaging him—whoever he is—is that it isn't about if he's The Suit or The Rebel anymore. It's become more about the man I've gotten to know. The man who's opened up, who's joked, and who's stolen my little romantic heart with his gestures and words.

Feeling sad there isn't a message from him, I decide to type my own message out.

NY152,
I've had an obsession lately, and I'm not about to tell you this so you start sending me baskets full of them, but

because I want to know if you happen to have the same taste buds as me.
   Do you . . . like Butterfingers? (holds breath)
   Noely

I press send and wait for a response. Looking toward the ocean, I think about one of NY152's previous messages, about how childhood seems so close, yet so far away. I can remember going to the beach with my parents, with Alex, building sand castles, burying our dad in the sand, and running through the short waves on the shoreline, never letting the water get past my knees. They were simpler times, times where you didn't have to worry about things like finding someone to share your life with, or worrying about a job, or winding up alone. It might sound ridiculous, to worry about finding the counterpoint to your soul with all the other things happening in the world. But growing up with loving parents, parents who still adore each other, they set the bar high for me. They're what I so desperately want to replicate.
   Ding.
   A message.
   Smiling, I open it up.

Noely,
   Butterfingers, hmm . . . what if I told you I had a bag of them in my cabinet right now? Would that score me some brownie points?
   Me

Not able to hold back my smirk, I type him back.

. . .

N*Y152,*
Are you saying that just to say that? Or do you really have Butterfingers in your cabinet? If so, we might be a match made in heaven.
Noely

Exiting out of the app, I set my phone down on my lap and reach for my drink just in time to see a familiar figure walking in my direction.

"Oh my God," I whisper.

"What?" Dylan asks, eyes still trained on her e-reader.

Walking up to us, wearing worn, tight-fitting jeans and a light blue button-up shirt with the sleeves rolled to his elbows, is Jack Valentine. Boy, does he look good.

"I thought that was you," he says when he reaches our beach chairs. Dylan lowers her sunglasses and eyes Jack up and down. A noncommittal grunt comes from her before she turns back to her e-reader.

"Jack, what are you doing here?"

"I was just about to ask you the same thing."

"What do you mean?" I ask, adjusting my shirt as I turn to face him in my chair.

He motions to the house behind us. "Well, this is my neighbor's house, and this is his private beach. He's out of town, and said I'd keep an eye on his house for him. When I saw two women camping out in his sand, I figured I'd see who the squatters were. To my surprise, it's the hosts of Good Morning, Malibu." He searches around, a smirk at the corner of his lips. "Are you two doing a segment on a weekend I don't know about? How to break into someone's private beach?"

"Ehhh . . ." I look at Dylan who doesn't seem to care at all about what's going on. With my foot, I poke her to gather her attention, but she swats me away. Nervously laughing, I shrug my shoulders, "Uh, is this not the proper thing to do? Crash out on private beaches?"

Jack's smile lights up his entire face as he shakes his head. "No. It can actually get you put in jail, you know, trespassing on private property. That's if someone calls you in." He reaches in his pocket, takes out his phone and starts flipping it in his hand.

"You hearing this, Dylan?" I poke her again with my foot.

"Stop poking me. I'm at the good part where her milky breasts are revealed." Once again, Dylan swats at me, leaving me out to dry.

"You know"—Jack rocks on his heels—"how about this? I don't call the cops on you if you come up to my house for a drink."

Looking up to the cliff, to the residence behind us, I take in the two houses that flank each side, both beautiful, both houses I could only dream of having. I bet the view is amazing from up there.

Just to make his point clear, Jack adds, "Good Morning, Malibu's hosts being booked for trespassing doesn't necessary scream good ratings to me." He smiles, confident in his proposal.

"You wouldn't call the cops."

"Try me." He holds up his phone and even though I'm 99.9% confident he wouldn't make that call, I'm actually quite interested to see what his house looks like. Plus, we're friends now, right?

Standing from my chair, I gather my purse and phone. "Jail doesn't seem fun right now, so I'll take you up on that drink."

"Smart." He takes in Dylan. Pointing at her, he asks, "Is she going to be okay here?"

"She's going to be perfectly fine."

"After you, then," Jack says, his voice light, his demeanor almost giddy. It's odd, seeing him like this, but also kind of infatuating.

Have you ever looked up a realty website, stuck in the most expensive budget, and just drooled all over the houses you wish you could own?

Jack's house is one of those.

Whoever built his house spent every waking minute constructing it so no matter what room you were in, you had an almost panoramic view of the crystal-blue ocean. The living room has pocket doors that span the length of the house, opening up to a gorgeous deck with clear glass walls, white concrete flooring, and the most beautiful rectangular fire pit I've ever seen. And when I say fire pit, I mean fire comes out of glass rocks. It's so gorgeous. The bedrooms and bathrooms have stunning views as well, the master opening to the length of the deck, adding another outdoor/indoor living space. I've never seen anything like it.

The house is bright with its white walls, light grey accents, and chrome features. There isn't much on the walls, really anything at all actually. He's a minimalist, because it looks as if he just moved in.

Jack opens one of the most expensive-looking fridges I've ever seen and asks, "What would you like to drink?" Taking a glance in his fridge he cringes. "Damn, I should have thought this through. I have water and that's pretty much it."

"Water is fine."

He hands me a bottle and smiles sheepishly. "Sorry, I kind of just moved in, so I'm still working on stocking up on things."

Just moved in . . . huh.

"Uh, that's okay. No problem at all." I uncap my water and take a sip of it. "I guess that would explain the lack of décor on the walls."

He chuckles. "Yeah, still working on that as well. I've never been much of a decorator, so I have no idea what I'm doing. I might hire someone to do it all for me."

"No, don't do that." I shake my head and start nervously peeling the label off my water bottle. "For some reason—even since our dressing room bang—Jack makes me incredibly nervous, but not in a bad way. From the moment I met him, there's been a nervous, electric energy that's pulled me toward him. "Take your time learning your style, find pieces and décor you like and slowly put it together. You're going to be so much happier if you're the one who decorates your house over time rather than a random stranger coming in and trying to decipher your taste."

"But I know nothing."

I shrug. "Doesn't matter. It's your house, you don't have to know anything except what you like."

Leaning on the counter, his dark eyes sparkle at me. "You're right." He shakes his head and continues, "I don't know why I thought I needed to impress anyone. I should do what I like, so if I want to put up a poster of Superman, I can."

"Wait a minute now." I tamp him down with my hand. "You should decorate with what you like, but in good taste. If you decorate with Superman posters, you can guarantee your chances of getting laid will go down at least forty percent. I don't know if that's a percentage you're willing to risk."

He sips from his water bottle, the water making his Adam's apple bob up and down. Why that's sexy to me, I will never know.

When he caps his water, he looks me dead in the eyes and says, "Noely, there is only one person on my mind when I think about getting laid."

Those eyes, that jaw, his lips, oh hell, my body is drawn toward him.

"Care to join me on the deck?" He nods behind him.

"Uh, sure." I swallow hard and roll up the water bottle label in my hand. "Where's your trashcan?"

"Under the sink." Turning to the sink behind me, I open the cabinet and pull out the trash can and toss my water bottle label on top of a Butterfinger wrapper.

Still, as if the air around me is disappearing, I stare at that wrapper, wanting to rub my eyes to make sure I'm not seeing things. Looking up, I glance around his kitchen.

THREE BLIND DATES

A candle.

Leather scent.

Turning, I take in his living room.

A wicker basket holding magazines.

Holy shit.

HOLY SHIT!

"I need to pee," I panic shout, standing tall and accidentally slamming the cabinet door shut too loudly.

"Uh, is everything okay?" Jack asks, moving from the deck opening back to me.

"Peachy." I laugh uncomfortably. "Everything is nice, just nice. But I have to pee pee, like now." *Christ, don't say pee pee.*

"Bathroom is down the hall," he says, pointing to where I need to go.

"Yep." Half-sprinting, half-walking, I make my way to the bathroom, shut the door, and turn toward the mirror, which is almost non-existent thanks to the span of windows overlooking the ocean.

"Oh my God," I whisper, trying to get my head around this.

The new house, the Butterfingers, the leather candle, the wicker basket . . . *he's* NY152. The Suit, Jack Valentine, the man who wanted nothing to do with me after our first date, is the one who's been making my heart melt, causing my little romantic heart to go pitter-patter. He's the one who's been making me fall for him through his words and wooing ways.

Did I already say . . . *holy shit?*

It's all making sense now. His mixed signals every time I ran into him, his ability to create a new profile on the app—hello, he owns the damn thing—his urging to want to be friends, to want to get closer to me.

Jack Valentine is NY152; he's my very own Joe Fox.

To say my mind is blown is an understatement. From the way things ended with us, I never considered it could be Jack. Especially after seeing Beck the other day. *But he came after me in the dressing room. He took me because he couldn't resist any longer. He asked me to go out with him.*

Hand pressed to my forehead, I look out the window, almost feeling dizzy from the realization. That's when I spot Jack, leaning over the glass wall of his deck, hands typing away on the screen of his phone, a smile on his face.

His posture seems so much more relaxed, at ease, as if he's finally happy.

Ding.

I pull my phone out of my pocket and see a notification. Looking back at Jack, I watch as he puts his phone in his pocket and then stares out at the ocean, hands pressed in front of him.

HOLY SHIT!

Unable to wait a second longer, I open my app and read his message.

Noely,
From the get-go, I've thought we're a match made in heaven. I'm trying to get you on board and if that means I have a lifetime supply of Butterfingers in my cabinet at all times, then I'll start ordering right now.

Me

I read his message a few times, my heart pounding out of my chest, my breath catching in my throat with each pass. Needing to talk to someone, I quickly dial Dylan and pray she picks up.

"If he's captured you, tied you up, and is asking for ransom, then that's the only reason I won't be mad at you for calling when I'm reading my stories."

"Dylan," I whisper, not wanting to be too loud. "It's him."

"I'm hanging up now."

"Dylan, wait." I say in a panic. "Jack, he's NY152."

There's silence on the other end. I check my phone to make

sure I'm still connected and she didn't hang up on me, which she didn't.

"Dylan, please say something. I don't know what to do."

"Are you sure it's him?" she finally asks, sounding only marginally annoyed that I interrupted her "stories."

"Yes," I answer, my voice barely above a whisper. "There have been clues from our letters; it's too much to explain but it's definitely him. I just watched him send me a message through the app too."

"Really? Okay." I can hear her shift on her chair. "Where are you now?"

"In the bathroom." I watch Jack, whose back muscles are rippling under his shirt with every movement he makes. "I excused myself when I figured it out. I don't know what to do now. Should I leave?"

"Do you want to leave?"

"Um, I mean . . . not really." And if that truth doesn't shock me, I don't know what will. I've done everything in my ability to avoid this man, but for some reason, I keep finding him in my presence. *Or perhaps, he has kept finding me.* Could the *Going In Blind* app really be right? The first date *is* the best match. Despite my turbulent feelings toward The Suit, it's NY152 I've gotten to know, who I've started to fall for.

"Okay, then go enjoy yourself. What's the problem?" She makes it seem so simple, but for some reason, it feels less than simple.

"But, do I tell him I know? Do I confront him?"

"No," Dylan's voice is stern. "He clearly has a plan, something he's trying to execute. You didn't think you'd ever want to go out with him again. You couldn't stand him. And from the way you treated him, I wouldn't blame him wanting to take a different approach when it came to winning your affection. Let him do his thing."

"So, just go on as if I know nothing? Won't that be weird?"

"Only if you make it weird. Instead of worrying about the romantic gesture he's making, enjoy his company. Try to find the chemistry you had when you went out on your first date, because I don't think I've ever seen you so happy than after your first date with him."

She's right, she's absolutely right.

"Let it happen, Noely. Don't overthink it; let it be."

Hanging up with a goodbye and thank you, I take one last look in the mirror and fluff my hair, mentally giving myself a pep talk as butterflies start to float around in my stomach for this man once again.

I don't know why I'm so nervous. We've been on a date. Hell, he's seen me with a horrible perm, he's had his way with me in my dressing room, and he's made it quite clear his intentions are to get to know me all over again. So what's holding me back? A miscommunication? He's already explained his reasoning. So it can't be that.

Maybe it's what Beck said. Maybe I'm too scared about failing, I'm not quite ready to give my relationship with Jack another go in fear it won't work out.

But . . . what if it does?

At this point, the positives are outweighing the negatives of my internal dialogue. I'm going to do what Dylan suggested. I'm going to let Jack do his thing and, in the meantime, get to know him on a more personal level.

CHAPTER THIRTY-FIVE

NOELY

"Everything good?" Jack asks as I approach him.

"Yeah." I let out a shaky breath. The man I've slowly started to fall for is actually real. I can put a familiar face to the beautiful words he's written to me, to the funny messages, and thoughtful gifts, even the wasp spray.

Motioning with his head, he says, "Come here."

Walking up to him, I watch his gaze roam my body and land on my eyes when I lean against the rail with him. "This is beautiful. Absolutely gorgeous."

"It's everything I ever dreamed of having," he answers honestly. "It reminds me so much of my grandparents' house. It really feels like home."

"And once you get some of your favorite things hung on the walls, it will truly feel peaceful here."

"It will." Still leaning on the railing, he smiles at me. "I was only in your house briefly, I barely remember it. Maybe because I was distracted by something else—"

"My hair, I know. What a mistake that was," I tease.

He shakes his head. "No, it wasn't your hair." He stares directly at my lips, and his unabashed and obvious longing thrills me. Taking a second, he lets a breath of silence fall between us before saying, "What's your favorite thing in your house? The thing you would grab if your house was on fire? What is irreplaceable?"

"Hmm." I rest my chin in my propped-up hand and look toward the ocean, images of my house flashing in my head. "Just one thing? Or can it be like a group of things?"

He chuckles. "It can be whatever you want, Noely."

"Then it would be my grandma's doilies. You know what those are, right? The frilly little lace linens you usually find under lamps."

"My grandma had them all over. I always thought they were weird, but now when I see one, they make me feel at home."

His reply makes my heart ache, especially from the way he's gently pressing his hand against mine. Comfort.

Feeling warm and all sorts of tingly, I joke, "Must be a grandma thing."

"Has to be. Do they remind you of your grandma?"

I nod. "Yes, but they also remind me of all the good times we had. I used to visit my grandma when I was little, and there was always a tea party waiting for me. She would deck out her table in doilies, her best china and silverware, and she would serve tea with scones, her famous cinnamon-chip scones. And before we could sit down, she would take me to the guest room where we would dress to the nines in dress-up clothes, long velvet gloves, and gaudy hats with feathers. She would let me wear her pearls and heels, then she would take me to the table where we discussed everything from the weather, to the type of Play-Doh she had waiting for me to play with after tea time." I smile wistfully, my grandma's loving face coming into vision. "She was a beautiful woman who gave me the world. Those doilies, they remind me of everything about her and the time she spent with me."

Jack endearingly smiles, his hand now on my back, gently rubbing it, his body closer than I remember. "I had the same relationship with my grandma." His voice is low, but engaging, almost as if he's never really shared this with anyone but is eager to. "My

THREE BLIND DATES

grandpa would take me fishing, we would go on hikes, and share a Snickers bar whenever we were away from my grandma. But when it came to the woman of the household, the woman who held all the cards, my grandma treated me like a prince." He chuckles and shakes his head. "I don't know why I'm going to tell you this, but she taught me to quilt. We spent a whole summer making a quilt together. I would skip fishing trips with my grandpa to make sure I finished my blanket. Once it was done, my grandma stitched a little message in a square." Jack pauses, his thumb gently rubbing up and down on my back. "That would be the thing I would grab if my house was on fire. Not the fishing poles my grandpa left me, but my quilt, because after it was done, it was something my grandma and I shared creating. On movie nights, my grandparents and I would snuggle under my quilt and watch movies together, me sitting in the middle, the crashing of waves in the background. Those are the nights I will never forget, watching old movies like The Thin Man." He lets out a low, steady breath. "I miss them."

His story, the image he's created in my head, awakens a new type of feeling for him, one I don't think I've felt before when it comes to Jack Valentine. It's . . . anything but scary, more reassuring. He's not cold, he's not unflappable, he's actually real and sincere. I'm thinking there aren't many men like him.

"That's so sweet," I reply. "Can I see the blanket?"

"Of course. One second." Once Jack retreats, I take a moment to observe his surroundings. Straight lines, cool colors, chrome accents. His house matches the exterior of his personality, but the warm fire popping up over the smooth glass rocks in the fire pit . . . that's the warmth I'm feeling from him now, the warmth that's drawing me in closer and closer.

"It's a little worn," he says, walking up behind me.

I take the blanket in my hands, the fabric a little threadbare but still holding together nicely. The colors have faded, but I can tell it used to be a very vibrant quilt constructed with . . .

I raise an eyebrow at him. "Looney Tunes?"

He chuckles and runs a hand over his face. "It was cool-ish

back then." Sighing, he continues, "It was the only thing I was allowed to watch at my grandparents' house, so I became a little obsessed. And before you ask, I was a Bugs Bunny fan. Classic. Daffy was a close second."

"Oh my God." Humor pours out of me. "Why does this make you really, really cute?"

"Cute? Not devastatingly handsome?" He playfully wiggles his eyebrows at me.

"Just cute." No way in hell am I going to tell him I think he's devastatingly handsome, or that I've thought that from the very beginning.

We exchange a look, a heated look, and before I can say anything to cut the tension, he asks, "Want to order some Chinese food? Have a little fire with me and maybe a game of Monopoly?" There is a smile on his face but insecurity in his eyes, too. Strange. And that's when it really hits me. *I truly regret what I did, because every time I run into you, I see the beautifully intelligent and dynamic woman I foolishly let slip from my grasp.*

He truly regrets letting me go.

That insecurity has been present in his stare every time we've run into each other. Even when he was deep inside me, I saw the same look. Despite his cool, alpha businessman demeanor, he's insecure when it comes to me.

Which only means one thing.

He really likes me.

And hell . . . I really like him.

Crazy, I know!

But . . . look at him. It's not just his looks, his stoic posture, or the way he can slice you into a million pieces with a once-over from those dark, stormy eyes; it's his heart.

As he waits for an answer, I chew on my bottom lip and nod yes. His eyes light up, his smile grows to a full-on panty-melting grin, and he lifts off the railing, placing his hand on my lower back. "For some reason, I think you might annihilate me at Monopoly."

"I'm ruthless, so you better watch out, Suit."

THREE BLIND DATES

"Come on five, come on five," Jack chants, fingers crossed, looking entirely too adorable under the glow of the fire.

Over my lap, I have Jack's Looney Tunes quilt, keeping me warm as well as the fire in front of me, and the hoodie Jack let me borrow that smells just like him. Oh, girls, let me tell you, it smells like absolute heaven. I pulled the hood over my head so I could take in his smell even more.

"You know, you don't have to gloat." I shake the dice in my hands, praying I don't roll a five, not with Jack's prime real estate on the yellow and green squares. I own Park Place and Boardwalk and spent all my money building my real estate on those two blue squares. But guess what, they're not winners.

Nooooo, Jack has skipped over them every time and they have been nothing but a drain of cash. And thanks to Jack's proper planning, he's been able to slaughter me with his yellow and green squares that flank the go to jail block. And you know it's bad when you're hoping to land in jail.

"Not gloating, just hoping to take the rest of your money."

"Just you wait." I continue to shake the dice in my hands, as if the extra shake will steer me away from a five. "I'm going to get past your luxury resorts as you like to call them, collect my two hundred dollars, and turn this board game around."

"You say that every time you try to pass my luxury resorts, but face it, baby, you can't seem to pass up my hospitality."

"Don't flatter yourself." I toss the dice and inwardly pray I don't roll something that will have me once again feeding his bank.

The dice roll to a stop and show a set of twos.

"Four," I announce then panic for a second when I check out the board. "Ah-ha!" I count out my four squares and land on Community Chest, avoiding the luxury resorts—thank God. I pick up a card and read out loud. "You inherit one hundred dollars." I do a little happy bounce and hold my hand out to the banker.

"Looks like my luck is about to change, and since I rolled doubles, I get to go again."

Jack hands me a one-hundred-dollar bill and the dice. "Don't get cocky now."

"Ha, coming from the cockiest player tonight."

He shrugs. "I've got to be cocky, babe. It's in my nature."

That's what he likes to think, but after talking to him, after all his messages, I know it's not the only part of him. No, he's not a cocky man, but it is the persona he likes to project. I can see right through it.

I roll again and make my way past Go, collect my money, and sit pretty with an extra three hundred in my bank, money I needed desperately.

Continuing to switch back and forth between rolls, I say, "I like that you have original Monopoly. There are so many different versions of the game, and I feel like it's rare when you see original, or rare when you even play Monopoly."

"I'm classic." He shrugs. He nods at the table next to me. "You never ate your fortune cookie. Do you not like them?"

I hold my stomach. "I was digesting. I think I ate my half of Chinese food and yours as well."

"You sure did woof it down." He smiles mischievously.

I point at him. "Watch it, mister."

He holds his hands up in defense. "I apologize."

Setting the dice down, I pick up my fortune cookie and open it up. I pop a piece of the cookie in my mouth and read the fortune out loud. "Look around, happiness is trying to catch you." My heart sputters in my chest when I glance at Jack. His gaze is locked on mine, the atmosphere almost morphing into something else, something I don't know I'm prepared for, something I know I will easily fall for.

"I couldn't agree more with that fortune." Jack leans back and takes a sip of his water, cockiness firmly in place.

"You didn't have to take me home. I didn't mind grabbing an Uber," I say as Jack parks in front of my house.

"I would never have allowed that." He puts the car in park, turns it off, and exits his side of the vehicle.

He's going to walk me to the door. Why does that give me butterflies?

Maybe because I know what kind of things happen when attractive men walk you to your door.

Kisses.

That's right, all the kisses happen. Lips against lips, tongues tangling with tongues. A walk to the door is a guaranteed make-out session, or at least it gives you the go-ahead for a little peck. Either way, butterflies are fluttering.

And not because I haven't kissed him already. You and I both know his lips have touched mine, but that's not what's making little butterflies flutter in my stomach from the prospect of Jack walking to my door. It's the fact that the man who will be walking me to my door, the one who will possibly kiss me tonight isn't just Jack. He's NY152. And that's a big freaking deal.

Jack opens my door and holds out his hand, which I take. Helping me to my feet, he shuts the car door once I'm out of the way. Hand still clasped with mine, he walks me down the narrow walkway of my front yard and stops in front of my entryway where he lets go of my hand. I notice the loss of his warmth immediately.

"Thanks for hanging out tonight, *friend*." The way he emphasizes the word friend with that smirk on his face, well hell, it makes me feel weak in the damn knees.

"Thanks for having me," I answer awkwardly, pulling on the sweatshirt I borrowed. "Oh, I should probably give this back to you."

"Hold on to it for now. You can give it back to me another time."

"There's going to be another time?" I ask, a little flirtation in my voice.

He shrugs non-committedly. "We're friends after all, right?"

"I guess we are." I chuckle and shake my head in disbelief.

"What?"

"I just never expected us to be friends, that's all. I mean we've had kind of a weird relationship, don't you think?"

"More like unique, in a good way. Sometimes the strongest bonds are formed during off-the-beaten-track experiences." He pushes a strand of hair behind my ear. "I'll see you around."

He takes a step backward and my heart starts to sink. Oddly, I don't want this evening to end, but from the friendship remarks, I'm going to assume Jack wants to keep this platonic. For now . . . at least until he reveals himself. That's what I'm hoping.

"Wait," I say before he can put too much distance between us. Smiling at me, he waits for my next move. Before I can stop myself, I throw my arms around him and rest my head on his chest, hugging him tightly. Not making me wait, Jack wraps his arms around me as well and pulls me in close.

Warm, woodsy, and clean. That's how I describe his scent.

In a flash, our first date crosses my mind, the amazing night we had on the beach, dancing, the card game we played. That night was a pinnacle in my life, a life-altering night, a night that has lived with me since. I haven't been able to forget it, because it's the date that told me he might very well be the one.

After tonight and all his messages, I can see why my intuition was so strong. Jack Valentine is my perfect match.

"I could get used to this." He chuckles, his chest rumbling beneath me.

I squeeze him tighter. "I just wanted to let you know I had a good night. I'm glad we're friends." I look up at him, and oh God, his lips tempt me.

"Yeah?" His smile sears me in two, his teeth so white, his scruff so sexy.

"Yeah." I squeeze him once more and then step away, feeling a little awkward from my impromptu embrace. I needed something a little more than a verbal goodbye.

THREE BLIND DATES

Stepping back, he grips the back of his neck, almost a tortured look on his face when he says, "Have a good night, Noely."

Waving, I reply, "You too, Jack."

With a heavy sigh, I turn to my house and wish my night with Jack didn't have to come to an end. But perhaps because he wants my nights in the future—*and I know in my heart that I absolutely want that too*—I can be content tonight.

CHAPTER THIRTY-SIX

NOELY

N*oely,*
Have you ever wondered what your life will look like in ten years? Where you'll be? What kind of life you'll be living? Do you think you'll still be hosting Good Morning, Malibu? Or do you think you'll be living in New York City, working on Good Morning, America, living in some swanky apartment with an orange tabby cat and a rotation of male models going in and out of your apartment?
Me

N*Y152,*
Rotation of male models, don't mind if I do! Thanks for the suggestion.
As for the rest of my life, I don't know. I can't imagine living in New York. Not only does the cold weather not suit me, I can't imagine living in such a big city. I like how Malibu feels like a small town when it really isn't. If that makes sense.

THREE BLIND DATES

I guess I haven't thought about ten years ahead. I'm still working on the here and now. What about you?
Noely

Noely,
There better not be a rotation of male models going in and out of your door. That would be a joke gone wrong.
Hmm . . . ten years from now? That's easy, I want to be a family man. Kids, soccer games on the weekends, Friday night pizza nights, waffles every Sunday morning, and rocket ship rides to bed every night, with the obvious crash landing into the mattress. I want to be able to kiss my kids good night and then hold my girl for the rest of the evening either playing cards or watching a movie.
I'm not saying this to win your heart. I'm telling you this so you know where I'm at in my life, where I want to be. Does that scare you?
Me

NY152,
That doesn't even scare me in the slightest.
Noely

~

Noely,
What's your favorite recipe you stole from your show?
I tried making that lamington recipe the other day that you made with that Australian baker and failed miserably. My coconut wouldn't stick, and when it came to the coconut, my heavy hand flattened my squares. It tasted okay, maybe because I used olive oil instead of vegetable oil, or maybe

because I swore the entire time while making it. Either way, it didn't come out the way it did on your show.
Me

NY152,
You made lamingtons? I don't know why I think that's so adorable. It's really not that hard to make, so I'm actually surprised you messed it up.

And my favorite recipe from the show? Hmm, probably the cranberry orange pancakes we made last year during the fall. Oh my God, they are so good. Maybe one day, I'll make them for you.
Noely

Noely,
Don't fucking tease me.
You know I would take you up on making me pancakes so fast, especially if it meant gaining a second chance with you.
Me

NY152,
Are you really worried about a second chance? Don't you think you'd get one by now?
Noely

Noely,
Honestly, I have no idea. I let you get away once. A second time would just about wreck me. It's a chance I'm not sure I'm ready to take.
Me

THREE BLIND DATES

~

"**G**reat show, Noely."

"Thank you," I reply, walking through the halls of the studio with one thing on my mind: tacos. I want all the tacos in my mouth right now. And queso. Tacos and queso. I'm skipping my gym session and I'm stuffing my mouth with chips, queso, and freaking tacos.

My heels click loudly across the cement floor as I approach my dressing room door.

"Noely." Kevin's annoying voice rings through the hallway.

Hand on doorknob to my dressing room, I ask, "What?"

"Next week, we have Turk coming in to discuss decorating your Christmas tree. Are you going to be okay with that?"

I roll my eyes. Turk Gunderson and I had a little spat off air last time he was here. It was a pointless fight about stepping on his toes during his segment and me telling him to grow up. Not my finest moment, but really, you're going to get mad about me stepping on your toes? Ridiculous.

"If I said I wasn't okay with it?"

"Then I would tell you to suck it up. Whenever Turk is on the show, we have amazing ratings."

Exasperated, I say, "Then why even ask?"

He shrugs. "Not sure. Maybe to get on your nerves."

I shake my head. "You're seriously the worst. Pushing my buttons for the hell of it has never gotten you anywhere, Kevin. And now all you've done is ruined my mood to eat tacos. Damn you."

He dusts off his hands and says, "Then my work here is done." With a giant, annoying smirk, he spins on his heel and heads to his office, man muffins hanging over his pants and everything.

God, he's annoying.

Irritated, I walk into my dressing room with a sour taste on my tongue. Stupid Kevin.

"Hey Noely."

"Ah," I scream, holding my hand to my chest while staring right into Jack Valentine's eyes. "Oh my God, what is wrong with you?"

Chuckling, he stands from my couch and swaggers toward me, his suit caressing his fit body. Flashes of the last time we were in this room together run through my head, heating my veins to dangerous levels.

Without saying a word, Jack pulls me into a hug, and the tension I was experiencing evaporates under his touch.

"I meant to surprise you, not scare you." Putting some distance between us, he adjusts his tie and gives me a once-over. "You look beautiful. Yellow is a gorgeous color on you."

"Uh, thank you," I answer shyly. "What are you doing here?"

"Thought I would take my *friend* out for lunch. Are you free?"

"Well . . . I did have a date with tacos."

"Yeah?" Jack raises his brows at me. "Then let's get you some tacos."

I have just enough time to snag my purse and phone before he takes my hand, ushers me out the door, and down the hallway.

I allow him to guide me through the halls of the studio, because I'm so focused on what his large hand feels like wrapped around mine. It makes me feel warm, taken care of, *and* that I don't want him to let go of it.

It reminds me of just how happy I am to see him.

God, am I happy to see him.

Once we're in his car, the smooth leather beneath me, the smell of his cologne engulfing me, he says, "I know a great place for tacos. Do you trust me?" His hand is on the gearshift, his other gripping the steering wheel, looking sexy powerful.

I nod. "I trust you." There is no way I can't. "Yes, take me to tacos."

We zip through the streets of Malibu, and it's fun watching tourists take in the expensive car. Jack pulls off the street and parks next to a meter. I'm surprised when I see a little hole-in-the-wall place with a neon sign in the window that says tacos. I would never think about stopping here, but from the look of contentment on Jack's face, I'm going to assume this place is really good.

Taking my hand when we're out of the car, we make our way into the restaurant, pass the hostess stand with a sign that says seat yourself, and through a black curtain that opens into a cantina-style courtyard. Palm trees provide the space shade and little wrought iron bistro seats are scattered around the cobblestone ground.

"Oh my God, this place is so not what I expected."

Jack squeezes my hand. "You can't judge a book by its cover, Noely. Just because it doesn't have a picture on the front, doesn't mean it isn't going to be the most amazing thing you ever experience."

"Noted." Looking around, I point to table in the corner. "Want to sit over there?"

"Sure." With his hand on my lower back, he walks us over to the corner table and pulls the chair out for me. Such a gentleman. When he sits across from me, he undoes the button of his suit jacket and picks up the menu. "The shrimp tacos with garlic lime sauce are so damn good."

"I love shrimp. Should I even look at the rest of the menu?"

He shakes his head. "No need, these will be just what you're looking for. Want some guac and chips as well?"

"Uh, yeah. It's not a taco party without chips and guac."

"And a margarita." He wiggles his eyebrow. Jack retreats behind the curtain where I'm assuming he's going to order, giving me time to take in more of the restaurant.

Interesting place with the indoor-outdoor feel, the big bulb lights strung along the perimeter of the space, and the ivy climbing up the stucco walls. It's quaint, charming, a place I would love to visit at night.

Once Jack's sitting across from me again, I can't help but stare at him. Clean-cut scruff around his jaw, his hair styled to the side, so full and dark, and those lips . . . they're calling to me. All I want is to feel his lips on mine again.

"Are you dating right now?" Jack asks, throwing me out of my reverie and into a serious tailspin.

"What?" I ask, confused.

"Have you started dating again?" He leans back in his chair, just as someone brings us salt-rimmed margaritas and water glasses. Keeping his gaze on me, he brings his margarita causally to his lips and takes a sip.

What is he doing? What's his game? He should know I'm not dating, that I'm kind of waiting for him to spill the beans about the whole NY152 thing. Soooo why is he asking me if I'm dating?

Unless . . .

He's not NY152.

I chew on that thought for a second before nixing it. He's NY152. I can't be wrong.

So why is he asking me if I'm dating? There is only one way to find out.

"No, but I'm talking to someone on the app."

His eyebrows rise in curiosity. He's so hard to read right now, and it's driving me a little crazy. "Is that so? You're talking to someone. Are you interested in him?"

Is he feeling me out? Trying to see if I could fall for him, seeing if he's done his job and I'm ready to fall head over heels for him.

"I am," I answer honestly. "Very much so."

Face impassive, he nods and takes another sip of his drink. "How long have you been talking?"

"Long enough to know I want to have more than a relationship through messages."

Studying me, his eyes growing more intense with each passing second, he says, "It seems like you really like this guy."

Knowing if I want this little tête-à-tête to end, I need to encourage him. "I do. He's sweet, kind, funny, and has a beautiful heart. As my friend, I think you'd approve."

"You think? I don't know about that." Jack rubs his jaw in thought. "Why are you still talking on the app then? Why not go on a date?"

Okay, his questions are really starting to throw me for a loop here.

Feeling a little shy now, even though I'm almost positive NY152 is Jack, I say, "He, uh, he wanted to take some time to get to know me."

"And has he?"

"I think so. I at least hope so, because I'm starting to get a little impatient." I lift my gaze and look at Jack through my eyelashes. "He's kind of captured my mind and soul. I want more from him now."

"I see." Jack takes another sip from his margarita, so I do the same but instead of a sip, I take one giant gulp. "This guy, he seems to know what he's doing, as if he's getting you to a point in conversation where you have no choice but to beg to finally meet him."

"Well, begging seems a bit aggressive."

"But from the sparkle in your eye when you talk about him, I can see he's on your mind; he really has captured you."

You have, I want to scream. I want to throw this table to the ground, hop on his lap, and kiss him senseless.

"You know, I wonder where we would be right now if I didn't foolishly break things off with you. If I'd talked to you rather than run away."

Feeling sad about all the wasted time we've endured, I say, "We wouldn't be just friends, Jack."

"No we wouldn't." He humorously shakes his head. "We would be a hell of a lot more than just friends." Running his hand over his face, he blows out a long breath, as if he's truly distraught over our situation.

Before I can break the silence and question him, our food is placed in front of us, and the smell of shrimp tacos consumes us. For the rest of the "date" we talk about unimportant things like my work, and the weather, things that go nowhere to digging deep.

The ride to the studio is just as awkward and instead of a hug goodbye, Jack gives me a small wave from his side of the car.

That night, I don't receive any messages from NY152, nor do I receive any from him the next day, or the day following.

What on earth is going on? Does he really not know that I believe NY152 is him?

Was I wrong? Have I lost Jack?

Again?

CHAPTER THIRTY-SEVEN

JACK

NY152,
You know that scene in You've Got Mail where Tom Hanks and Meg Ryan are at that party together where Meg Ryan finds out Tom Hanks is in fact, Joe Fox, and they are both getting food from the table. Tom Hanks grabs all the caviar off one of the plates and Meg Ryan yells at him, telling him the caviar is a garnish? Do you remember that? Well, I had caviar today for the first time and I've come to the conclusion that it should be a garnish and nothing else.
Ugh, I can't get the taste out of my mouth.
Help!
Noely

NY152,
On the show today, Turk Gunderson came and did a piece about Christmas trees and how to decorate them. He was insistent about using fake fiber-optic trees because they glistened and shimmered rather than glowed.

When did glistening and shimmering become better than glowing? I always thought glowing was the optimal way to shine light. Are you a glower, glistener, or shimmer-er? In my head, you're a glower, but maybe that's because I hold you in a higher regard.

Noely

NY_{152},
My brother made duck last night for our little family dinner. Duck, like the little quack, quack ducks you can feed at a pond.

I wasn't a fan of his menu selection, nor was I fan of him using the head of the duck as a "decoration." Hell, I would have rather seen the caviar gracing the plate at that point.

When he brought it out, all I could think about was the end scene in A Christmas Story when they are at the Chinese restaurant, singing Fra ra ra ra all night long.

Despite the fun memory, and that song playing on repeat in my head, I still couldn't get over the dead duck head. Why my brother had to do that, I have no idea. Thankfully, he got an earful from his wife when their daughter buried her body under the table and would not reappear for dinner.

He doesn't think things through sometimes.

Noely

NY_{152},
I'm not sure why you've been so silent lately, but please know this. I've missed you and your messages. I've missed the way you make me laugh, and the sweet words you say. I'm not sure if I said something wrong, or if you're pulling away, but whatever it might be, I hope you tell me because honestly, I've missed you.

Hope to hear from you soon.

ShopGirl

I close out of the app and run both hands over my face, squeezing my eyes shut in the process. God, I miss her too.

I miss her so damn much, just as much as I missed her when I stopped us from going further the first time.

Why the hell did I do that?

Hmm . . . maybe because I'm a scared asshole with a tendency to run when things get complicated. Just like they are now.

Fuck, are they complicated.

I didn't think this through, not even in the slightest.

When we went out for tacos the other day, I wanted to gauge where she was at, to see if there was any inkling that I could be the guy she's messaging. But when she talked about it, when she talked about "him" it seemed like she was talking about someone completely separate from me, and that's what is terrifying me.

I thought I'd been winning her over during the past few weeks. I thought I was doing a really good job at it actually, turning our sour encounter into a relationship to last for years to come. But now, now I wonder if I inadvertently friend-zoned myself?

Is she thinking The Rebel is who she's been talking to? Is The Rebel the one who's captured her? If only she would give me some sort of hint, because frankly, I'm terrified to meet up with her as NY152 and for her to be tremendously disappointed.

"Shit," I mutter and walk out to my deck. What I wouldn't give to have Noely here right now, laughing and teasing me.

I didn't mean to meet anyone with the app. My profile was just a test profile, to make sure we had everything setup properly, but when the system matched me with Noely, and I read everything about her, I was intrigued. I had to meet her, so I said yes to a date.

Best decision of my life.

That night we spent together, hell, I haven't stopped thinking about it.

Scratch that, I haven't stopped thinking about the kiss we shared in her house, with her hair crazed with curls.

Wait, no. I haven't stopped thinking about what we did in her dressing room. God, she'd felt perfect in my arms. So damn perfect. The taste of her. The feel of her wrapped around me. The softness of her skin. *Fuck. How did I mess this up so badly?*

I rub the scruff on my jaw, contemplating what I should do next. I thought using the *You've Got Mail* identities would make it so easy for her to know it was me. Wasn't it the first thing we really connected on? The first big tick that said she and I were so suited? *Had she actually found that in common with The Rebel as well?*

I have two options, I can continue to be Noely's friend, or I can nut up and message her back, ask her out on a date.

Knowing I can't drag this on anymore—I've reached my breaking point—I pull my phone from my pocket.

Noely,
I'm so sorry about the silence recently. To be honest, I was trying to come up with different excuses as to why not to answer you, but they were all lies and you deserve better than that. So to tell you the truth, I took some time to do some serious thinking about what's to come, about us, if there even is an us.

Despite being a strong and confident man, you've bewitched me. You've invaded my mind and turned it into a dusty fog, a place where nothing but your beautiful eyes and smile exist.

But even that is not an excuse, so I deeply apologize if I bewildered or upset you in any way. Please don't think I'm not thinking about you, because your mouthy remarks and funny banter ring through my head every damn day.
Me

. . .

I hit send and take in a deep breath. I've never been this edgy about a girl in my life. Hell, I've never been nervous about anything really for that matter. Million-dollar business deals barely grant me a perspiration, but Noely in a tight red dress with matching lipstick? Fuck, she had me sweating from my hands to my feet.

Below me the waves crash onto the shore, calming my racing heart just as a message pings on my phone. That was quick, but I'm glad. I don't know if I can wait very long for a response.

NY152,
Some serious thinking? What were you thinking about? It kind of makes me nervous that you took a while to respond because of thinking.

If we're being honest, I like you, a lot, and if you were thinking about possibly ending this messaging relationship without even meeting, it would probably crush me.

Noely

Fuck. I run my hand through my hair. I have her just where I want her, liking the man who has won her soul over, but the only question is, is she going to like the man who's behind the messages?

How on earth did Tom Hanks do this in *You've Got Mail*? I know it's fiction—a movie no less—but it took some serious guts to win Meg Ryan over after he put her out of business. I would feel way more confident if The Rebel wasn't in the picture. I know nothing about him. For all I know, *he* could be her soul mate.

Yes, I could have looked him up in the system, since I created it, but that would be a gross invasion of privacy. Now I'm second-guessing that decision.

My lips twist to the side as I think about my options. Well, option . . . because there really is only one.

It's time to come clean. I hope that when she sees who NY152 is, she's not disappointed.

Gathering myself, I open the app back up and click on the date request for ShopGirl. When I hit send, I go to the message bar and type her a quick message.

Noely,
Ending our messaging, no. I could never do that without at least taking you out on one more date, without giving myself one more chance at winning over your heart.

So, will you do me the honor and go out with me this Friday night? If you'd like to, accept my date request and I'll see you at Going in Blind. Until then, sleep well, beautiful.
Me

Pressing send, I take a deep breath and let it out slowly as I stare out at the ocean, trying to let the crash of the waves calm my nerves. Unfortunately, I'm at a point where nothing is going to soothe me, not until Noely is once again in my arms. Not until she is truly mine. Because when she is, I am never letting her go.

CHAPTER THIRTY-EIGHT

NOELY

"You smell nice."

"Uh, thank you," I reply to the Uber driver taking me to the restaurant. I'm glad I smell good, because from the way I've been sweating ever since I put on this dress, I'd think I smelled like a pungent Vidalia onion.

"Are you meeting someone special tonight?"

Staring out the window, I answer, "Yeah, someone very special."

When I heard back from Jack—or NY152—I felt relief. *Initially*. I know it's Jack who's behind all of this, but he second-guessed our relationship, questioned whether we were an *us*. As a result, I lost some of my confidence. Again. I hope that when we finally admit how we truly feel about each other, that this discomfort will go. I told him it would crush me if he backed away, and I wasn't lying. He's become someone so important to me. Those days without him were . . . agony.

I've tried to remind myself of how well we connect. The fun and deep conversations, the laughs, the games, the teasing . . . the . . . well, you know, what we did on my dressing room table. Let's not go into detail about *that* weak moment, even though it was a deliciously weak moment, a moment I wouldn't mind repeating, not even in the slightest. Honestly, it shouldn't be that big of a deal. I mean, we've spent a lot of time together and we, you know, did it on my dressing room table.

"Oh, he must be a very lucky man." As she pulls up to the curb, the Uber driver, a sweet older lady, turns in her seat and says, "Do you want to touch-up your lipstick?"

Eyes wide, I press my fingers against my lips. "Does it need touching up?"

"No." She shakes her head. "It looks great."

Okay . . . then why say that? Now I feel self-conscious.

"Smile for me, sweetheart. Let me see if you have lipstick on your teeth. I'm notorious for having a large line across mine."

Probably because she uses lipstick from the fifties.

Awkwardly, I smile at her, showing my teeth. In return, she gives me a thumbs up. "All clear, honey." Clapping her hands, she says, "I hope you have a wonderful night."

"Thank you." I gather myself and open the door. "Have a good one."

"You too, knock him dead!"

She's still giving me the thumbs up as I walk toward the restaurant. I smile to myself, happy for the small distraction from my nerves.

Last time I was here, I was drunk. No, that's not quite the way to put it. I was absolutely cabbaged. Trying to make Jack jealous while acting like an ass in front of Hayden. Why he continued to go out with me, I have no idea. Maybe I was entertaining in my turtleneck. Can't hate on a girl who rocks a turtleneck like it's a laced-up bustier.

I open the door to the restaurant, the white exposed brick calming me from its familiarity. Veronica smiles brightly.

"Miss Clark, what a pleasure to see you again."

"Hi." I wave with a tight smile, feeling a little embarrassed. "Lucky number four." I cross my fingers and she smiles kindly.

"Shall I show you to the bar?"

THREE BLIND DATES

I hold up my hand. "I think I've got it, thank you, though." I turn toward the bar when I stop and say, "Veronica, can I ask you a question?"

"Of course, Miss Clark." She's so pretty and sweet; I have a slight crush on her.

Only a slight one.

"Are you with someone?"

She nods with a bright smile. "I am." She glances in Danny's direction and I put two and two together.

"You're with Danny? Wow, that's . . . that's great."

"Thank you." She smiles and eyes Danny for a second before turning back to the screen in front of her. "Is there anything else I can assist you with?"

"You don't happen to have any dating advice for me, do you?"

Chuckling quietly, she says, "Just be yourself, Miss Clark."

With that, she turns back to the screen. Just be myself, well, that's easy.

I walk over to the bar where Danny is filling a tumbler with the bar gun and take a seat.

"Miss Clark, what a pleasant surprise. How are you?"

It's nice they know me by name here, but also slightly embarrassing. It's not like a coffee shop where they know my order the minute I walk up; it's a dating restaurant.

"I'm doing okay, a little tense."

"I would be shocked if you weren't. Going on a first date is always nerve-racking, but isn't it a little thrilling?"

"No." I shake my head and laugh. "Not at this point. I'm just . . . really nervous."

Setting the glass down, Danny leans on the bar in front of me, his hands gripping the edge. "Sometimes, we can be blind to what's right in front of us because of all the nerves and anxiety of meeting someone new, but the heart"—he taps his chest—"is never blind, so listen to what it's telling you." He winks and walks to the other side of the bar to hand someone their drink. Why are the employees here so damn insightful? Was that a requirement?

Must be great at making patrons feel at ease. If so, well done, Jack, well done.

Tapping the top of the bar countertop, I look around the restaurant, listening to the light hum of conversation. There are old couples, young, gay, and bi-racial with, I presume, one giant thing in common: they are looking for love. I'm glad I'm not the only one.

There is a tap on my shoulder and immediately my stomach flutters with nerves. This is it. Deep breath.

Shaking slightly, I turn around where I'm greeted by a cocky smirk that is all too familiar.

"Hey there, Sassy."

Beck.

What the . . .

Stunned and caught off guard, I sit a little taller.

"Beck." I clear my throat, feeling . . . God, I don't even know what I'm feeling. I wasn't expecting to see that leather jacket and motorcycle helmet tonight. I was expecting to be greeted by a Windsor knot. "Wow, I didn't expect to see you here."

"I don't know if I should be insulted or not." He winks and pulls my hand to his mouth where he lightly kisses it.

I just . . . I don't . . .

I mean . . .

Beck is NY152? I don't understand how that is even possible. All the clues hinted toward Jack. He had Butterfingers in his trashcan for crying out loud. He had a new house. He had a wicker basket.

Maybe it was all coincidence. One giant coincidence. Orrrrrr, it could be the dating gods messing with my head. Surely Beck isn't here on a date yet. He propositioned *me* recently. *Why are men so confusing?* Was I just seeing things in Jack's house because I wanted it to be him? Was I trying to convince myself that NY152 was Jack because deep in my heart, he's the one I want?

When Beck's lips press against the back of my hand, I feel . . . nothing. Absolutely nothing. Not like I used to. Not like when Jack is in the room, or when he looks at me, his dark eyelashes blanketing his irises causing a serious wave of heat to erupt all over my body.

"You look gorgeous."

I glance at the deep purple dress I chose to wear tonight along with my black strappy heels.

"Thank you." Still stunned, I sit back and say, "I had no idea." I feel like I should follow up my sentence with something like "but I'm pleasantly surprised," but I don't think I am. So instead, to make this awkward, I place my hand on his chest above his heart that seems to be beating at a normal pace, unlike mine that almost feels like it's going to pop out of my chest.

Beck's brows draw together just as I catch a movement of navy blue behind him. Looking over his shoulder, I make eye contact with deep chocolate eyes. Eyes that have caressed me as they've wandered up and down my body. Eyes that have haunted my dreams, made me dizzy in lust. Eyes I want to wake to daily.

Jack.

And just like that, my stomach flips, my veins buzz, and in my heart, I know. He's the one.

But just when my excitement starts to get the best of me from seeing him, he slowly backs away, his eyes cast on Beck.

Oh crap.

"You had no idea about what?" Beck asks, pulling my attention toward him.

"Uh." I look over Beck's shoulder again to see Jack give Veronica a curt nod and head outside.

Crap, crap, crap.

I hop off my chair, purse in hand, and start toward the door, but Beck snags my arm before I can get any farther. "What's going on, Sassy?"

I glance at the door, willing Jack to come back before I respond to Beck. "Long story." I shake my head. "But the man I want in my life just walked out that door and if I don't go after him, I'll lose my chance at being with him."

A small smile plays over Beck's lips. "Then what are you waiting for, Sassy? Go get him."

Letting me go, he steps aside before giving me a playful nudge toward the door. "Go."

Not wasting any more time, I run past Veronica—who has a bright smile on her lips—out the door and onto the street. Out front, I look in both directions until I find Jack's retreating back, his shoulders tense, but his head held high.

I take off after him, my heels pounding on the cement beneath me. "Jack," I call out, as if I'm in my very own movie, the music coming to a crescendo, building and building. "Jack, wait!"

The moment he turns around, I know he's the one because my heart skips a beat.

Your heart is never blind.

This couldn't be more true. Jack is the one, my match, the man I'm supposed to be with, and my heart is showing me loud and clear.

When I reach him, there is an unsure look on his face, almost as if he isn't entirely confident in the bond between us.

"Jack," I breathe out and put my hand on the lapel of his smooth suit jacket, the fabric so rich. "It's you, isn't it?"

Lips pressed together, he looks at the ground and nods.

Wanting to see those eyes of his, I lift his chin and say in my best Meg Ryan voice, "I wanted it to be you. I wanted it to be you so badly." The famous quote from *You've Got Mail* at the end of the movie when they finally meet in the park is the only thing I can think to say at this moment.

The tension in Jack's shoulders ease, and the most beautiful smile I've ever seen crosses his face. Pulling me in tightly by the small of my back, he presses his forehead against mine. In a sultry voice, he asks, "Will you go out on a second date with me, ShopGirl?"

Wrapping my arms around his tapered waist, I take no time in answering him. "I would want nothing more than to date you, NY152."

THREE BLIND DATES

"Thank you, Tom Hanks." Chuckling, he brings my chin up with his index finger and studies my eyes right before his lips press against mine, sending my heart into a tailspin of lust.

It's him. It's him.

It's what my heart keeps pounding out, telling me. This is the man I need to be with, the man I'm meant to be with.

He's my very own love story.

EPILOGUE

JACK

Two weeks later...

I shift on my feet, flowers in hand, anxious for Noely to open the door. I hear her running down the hallway followed by the sound of the door being unlocked. When she opens the door, she acts casual, but from the glint in her eyes, I can tell she's excited to see me. Hell, I'm just as excited to see her.

"Hey, beautiful."

"Hey." She bounces on her bare feet and then throws her arms around me.

This will never get old.

Her face presses against my chest, her small body wrapping around mine. I kiss the top of her head. God, this feels so right. "I brought you flowers, and food should be here any minute. Can I come in?"

Looking up at me, she beams. "Of course."

THREE BLIND DATES

She takes the flowers from me and walks into her kitchen. I follow closely behind her, making sure to shut the door. I lean against the counter, taking in her pajama-clad body while she puts the flowers in a vase. "How was your day?"

"Much better now that you're here." She plops the flowers in water and turns toward me. Without a second thought, she buries her lithe body against mine, her arms wrapping under my suit jacket.

Two weeks of this, two weeks of calling this woman mine, two weeks of dinners, dates, and long walks on the beach, stopping occasionally to dance beneath the stars. It's been incredible, everything I could have asked for when it comes to a partner in life.

"I caught the show this morning."

"Yeah?" She guides me to her couch where she pushes me down on the cushions and takes a seat on my lap. "Did you like the segment we did on booze in eggnog?"

"Watching Dylan's face while taking a sip of each spiked drink was priceless." I chuckle. "But that's not what I wanted to talk about."

"No?"

I shake my head, my hand playing with the hem of her short pajama shorts, my fingers grazing under the fabric occasionally. From beneath her shirt, I catch the puckering of her nipples, and yes, immediate hard-on.

"No, I wanted to discuss that little dress you had on today."

"The green sequined dress?" She plays with my tie, starting to undo the tightly wound Windsor knot.

"Yeah, that dress." I move my hand up her thigh, under her shorts where I find she's not wearing any underwear. "It was quite short, don't you think?"

Expertly her fingers free my tie and she pulls it from around my neck only to toss it on the floor. "I don't think it was short at all."

"Really? That's interesting, because from the way I saw it, it almost seemed like you were trying to tease me while you were on the show today. You know how much I love a short dress on you." Some men like a low-cut dress, but me, hell, there is something about Noely in a short dress that about makes me lose all concentration. To say I was useless for the rest of the day was an understatement. *All* I could think about was my girl in that dress.

While she fiddles with the buttons on my dress shirt, she smiles seductively. "I might have chosen it with you in mind, hoping you caught the show."

"That doesn't surprise me in the slightest." I move my hand out from her shorts and up her shirt where my fingers graze her bare stomach. "You in that dress distracted me all day."

She giggles. "My mistake."

"Yeah, right." In one swift movement, I pin her to the couch and hover above her where I take off my dress shirt and then position my hands on both sides of her head. Her eyes rake over my bare chest, filling with heat while her tongue wets her lips with a smooth stroke. I brush a piece of hair off her face. "You're so beautiful, Noely."

Moving closer, I bring my lips to just above hers where I hear a hitch in her breath. "But because you tortured me all day long with that image, I think I might have to torture you now."

She wraps her arms around my neck and brings me in even closer. Whispering, she says, "Do your best work."

God, this woman. So fucking addicting.

I don't waste any time. I plunge forward, my lips on hers, my tongue spreading her mouth, granting me access. One of my hands reaches below and moves the hem of her shirt up where I find that she isn't wearing a bra either. She knew what she was doing all along, tempting me, torturing me . . . and hell if I don't like it.

As my mouth tangles with hers, my hand connects with her breast, and I pluck and squeeze her nipple, forming it into a tight little bud. Her back arches, filling my hand with more of her breast, her moans fresh off her tongue, rolling into my mouth, making this moment that much hotter.

Reaching between us, Noely unbuckles my pants and pushes them down over my ass along with my boxer briefs, exposing my hardened length. Pressing forward, before she can grip me, I run my cock along her flannel-covered crotch and revel in how I can feel her arousal beneath me, how I can feel how wet she is.

"Yes," she moans again, now tilting her chin up, giving me access to her neck. I take advantage of her offering and bring my tongue down the sweet, silky column, before I remove her shirt up and over her head.

While I move my lips to her breasts, she shucks her shorts, twisting her legs in and out of mine until she's free of all fabric. Lying completely naked beneath me, writhing, and clinging to my hard body, she begs for more.

From the night we had our second date until now, we haven't been able to keep our hands off each other. Almost every night we've stayed at each other's houses, starting with conversation —*usually*—and then fucking each other on every surface possible. Tonight is no exception.

"I missed you today," she rumbles beneath me.

"I missed you, baby," I whisper in her ear, moving my lips to her mouth before I move my hardened length over her slick arousal.

"Mmm," she moans, her hips rocking against me, the feeling so fucking good. "More."

I know I said I was going to tease her, but there is no way in hell I can stop myself now. I need inside her right fucking now.

Grabbing the base of my cock, I find her center and, in one thrust, plunge myself forward. I swallow her moan with my mouth, eating up every last piece of pleasure rocketing through her as I bury myself so deep, so fucking deep.

Tight and smooth, so good, so addicting, so everything.

Using the couch as leverage, I grip the cushion below her, and play with her nipple with my other hand while I pull away from her mouth and stare at our connection, rocking in and out of her, in and out.

She tightens around me, her moans growing louder, her grasp on my arms magnetic. Moving quicker now, our impending orgasms on the brink, I keep my eyes fixed on our connection and every once in a while glance up to see Noely writhing beautifully, her lips parted, her breath gasping, and her eyelashes fluttering shut.

Faster, harder, longer . . . I swivel my hips and pinch her nipple. Her walls contract around my cock, the feeling so constricted, like there is no more room left to go. But I push in harder only to hear her gasp out my name, her back arching, and her fingers digging divots into my skin.

"Yes, God, yes!" Her body stiffens, her center thrumming around me, squeezing me so damn tight it only takes a few more pumps until I reach my orgasm. Gripping the couch tightly, I still as pleasure ricochets up my legs to my core and then down my arms, consuming me in euphoric bliss.

It has never been this good. *Ever.* There is only one reason why.

Snuggling in close, I fall to the couch and wrap my body around Noely, shucking my pants with my feet so they aren't in the way. I bury my head in her hair and squeeze her tight, which makes her giggle.

"What's so funny?" I ask, talking to her hair.

"You're such an oxymoron."

"Why's that?" She smells so fucking good.

"Because, you act like this tough, stern businessman, when in reality, you're just a giant softy who loves to cuddle."

"And you're complaining because?" I kiss along her neck.

"Not complaining at all, just making a statement, letting you know I'm onto you, Jack Valentine."

I take a deep breath. "You should have known the first day we met I wasn't truly the man I project on the outside, especially when we spent some of the night dancing under the stars while the waves crashed at our feet. I may be ruthless between office walls, but I'm a true romantic at heart."

"You're so right." She turns in my arms and presses her soft hand against my rough jaw. "From the very beginning, I should have known you were NY152. It makes the most sense. The grand gesture, the love for Tom Hanks and using him as a way to reach my heart. Then you were able to make another profile. I guess in the moment I was blind. Scared."

"But your heart wasn't." I kiss her lips.

"It wasn't even in the slightest bit blind. It was incredible really. *Every* time you were around, even when I was on dates with the other guys, when I ran into you, my heart started pounding like I'd just finished running a marathon. I don't think I told you about my date in the themed kitchens. But I was so confused that night. My heart beat loudly for you in your presence, when I ran into you blocks away from the venue. But I now think my mind protected my heart a little when out of range. I hate that we wasted precious time, but I also think it made us work harder to ensure we were certain about us." This isn't our first discussion about this. Maybe second or third. But it never gets old knowing from the very beginning, her heart connected with mine. *And knowing she doesn't hate me for stalling us.*

"Is it pounding now?" I run my hand between her breasts, loving how soft they feel, and press my hand against her chest, the beat of her heart thrumming into my palm.

"Always when you're around, Jack."

I snuggle into her some more, because now? I can. I will never let go.

~

One Month Later...

"Babe, if you don't get your pretty little ass out here in the next five minutes, we're going to be late."

"Almost done."

Yeah, that's what she said ten minutes ago.

Feeling impatient, I take another look at my watch, the second hand ticking away, causing a light sheen of sweat to form on my brow. We can't be late. What is taking her so long?

"I'm sure you look great, Noely. No need to spend too much time in front of the mirror."

"Jack, don't you dare rush me."

I run my hand over my face, calming my temper. "Well, maybe if you didn't spend two hours at Dylan's today you wouldn't be running late."

Note to all men out there: don't take the route I am when trying to usher along your girl so you're not late. *Fuck, that's not going to go over well.* I should have taken my own advice.

"Excuse me?" Noely calls out, anger etched in her voice.

I'm already deep with that comment so might as well keep digging.

"You knew we had this party tonight," I say casually but with a slight hint of nagging. Yeah, nagging. That's what I'm resorting to at this point.

"And Dylan had an emergency and needed my help."

"Don't you think her husband could have helped her out? Finding a wart on your foot doesn't necessarily scream best friend emergency to me. That's more of a run to the store moment for wart removal."

"Jack." Oh, *that* tone. Shit. Noely raises her voice. "It's a wart, a WART! We soderized that bitch right off her foot."

"Now when you say we, you make it sound like you two actually did it, when the doctor just lasered it off. You didn't have to be there."

"Are you insane?" Noely is still calling out from the bathroom. Time is ticking away. Can't we argue in the car on the way to the party? "A laser was coming at my friend, a freaking laser. Of course I was going to be there and hold her hand. She's terrified of lasers."

"And this party is important to me. You knew that."

Is this our first fight? It seems like it, unless this qualifies as a disagreement.

There is a slam of the door and Noely's heels click down the hall to the living room where I'm sitting on the arm of my couch. Hair bouncing with curls and her lithe body tucked into that goddamn green sequined dress, she puts her clutch under her arm and gestures toward the door, anger in her movements. "Well, let's go before you have a coronary."

She strides toward the front door, but I stop her by her elbow. Her scent is the first thing that hits me, sweet and seductive, then her hand comes to my chest from the abrupt stop in her movements.

I tilt her chin up so she has to look at me. "Hey, you look beautiful."

"Nope." She shakes her head. "Not going to happen, mister. I'm mad at you."

I move my hands down her back and cup her ass, the green sequins burying into my palms. "You can't be mad at me when I'm mad at you."

"What?" She pushes against my chest but I keep my hold on her, not letting her budge. "How on earth are you mad at me? For being a good friend?"

"No, for putting Dylan over me. You knew this was important to me, Noely." My hands slip further down her dress to the hem and then slowly start to pull the tight fabric up.

"I didn't put Dylan first. I'm ready, aren't I? I'm here, ready to go."

"That's not what I mean. We had plans for today. We were supposed to watch *Catch Me if You Can* and have pizza before this party." I slip the dress up and over her butt and she barely flinches when I grip her bare ass, causing a wave of lust to shoot up my spine. "Instead, I ate a peanut butter and jelly sandwich and watched a rerun of some Hallmark movie on TV by myself."

The anger that once laced her eyes morphs into understanding as she steps into my embrace even closer. "Are you telling me, you wished we'd hung out today instead of you being alone? Did you wonder if I was going to make it to your party?"

"Yes, that's exactly what I'm saying. When we get the chance, which is usually on the weekends with our schedules now, I want to spend as much time with you as I can get."

She stands on her toes and presses a kiss against my chin, not even caring that I'm moving her dress even farther up her body . . . to her ribcage.

"Aw, you were lonely today."

"I was." I pout, loving the affection she's bestowing upon me. I know, a pouting businessman, what's that about? You'll see in a second.

I move her dress up even higher until I reach her breasts. "You know, any higher and that dress is going to be off my body. That's really going to make us late."

"That's the point, babe. You know you can't wear this dress and get away with me not taking it off the minute I see it." I undo the zipper on the side and peel off the rest of the dress until she's standing in front of me completely naked. I am such a fucking lucky bastard. Standing back for a second, I run my hand over my jaw and study her. "Well, fuck. What am I supposed to do now?"

Closing the distance between us, she presses her body against mine and says, "I owe you a little loving, don't I? I don't like to make you sad."

She rubs against my body, my cock swelling instantly. See, this is what a simple pout can get you. But don't overuse it. It's a powerful tool only to be used when absolutely necessary. *Like* when you're late for a party but want to fuck your girl so bad that you fake being sad so it's okay.

I take in the time on my watch and then smile at her. "Looks like we're going to be late."

∼

THREE BLIND DATES

T*wo Months Later...*

I stand behind the cameras, hand in pocket, watching Noely light up the room and the cameras pointing directly at her. She's electric, so full of life, funny as hell, and compassionate. Not to mention incredibly beautiful on the inside and out.

When I originally started the *Going in Blind* restaurant, I never expected to find love. I only put myself in the running so we had a few profiles to test, but the second I saw that I matched with Noely and reading her profile, and then secretly watching her "casting" video, the one only staff are allowed to view, I had to go out on a date with her, even though I wasn't looking to be matched. I knew at that moment I had to get to know this woman, and hell am I glad I did, because the woman who's horribly trying to juggle her mimosa glass and a hedgehog has etched her way into my heart.

She's the one.

Easily.

Hands down, I'm going to marry her one day.

I'm going to marry her so fucking hard.

"Thank you for stopping by today, James. We always enjoy having you on the show," Noely says. Turning toward the teleprompter, she reads, "Until next week, Malibu, have a beautiful day."

A ringing sound echoes through the set as Kevin starts wrapping up the crew. I stand off in the back as Noely wraps up and removes her mic, all the while eyeing me from behind the obtusely large cameras. Dylan says something to her I can't make out, which makes Noely laugh loudly, the sound so beautiful. Her smile lights up my heart, and the way she speaks so kindly to the crew around her, it reminds me of how kind her heart is.

When she finally breaks free from the set, she runs up to me, her heels echoing against the cement floor. She flies into my arms and kisses me hard before pulling away and entwining her fingers behind my neck.

"You're back."

"I am." I link my arms at her lower back, loving the feel of her in my arms again.

"How was Japan?"

"Would have been better if you were there."

"Did you bring anything back for me?" She presses another kiss against my lips, this one chaste and entirely too short for my liking.

"I did."

"What is it?"

"A silk kimono just like you asked for, but there is one rule you have to follow when wearing it. You have to be completely naked underneath it," I whisper in her ear.

Her short intake of breath does something to my insides. *God, this girl.* Irresistible.

"Is that so you can feel me up anytime you want?"

"Pretty much." I nod toward the exit. "Come on, I have two more things to give you."

For a brief second we stop in her dressing room to get her purse and then head to my car where I help her into the passenger side. When I join her, instead of turning the car on, I face her and can barely hold back the grin stretching across my face.

She pokes my cheek. "Why are you so happy?"

"I missed my baby." I grip the back of her head and bring her lips closer to mine where I nibble on them for a few seconds before pulling away, just as she was starting to deepen the kiss.

"More kisses," she says, trying to bring me closer to her again.

I hold up my finger. "In a moment. First, I want to give you this." I reach into the glove compartment and hand her a piece of paper that she unfolds. On the inside, I've scribbled down every single Tom Hanks movie and point to the movie title on the bottom.

"What this?"

"We've watched every Tom Hanks movie together besides one."

She scans the list and then shakes her head. "Not possible. We've watched that together."

"We haven't. I've kept track. Ever since our second date, I knew I wanted to watch every movie with you, so that's when I made this list. And every movie we've watched, I've checked them off."

"So you're telling me, we've never seen *You've Got Mail* together?"

I shake my head. "Never."

"Well, that's just . . . that's . . . God, that's so wrong."

"Tell me about it." I chuckle. "Which brings me to your second gift." I reach into my pocket and pull out a small box.

"What's this?" she asks, looking stunned.

"Not what you think it is. Believe me, when I ask you *that* question, it won't be in my car outside your work." I nod at the box, "Go ahead. Open it."

Chewing on the side of her lip, eyeing me, she opens the box and pulls out a key. "What's this?"

"You know, Japan to LAX is a really long flight and it got me thinking. Why the hell are we splitting our time between two houses when we can just have one?"

Smiling brilliantly, she asks, "Are you asking me to move in with you, Jack?"

"I am. I'm asking you to move in with me and watch *You've Got Mail*. I can't think of a better way to commemorate moving in, can you?"

She shakes her head. "You're unreal, Jack."

"So is that a yes?" I smile, hoping it is.

"There is no way in hell I could possibly say no to you." And with that, she closes the space between us once again and kisses me. She kisses me so fucking hard that I feel dizzy from lust, lust for this woman, the one who so easily captured my heart and showed me that the saying is true, your mind might be blind, but your heart never is.

From the very beginning, our hearts knew, we were meant for each other. It only took a date with a suit, a rebel, and a jock to figure it out.

THE END

Made in the USA
Middletown, DE
26 July 2024